LANTERN CITY ™

Published by

 ARCHAIA

 MACROCOSM

Macrocosm Entertainment, Inc.

TREVOR CRAFTS CEO & Founder

ELLEN SCHERER CRAFTS COO

MATTHEW DALEY VP of Development

LANTERN CITY Volume One, March 2016. Published by Archaia, a division of Boom Entertainment, Inc., 5670 Wilshire Boulevard, Suite 450, Los Angeles, CA 90036-5679. Lantern City is ™ & © 2016 Macrocosm Entertainment, Inc. Originally published in single magazine form as LANTERN CITY No. 1-4. ™ & © 2015 Macrocosm Entertainment, Inc. All Rights Reserved. Archaia™ and the Archaia logo are trademarks of Boom Entertainment, Inc., registered in various countries and categories. All characters, events, and institutions depicted herein are fictional. Any similarity between any of the names, characters, persons, events, and/or institutions in this publication to actual names, characters, and persons, whether living or dead, events, and/or institutions is unintended and purely coincidental.

BOOM! Studios, 5670 Wilshire Boulevard, Suite 450, Los Angeles, CA 90036-5679. Printed in China. First Printing.

ISBN: 978-1-60886-827-8, eISBN: 978-1-61398-498-7

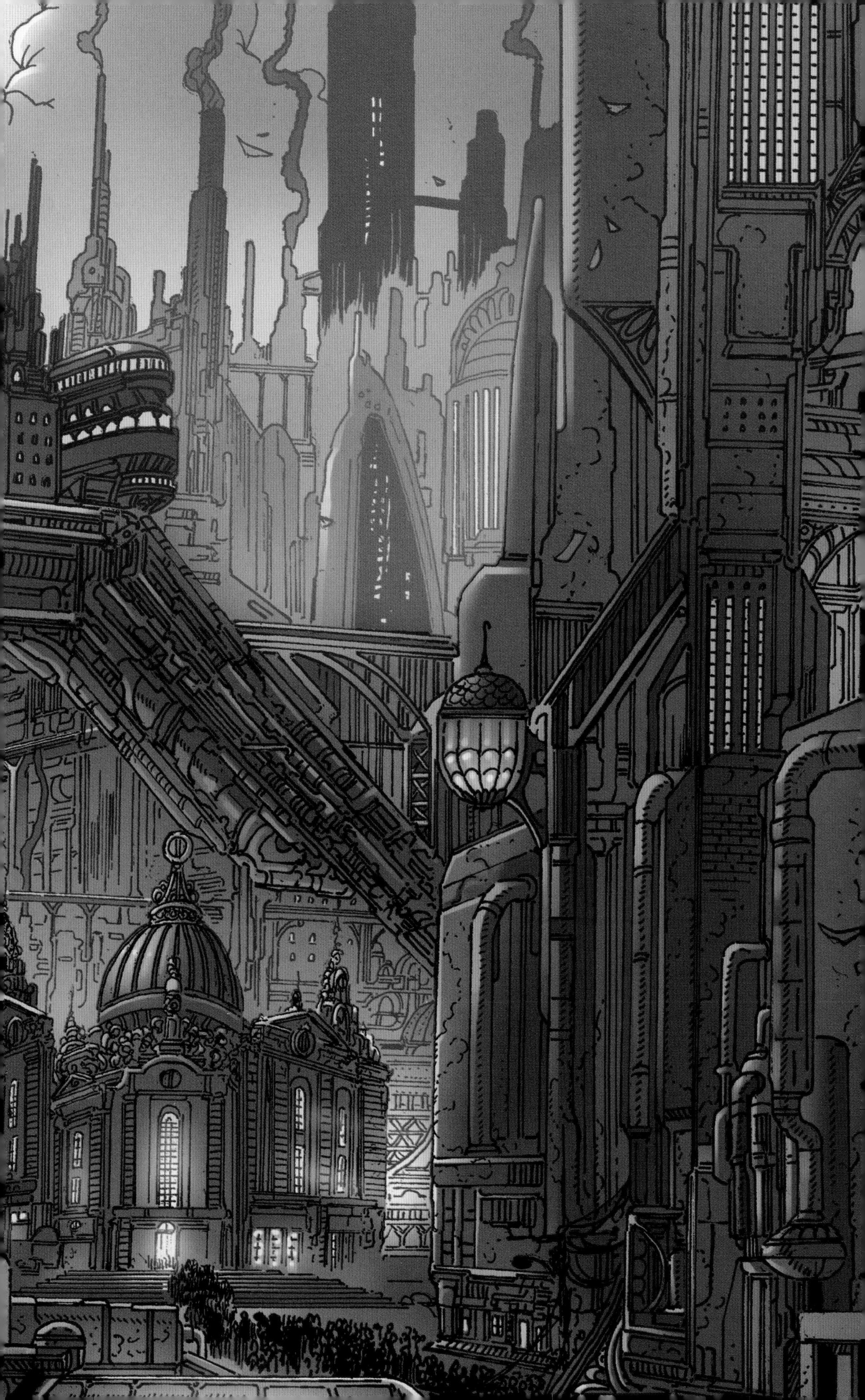

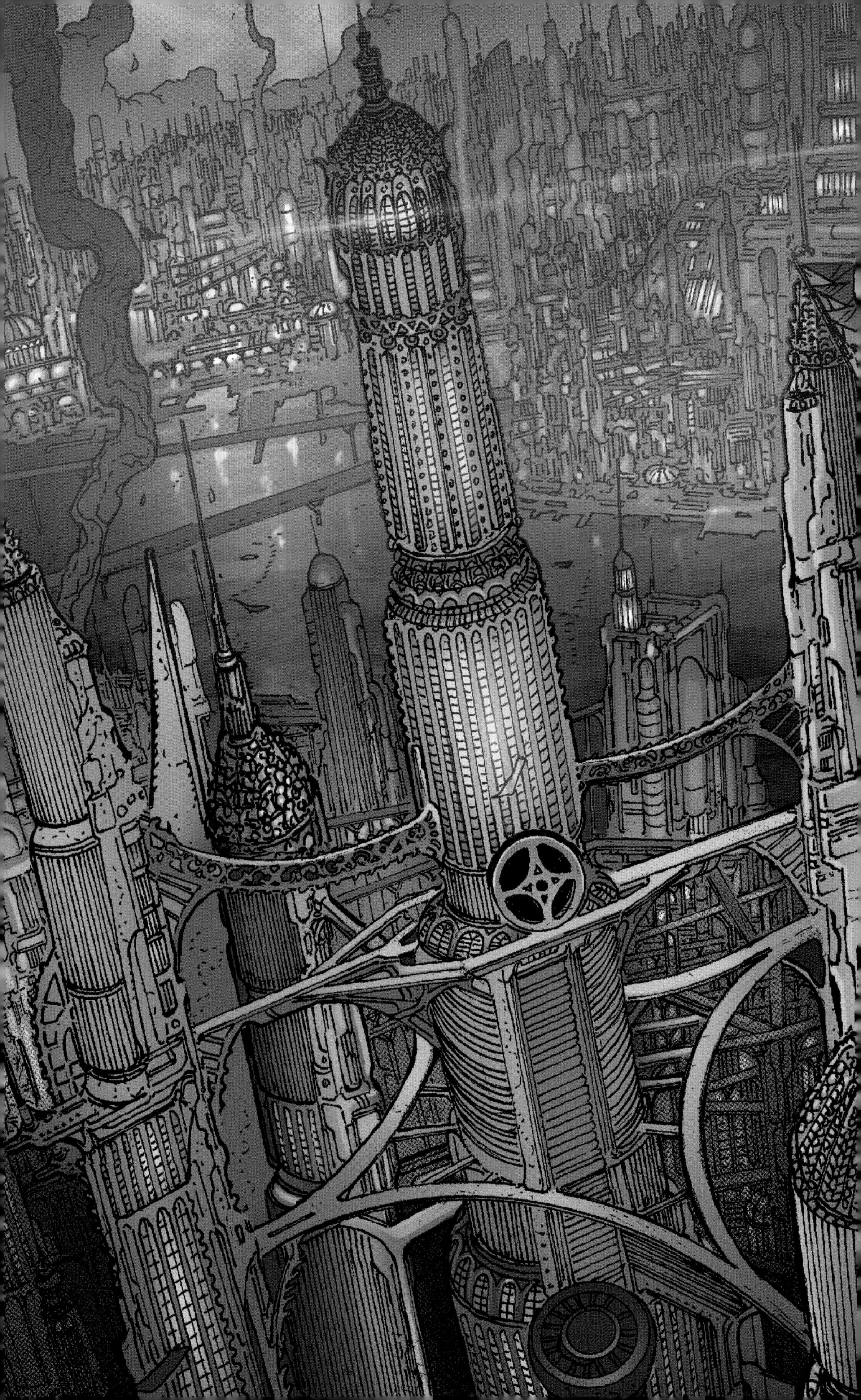

CREATED BY
TREVOR CRAFTS

CO-CREATORS
MATTHEW DALEY
BRUCE BOXLEITNER

CHAPTER ONE WRITTEN BY
PAUL JENKINS &
MATTHEW DALEY

CHAPTER TWO WRITTEN BY
MATTHEW DALEY

CHAPTERS THREE AND FOUR WRITTEN BY
MATTHEW DALEY &
MAIRGHREAD SCOTT

ILLUSTRATED BY
CARLOS MAGNO

COLORS BY
CHRIS BLYTHE

LETTERS BY
DERON BENNETT

COVER BY
DAVE DORMAN

DESIGNER KELSEY DIETERICH
ASSISTANT EDITOR MARY GUMPORT
EDITOR DAFNA PLEBAN
SPECIAL THANKS TO REBECCA TAYLOR

CHAPTER ONE

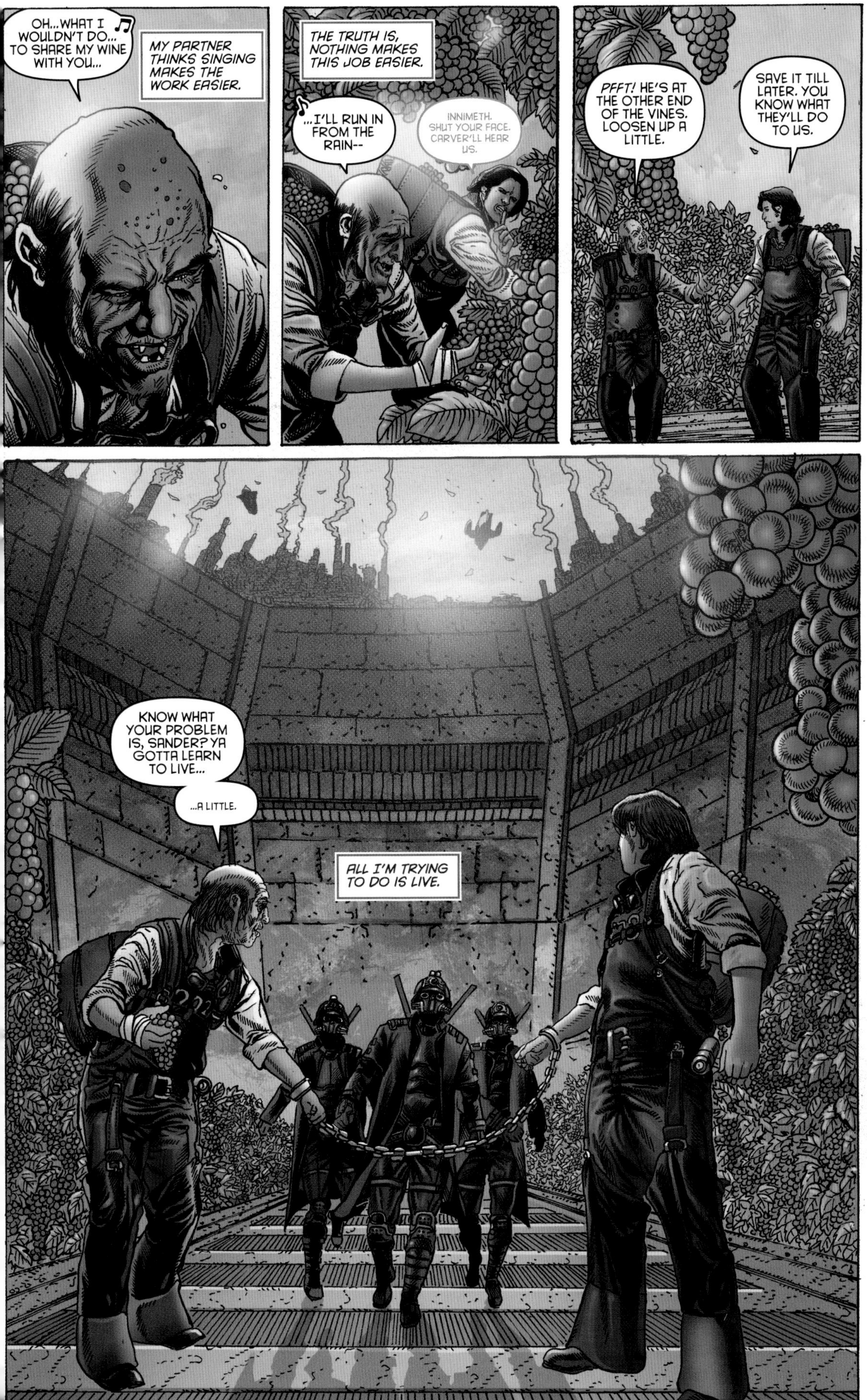
OH...WHAT I WOULDN'T DO... TO SHARE MY WINE WITH YOU...
MY PARTNER THINKS SINGING MAKES THE WORK EASIER.
THE TRUTH IS, NOTHING MAKES THIS JOB EASIER.
...I'LL RUN IN FROM THE RAIN--
INNIMETH. SHUT YOUR FACE. CARVER'LL HEAR US.
PFFT! HE'S AT THE OTHER END OF THE VINES. LOOSEN UP A LITTLE.
SAVE IT TILL LATER. YOU KNOW WHAT THEY'LL DO TO US.
KNOW WHAT YOUR PROBLEM IS, SANDER? YA GOTTA LEARN TO LIVE...
...A LITTLE.
ALL I'M TRYING TO DO IS LIVE.

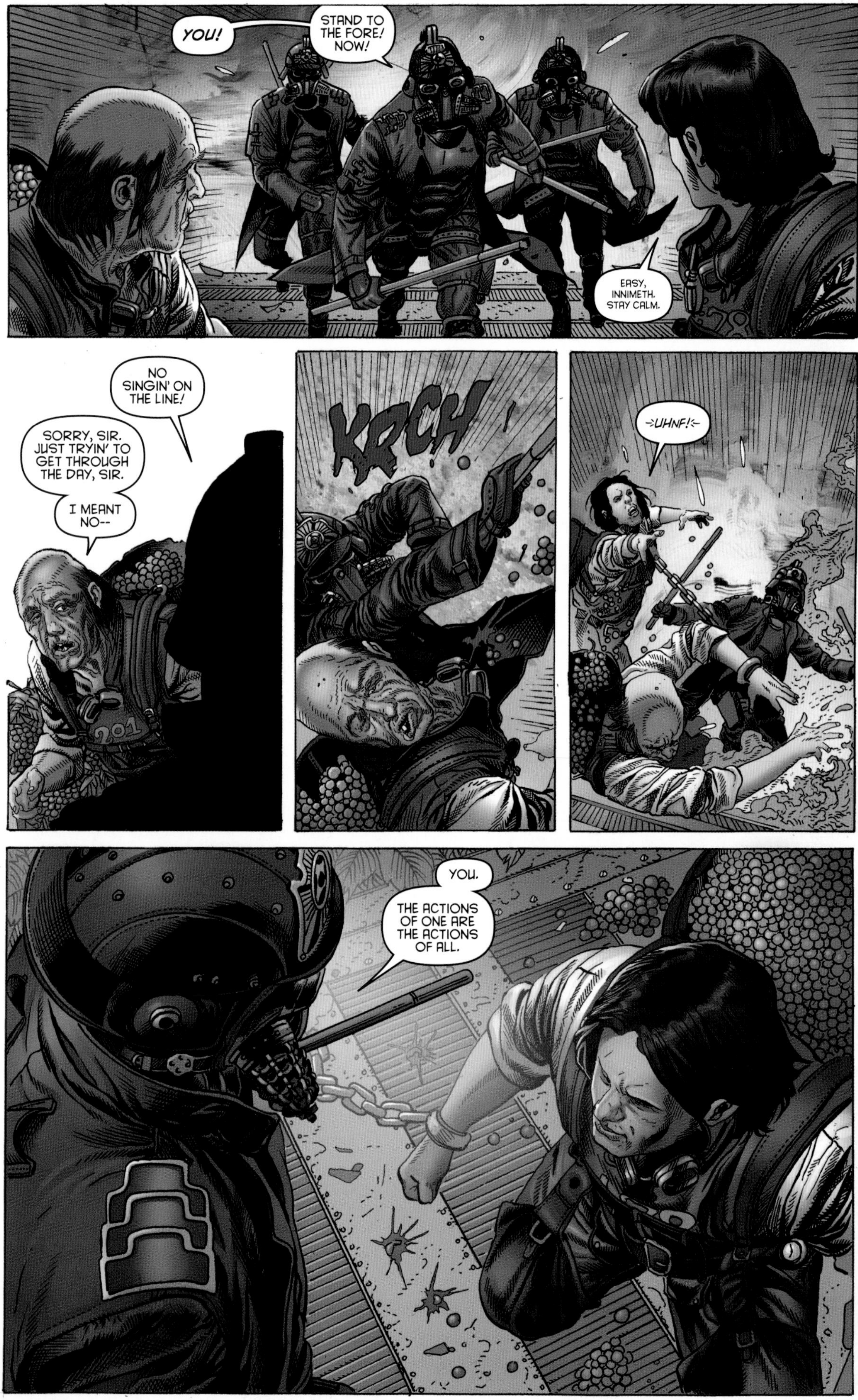
YOU!
STAND TO THE FORE! NOW!
EASY, INNIMETH. STAY CALM.
NO SINGIN' ON THE LINE!
SORRY, SIR. JUST TRYIN' TO GET THROUGH THE DAY, SIR.
I MEANT NO--
201
KRCH
UHNF!
YOU.
THE ACTIONS OF ONE ARE THE ACTIONS OF ALL.

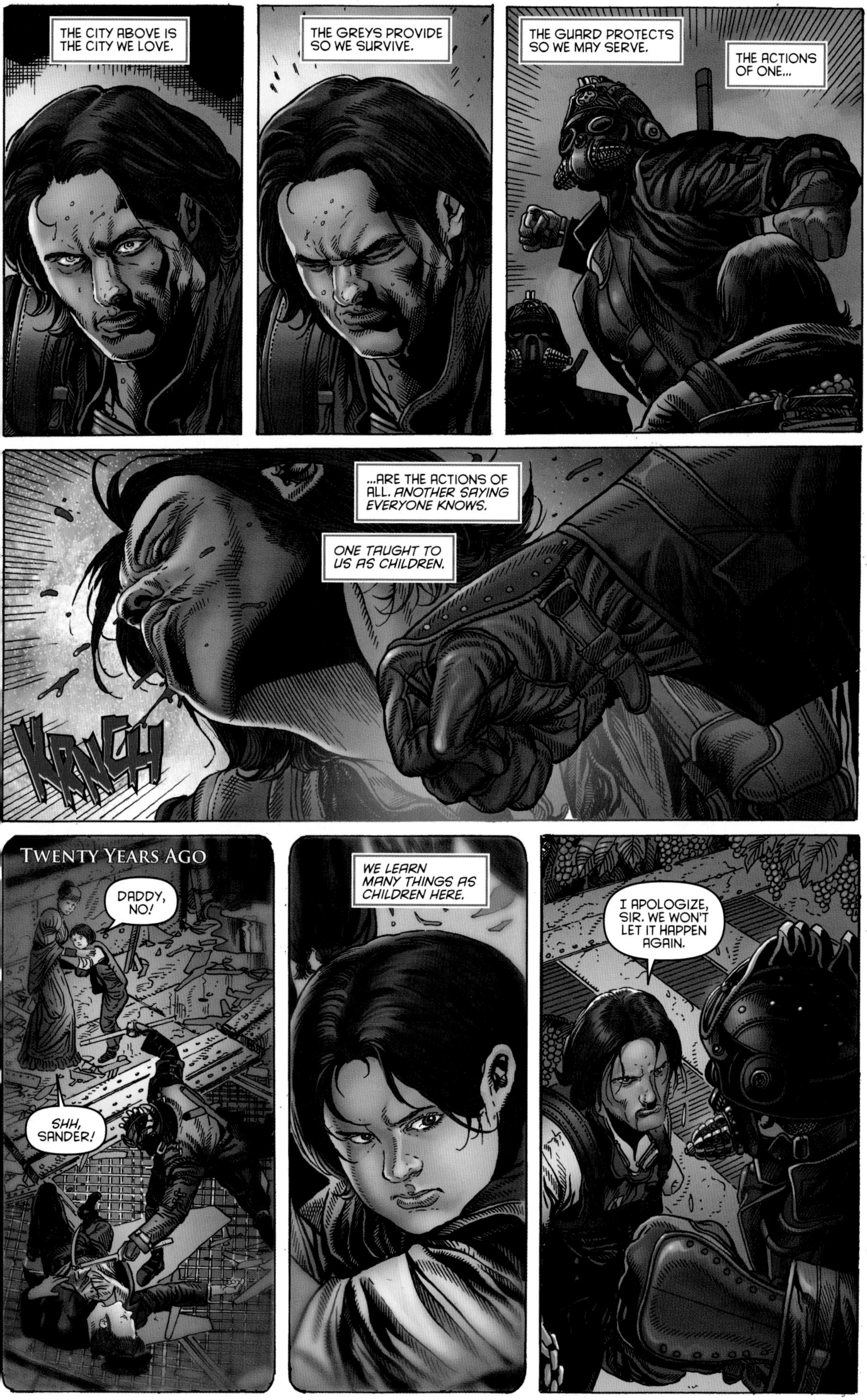
THE CITY ABOVE IS THE CITY WE LOVE.
THE GREYS PROVIDE SO WE SURVIVE.
THE GUARD PROTECTS SO WE MAY SERVE.
THE ACTIONS OF ONE...
...ARE THE ACTIONS OF ALL. ANOTHER SAYING EVERYONE KNOWS.
ONE TAUGHT TO US AS CHILDREN.
KRNCH
TWENTY YEARS AGO
DADDY, NO!
SHH, SANDER!
WE LEARN MANY THINGS AS CHILDREN HERE.
I APOLOGIZE, SIR. WE WON'T LET IT HAPPEN AGAIN.

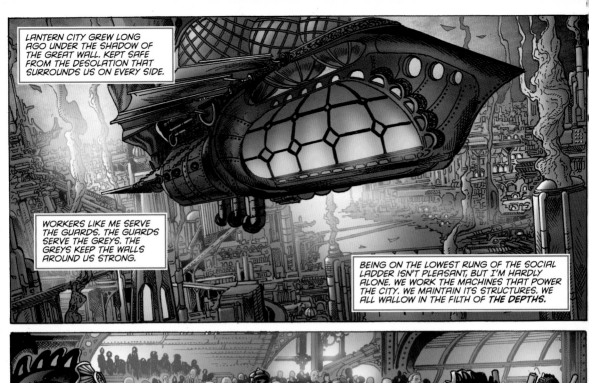

LANTERN CITY GREW LONG AGO UNDER THE SHADOW OF THE GREAT WALL. KEPT SAFE FROM THE DESOLATION THAT SURROUNDS US ON EVERY SIDE.

WORKERS LIKE ME SERVE THE GUARDS. THE GUARDS SERVE THE GREYS. THE GREYS KEEP THE WALLS AROUND US STRONG.

BEING ON THE LOWEST RUNG OF THE SOCIAL LADDER ISN'T PLEASANT, BUT I'M HARDLY ALONE. WE WORK THE MACHINES THAT POWER THE CITY. WE MAINTAIN ITS STRUCTURES. WE ALL WALLOW IN THE FILTH OF *THE DEPTHS*.

I'M ONE OF THE LUCKY ONES PERMITTED TO WORK THE FIELDS. BETTER THAN BEING STUCK INSIDE, TRAPPED IN THE SHADOWS OF GREY TOWERS.

WHEN THE WORK IS DONE, WE LIVE OFF THE CRUMBS THAT FALL FROM ABOVE.

HUNGER AND SICKNESS ARE ALWAYS RIGHT AROUND THE CORNER.

BUT IF THERE'S ONE THING LIVING IN THE DEPTHS TEACHES YOU...

...IT'S THAT THINGS COULD ALWAYS BE WORSE.

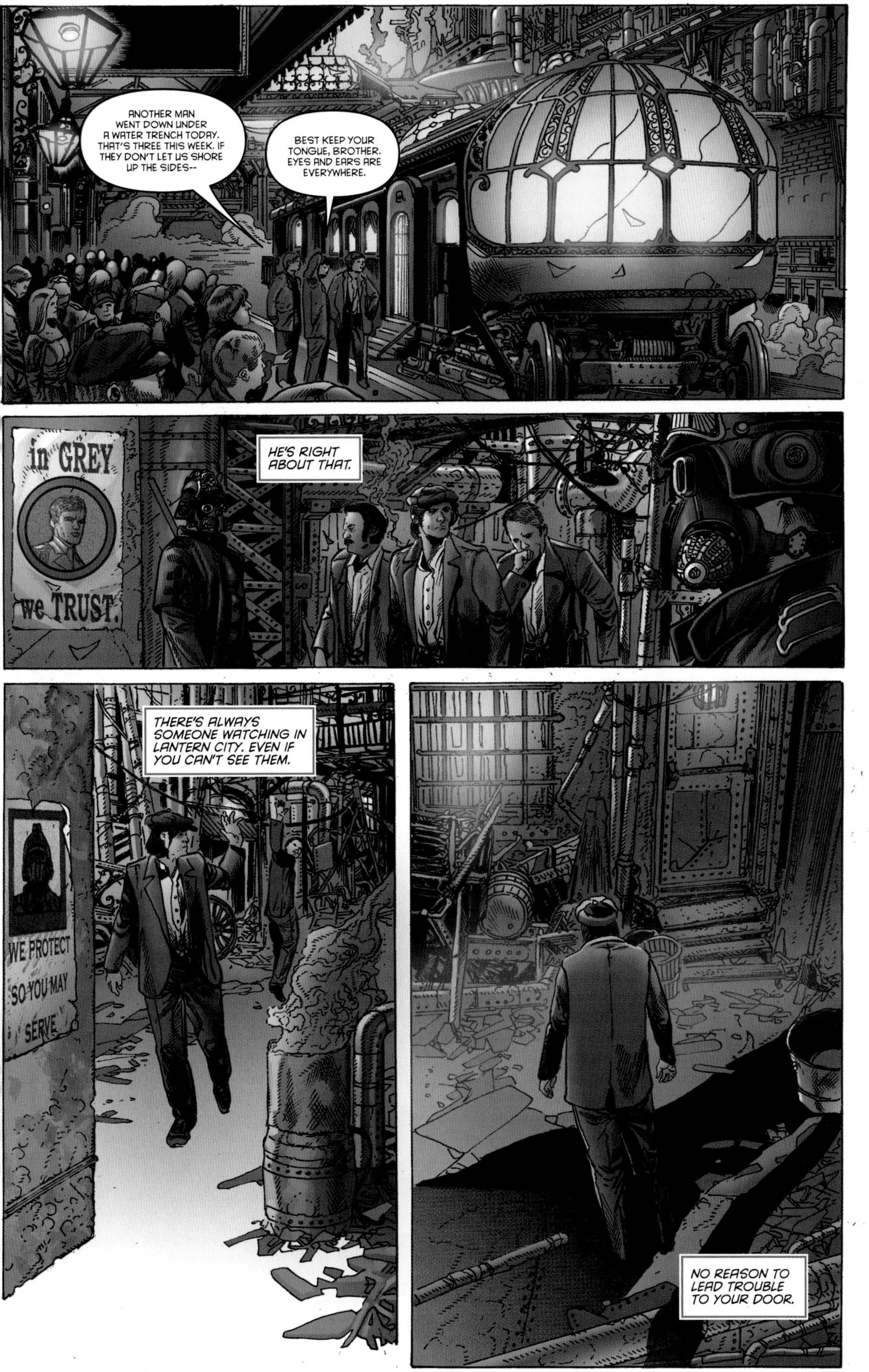
ANOTHER MAN WENT DOWN UNDER A WATER TRENCH TODAY. THAT'S THREE THIS WEEK. IF THEY DON'T LET US SHORE UP THE SIDES--
BEST KEEP YOUR TONGUE, BROTHER. EYES AND EARS ARE EVERYWHERE.
in GREY
we TRUST.
HE'S RIGHT ABOUT THAT.
THERE'S ALWAYS SOMEONE WATCHING IN LANTERN CITY. EVEN IF YOU CAN'T SEE THEM.
WE PROTECT SO YOU MAY SERVE
NO REASON TO LEAD TROUBLE TO YOUR DOOR.

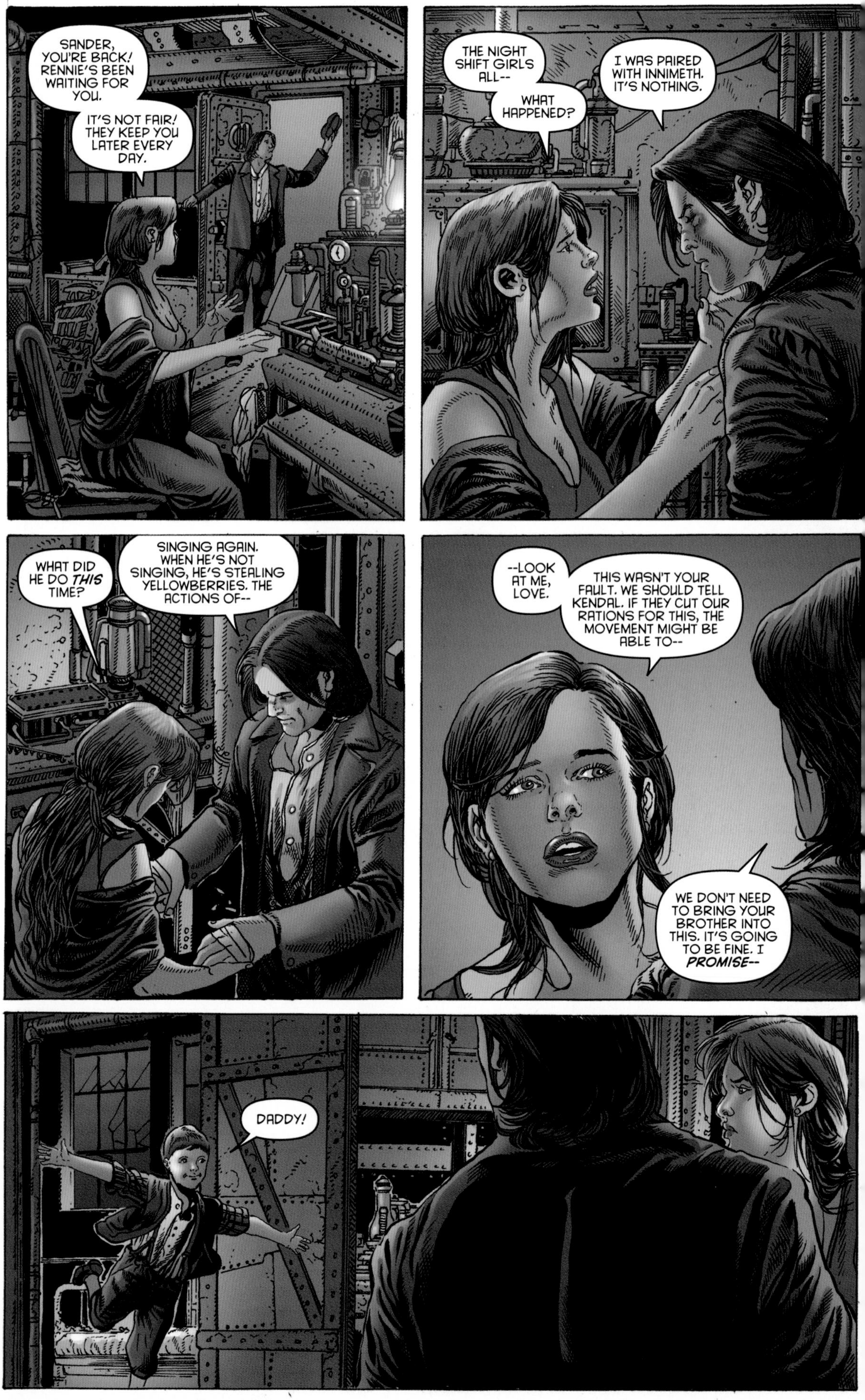
SANDER, YOU'RE BACK! RENNIE'S BEEN WAITING FOR YOU.
IT'S NOT FAIR! THEY KEEP YOU LATER EVERY DAY.
THE NIGHT SHIFT GIRLS ALL--
WHAT HAPPENED?
I WAS PAIRED WITH INNIMETH. IT'S NOTHING.
WHAT DID HE DO *THIS* TIME?
SINGING AGAIN. WHEN HE'S NOT SINGING, HE'S STEALING YELLOWBERRIES. THE ACTIONS OF--
--LOOK AT ME, LOVE.
THIS WASN'T YOUR FAULT. WE SHOULD TELL KENDAL. IF THEY CUT OUR RATIONS FOR THIS, THE MOVEMENT MIGHT BE ABLE TO--
WE DON'T NEED TO BRING YOUR BROTHER INTO THIS. IT'S GOING TO BE FINE. I ***PROMISE--***
DADDY!

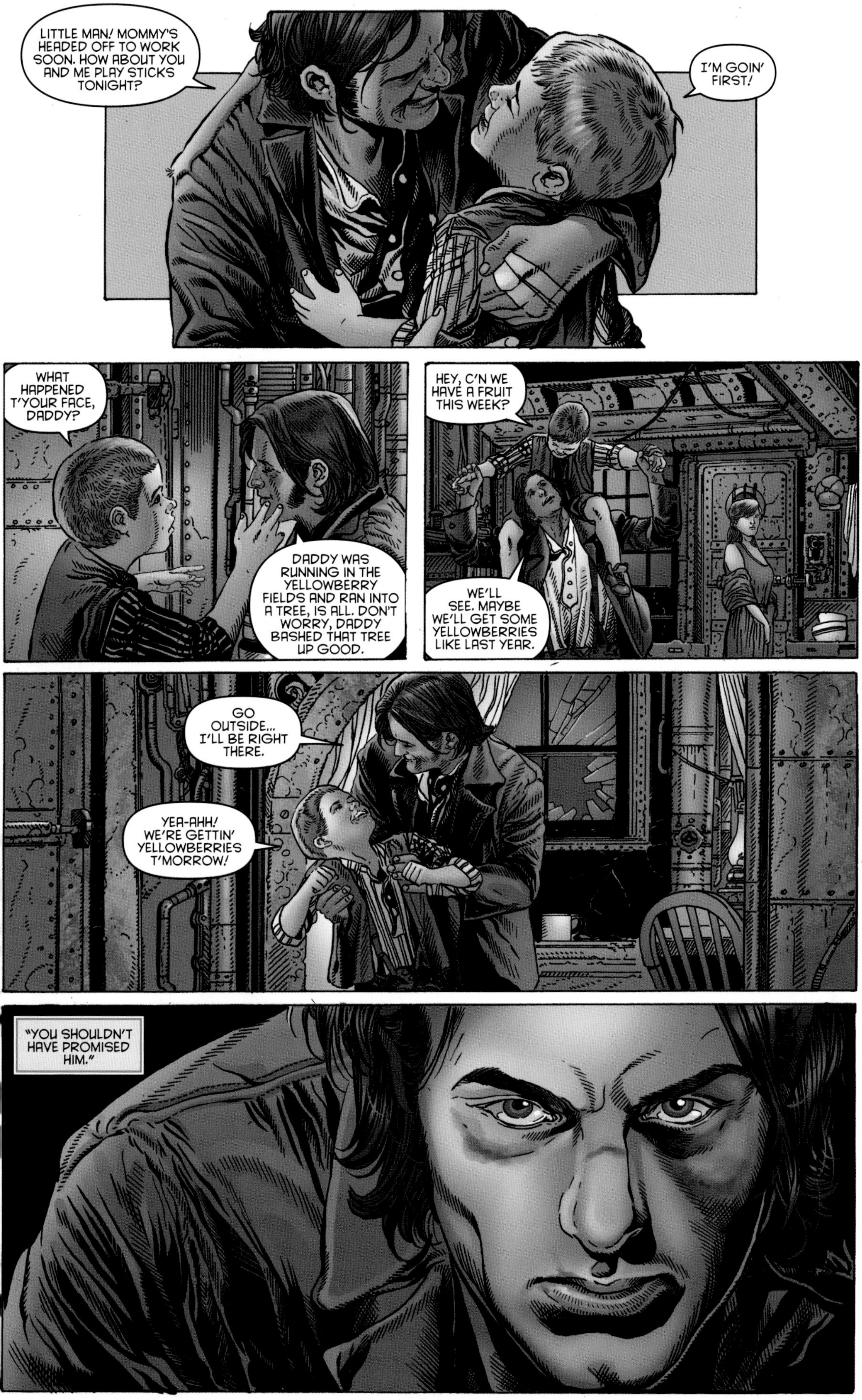
LITTLE MAN! MOMMY'S HEADED OFF TO WORK SOON. HOW ABOUT YOU AND ME PLAY STICKS TONIGHT?
I'M GOIN' FIRST!
WHAT HAPPENED T'YOUR FACE, DADDY?
DADDY WAS RUNNING IN THE YELLOWBERRY FIELDS AND RAN INTO A TREE, IS ALL. DON'T WORRY, DADDY BASHED THAT TREE UP GOOD.
HEY, C'N WE HAVE A FRUIT THIS WEEK?
WE'LL SEE. MAYBE WE'LL GET SOME YELLOWBERRIES LIKE LAST YEAR.
GO OUTSIDE... I'LL BE RIGHT THERE.
YEA-AHH! WE'RE GETTIN' YELLOWBERRIES T'MORROW!
"YOU SHOULDN'T HAVE PROMISED HIM."

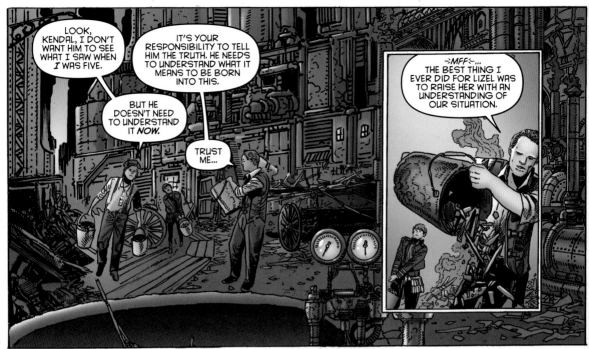

LOOK, KENDAL, I DON'T WANT HIM TO SEE WHAT I SAW WHEN *I* WAS FIVE.

IT'S YOUR RESPONSIBILITY TO TELL HIM THE TRUTH. HE NEEDS TO UNDERSTAND WHAT IT MEANS TO BE BORN INTO THIS.

BUT HE DOESN'T NEED TO UNDERSTAND IT *NOW*.

TRUST ME...

→MFF←... THE BEST THING I EVER DID FOR LIZEL WAS TO RAISE HER WITH AN UNDERSTANDING OF OUR SITUATION.

IF RENNIE DOESN'T LEARN WHAT LIVING IN THE DEPTHS MEANS SOON, FINDING OUT COULD GET HIM *KILLED*.

LIZEL! GO BACK TO THE HOUSE. TELL AUNT KARLA THAT UNCLE SANDER AND I WILL BE ALONG FOR FOOD IN A WHILE.

I'LL GO IF YOU LET ME HAVE A SWIG.

I TOLD YOU NOT TO TOUCH THIS STUFF.

YOU ALSO SAID TO LEAD BY EXAMPLE.

DAUGHTERS AREN'T SUPPOSED TO LISTEN TO THEIR FATHERS.

NOW DO AS I SAY.

THERE WON'T BE FOOD LEFT FOR *EITHER* OF YOU.

AFTER THE DAY YOU HAD, YOU NEED THIS.

BESIDES, A LITTLE GRAIN SOFTENS THE EDGES.

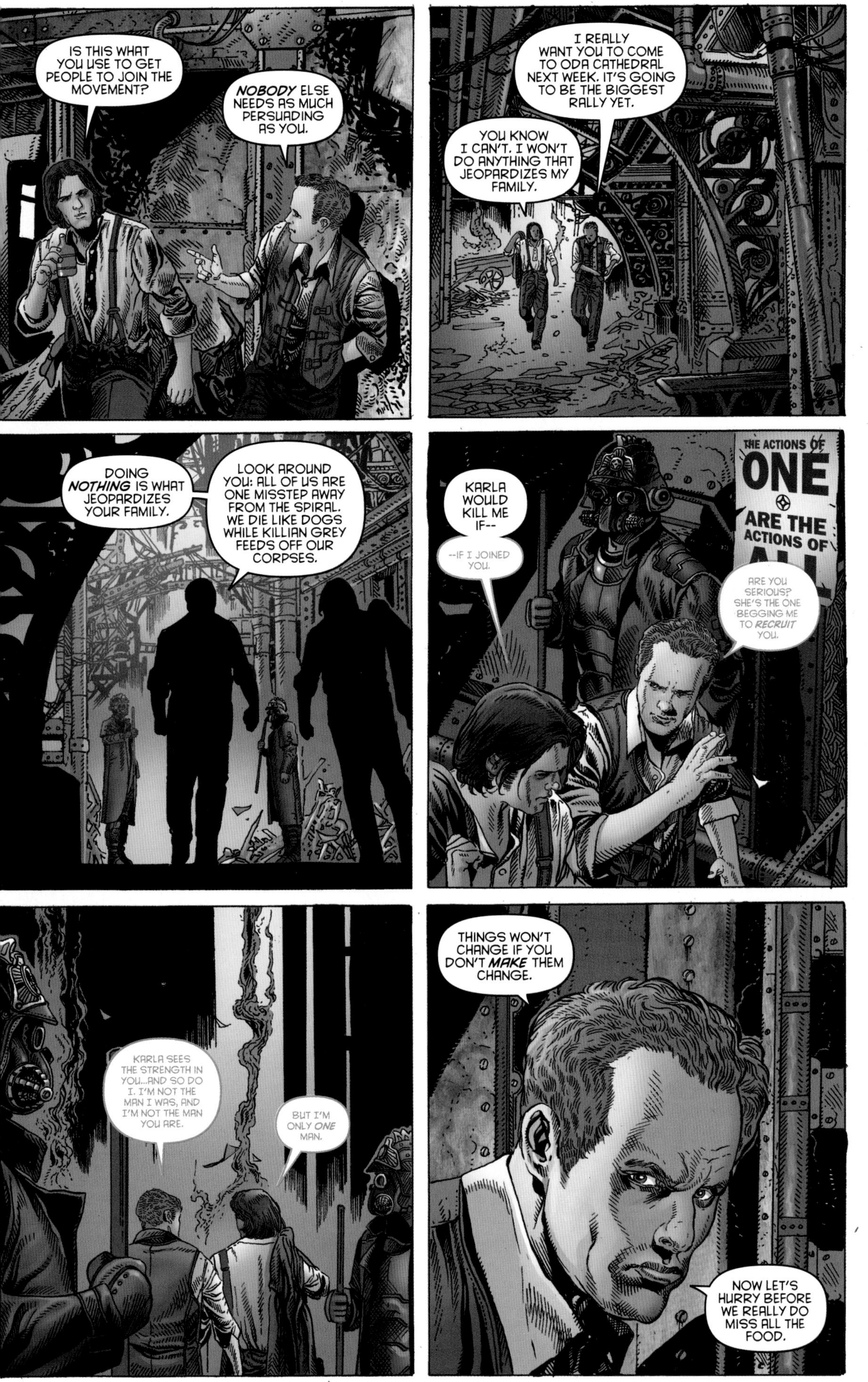
IS THIS WHAT YOU USE TO GET PEOPLE TO JOIN THE MOVEMENT?
NOBODY ELSE NEEDS AS MUCH PERSUADING AS YOU.
I REALLY WANT YOU TO COME TO ODA CATHEDRAL NEXT WEEK. IT'S GOING TO BE THE BIGGEST RALLY YET.
YOU KNOW I CAN'T. I WON'T DO ANYTHING THAT JEOPARDIZES MY FAMILY.
DOING NOTHING IS WHAT JEOPARDIZES YOUR FAMILY.
LOOK AROUND YOU: ALL OF US ARE ONE MISSTEP AWAY FROM THE SPIRAL. WE DIE LIKE DOGS WHILE KILLIAN GREY FEEDS OFF OUR CORPSES.
THE ACTIONS OF ONE ARE THE ACTIONS OF
KARLA WOULD KILL ME IF--
--IF I JOINED YOU.
ARE YOU SERIOUS? SHE'S THE ONE BEGGING ME TO RECRUIT YOU.
KARLA SEES THE STRENGTH IN YOU...AND SO DO I. I'M NOT THE MAN I WAS, AND I'M NOT THE MAN YOU ARE.
BUT I'M ONLY ONE MAN.
THINGS WON'T CHANGE IF YOU DON'T MAKE THEM CHANGE.
NOW LET'S HURRY BEFORE WE REALLY DO MISS ALL THE FOOD.

"THINGS WON'T CHANGE IF YOU DON'T MAKE THEM CHANGE."

THE THING IS, WE *CAN'T* MAKE THINGS CHANGE.

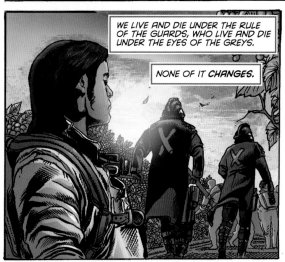

WE LIVE AND DIE UNDER THE RULE OF THE GUARDS, WHO LIVE AND DIE UNDER THE EYES OF THE GREYS.

NONE OF IT *CHANGES*.

BETTER TO JUST PROTECT OUR CHILDREN, ALWAYS KNOWING--BUT NEVER ADMITTING--THAT ONE DAY, THEY'RE SIMPLY NOT CHILDREN ANYMORE.

THEN, THEY'RE JUST ANOTHER ONE OF US: THE PEOPLE AT THE BOTTOM, HIDDEN IN THE BOWELS OF LANTERN CITY.

THE WORLD ABOVE US NEVER LOOKS DOWN. WHY TORTURE OURSELVES WITH LOOKING UP? WHY WISH FOR SOMETHING WE CAN NEVER HAVE?

AND WHY DO I FEEL LIKE I'M TRYING TO CONVINCE MYSELF OF THIS, EVEN WHEN I KNOW IT'S THE TRUTH?

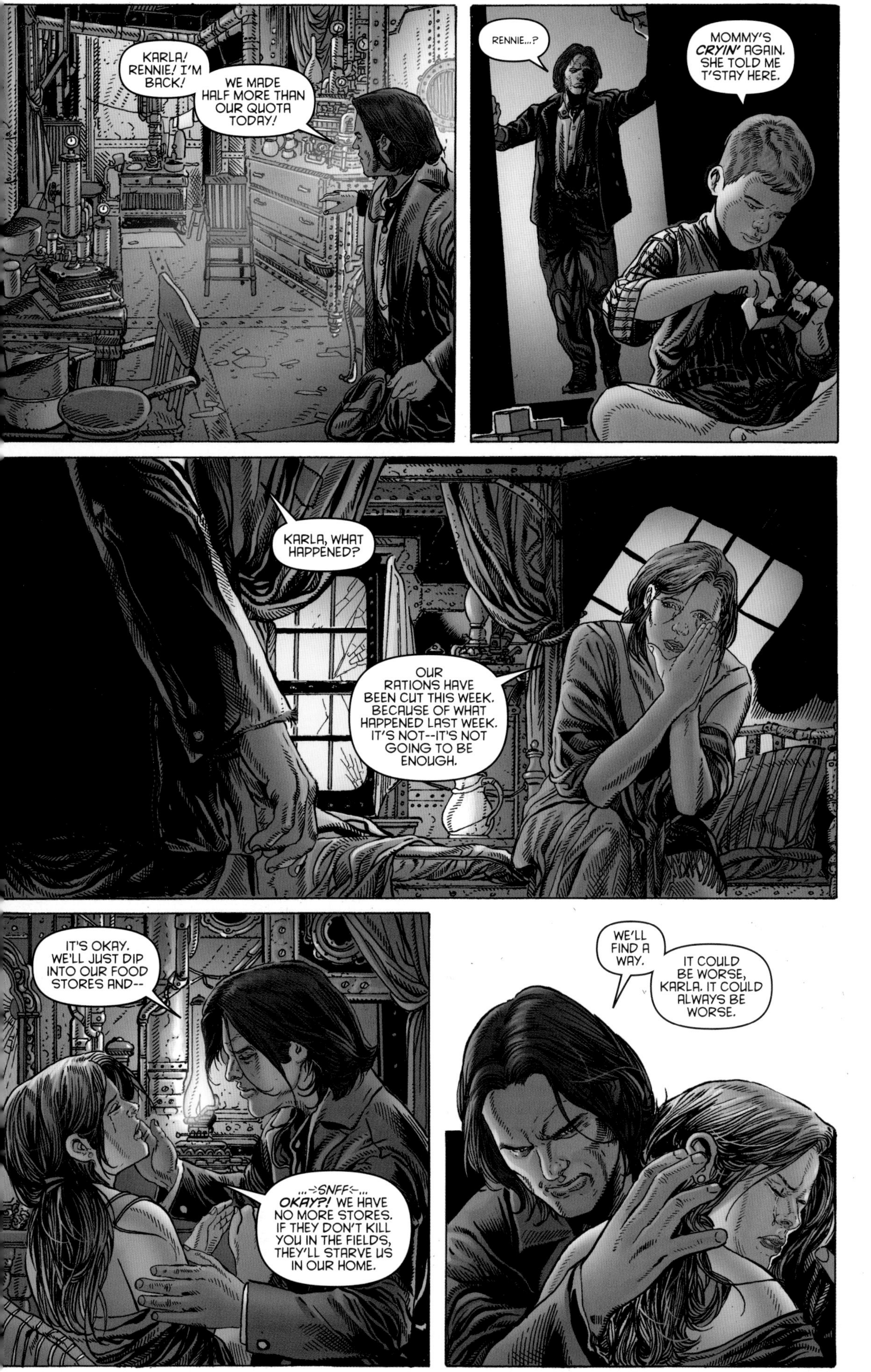
KARLA! RENNIE! I'M BACK!
WE MADE HALF MORE THAN OUR QUOTA TODAY!
RENNIE...?
MOMMY'S *CRYIN'* AGAIN. SHE TOLD ME T'STAY HERE.
KARLA, WHAT HAPPENED?
OUR RATIONS HAVE BEEN CUT THIS WEEK. BECAUSE OF WHAT HAPPENED LAST WEEK. IT'S NOT--IT'S NOT GOING TO BE ENOUGH.
IT'S OKAY. WE'LL JUST DIP INTO OUR FOOD STORES AND--
...SNFF... *OKAY?!* WE HAVE NO MORE STORES. IF THEY DON'T KILL YOU IN THE FIELDS, THEY'LL STARVE US IN OUR HOME.
WE'LL FIND A WAY.
IT COULD BE WORSE, KARLA. IT COULD ALWAYS BE WORSE.

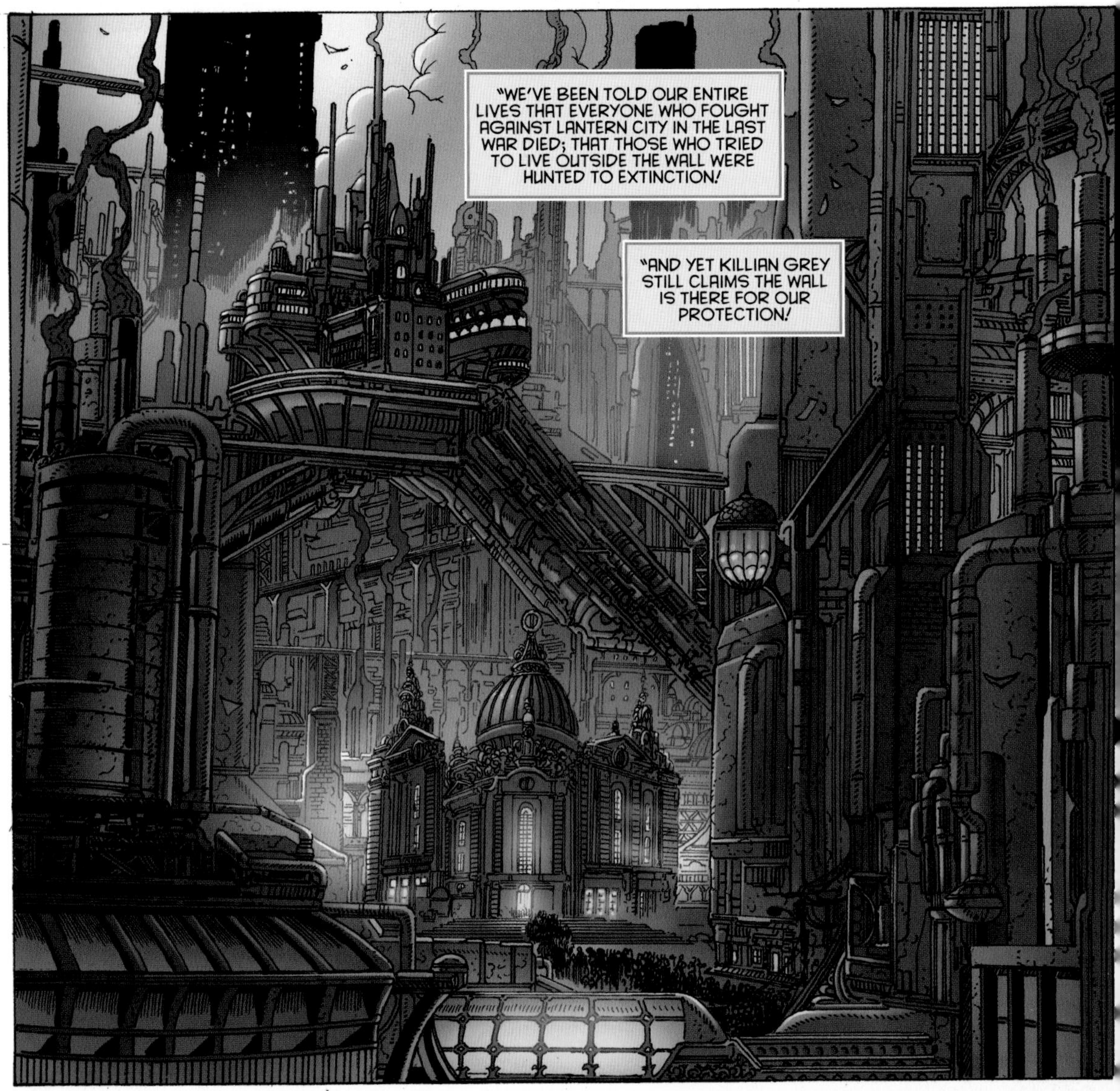
"WE'VE BEEN TOLD OUR ENTIRE LIVES THAT EVERYONE WHO FOUGHT AGAINST LANTERN CITY IN THE LAST WAR DIED; THAT THOSE WHO TRIED TO LIVE OUTSIDE THE WALL WERE HUNTED TO EXTINCTION!
"AND YET KILLIAN GREY STILL CLAIMS THE WALL IS THERE FOR OUR PROTECTION!

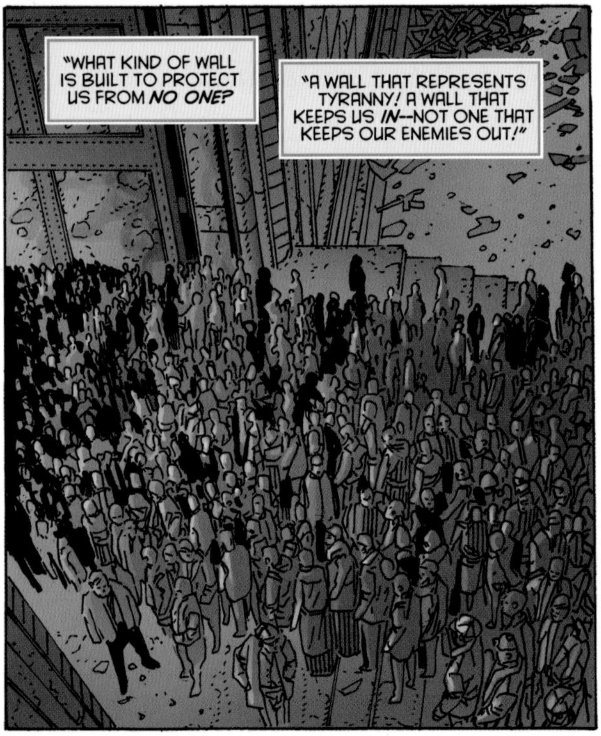
"WHAT KIND OF WALL IS BUILT TO PROTECT US FROM NO ONE?
"A WALL THAT REPRESENTS TYRANNY! A WALL THAT KEEPS US IN--NOT ONE THAT KEEPS OUR ENEMIES OUT!"

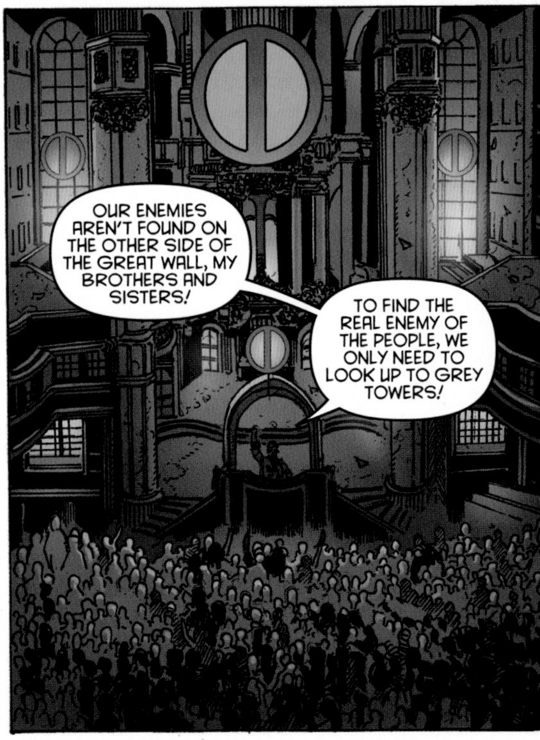
OUR ENEMIES AREN'T FOUND ON THE OTHER SIDE OF THE GREAT WALL, MY BROTHERS AND SISTERS!
TO FIND THE REAL ENEMY OF THE PEOPLE, WE ONLY NEED TO LOOK UP TO GREY TOWERS!

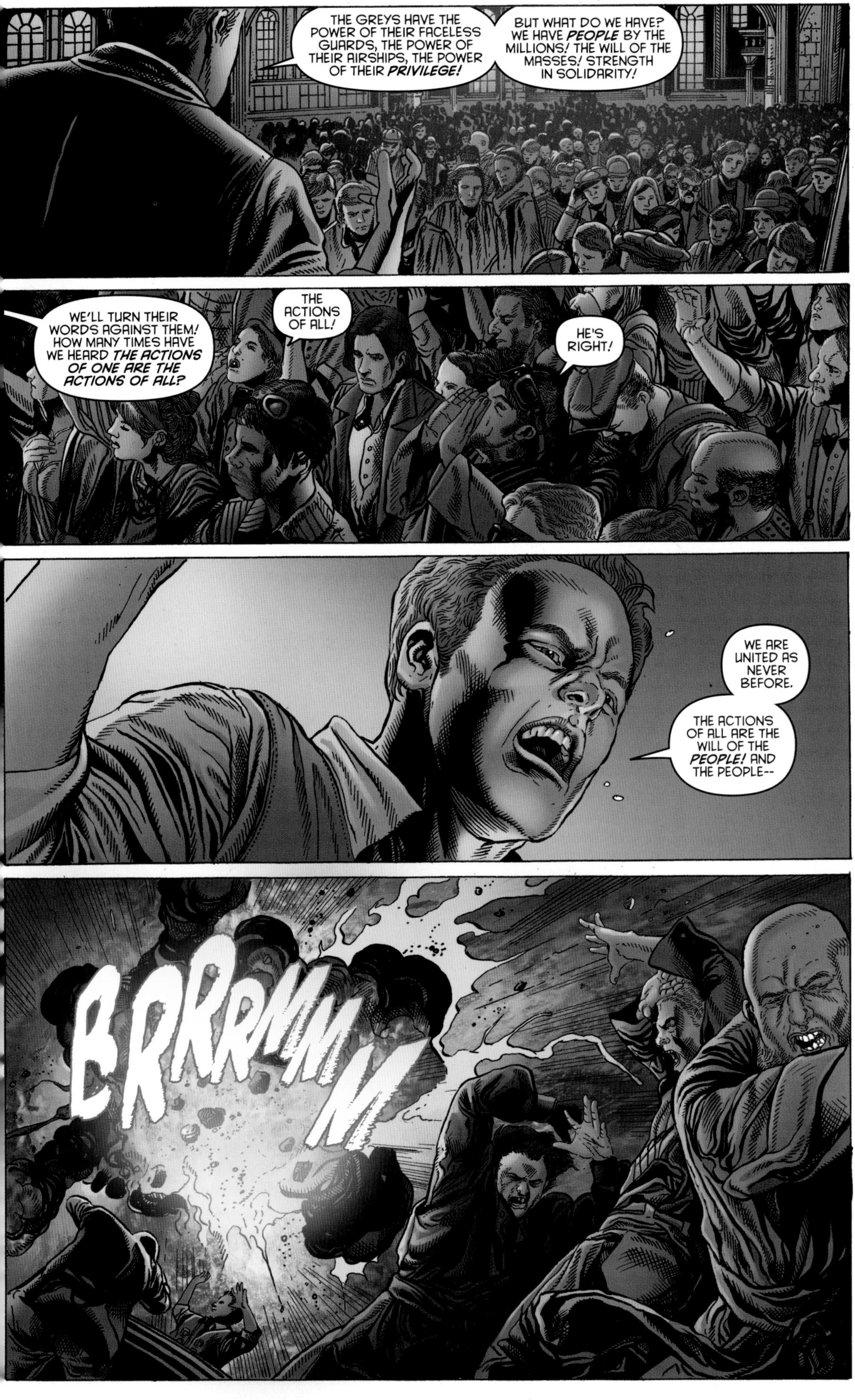
THE GREYS HAVE THE POWER OF THEIR FACELESS GUARDS, THE POWER OF THEIR AIRSHIPS, THE POWER OF THEIR *PRIVILEGE!*
BUT WHAT DO WE HAVE? WE HAVE *PEOPLE* BY THE MILLIONS! THE WILL OF THE MASSES! STRENGTH IN SOLIDARITY!
WE'LL TURN THEIR WORDS AGAINST THEM! HOW MANY TIMES HAVE WE HEARD *THE ACTIONS OF ONE ARE THE ACTIONS OF ALL?*
THE ACTIONS OF ALL!
HE'S RIGHT!
WE ARE UNITED AS NEVER BEFORE.
THE ACTIONS OF ALL ARE THE WILL OF THE *PEOPLE!* AND THE PEOPLE--
BRRRMMMM

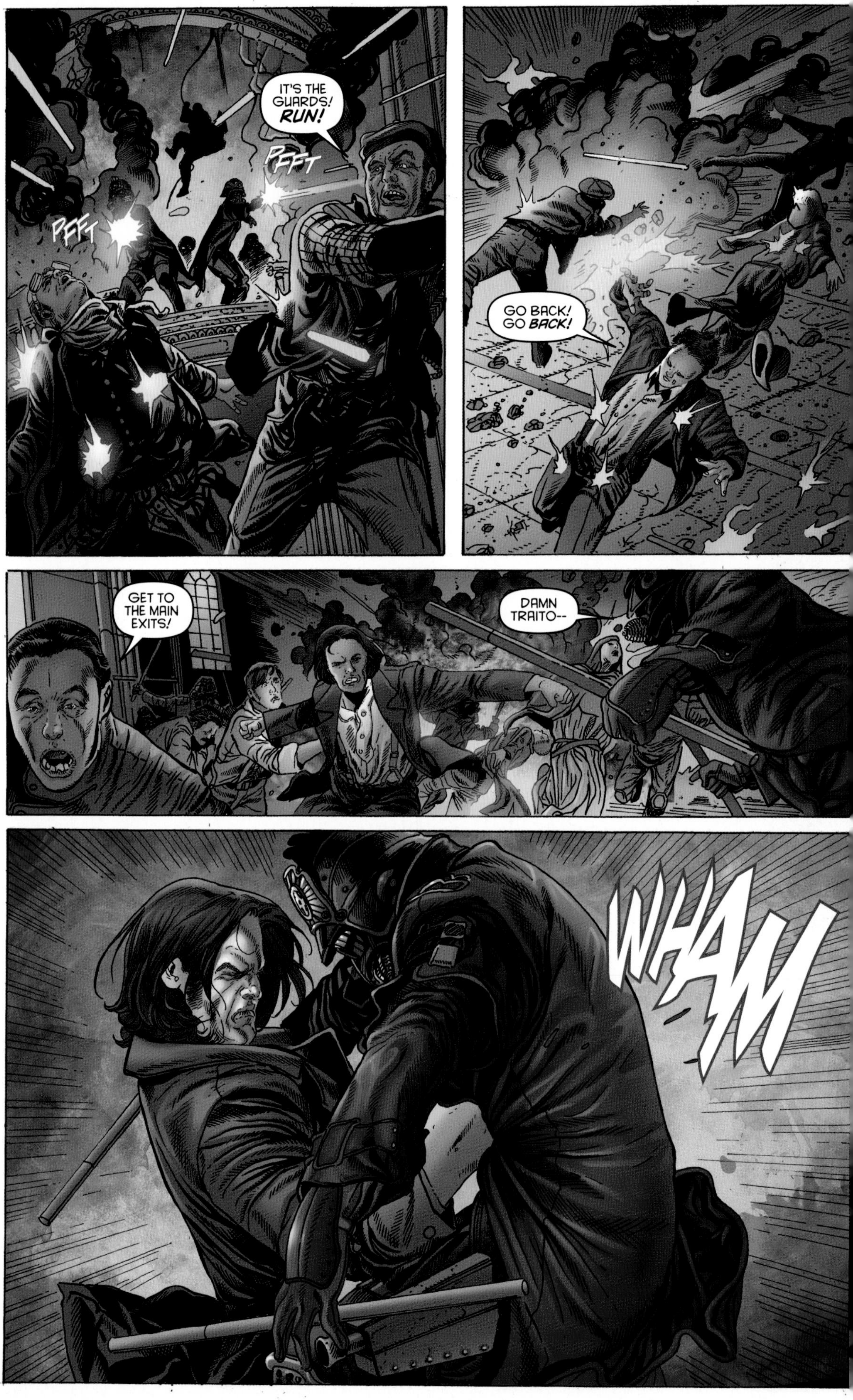
IT'S THE GUARDS! RUN!
PFFT
PFFT
GO BACK! GO BACK!
GET TO THE MAIN EXITS!
DAMN TRAITO--
WHAM

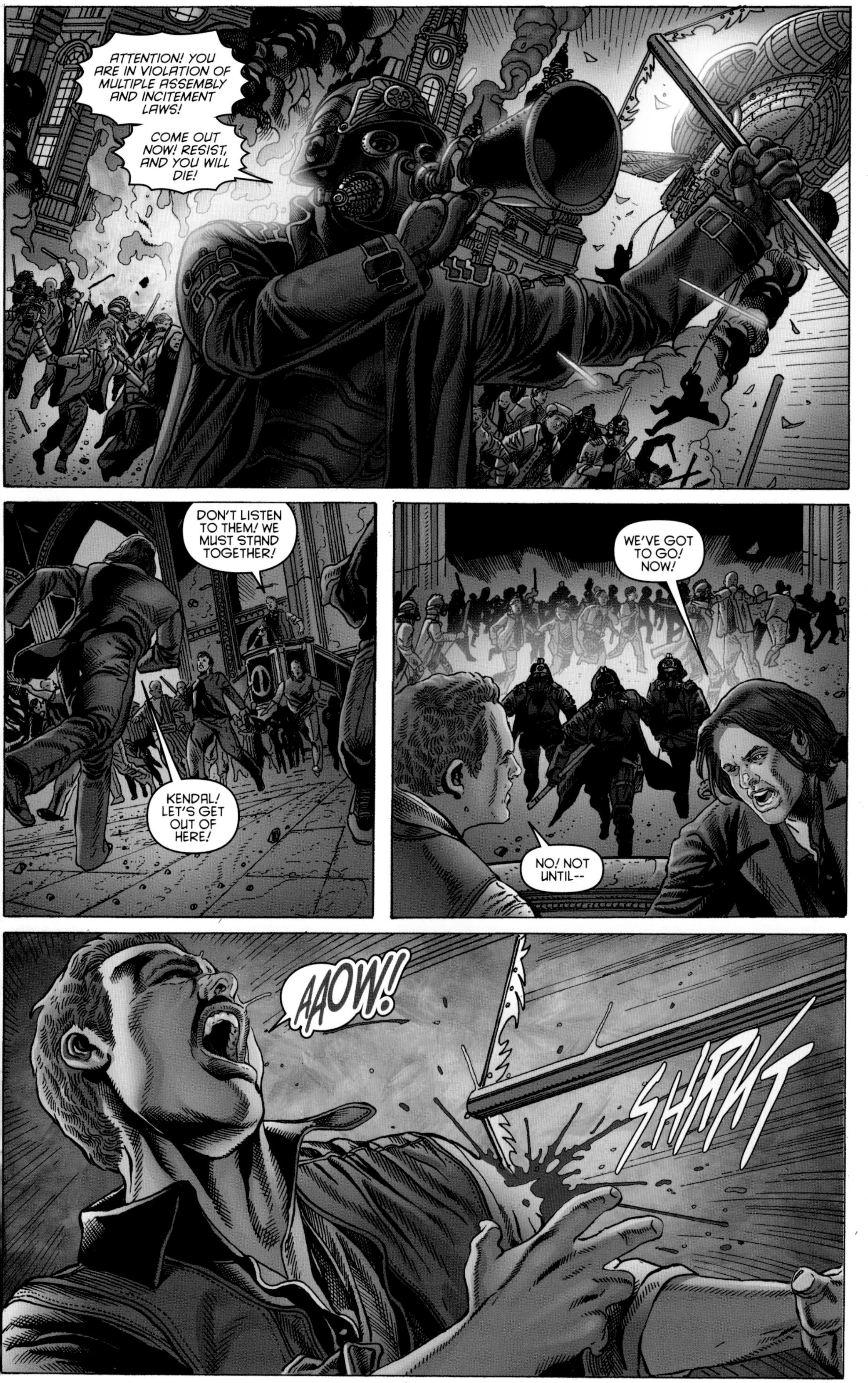
ATTENTION! YOU ARE IN VIOLATION OF MULTIPLE ASSEMBLY AND INCITEMENT LAWS!
COME OUT NOW! RESIST, AND YOU WILL DIE!
DON'T LISTEN TO THEM! WE MUST STAND TOGETHER!
KENDAL! LET'S GET OUT OF HERE!
WE'VE GOT TO GO! NOW!
NO! NOT UNTIL--
AAOW!
SHRAKT

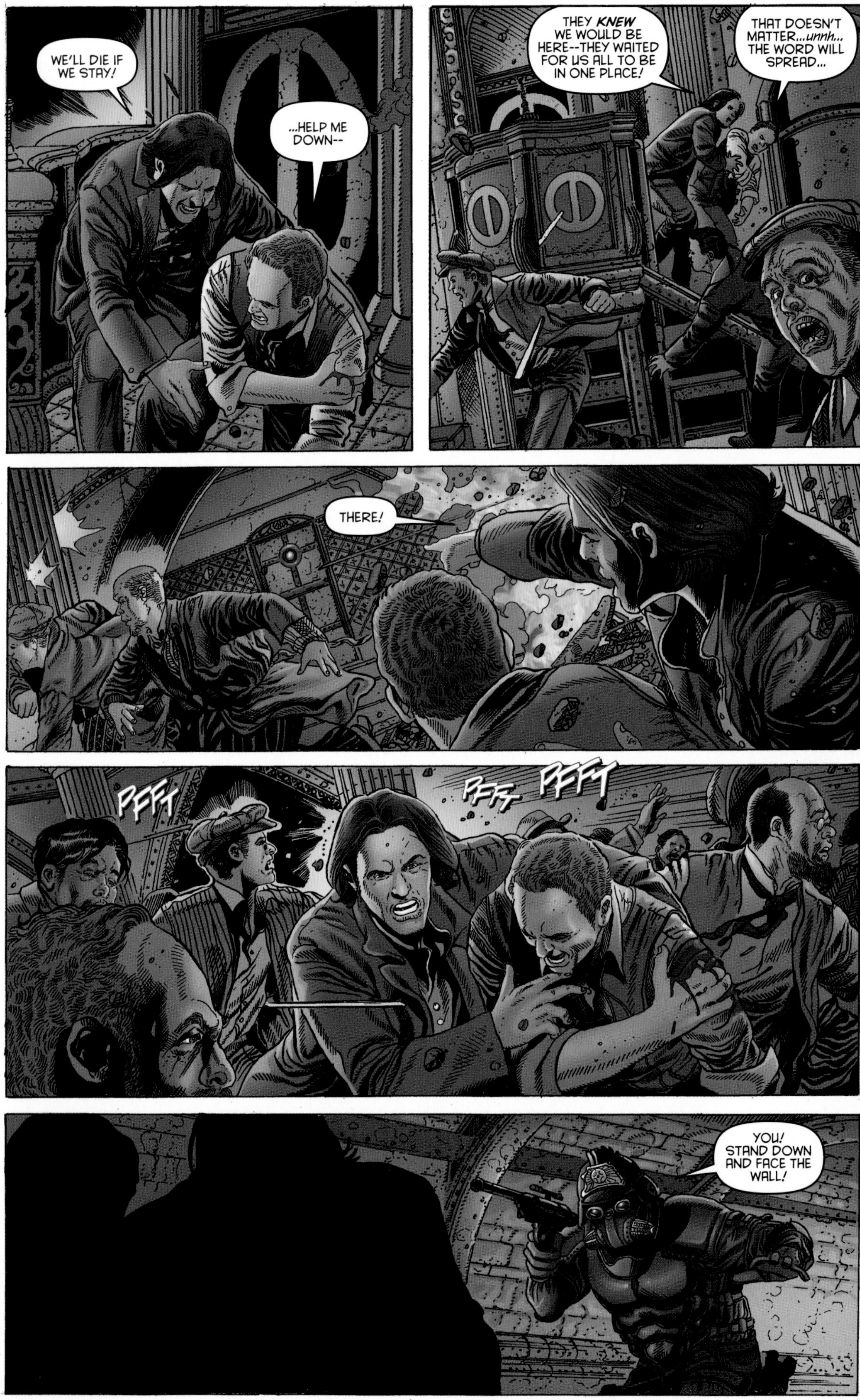
WE'LL DIE IF WE STAY!
...HELP ME DOWN--
THEY KNEW WE WOULD BE HERE--THEY WAITED FOR US ALL TO BE IN ONE PLACE!
THAT DOESN'T MATTER...unnh... THE WORD WILL SPREAD...
THERE!
PFFT
PFFT
PFFT
YOU! STAND DOWN AND FACE THE WALL!

CAPTAIN, CAN YOU EXPLAIN WHAT'S HAPPENING? WE CAME HERE TO WORSHIP--

SILENCE!

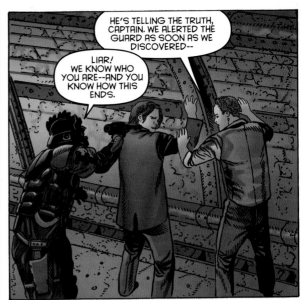

HE'S TELLING THE TRUTH, CAPTAIN. WE ALERTED THE GUARD AS SOON AS WE DISCOVERED--

LIAR! WE KNOW WHO YOU ARE--AND YOU KNOW HOW THIS ENDS.

FWOOM

HUNH?

SSSFFFFTTT

SHHKT

PEOPLE CAN SURPRISE YOU SOMETIMES.

YOU CAN SURPRISE YOURSELF.

SANDER... I...ehh...

FORGET IT--

WATCH MY BACK!

WHAT ARE YOU DOING?

HE'S *AIRBORNE CLASS*, THE BEST OF THE BEST--THE MOST RUTHLESS. AND HE'S A *CAPTAIN*.

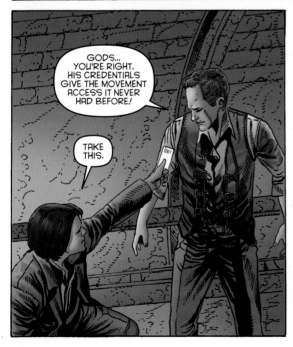

GODS... YOU'RE RIGHT. HIS CREDENTIALS GIVE THE MOVEMENT ACCESS IT NEVER HAD BEFORE!

TAKE THIS.

YOU KNOW, WHEN I WAS A KID, I DIDN'T THINK THEY EVEN HAD FACES.

SOMEHOW THIS MAKES IT WORSE.

YOU'RE ALWAYS TALKING ABOUT CHANGE, KENDAL. THIS IS YOUR CHANCE.

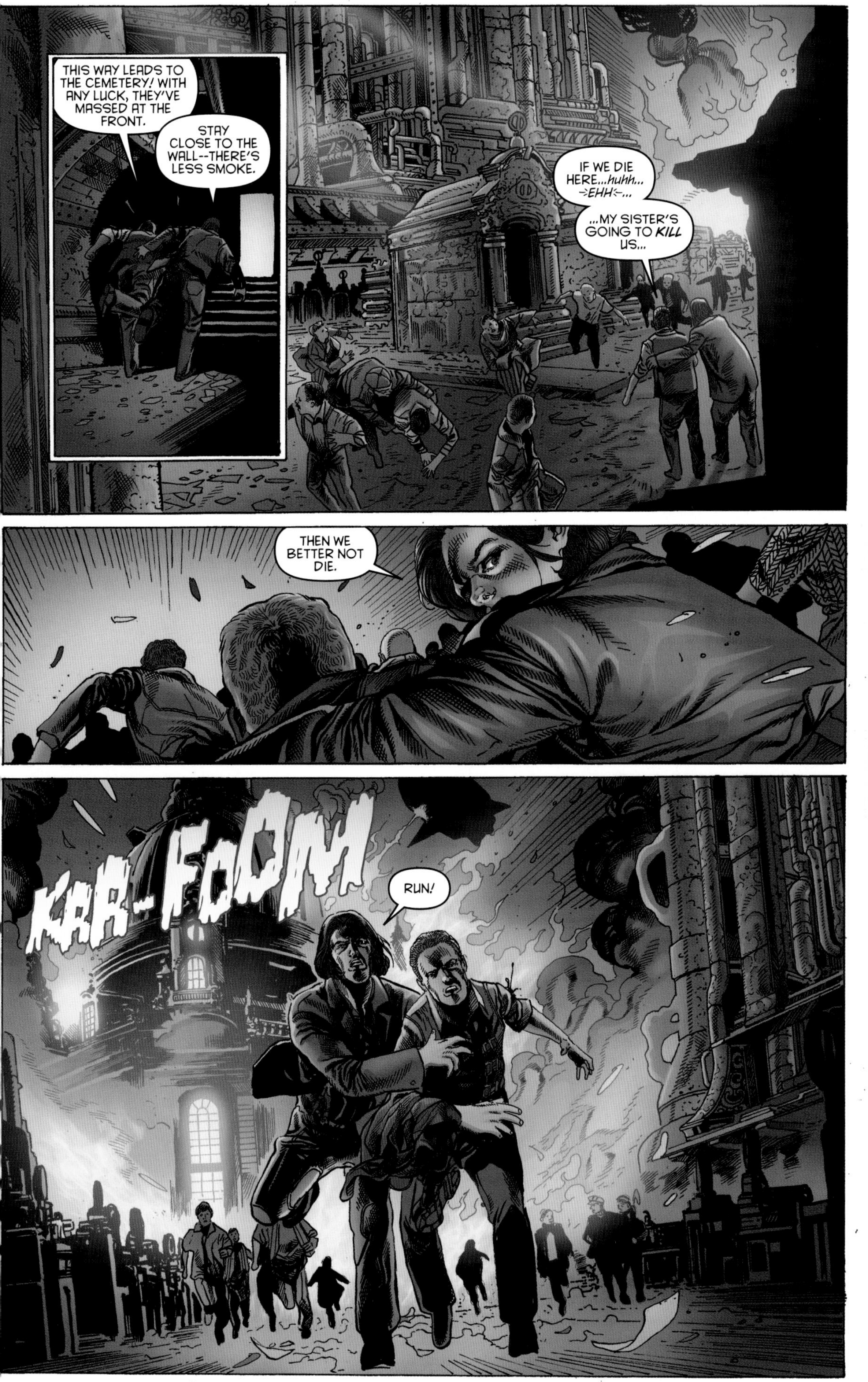
THIS WAY LEADS TO THE CEMETERY! WITH ANY LUCK, THEY'VE MASSED AT THE FRONT.
STAY CLOSE TO THE WALL--THERE'S LESS SMOKE.
IF WE DIE HERE...huhh... EHH...
...MY SISTER'S GOING TO KILL US...
THEN WE BETTER NOT DIE.
KRR-FOOM
RUN!

BE STILL, KENDAL. THIS GRAIN'LL CLEAN IT OUT.

...mmm...DON'T WASTE TOO MUCH...I *NEED* THAT BOTTLE...

THOSE GUARDS WERE AIRBORNE-- THEY WON'T REST TILL THEIR CAPTAIN IS ACCOUNTED FOR.

THEN WE BEST MAKE SURE THEY FIND HIM.

YOU'RE THE ONLY ONE WHO CAN DO THIS, SANDER. YOU HAVE HIS BUILD--

WHAT? THAT UNIFORM IS FOR *YOU.* I HAVE TO PROTECT MY--

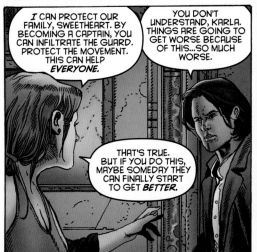

I CAN PROTECT OUR FAMILY, SWEETHEART. BY BECOMING A CAPTAIN, YOU CAN INFILTRATE THE GUARD. PROTECT THE MOVEMENT. THIS CAN HELP *EVERYONE.*

YOU DON'T UNDERSTAND, KARLA. THINGS ARE GOING TO GET WORSE BECAUSE OF THIS...SO MUCH WORSE.

THAT'S TRUE. BUT IF YOU DO THIS, MAYBE SOMEDAY THEY CAN FINALLY START TO GET *BETTER.*

WE CAN'T TELL ANYONE ELSE--NOT EVEN THOSE CLOSE TO ME IN THE MOVEMENT.

YOU NEED TO GET BACK BEFORE THE CAPTAIN IS REPORTED MISSING. IF HE'S DEAD, SO ARE OUR CHANCES.

YOU HAVE TO CHOOSE, SANDER. NOW.

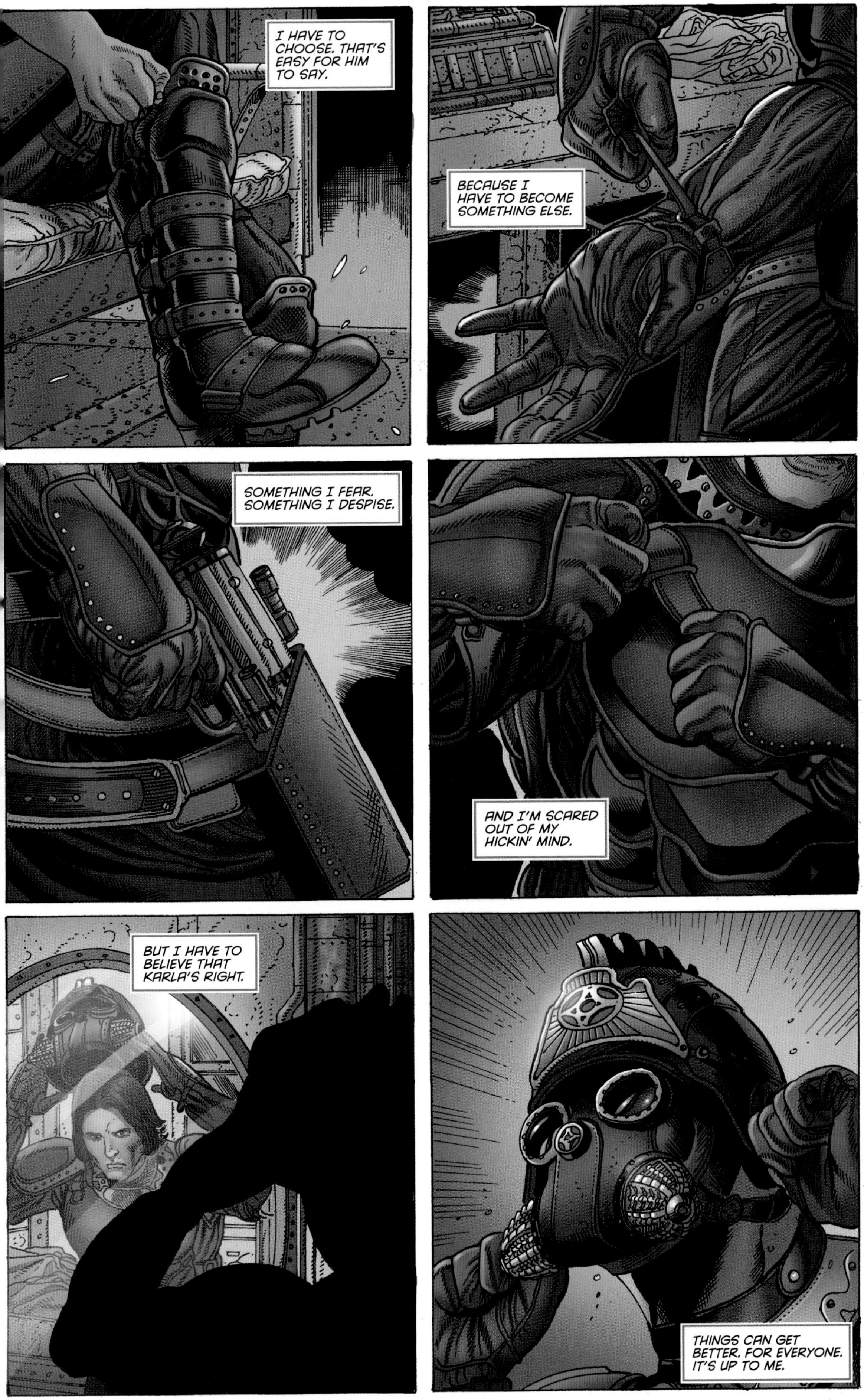
I HAVE TO CHOOSE. THAT'S EASY FOR HIM TO SAY.
BECAUSE I HAVE TO BECOME SOMETHING ELSE.
SOMETHING I FEAR. SOMETHING I DESPISE.
AND I'M SCARED OUT OF MY HICKIN' MIND.
BUT I HAVE TO BELIEVE THAT KARLA'S RIGHT.
THINGS CAN GET BETTER. FOR EVERYONE. IT'S UP TO ME.

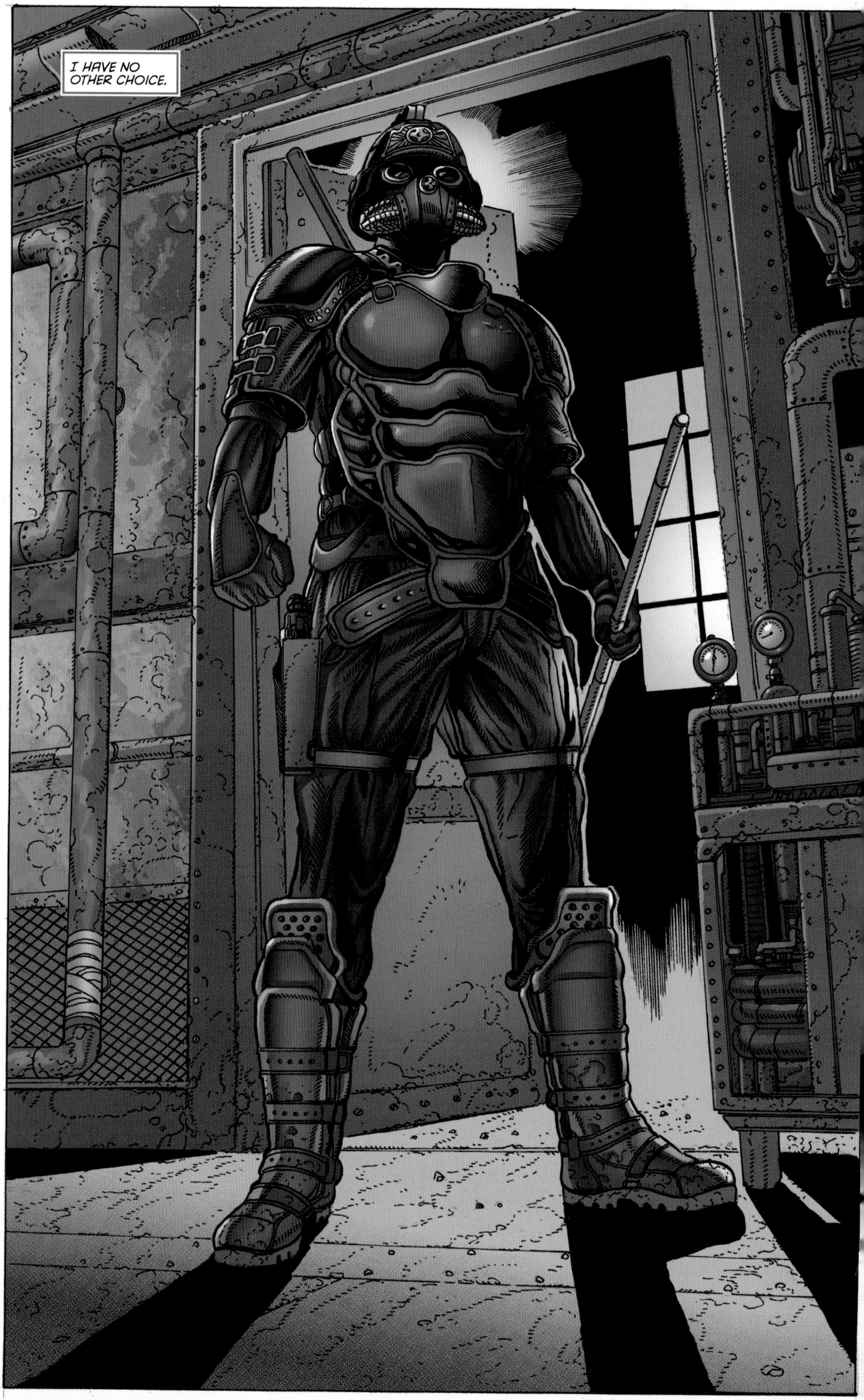
I HAVE NO OTHER CHOICE.

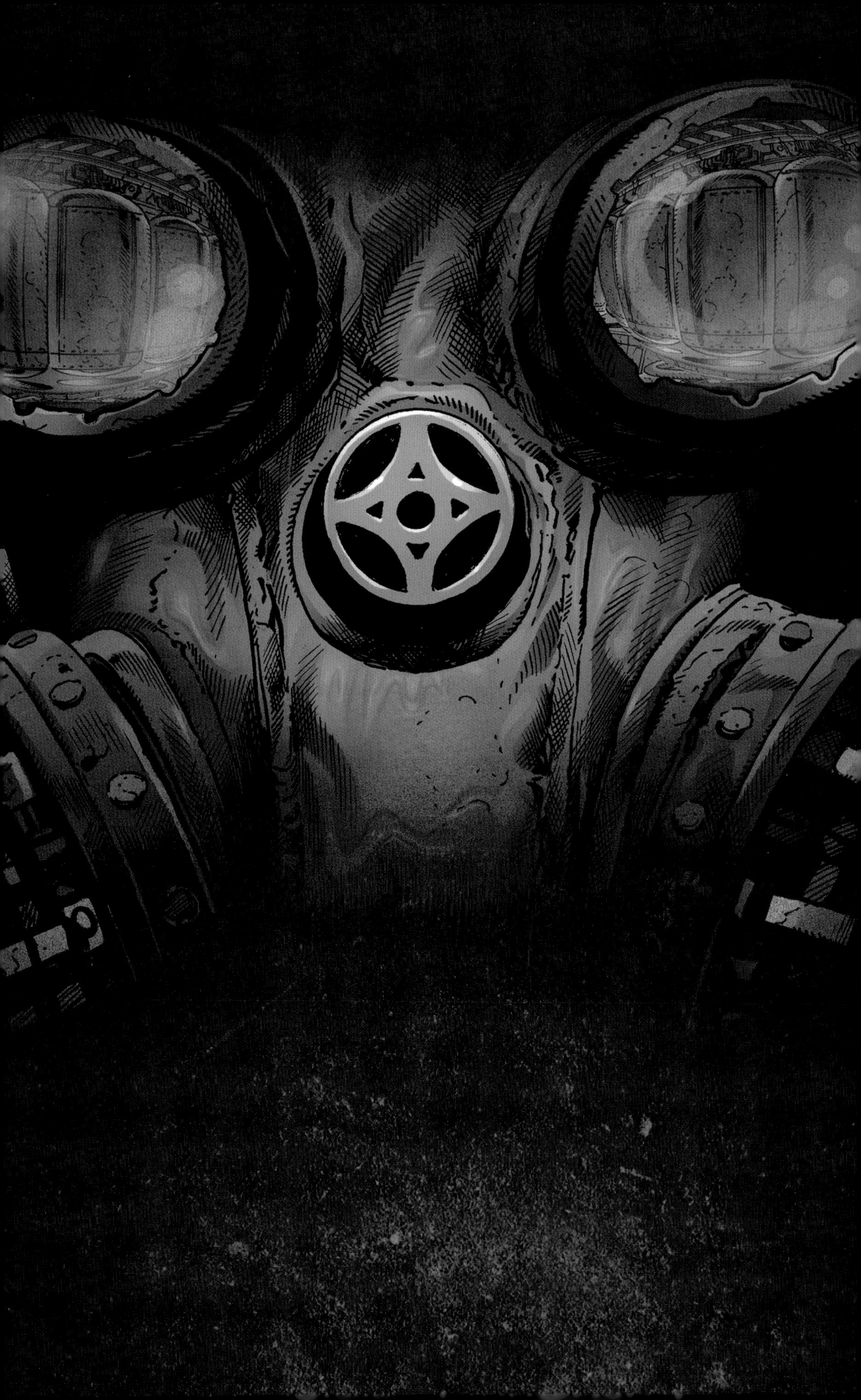

CHAPTER TWO

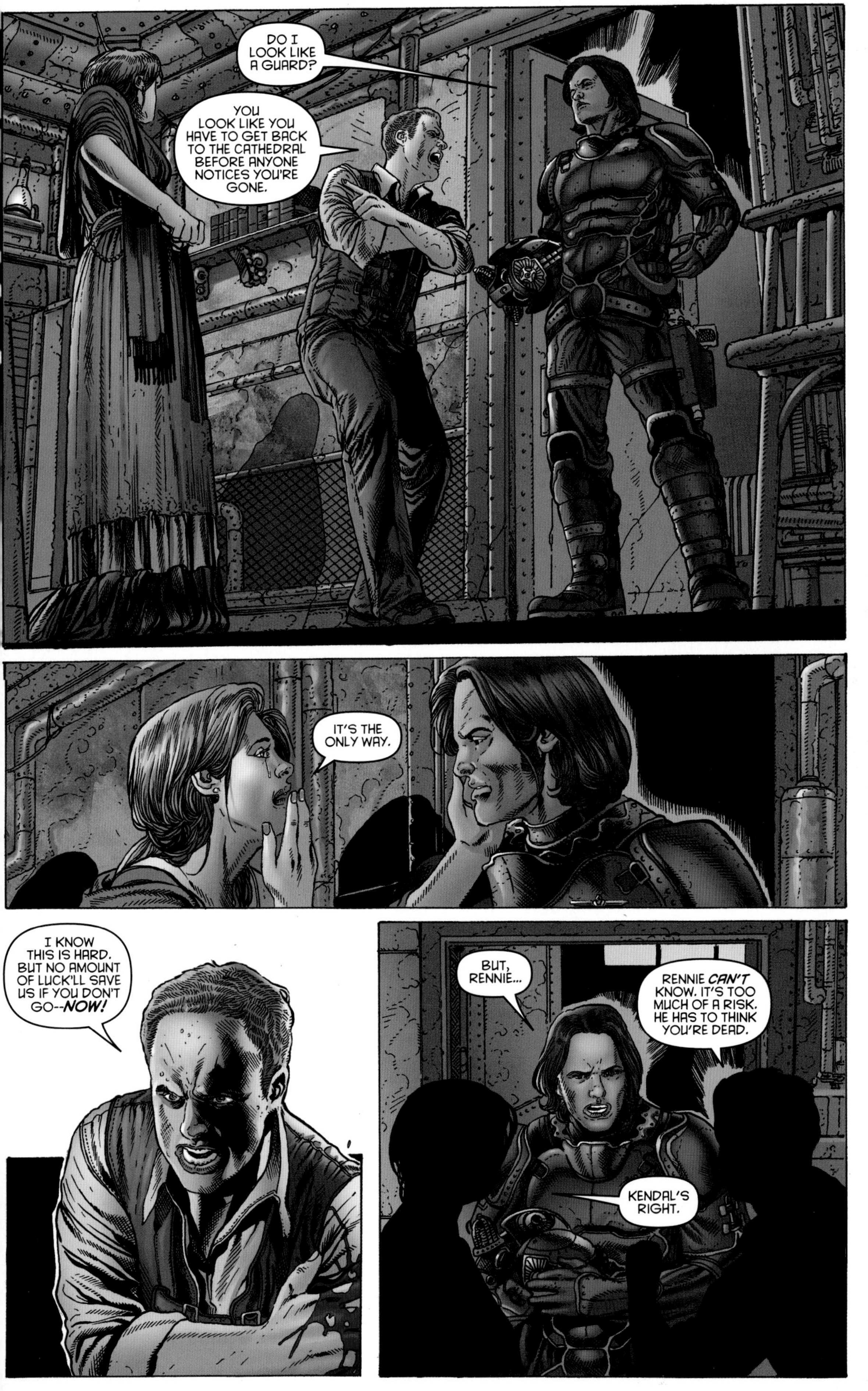
DO I LOOK LIKE A GUARD?
YOU LOOK LIKE YOU HAVE TO GET BACK TO THE CATHEDRAL BEFORE ANYONE NOTICES YOU'RE GONE.
IT'S THE ONLY WAY.
I KNOW THIS IS HARD. BUT NO AMOUNT OF LUCK'LL SAVE US IF YOU DON'T GO--NOW!
BUT, RENNIE...
RENNIE CAN'T KNOW. IT'S TOO MUCH OF A RISK. HE HAS TO THINK YOU'RE DEAD.
KENDAL'S RIGHT.

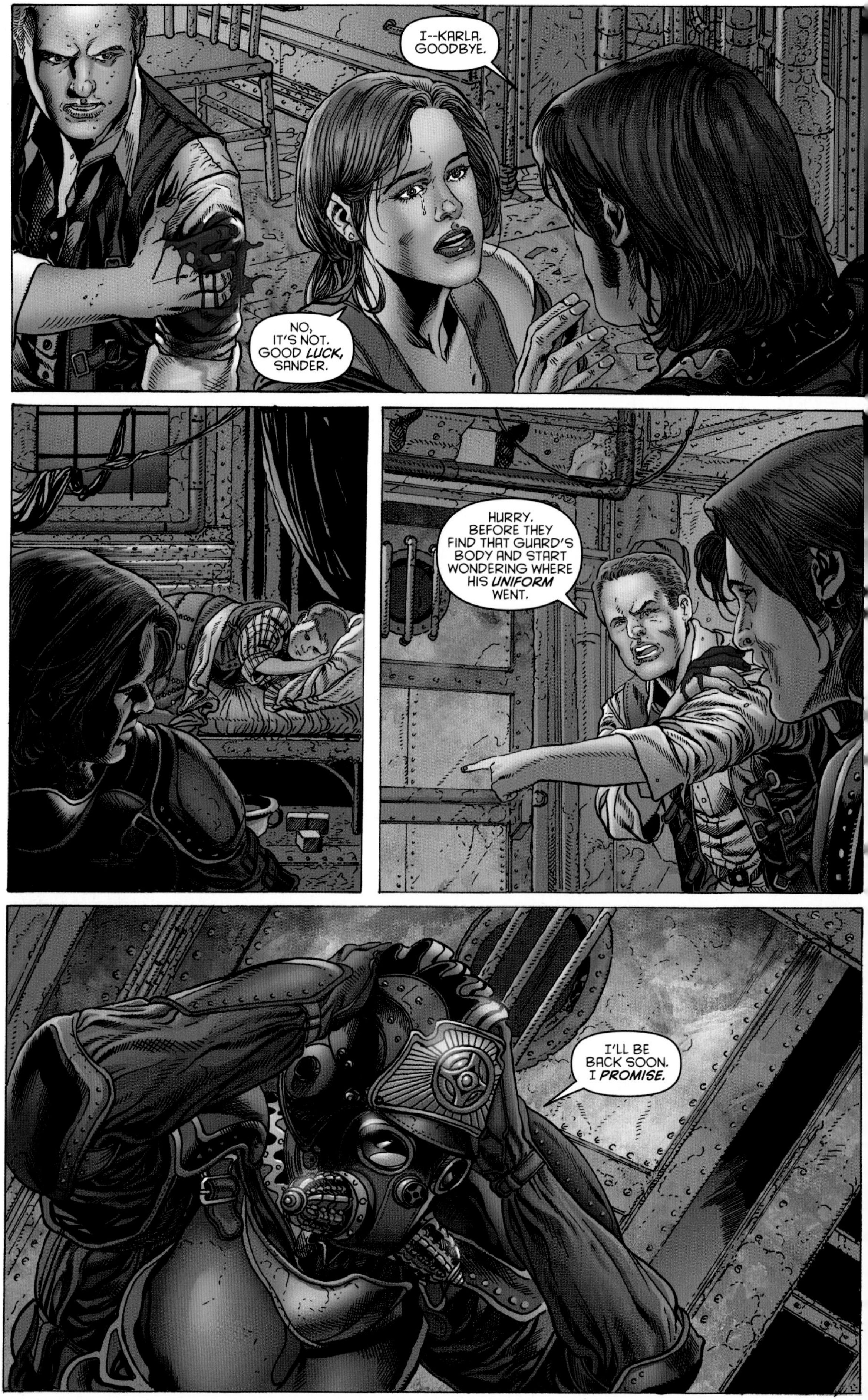
I--KARLA. GOODBYE.
NO, IT'S NOT. GOOD LUCK, SANDER.
HURRY. BEFORE THEY FIND THAT GUARD'S BODY AND START WONDERING WHERE HIS UNIFORM WENT.
I'LL BE BACK SOON. I PROMISE.

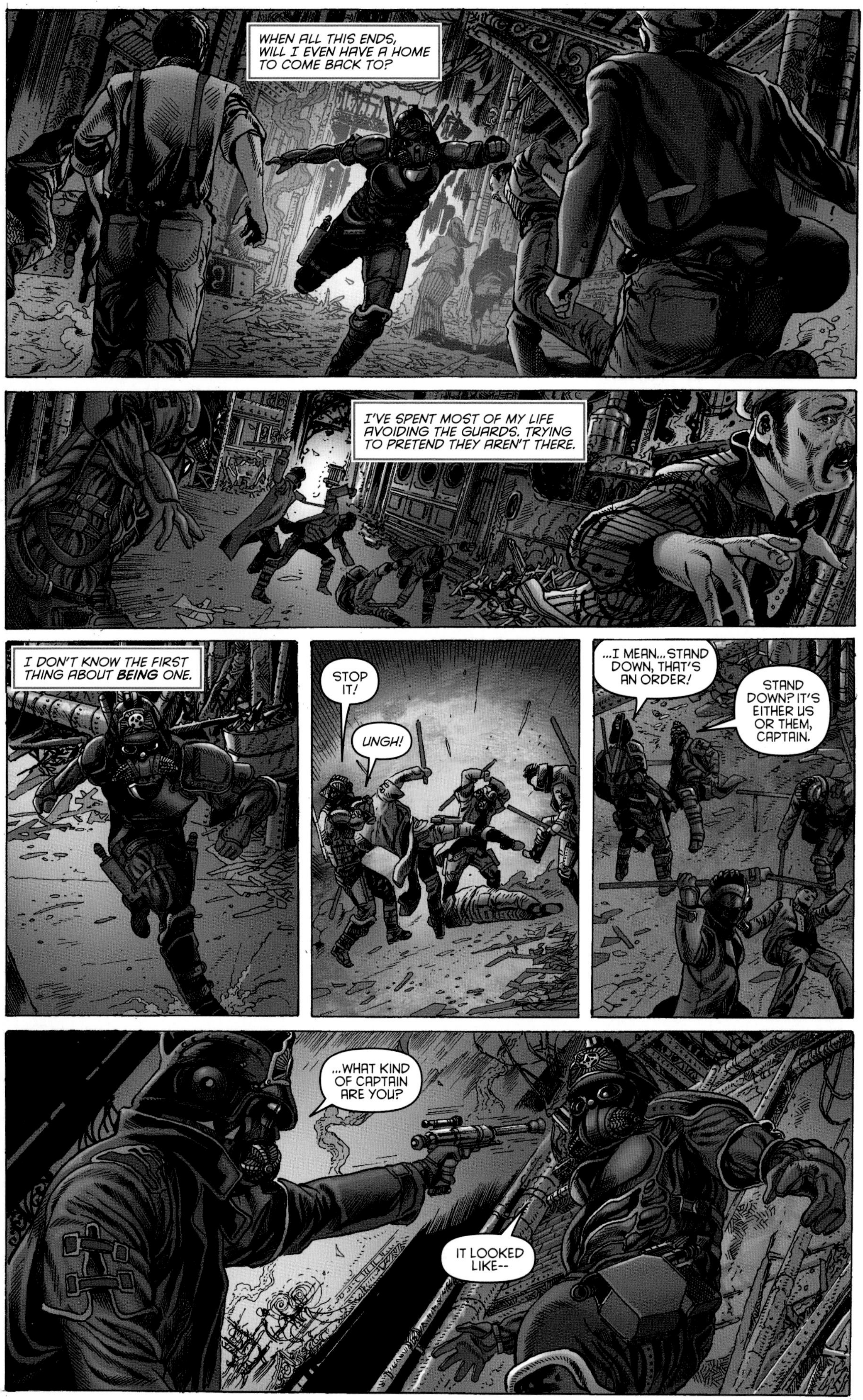
WHEN ALL THIS ENDS, WILL I EVEN HAVE A HOME TO COME BACK TO?
I'VE SPENT MOST OF MY LIFE AVOIDING THE GUARDS. TRYING TO PRETEND THEY AREN'T THERE.
I DON'T KNOW THE FIRST THING ABOUT BEING ONE.
STOP IT!
UNGH!
...I MEAN...STAND DOWN, THAT'S AN ORDER!
STAND DOWN? IT'S EITHER US OR THEM, CAPTAIN.
...WHAT KIND OF CAPTAIN ARE YOU?
IT LOOKED LIKE--

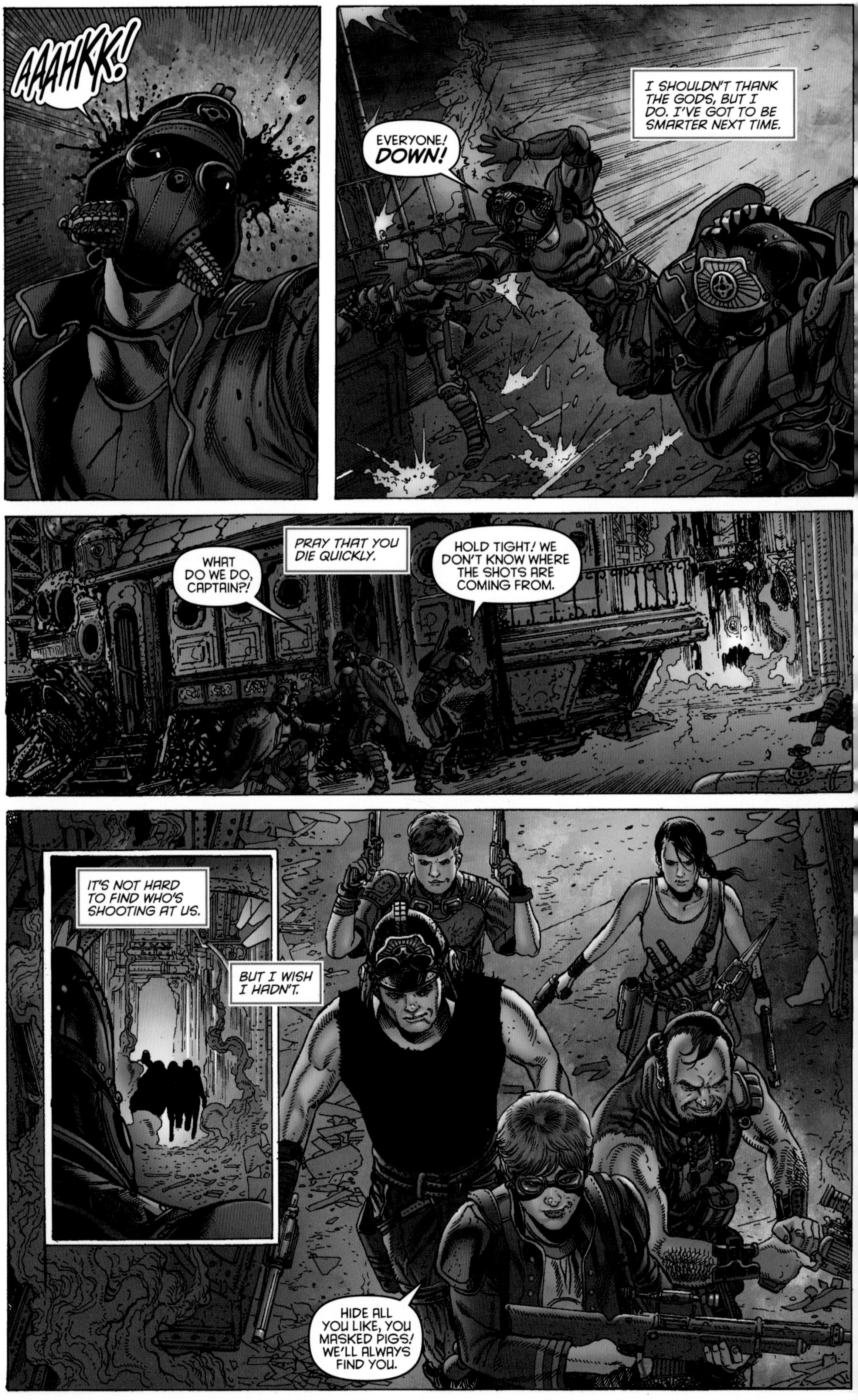
AAAHKK!
EVERYONE! DOWN!
I SHOULDN'T THANK THE GODS, BUT I DO. I'VE GOT TO BE SMARTER NEXT TIME.
WHAT DO WE DO, CAPTAIN?!
PRAY THAT YOU DIE QUICKLY.
HOLD TIGHT! WE DON'T KNOW WHERE THE SHOTS ARE COMING FROM.
IT'S NOT HARD TO FIND WHO'S SHOOTING AT US.
BUT I WISH I HADN'T.
HIDE ALL YOU LIKE, YOU MASKED PIGS! WE'LL ALWAYS FIND YOU.

NOW I NEED TO GET US **BOTH** OUT ALIVE.

THERE'S TOO MANY OF THEM. SPLIT UP. TRY AND LEAD THEM OFF. GO! GO!

REMEMBER-- AIM FOR THE NECK!

WHAAA!

I'M SORRY. I'M SORRY.

LIZEL, GET AS FAR FROM HERE AS YOU CAN!

SANDER? IS THAT YOU? WHAT ARE YOU--?

JUST GO! NOW!

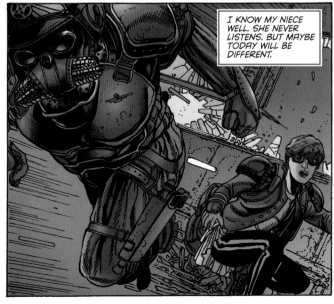

I KNOW MY NIECE WELL. SHE NEVER LISTENS. BUT MAYBE TODAY WILL BE DIFFERENT.

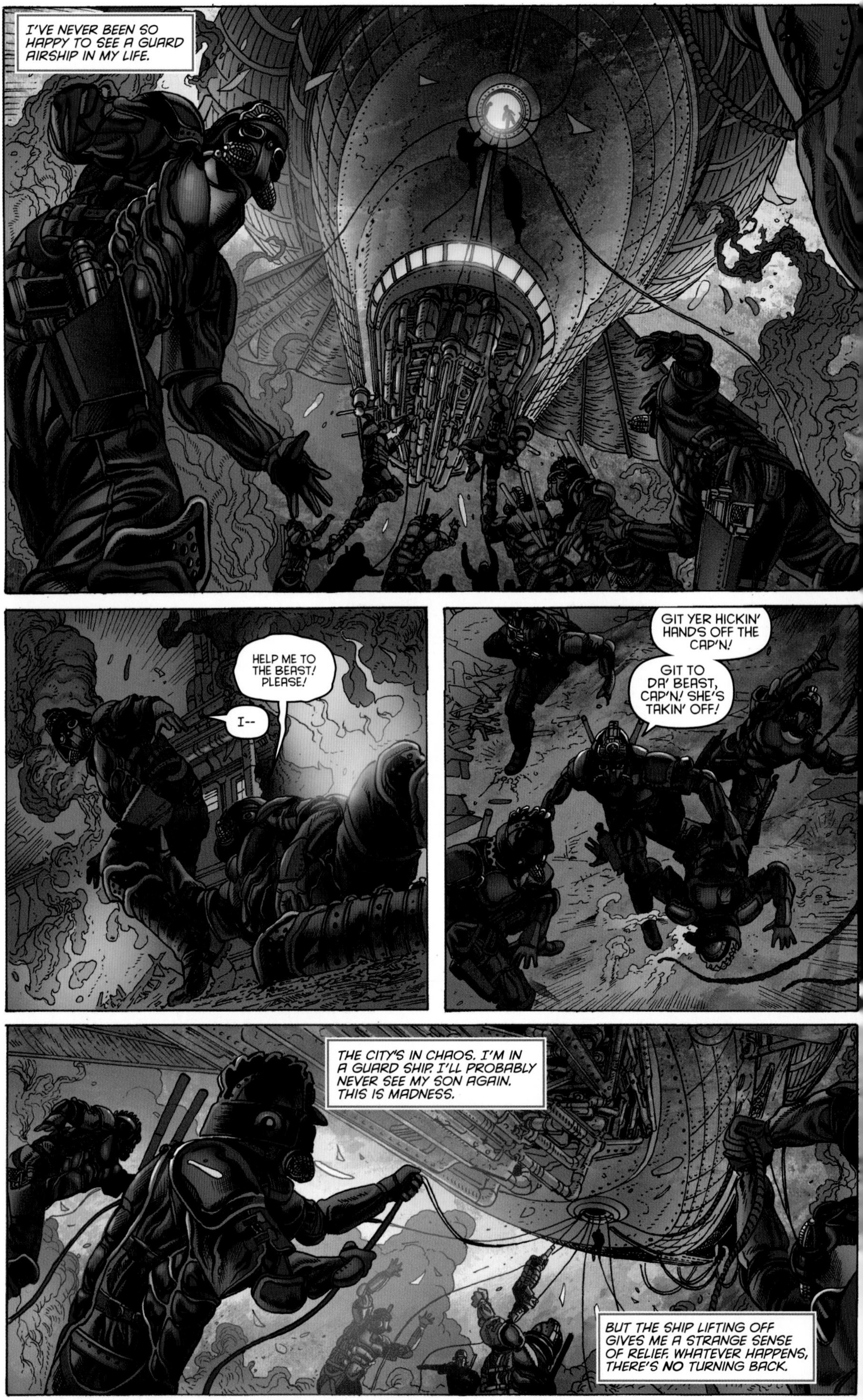
I'VE NEVER BEEN SO HAPPY TO SEE A GUARD AIRSHIP IN MY LIFE.
HELP ME TO THE BEAST! PLEASE!
I--
GIT YER HICKIN' HANDS OFF THE CAP'N!
GIT TO DA' BEAST, CAP'N! SHE'S TAKIN' OFF!
THE CITY'S IN CHAOS. I'M IN A GUARD SHIP. I'LL PROBABLY NEVER SEE MY SON AGAIN. THIS IS MADNESS.
BUT THE SHIP LIFTING OFF GIVES ME A STRANGE SENSE OF RELIEF. WHATEVER HAPPENS, THERE'S NO TURNING BACK.

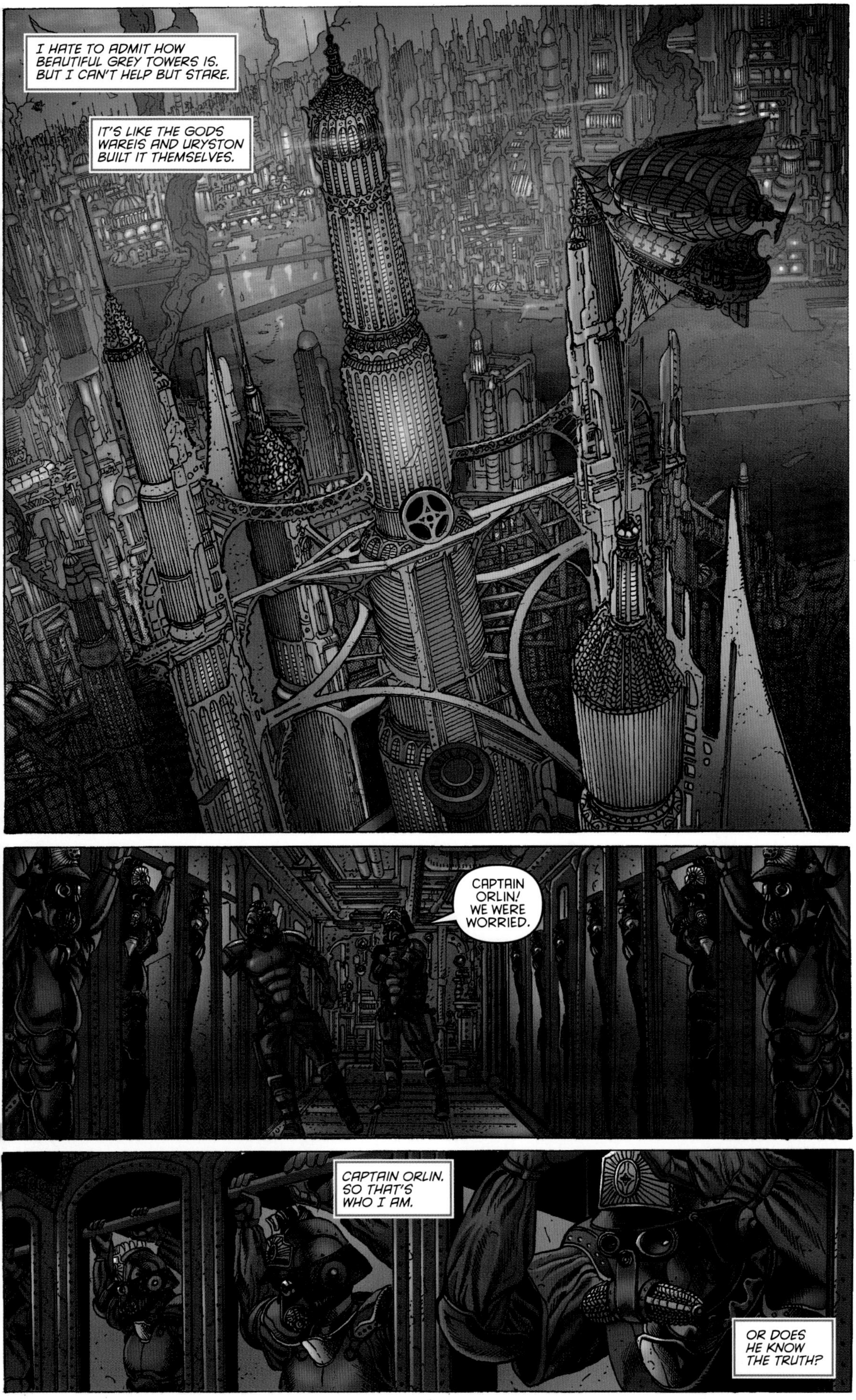
I HATE TO ADMIT HOW BEAUTIFUL GREY TOWERS IS. BUT I CAN'T HELP BUT STARE.
IT'S LIKE THE GODS WAREIS AND URYSTON BUILT IT THEMSELVES.
CAPTAIN ORLIN! WE WERE WORRIED.
CAPTAIN ORLIN. SO THAT'S WHO I AM.
OR DOES HE KNOW THE TRUTH?

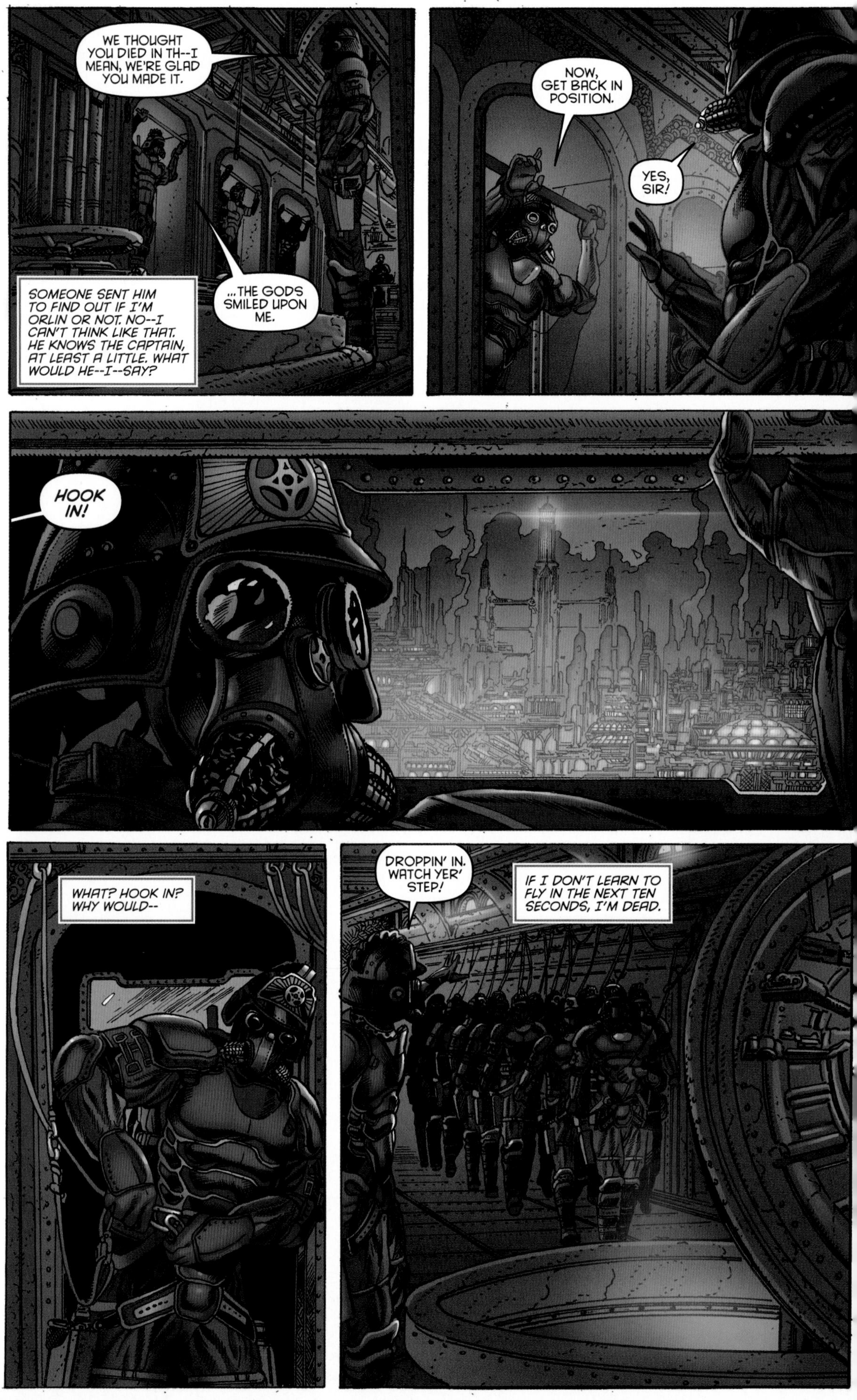
WE THOUGHT YOU DIED IN TH--I MEAN, WE'RE GLAD YOU MADE IT.
SOMEONE SENT HIM TO FIND OUT IF I'M ORLIN OR NOT. NO--I CAN'T THINK LIKE THAT. HE KNOWS THE CAPTAIN, AT LEAST A LITTLE. WHAT WOULD HE--I--SAY?
...THE GODS SMILED UPON ME.
NOW, GET BACK IN POSITION.
YES, SIR!
HOOK IN!
WHAT? HOOK IN? WHY WOULD--
DROPPIN' IN. WATCH YER' STEP!
IF I DON'T LEARN TO FLY IN THE NEXT TEN SECONDS, I'M DEAD.

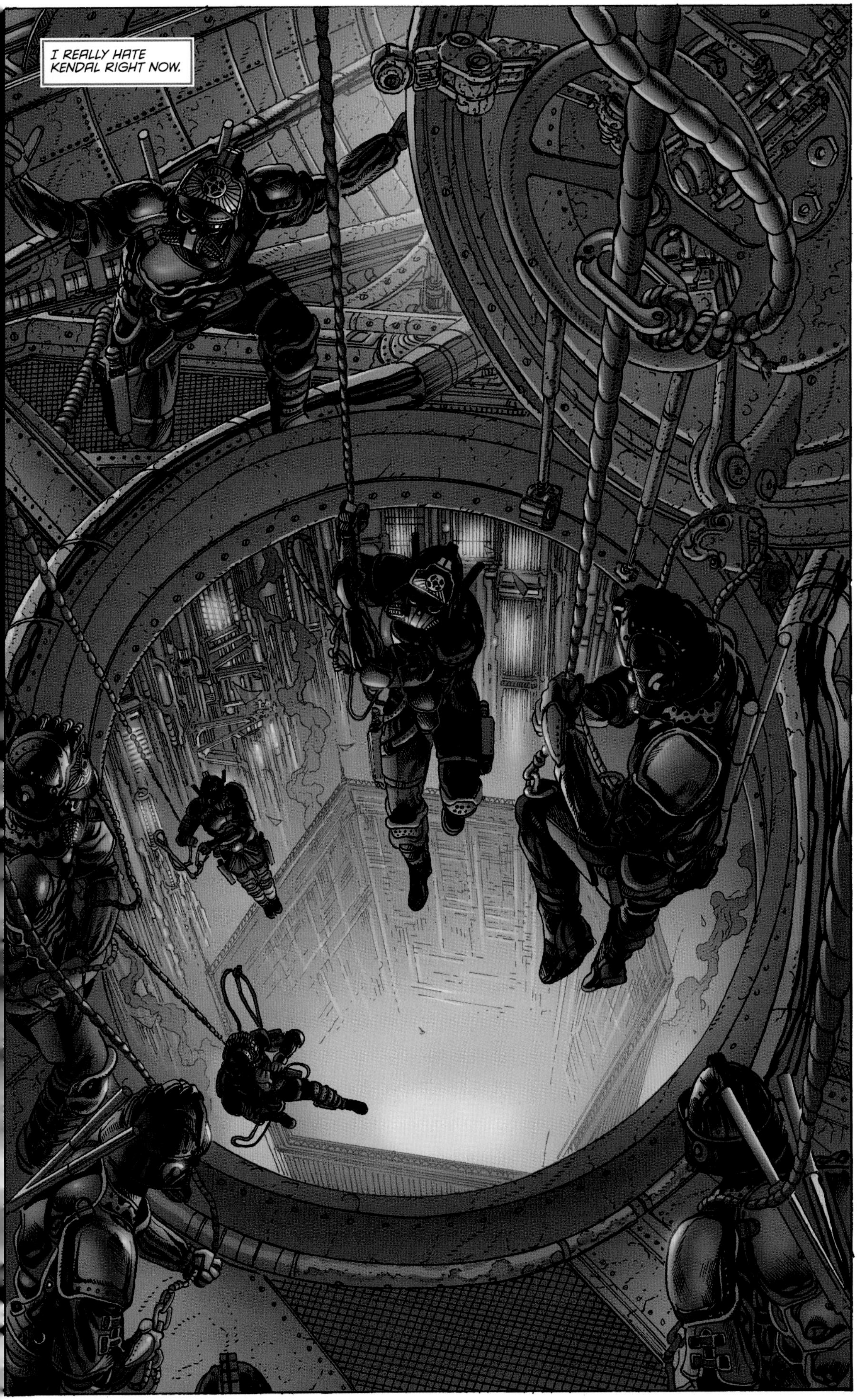
I REALLY HATE KENDAL RIGHT NOW.

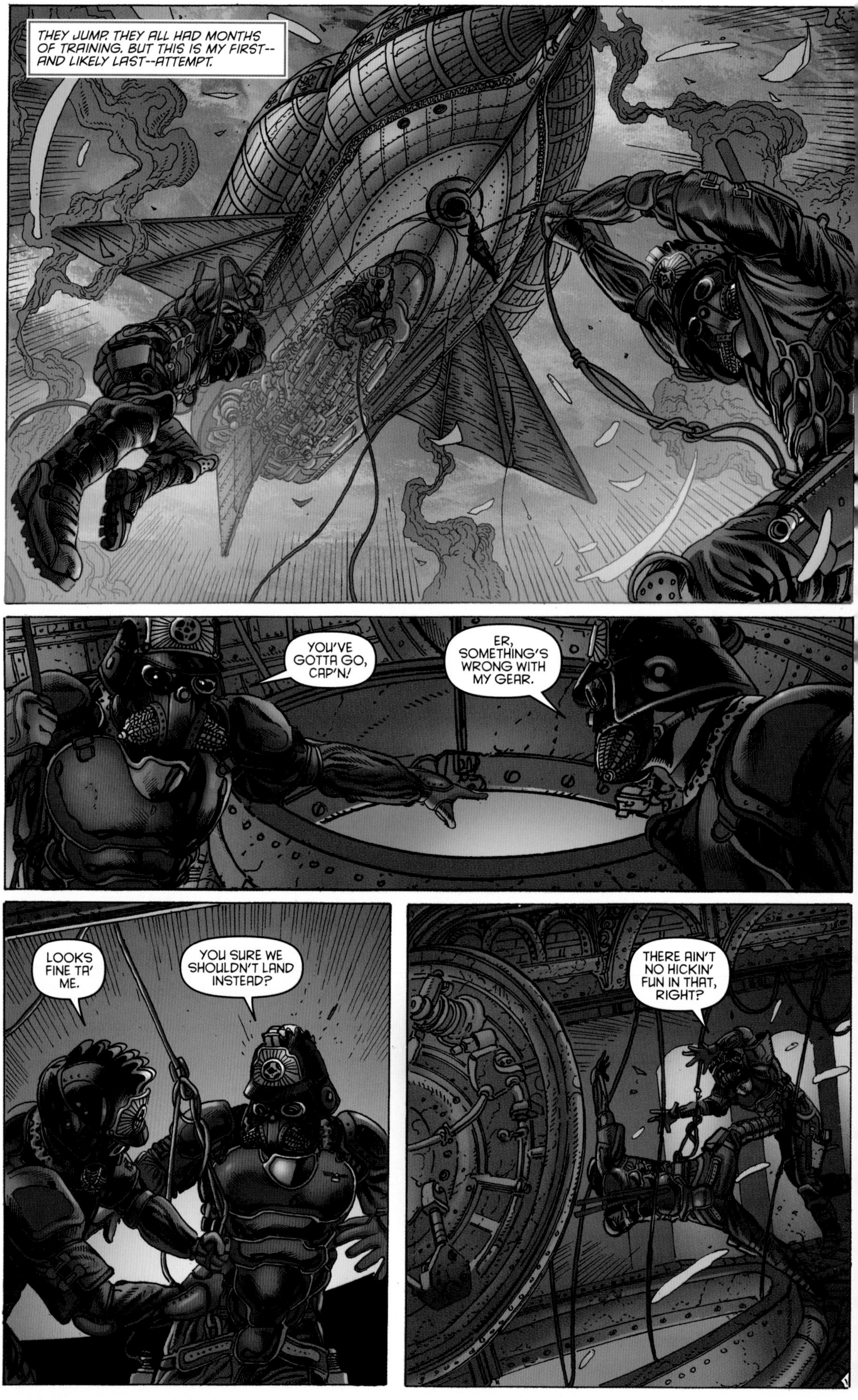
THEY JUMP. THEY ALL HAD MONTHS OF TRAINING. BUT THIS IS MY FIRST--AND LIKELY LAST--ATTEMPT.
YOU'VE GOTTA GO, CAP'N!
ER, SOMETHING'S WRONG WITH MY GEAR.
LOOKS FINE TA' ME.
YOU SURE WE SHOULDN'T LAND INSTEAD?
THERE AIN'T NO HICKIN' FUN IN THAT, RIGHT?

FALLING TRICKS YOU.

IT MAKES YOU FEEL FREE...

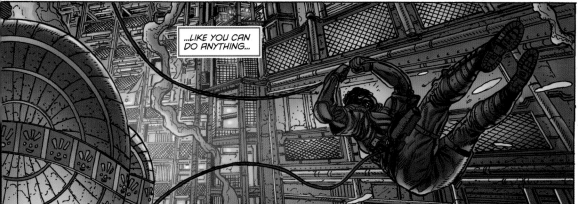

...LIKE YOU CAN DO ANYTHING...

...JUST BEFORE IT KILLS YOU.

WHAT? I'M CAUGHT, I--

SNTCK

I FALL A GRAND TOTAL OF SIX FEET.

I'M STILL PRETTY SURE I'M DEAD.

AHH!

ON THE STREETS, THEY CALL THIS PLACE *THE SIX.*

IT'S THE ONLY PLACE TOUGHER TO BREAK INTO THAN *GREY TOWERS.*

I ALWAYS SAID IF I GOT IN HERE, I'D FIREBOMB THIS HICKIN' PLACE TO ASHES. NOT THAT I HAD THE GUTS TO DO IT. BUT I SAID I WOULD.

FOR KILLING MY FATHER.

FOR ALL THE SUFFERING THEY'VE CAUSED ME AND EVERYONE BACK HOME.

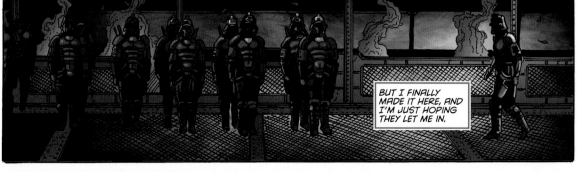

BUT I FINALLY MADE IT HERE, AND I'M JUST HOPING THEY LET ME IN.

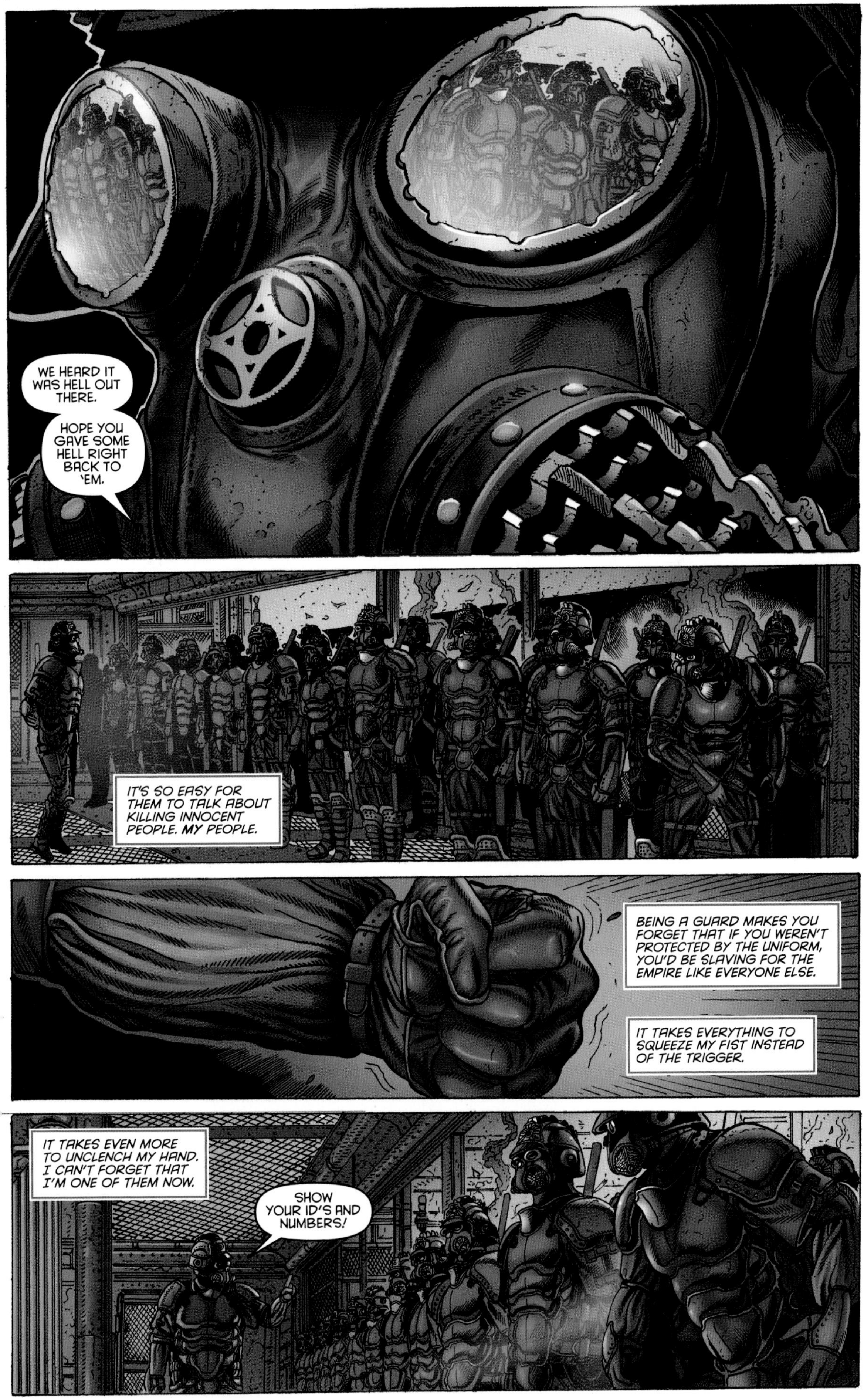
WE HEARD IT WAS HELL OUT THERE.
HOPE YOU GAVE SOME HELL RIGHT BACK TO 'EM.
IT'S SO EASY FOR THEM TO TALK ABOUT KILLING INNOCENT PEOPLE. MY PEOPLE.
BEING A GUARD MAKES YOU FORGET THAT IF YOU WEREN'T PROTECTED BY THE UNIFORM, YOU'D BE SLAVING FOR THE EMPIRE LIKE EVERYONE ELSE.
IT TAKES EVERYTHING TO SQUEEZE MY FIST INSTEAD OF THE TRIGGER.
IT TAKES EVEN MORE TO UNCLENCH MY HAND. I CAN'T FORGET THAT I'M ONE OF THEM NOW.
SHOW YOUR ID'S AND NUMBERS!

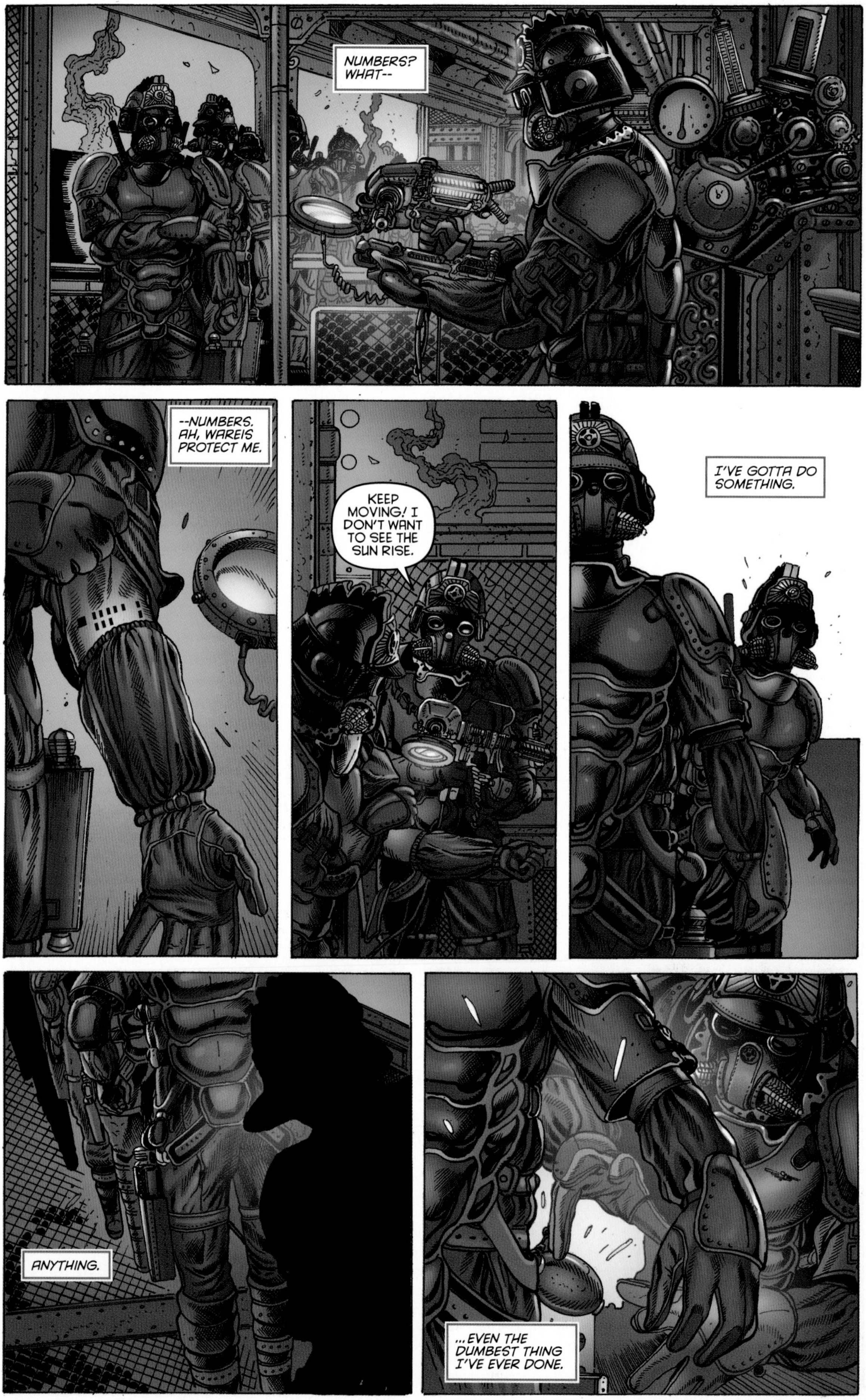
NUMBERS? WHAT--
--NUMBERS. AH, WAREIS PROTECT ME.
KEEP MOVING! I DON'T WANT TO SEE THE SUN RISE.
I'VE GOTTA DO SOMETHING.
ANYTHING.
...EVEN THE DUMBEST THING I'VE EVER DONE.

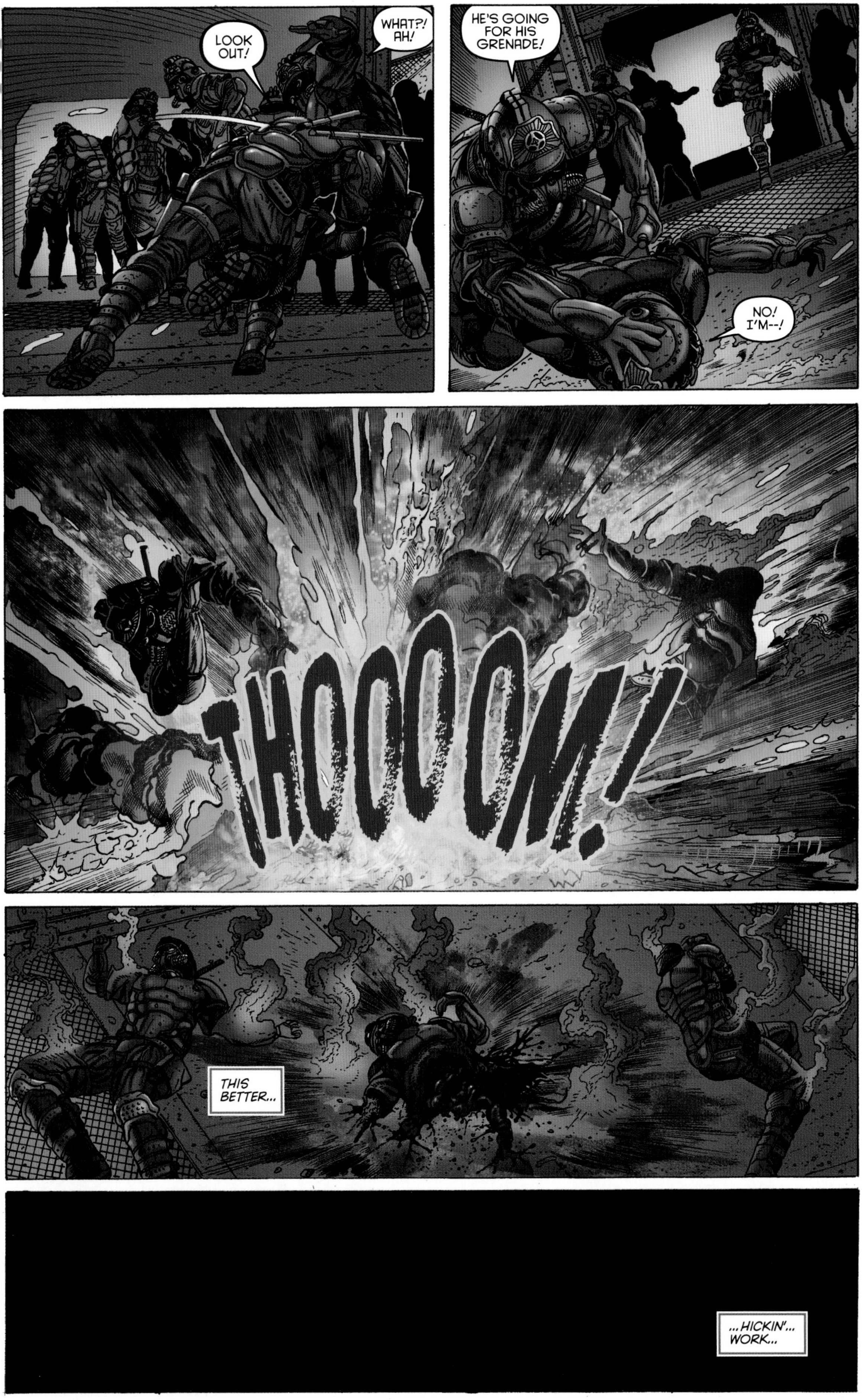
LOOK OUT!
WHAT?! AH!
HE'S GOING FOR HIS GRENADE!
NO! I'M--!
THOOOOM!
THIS BETTER...
...HICKIN'... WORK...

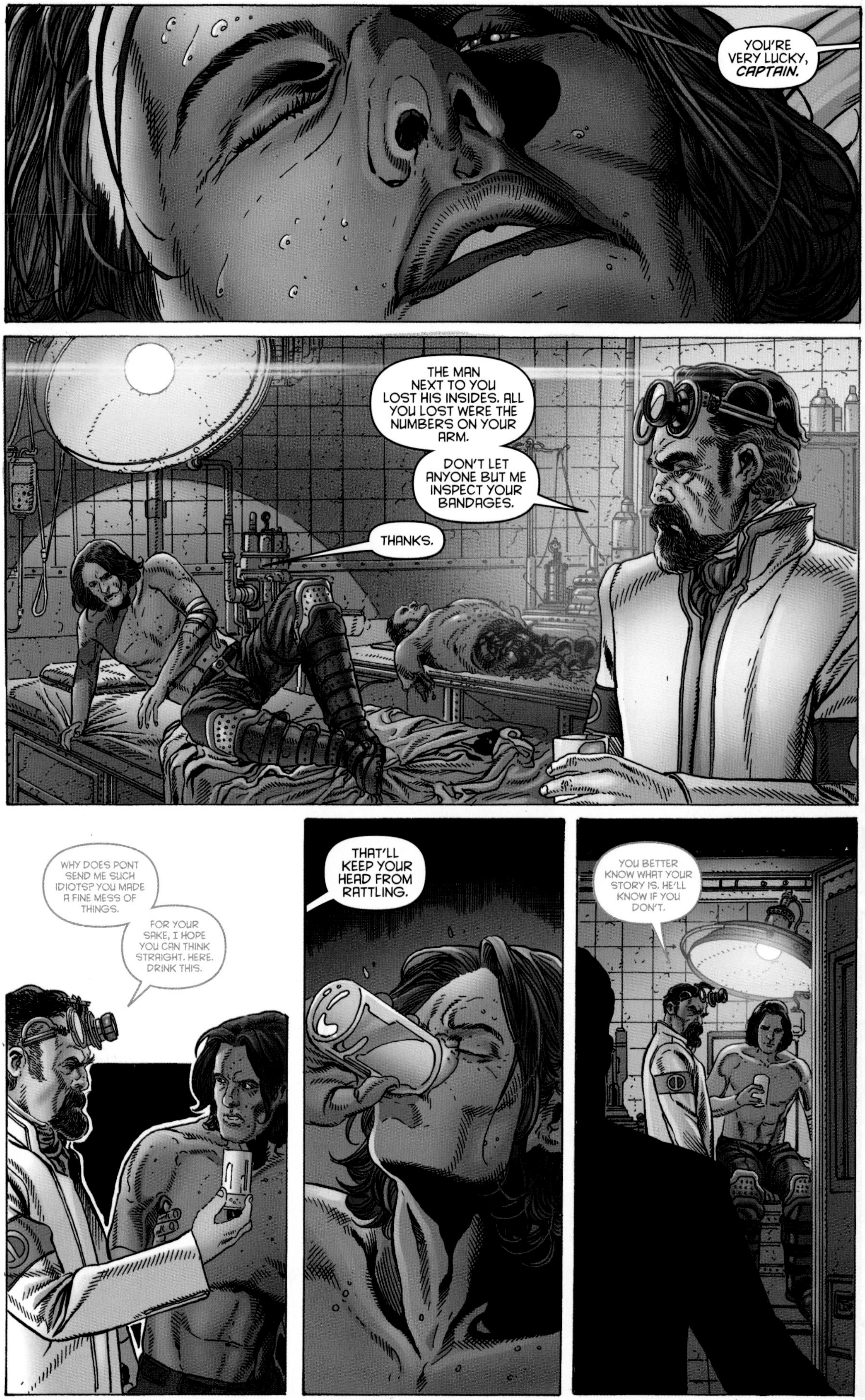
YOU'RE VERY LUCKY, *CAPTAIN.*
THE MAN NEXT TO YOU LOST HIS INSIDES. ALL YOU LOST WERE THE NUMBERS ON YOUR ARM.
DON'T LET ANYONE BUT ME INSPECT YOUR BANDAGES.
THANKS.
WHY DOES PONT SEND ME SUCH IDIOTS? YOU MADE A FINE MESS OF THINGS.
FOR YOUR SAKE, I HOPE YOU CAN THINK STRAIGHT. HERE. DRINK THIS.
THAT'LL KEEP YOUR HEAD FROM RATTLING.
YOU BETTER KNOW WHAT YOUR STORY IS. HE'LL KNOW IF YOU DON'T.

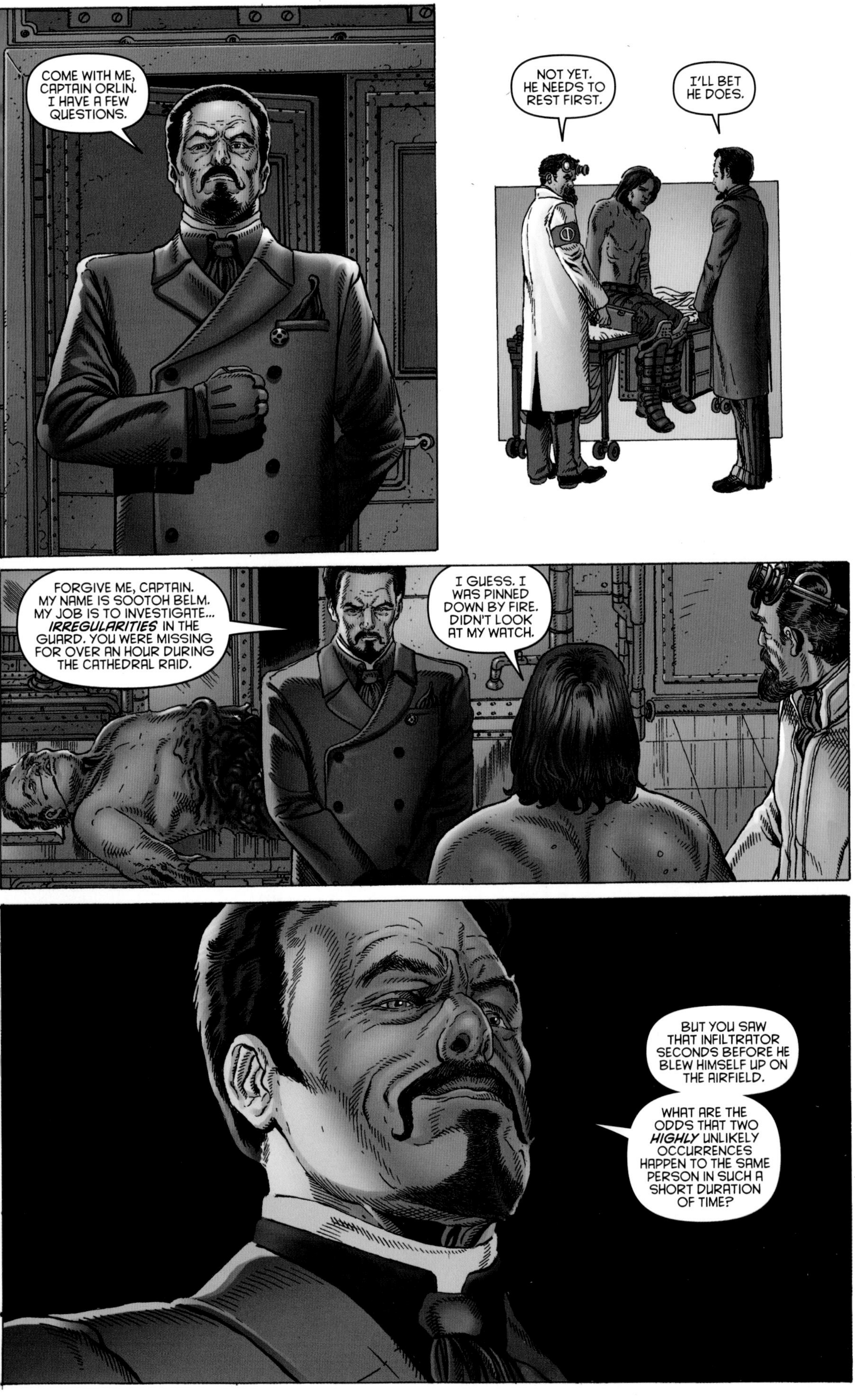
COME WITH ME, CAPTAIN ORLIN. I HAVE A FEW QUESTIONS.
NOT YET. HE NEEDS TO REST FIRST.
I'LL BET HE DOES.
FORGIVE ME, CAPTAIN. MY NAME IS SOOTOH BELM. MY JOB IS TO INVESTIGATE... IRREGULARITIES IN THE GUARD. YOU WERE MISSING FOR OVER AN HOUR DURING THE CATHEDRAL RAID.
I GUESS. I WAS PINNED DOWN BY FIRE. DIDN'T LOOK AT MY WATCH.
BUT YOU SAW THAT INFILTRATOR SECONDS BEFORE HE BLEW HIMSELF UP ON THE AIRFIELD.
WHAT ARE THE ODDS THAT TWO HIGHLY UNLIKELY OCCURRENCES HAPPEN TO THE SAME PERSON IN SUCH A SHORT DURATION OF TIME?

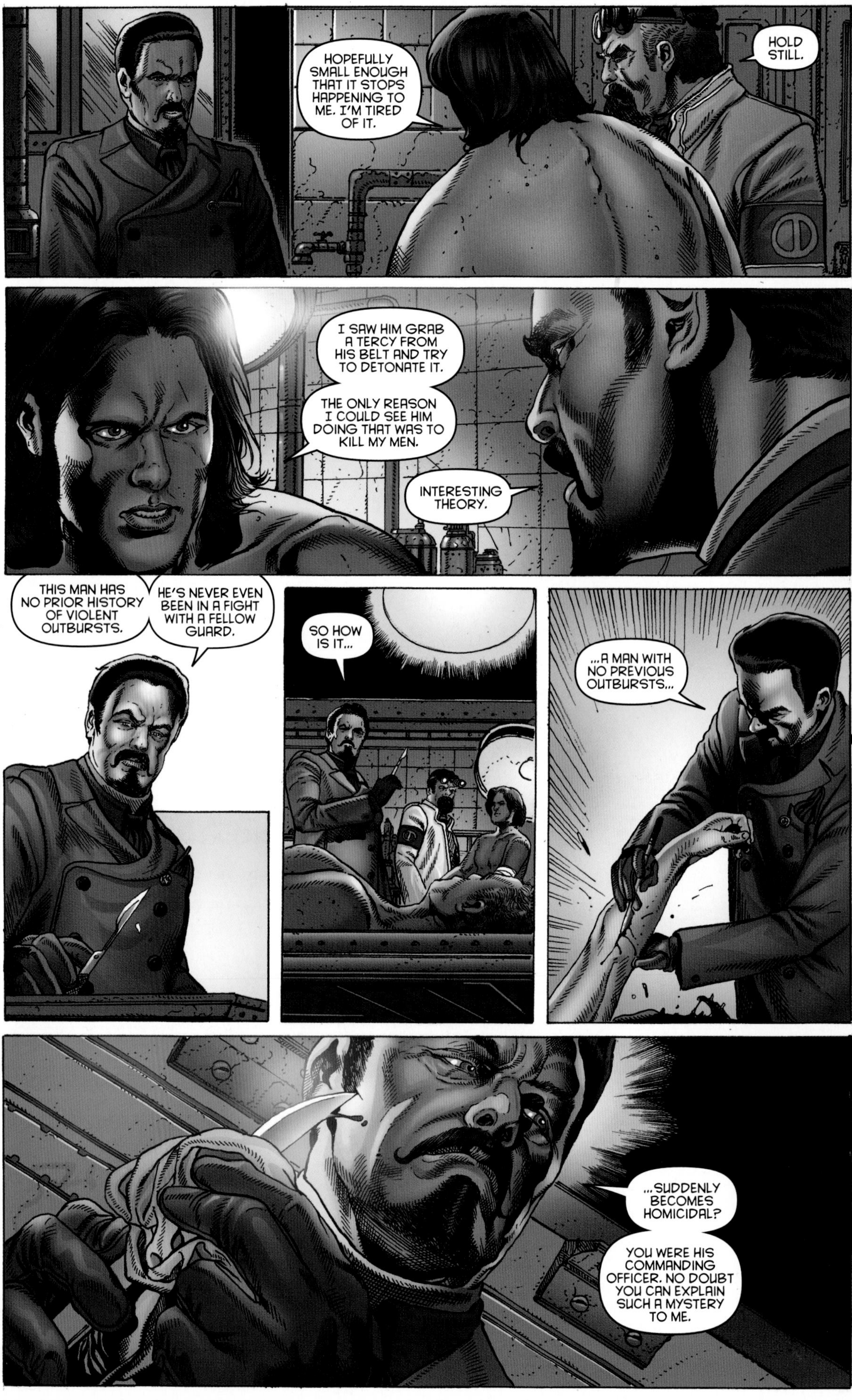
HOPEFULLY SMALL ENOUGH THAT IT STOPS HAPPENING TO ME. I'M TIRED OF IT.
HOLD STILL.
I SAW HIM GRAB A TERCY FROM HIS BELT AND TRY TO DETONATE IT.
THE ONLY REASON I COULD SEE HIM DOING THAT WAS TO KILL MY MEN.
INTERESTING THEORY.
THIS MAN HAS NO PRIOR HISTORY OF VIOLENT OUTBURSTS.
HE'S NEVER EVEN BEEN IN A FIGHT WITH A FELLOW GUARD.
SO HOW IS IT...
...A MAN WITH NO PREVIOUS OUTBURSTS...
...SUDDENLY BECOMES HOMICIDAL?
YOU WERE HIS COMMANDING OFFICER. NO DOUBT YOU CAN EXPLAIN SUCH A MYSTERY TO ME.

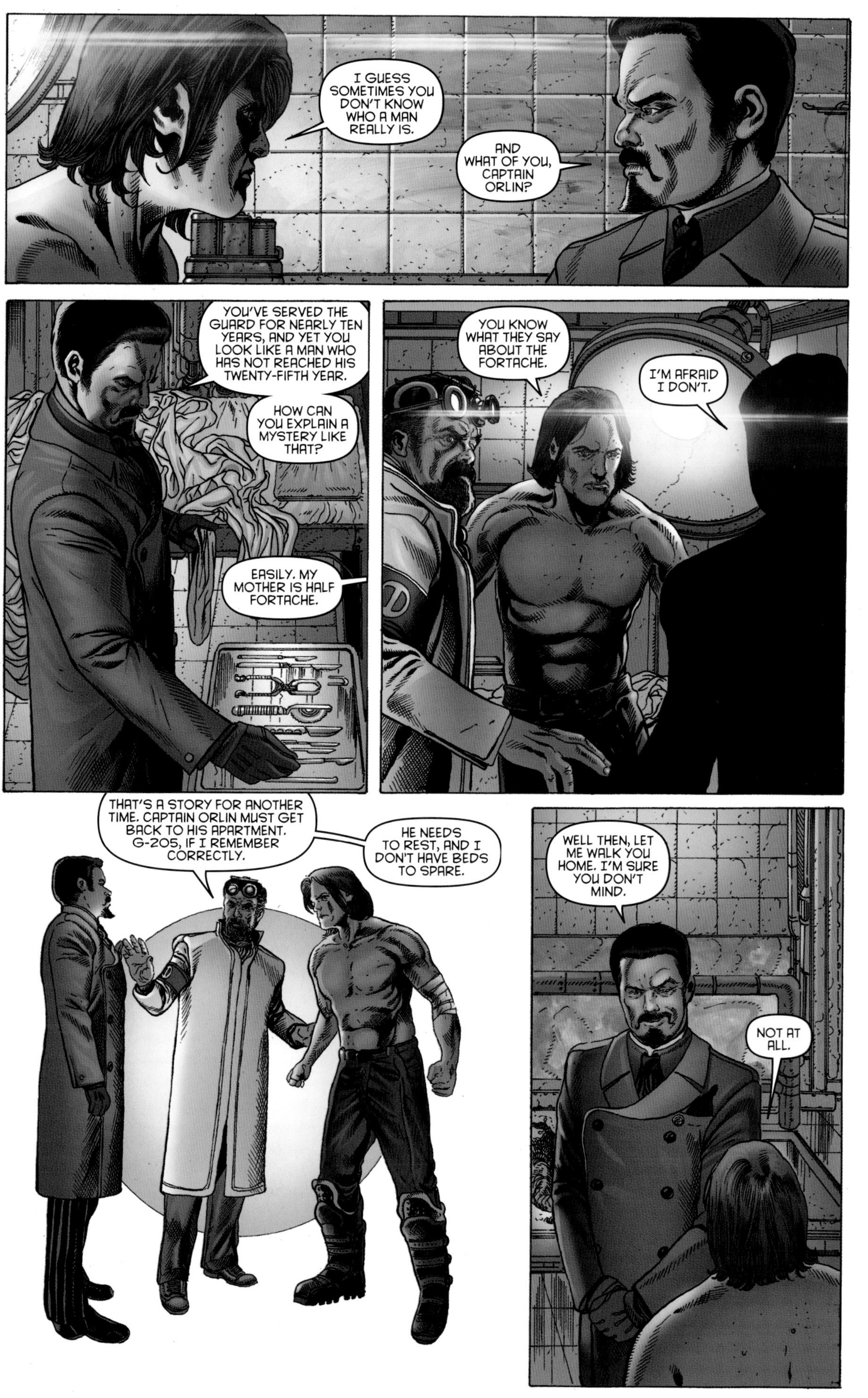
I GUESS SOMETIMES YOU DON'T KNOW WHO A MAN REALLY IS.
AND WHAT OF YOU, CAPTAIN ORLIN?
YOU'VE SERVED THE GUARD FOR NEARLY TEN YEARS, AND YET YOU LOOK LIKE A MAN WHO HAS NOT REACHED HIS TWENTY-FIFTH YEAR.
HOW CAN YOU EXPLAIN A MYSTERY LIKE THAT?
EASILY. MY MOTHER IS HALF FORTACHE.
YOU KNOW WHAT THEY SAY ABOUT THE FORTACHE.
I'M AFRAID I DON'T.
THAT'S A STORY FOR ANOTHER TIME. CAPTAIN ORLIN MUST GET BACK TO HIS APARTMENT. G-205, IF I REMEMBER CORRECTLY.
HE NEEDS TO REST, AND I DON'T HAVE BEDS TO SPARE.
WELL THEN, LET ME WALK YOU HOME. I'M SURE YOU DON'T MIND.
NOT AT ALL.

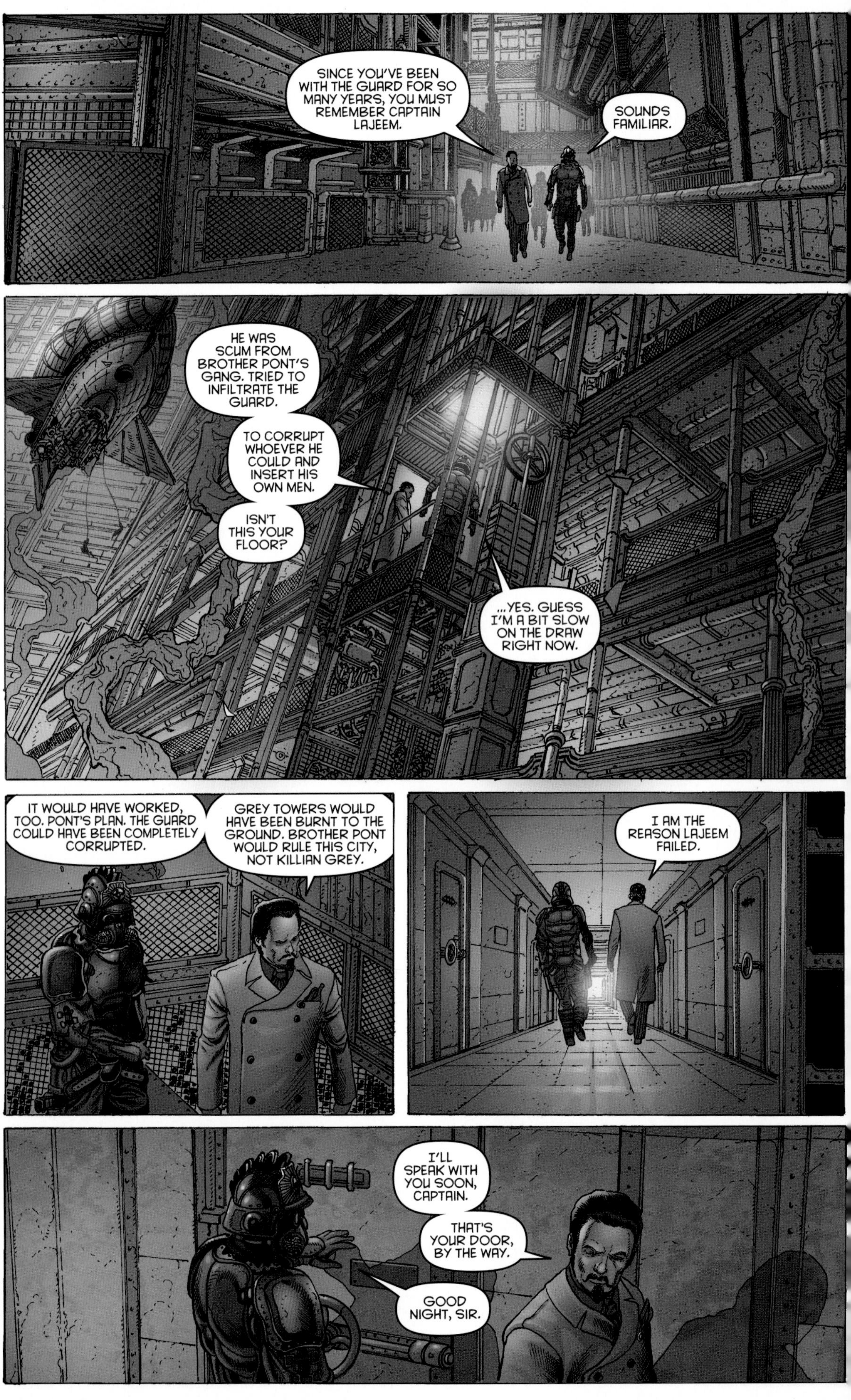
SINCE YOU'VE BEEN WITH THE GUARD FOR SO MANY YEARS, YOU MUST REMEMBER CAPTAIN LAJEEM.
SOUNDS FAMILIAR.
HE WAS SCUM FROM BROTHER PONT'S GANG. TRIED TO INFILTRATE THE GUARD.
TO CORRUPT WHOEVER HE COULD AND INSERT HIS OWN MEN.
ISN'T THIS YOUR FLOOR?
...YES. GUESS I'M A BIT SLOW ON THE DRAW RIGHT NOW.
IT WOULD HAVE WORKED, TOO. PONT'S PLAN. THE GUARD COULD HAVE BEEN COMPLETELY CORRUPTED.
GREY TOWERS WOULD HAVE BEEN BURNT TO THE GROUND. BROTHER PONT WOULD RULE THIS CITY, NOT KILLIAN GREY.
I AM THE REASON LAJEEM FAILED.
I'LL SPEAK WITH YOU SOON, CAPTAIN.
THAT'S YOUR DOOR, BY THE WAY.
GOOD NIGHT, SIR.

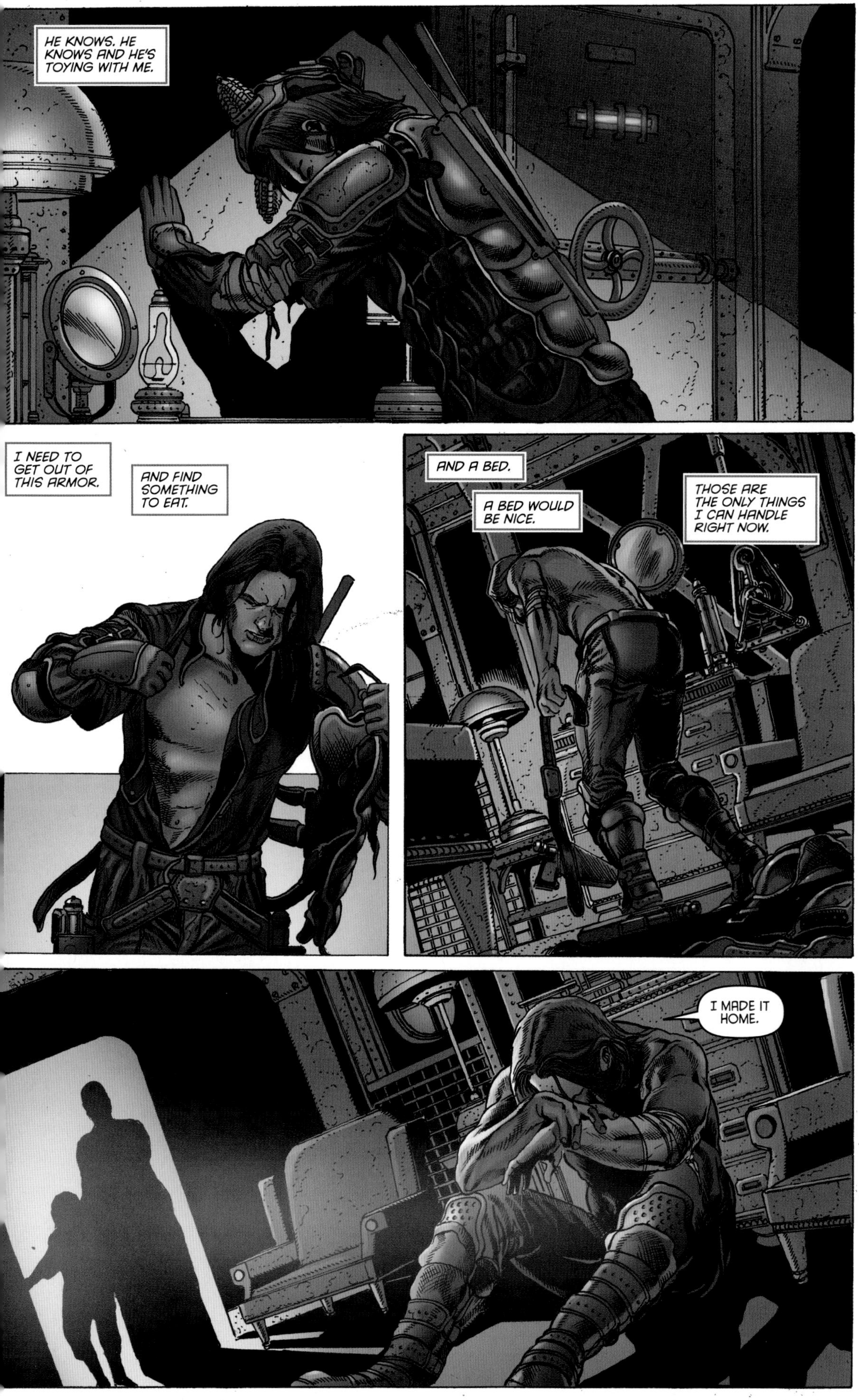
HE KNOWS. HE KNOWS AND HE'S TOYING WITH ME.
I NEED TO GET OUT OF THIS ARMOR.
AND FIND SOMETHING TO EAT.
AND A BED.
A BED WOULD BE NICE.
THOSE ARE THE ONLY THINGS I CAN HANDLE RIGHT NOW.
I MADE IT HOME.

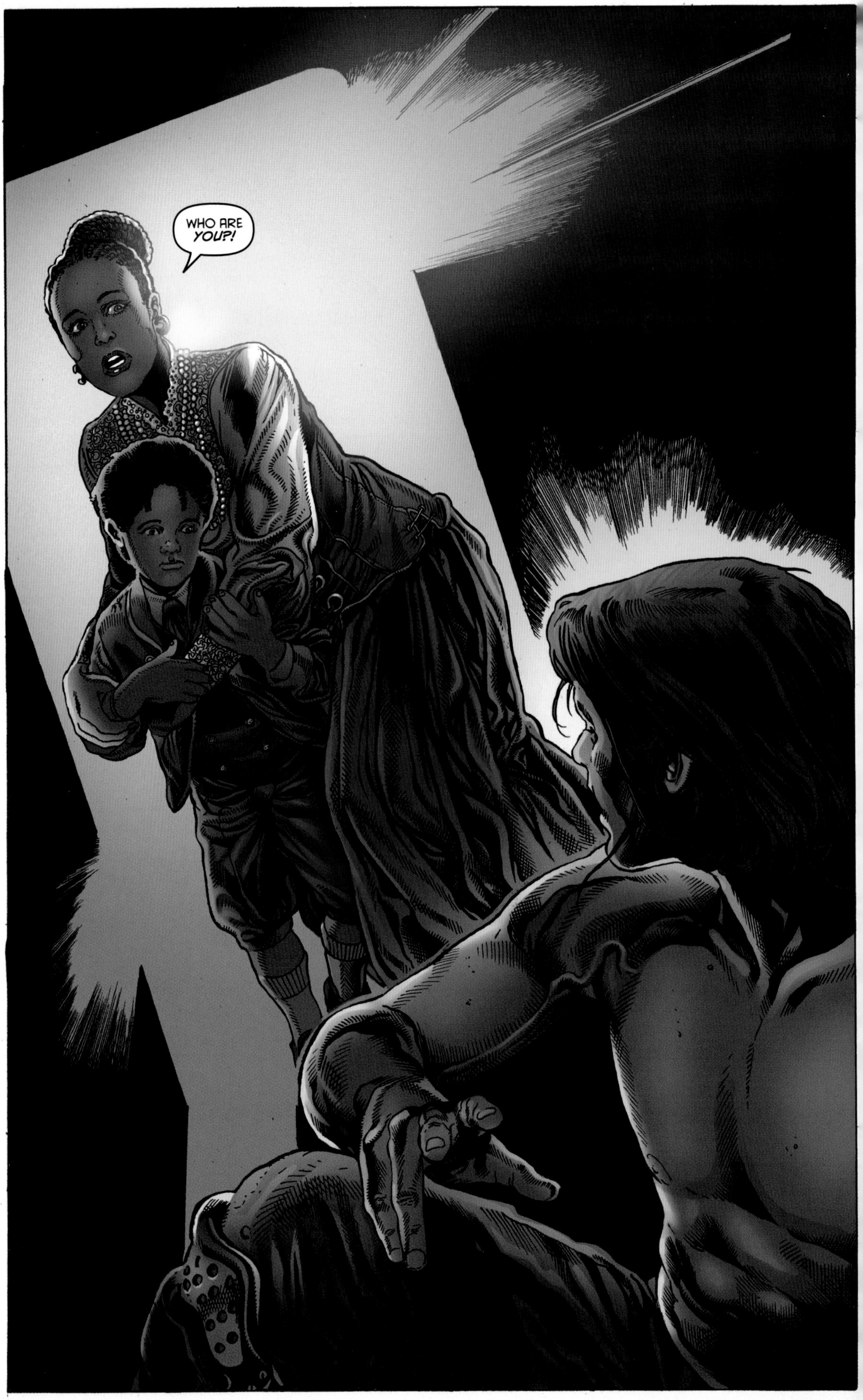
WHO ARE YOU?!

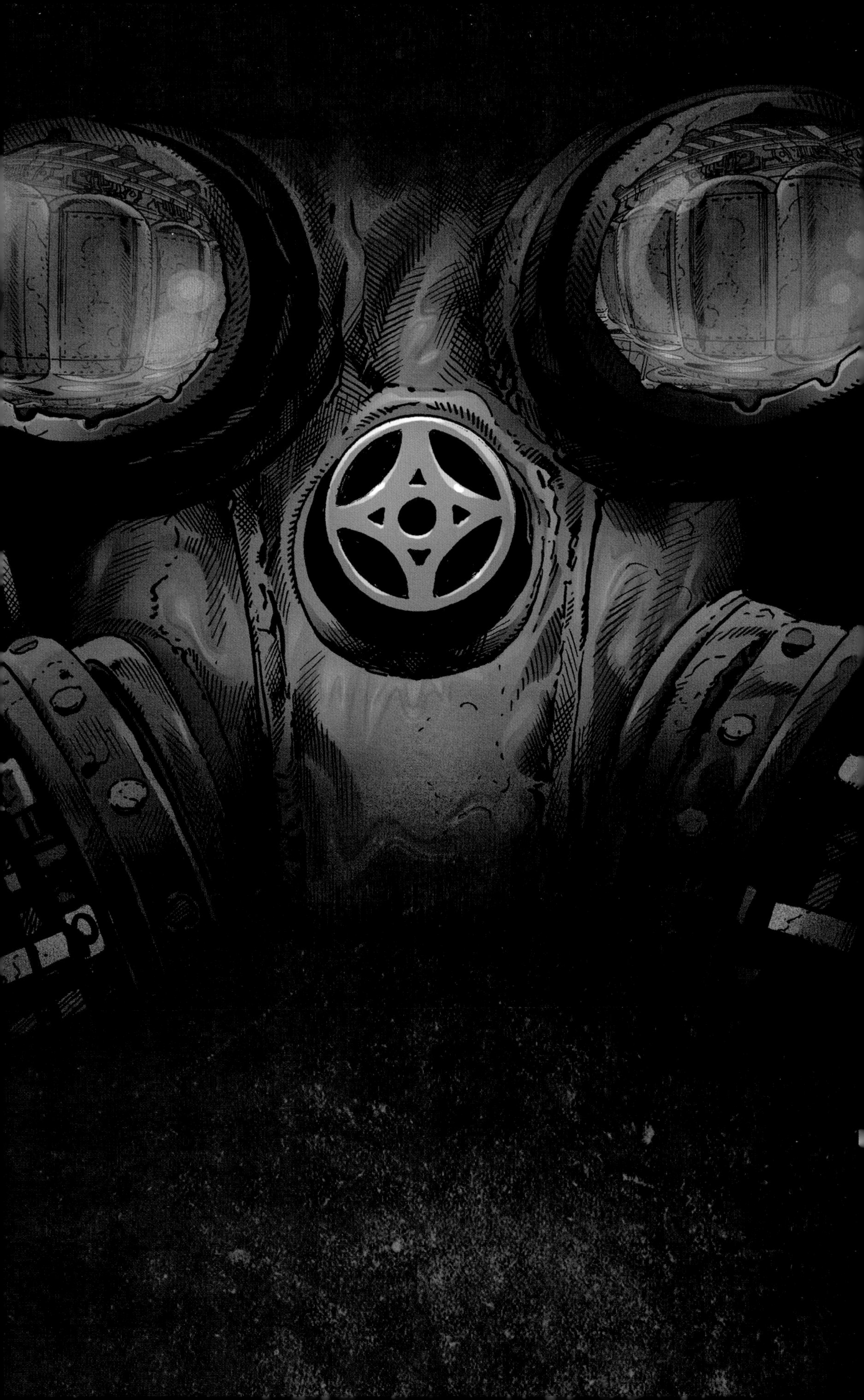

CHAPTER THREE

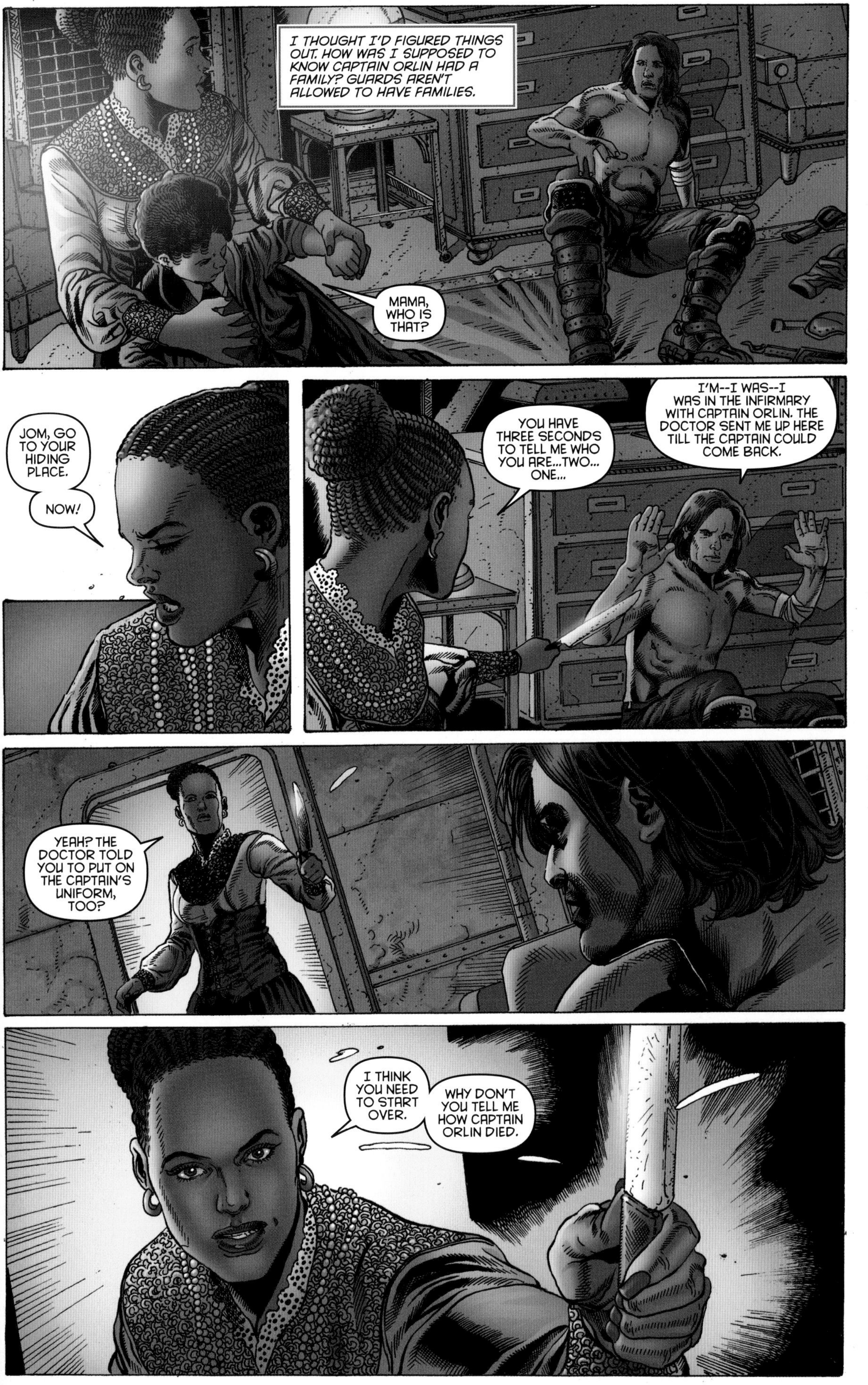
I THOUGHT I'D FIGURED THINGS OUT. HOW WAS I SUPPOSED TO KNOW CAPTAIN ORLIN HAD A FAMILY? GUARDS AREN'T ALLOWED TO HAVE FAMILIES.
MAMA, WHO IS THAT?
JOM, GO TO YOUR HIDING PLACE.
NOW!
YOU HAVE THREE SECONDS TO TELL ME WHO YOU ARE...TWO... ONE...
I'M--I WAS--I WAS IN THE INFIRMARY WITH CAPTAIN ORLIN. THE DOCTOR SENT ME UP HERE TILL THE CAPTAIN COULD COME BACK.
YEAH? THE DOCTOR TOLD YOU TO PUT ON THE CAPTAIN'S UNIFORM, TOO?
I THINK YOU NEED TO START OVER.
WHY DON'T YOU TELL ME HOW CAPTAIN ORLIN DIED.

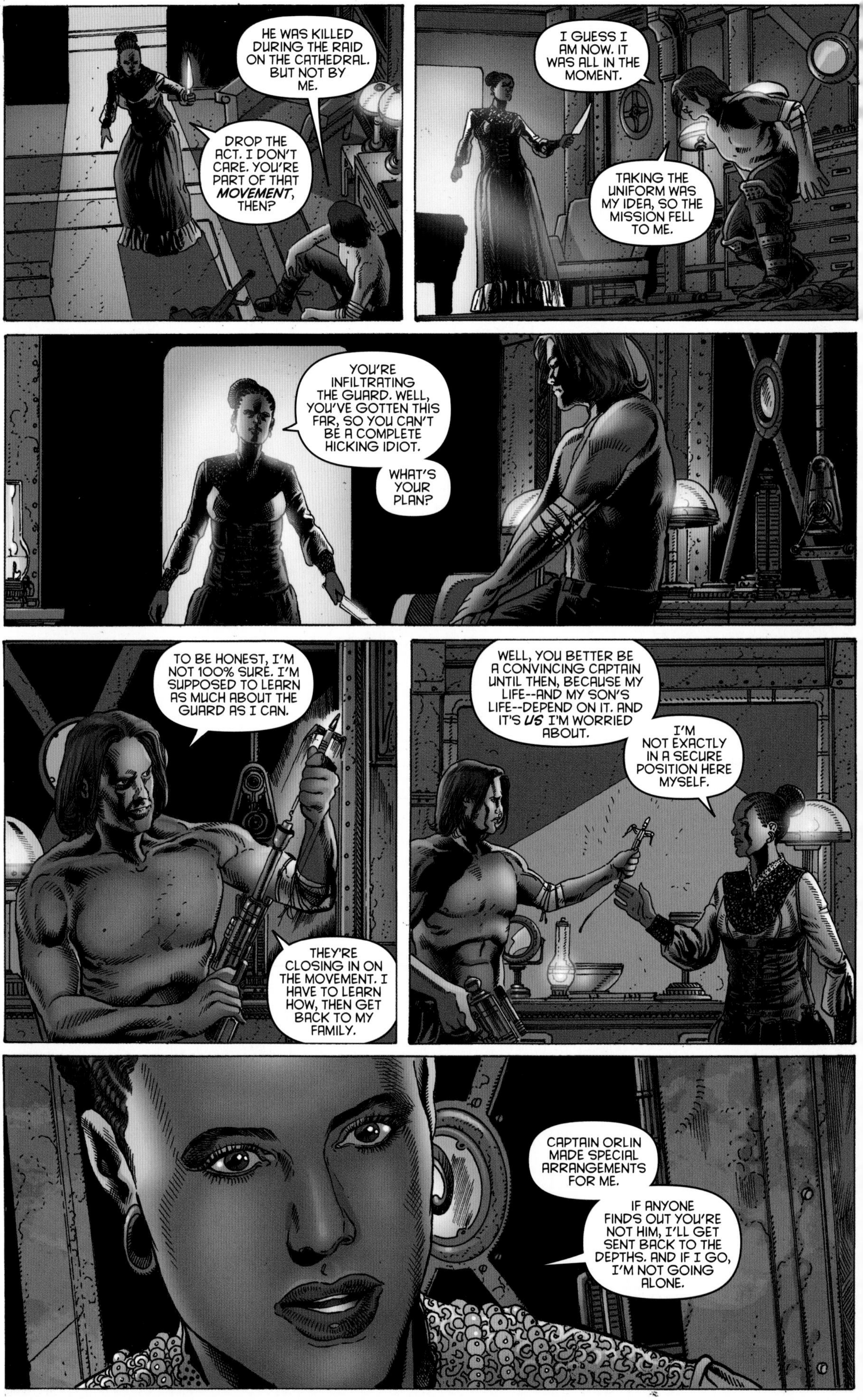
HE WAS KILLED DURING THE RAID ON THE CATHEDRAL. BUT NOT BY ME.
DROP THE ACT. I DON'T CARE. YOU'RE PART OF THAT *MOVEMENT*, THEN?
I GUESS I AM NOW. IT WAS ALL IN THE MOMENT.
TAKING THE UNIFORM WAS MY IDEA, SO THE MISSION FELL TO ME.
YOU'RE INFILTRATING THE GUARD. WELL, YOU'VE GOTTEN THIS FAR, SO YOU CAN'T BE A COMPLETE HICKING IDIOT.
WHAT'S YOUR PLAN?
TO BE HONEST, I'M NOT 100% SURE. I'M SUPPOSED TO LEARN AS MUCH ABOUT THE GUARD AS I CAN.
THEY'RE CLOSING IN ON THE MOVEMENT. I HAVE TO LEARN HOW, THEN GET BACK TO MY FAMILY.
WELL, YOU BETTER BE A CONVINCING CAPTAIN UNTIL THEN, BECAUSE MY LIFE--AND MY SON'S LIFE--DEPEND ON IT. AND IT'S *US* I'M WORRIED ABOUT.
I'M NOT EXACTLY IN A SECURE POSITION HERE MYSELF.
CAPTAIN ORLIN MADE SPECIAL ARRANGEMENTS FOR ME.
IF ANYONE FINDS OUT YOU'RE NOT HIM, I'LL GET SENT BACK TO THE DEPTHS. AND IF I GO, I'M NOT GOING ALONE.

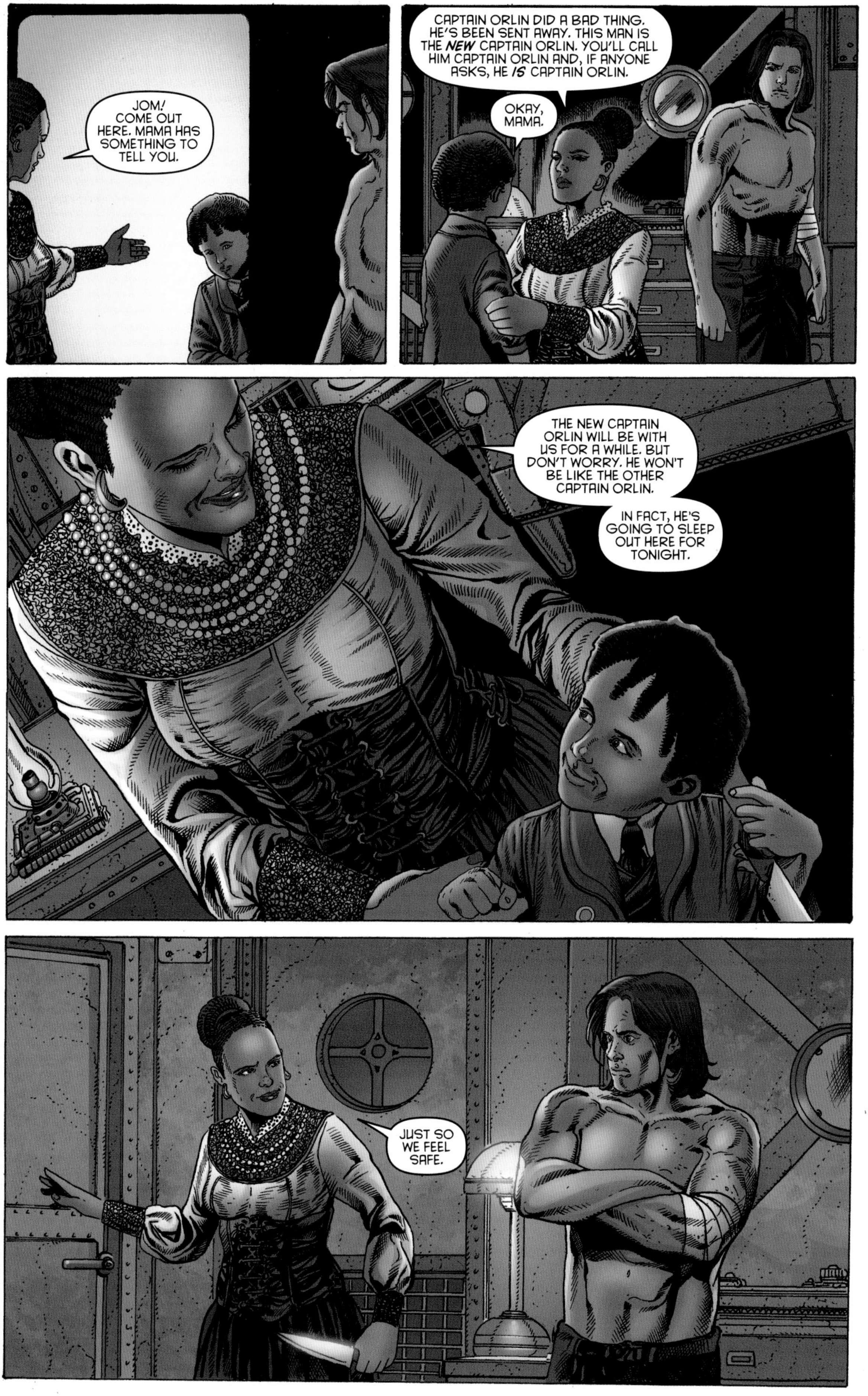
JOM! COME OUT HERE. MAMA HAS SOMETHING TO TELL YOU.
CAPTAIN ORLIN DID A BAD THING. HE'S BEEN SENT AWAY. THIS MAN IS THE NEW CAPTAIN ORLIN. YOU'LL CALL HIM CAPTAIN ORLIN AND, IF ANYONE ASKS, HE IS CAPTAIN ORLIN.
OKAY, MAMA.
THE NEW CAPTAIN ORLIN WILL BE WITH US FOR A WHILE. BUT DON'T WORRY. HE WON'T BE LIKE THE OTHER CAPTAIN ORLIN.
IN FACT, HE'S GOING TO SLEEP OUT HERE FOR TONIGHT.
JUST SO WE FEEL SAFE.

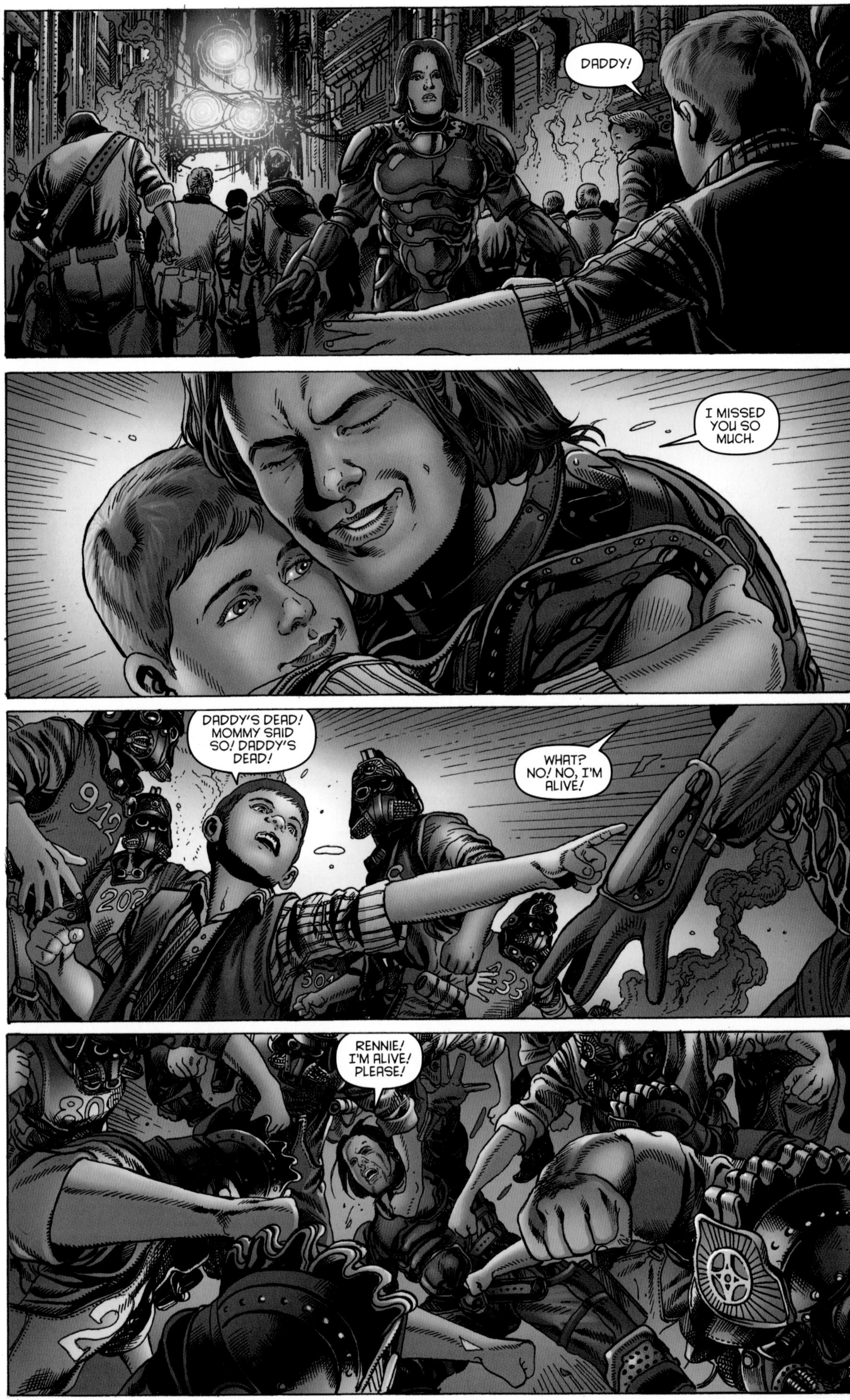
DADDY!
I MISSED YOU SO MUCH.
DADDY'S DEAD! MOMMY SAID SO! DADDY'S DEAD!
WHAT? NO! NO, I'M ALIVE!
912
202
501
433
RENNIE! I'M ALIVE! PLEASE!

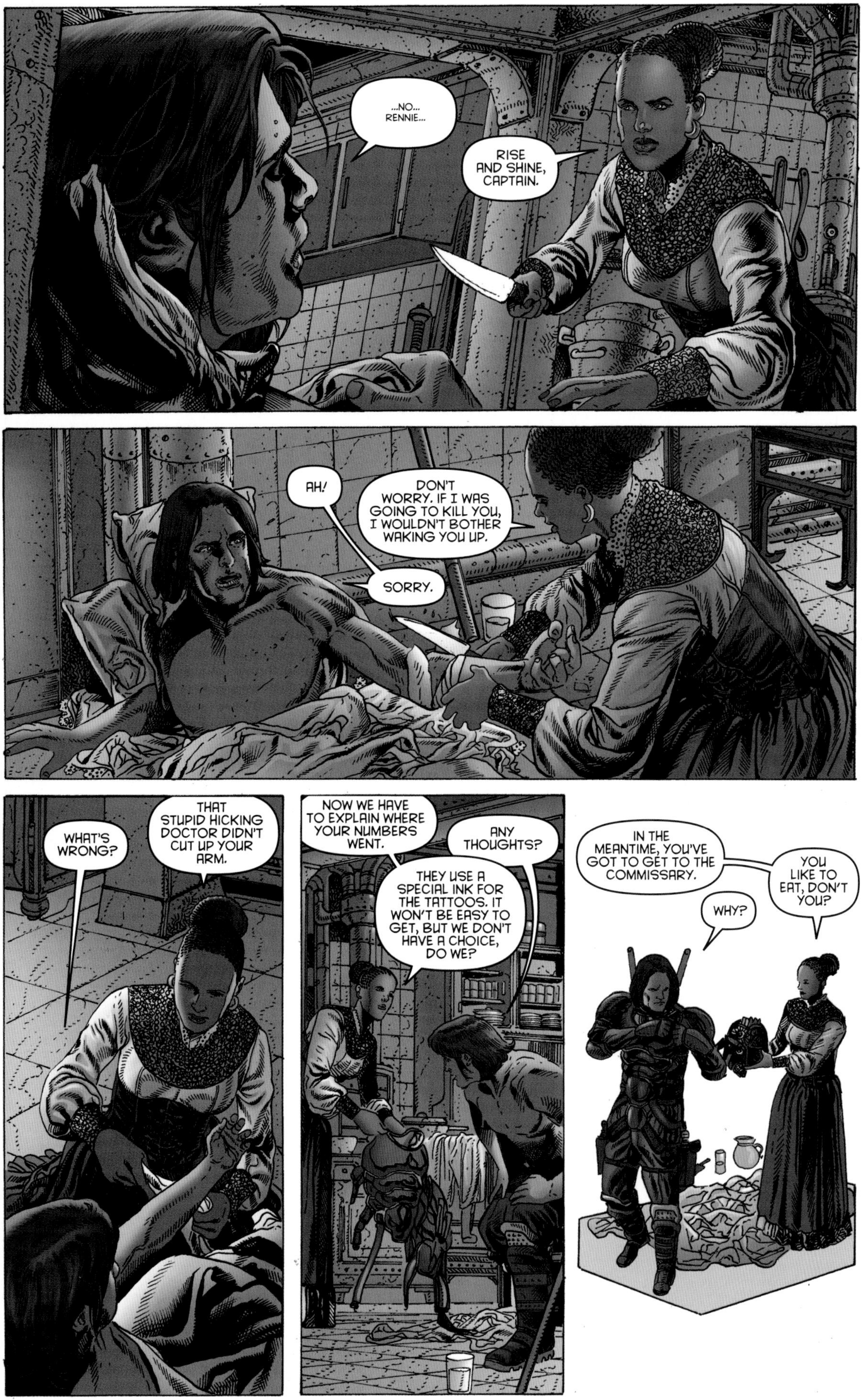
...NO... RENNIE...
RISE AND SHINE, CAPTAIN.
AH!
DON'T WORRY. IF I WAS GOING TO KILL YOU, I WOULDN'T BOTHER WAKING YOU UP.
SORRY.
WHAT'S WRONG?
THAT STUPID HICKING DOCTOR DIDN'T CUT UP YOUR ARM.
NOW WE HAVE TO EXPLAIN WHERE YOUR NUMBERS WENT.
ANY THOUGHTS?
THEY USE A SPECIAL INK FOR THE TATTOOS. IT WON'T BE EASY TO GET, BUT WE DON'T HAVE A CHOICE, DO WE?
IN THE MEANTIME, YOU'VE GOT TO GET TO THE COMMISSARY.
WHY?
YOU LIKE TO EAT, DON'T YOU?

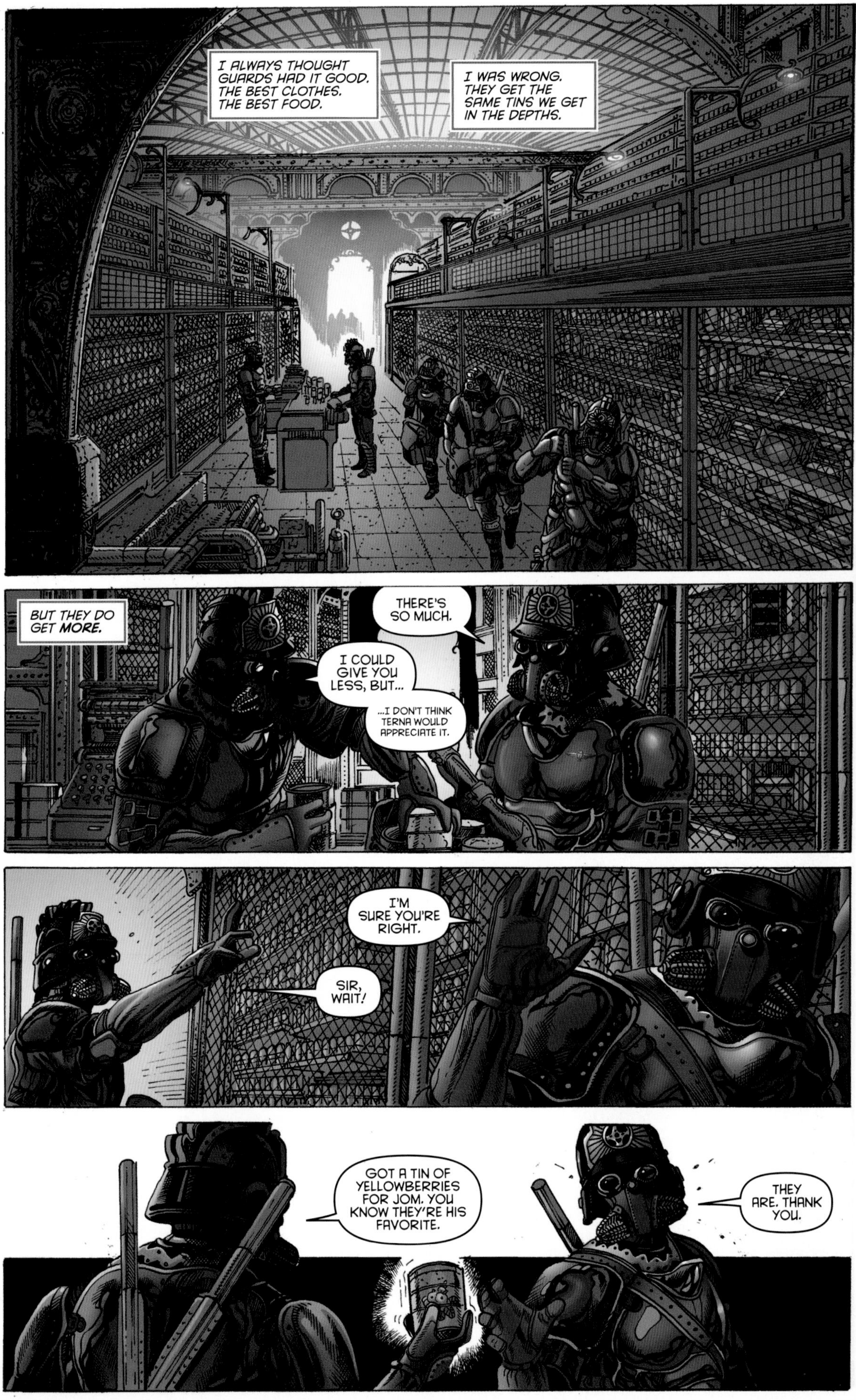
I ALWAYS THOUGHT GUARDS HAD IT GOOD. THE BEST CLOTHES. THE BEST FOOD.
I WAS WRONG. THEY GET THE SAME TINS WE GET IN THE DEPTHS.
BUT THEY DO GET MORE.
THERE'S SO MUCH.
I COULD GIVE YOU LESS, BUT...
...I DON'T THINK TERNA WOULD APPRECIATE IT.
I'M SURE YOU'RE RIGHT.
SIR, WAIT!
GOT A TIN OF YELLOWBERRIES FOR JOM. YOU KNOW THEY'RE HIS FAVORITE.
THEY ARE. THANK YOU.

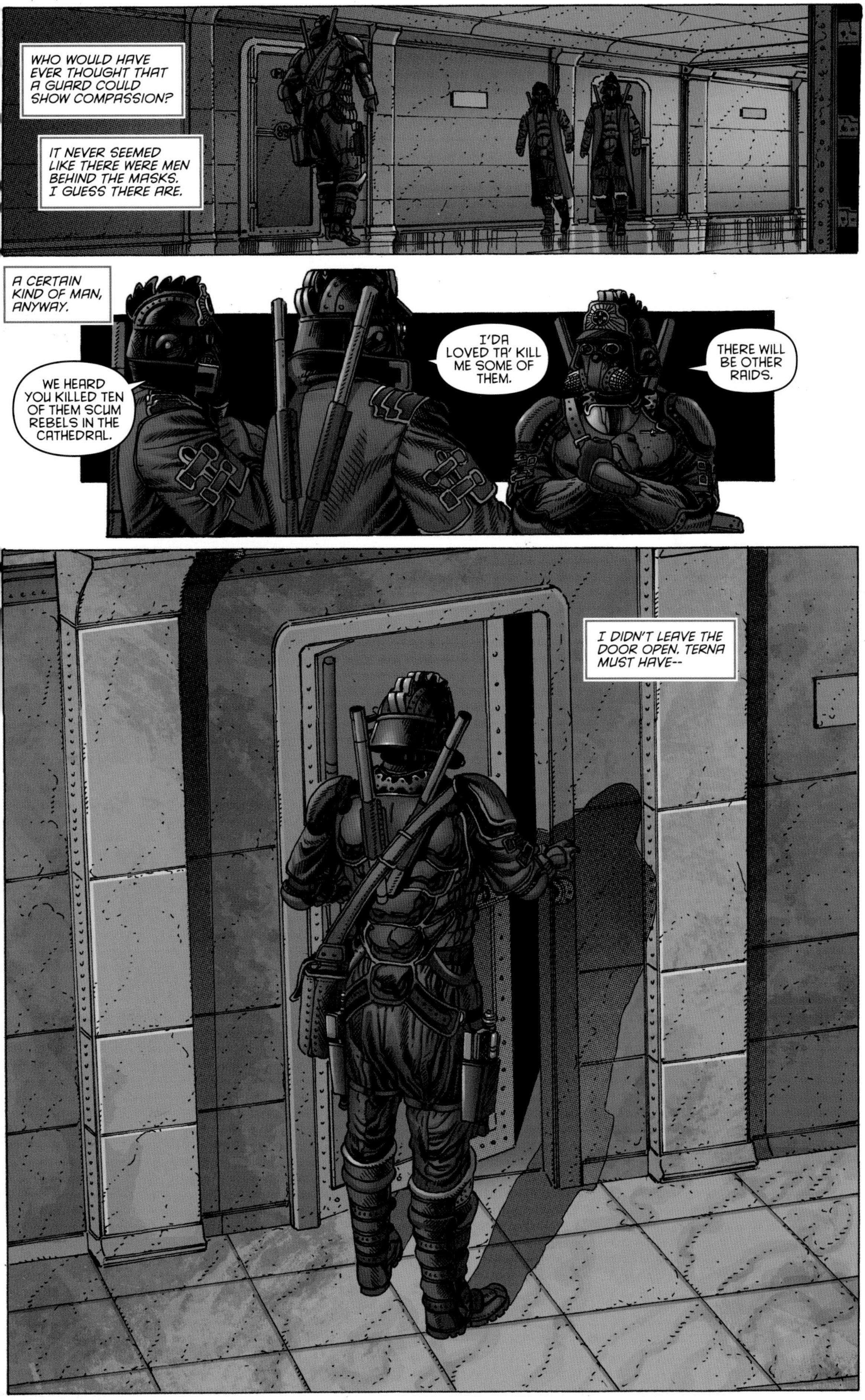
WHO WOULD HAVE EVER THOUGHT THAT A GUARD COULD SHOW COMPASSION?
IT NEVER SEEMED LIKE THERE WERE MEN BEHIND THE MASKS. I GUESS THERE ARE.
A CERTAIN KIND OF MAN, ANYWAY.
WE HEARD YOU KILLED TEN OF THEM SCUM REBELS IN THE CATHEDRAL.
I'DA LOVED TA' KILL ME SOME OF THEM.
THERE WILL BE OTHER RAIDS.
I DIDN'T LEAVE THE DOOR OPEN. TERNA MUST HAVE--

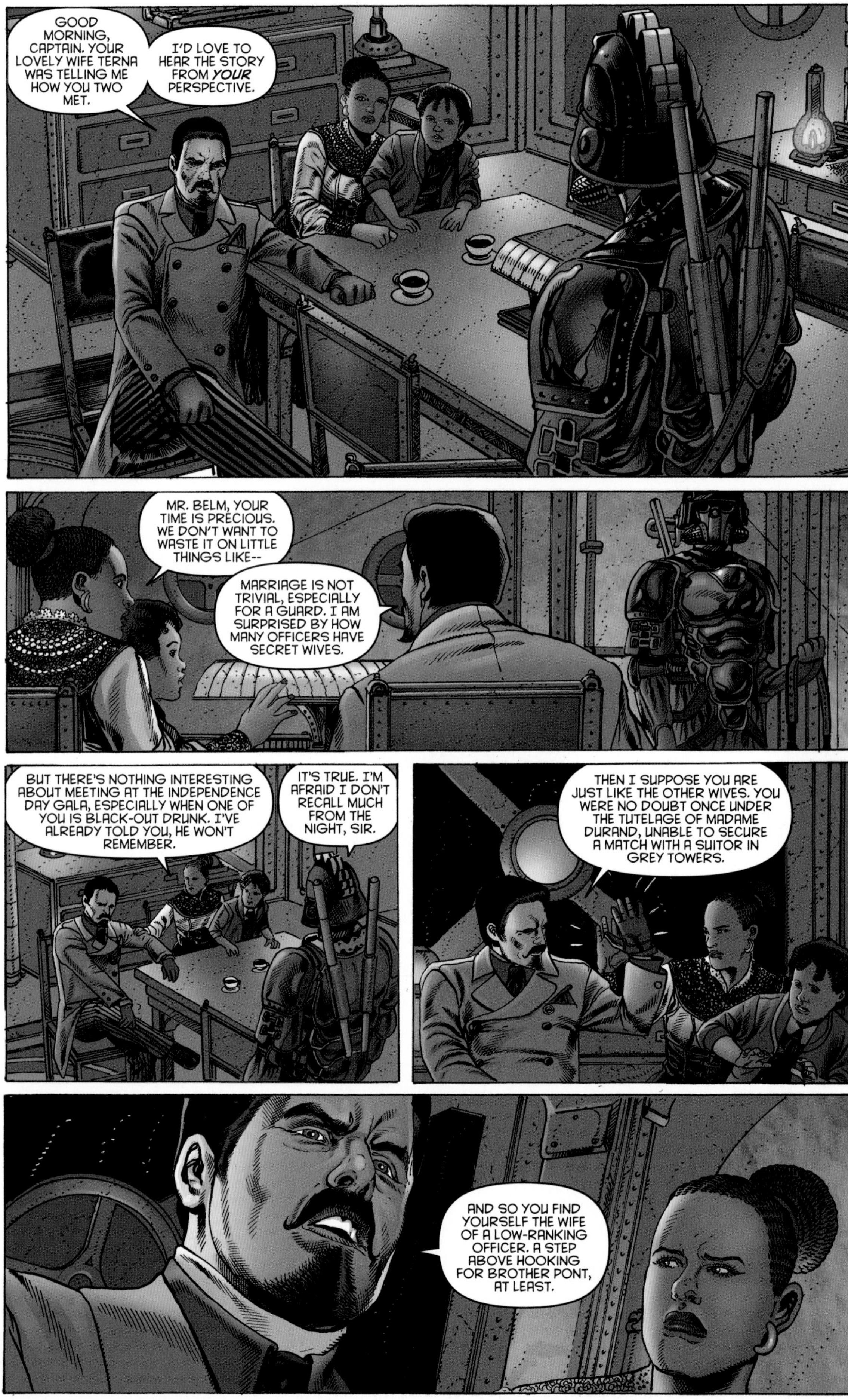
GOOD MORNING, CAPTAIN. YOUR LOVELY WIFE TERNA WAS TELLING ME HOW YOU TWO MET.
I'D LOVE TO HEAR THE STORY FROM *YOUR* PERSPECTIVE.
MR. BELM, YOUR TIME IS PRECIOUS. WE DON'T WANT TO WASTE IT ON LITTLE THINGS LIKE--
MARRIAGE IS NOT TRIVIAL, ESPECIALLY FOR A GUARD. I AM SURPRISED BY HOW MANY OFFICERS HAVE SECRET WIVES.
BUT THERE'S NOTHING INTERESTING ABOUT MEETING AT THE INDEPENDENCE DAY GALA, ESPECIALLY WHEN ONE OF YOU IS BLACK-OUT DRUNK. I'VE ALREADY TOLD YOU, HE WON'T REMEMBER.
IT'S TRUE. I'M AFRAID I DON'T RECALL MUCH FROM THE NIGHT, SIR.
THEN I SUPPOSE YOU ARE JUST LIKE THE OTHER WIVES. YOU WERE NO DOUBT ONCE UNDER THE TUTELAGE OF MADAME DURAND, UNABLE TO SECURE A MATCH WITH A SUITOR IN GREY TOWERS.
AND SO YOU FIND YOURSELF THE WIFE OF A LOW-RANKING OFFICER. A STEP ABOVE HOOKING FOR BROTHER PONT, AT LEAST.

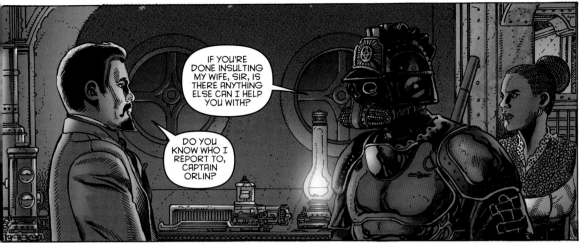

IF YOU'RE DONE INSULTING MY WIFE, SIR, IS THERE ANYTHING ELSE CAN I HELP YOU WITH?

DO YOU KNOW WHO I REPORT TO, CAPTAIN ORLIN?

THE LANTERN CITY COUNCIL. MORE SPECIFICALLY, *KILLIAN GREY* HIMSELF.

HE RECOGNIZES THE PROBLEMS WITHIN THE GUARD. HE WANTS TO ERADICATE THEM.

WHICH IS WHY THEY'VE PLACED ME HERE.

AND IT'S THE REASON YOU'LL BE REPORTING TO MY OFFICES TOMORROW. I NEED YOU TO EXPLAIN, IN DETAIL, WHAT HAPPENED DURING THE RAID AND ON THE AIRFIELD.

OR PERHAPS YOUR *SON* CAN--

I'LL BE THERE FIRST THING, SIR. BUT I'M VERY BUSY AT THE MOMENT.

INDEED.

ONE LAST THING...IN LIGHT OF YOUR HEROISM YESTERDAY, I SECURED YOU A POSITION AS THE LEADER OF A SPECIAL MISSION TO *THE SPIRAL.*

THERE'S BEEN ANOTHER RIOT, BUT I'M SURE YOU'LL HAVE IT CLEANED UP IN NO TIME. A MAN OF YOUR TRAINING.

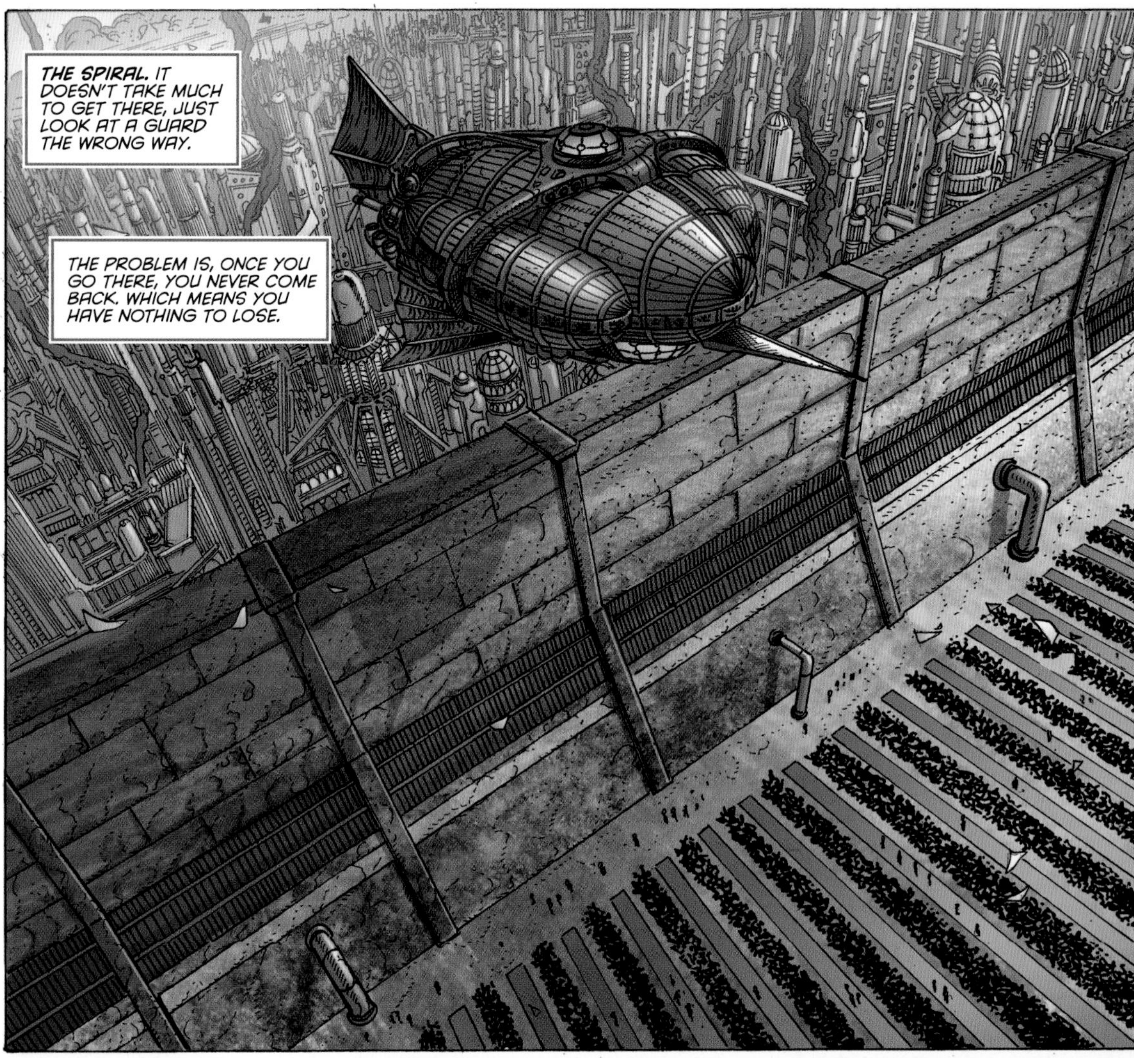
THE SPIRAL. IT DOESN'T TAKE MUCH TO GET THERE, JUST LOOK AT A GUARD THE WRONG WAY.
THE PROBLEM IS, ONCE YOU GO THERE, YOU NEVER COME BACK. WHICH MEANS YOU HAVE NOTHING TO LOSE.

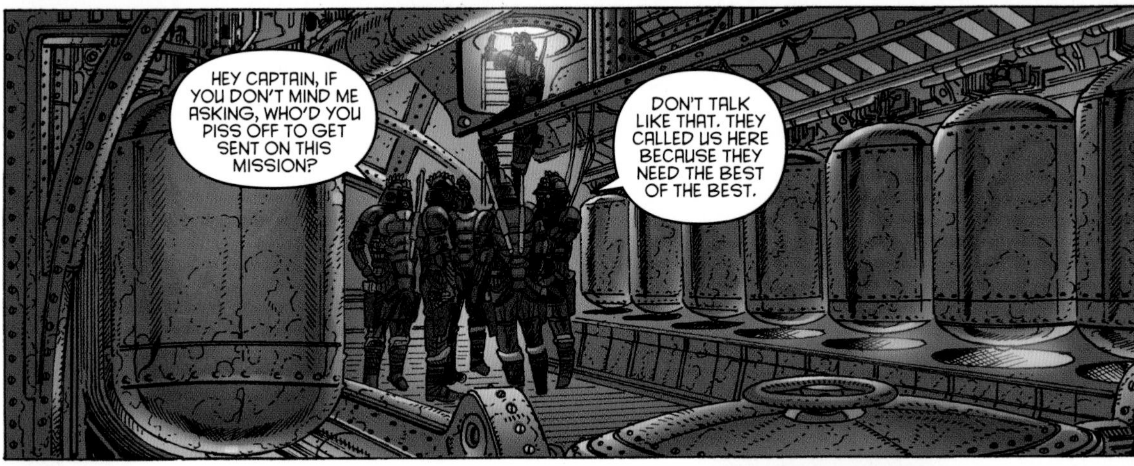
HEY CAPTAIN, IF YOU DON'T MIND ME ASKING, WHO'D YOU PISS OFF TO GET SENT ON THIS MISSION?
DON'T TALK LIKE THAT. THEY CALLED US HERE BECAUSE THEY NEED THE BEST OF THE BEST.

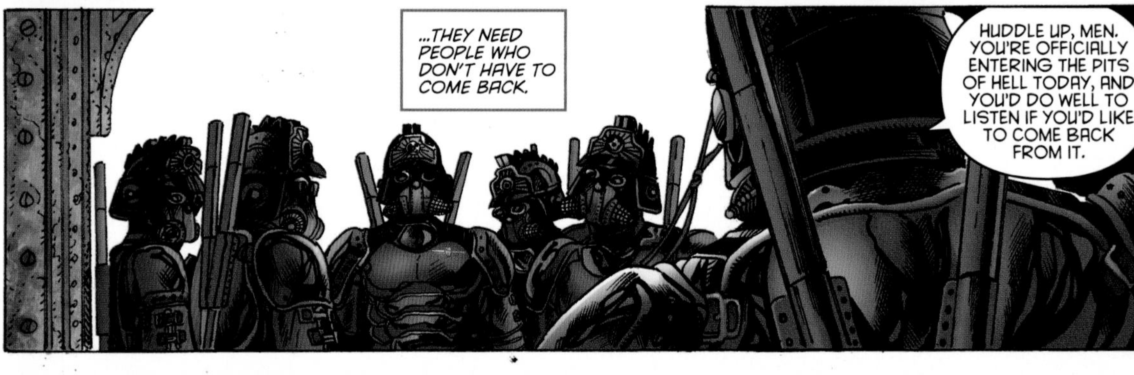
...THEY NEED PEOPLE WHO DON'T HAVE TO COME BACK.
HUDDLE UP, MEN. YOU'RE OFFICIALLY ENTERING THE PITS OF HELL TODAY, AND YOU'D DO WELL TO LISTEN IF YOU'D LIKE TO COME BACK FROM IT.

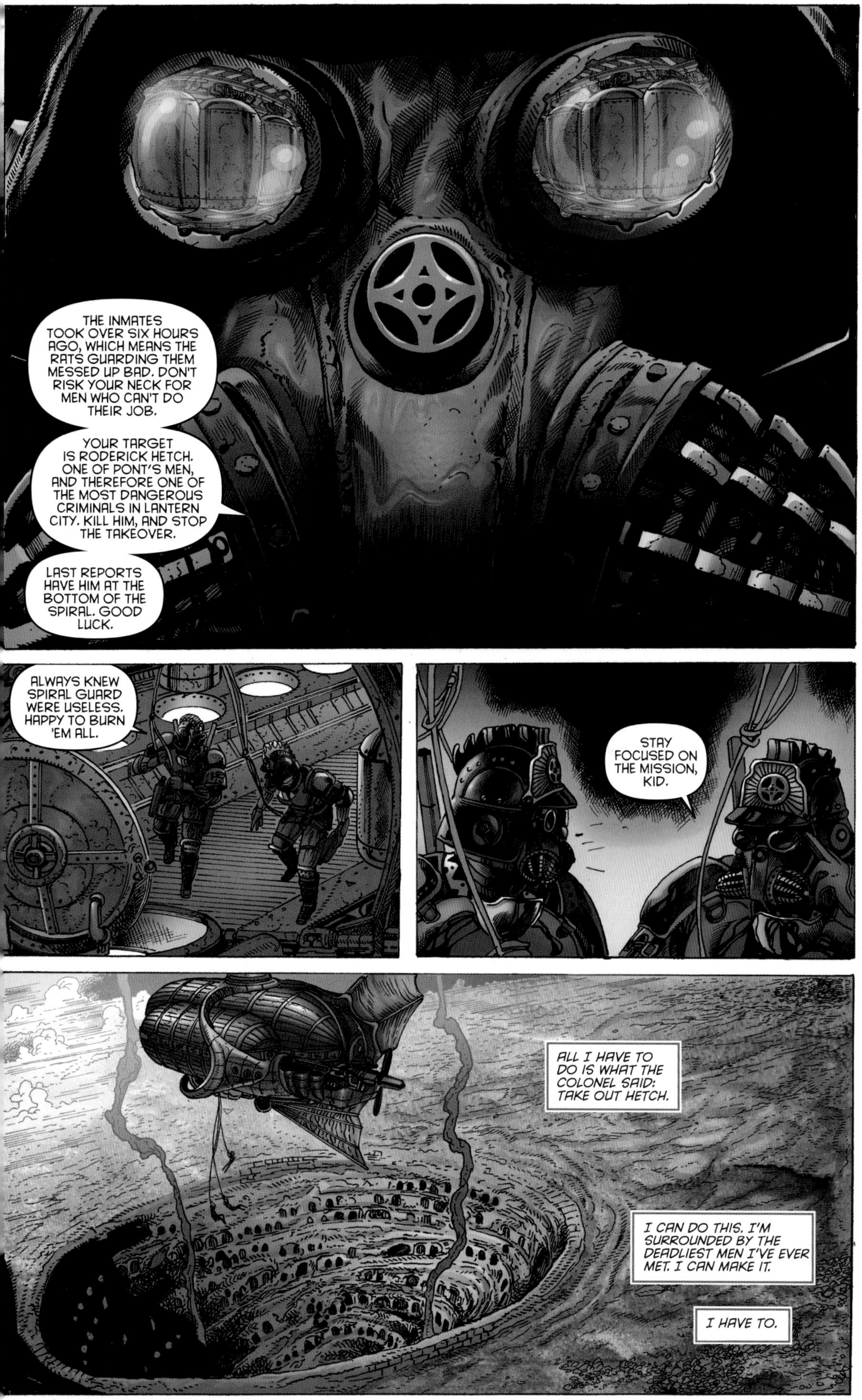
THE INMATES TOOK OVER SIX HOURS AGO, WHICH MEANS THE RATS GUARDING THEM MESSED UP BAD. DON'T RISK YOUR NECK FOR MEN WHO CAN'T DO THEIR JOB.
YOUR TARGET IS RODERICK HETCH. ONE OF PONT'S MEN, AND THEREFORE ONE OF THE MOST DANGEROUS CRIMINALS IN LANTERN CITY. KILL HIM, AND STOP THE TAKEOVER.
LAST REPORTS HAVE HIM AT THE BOTTOM OF THE SPIRAL. GOOD LUCK.
ALWAYS KNEW SPIRAL GUARD WERE USELESS. HAPPY TO BURN 'EM ALL.
STAY FOCUSED ON THE MISSION, KID.
ALL I HAVE TO DO IS WHAT THE COLONEL SAID: TAKE OUT HETCH.
I CAN DO THIS. I'M SURROUNDED BY THE DEADLIEST MEN I'VE EVER MET. I CAN MAKE IT.
I HAVE TO.

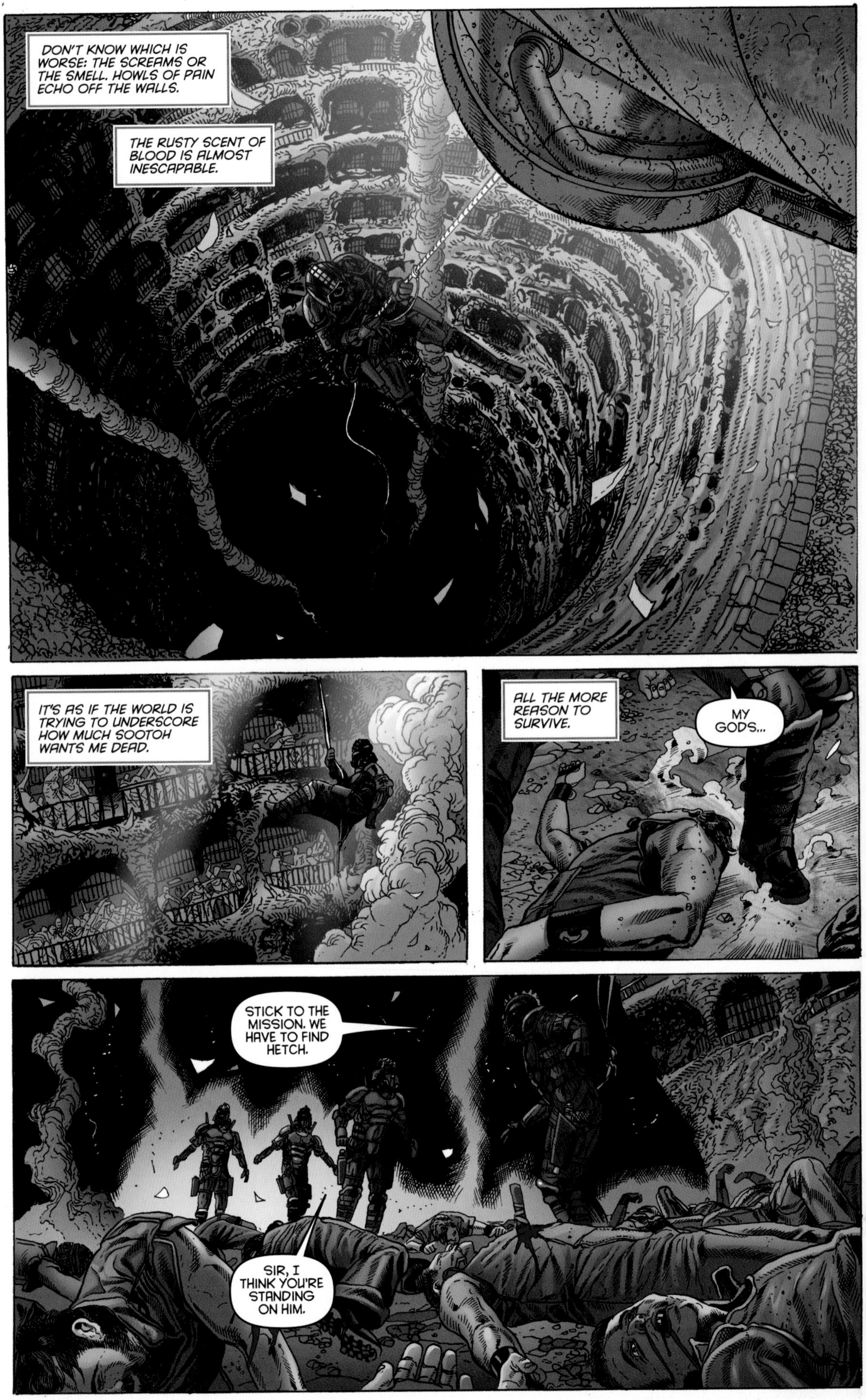
DON'T KNOW WHICH IS WORSE: THE SCREAMS OR THE SMELL. HOWLS OF PAIN ECHO OFF THE WALLS.
THE RUSTY SCENT OF BLOOD IS ALMOST INESCAPABLE.
IT'S AS IF THE WORLD IS TRYING TO UNDERSCORE HOW MUCH SOOTOH WANTS ME DEAD.
ALL THE MORE REASON TO SURVIVE.
MY GODS...
STICK TO THE MISSION. WE HAVE TO FIND HETCH.
SIR, I THINK YOU'RE STANDING ON HIM.

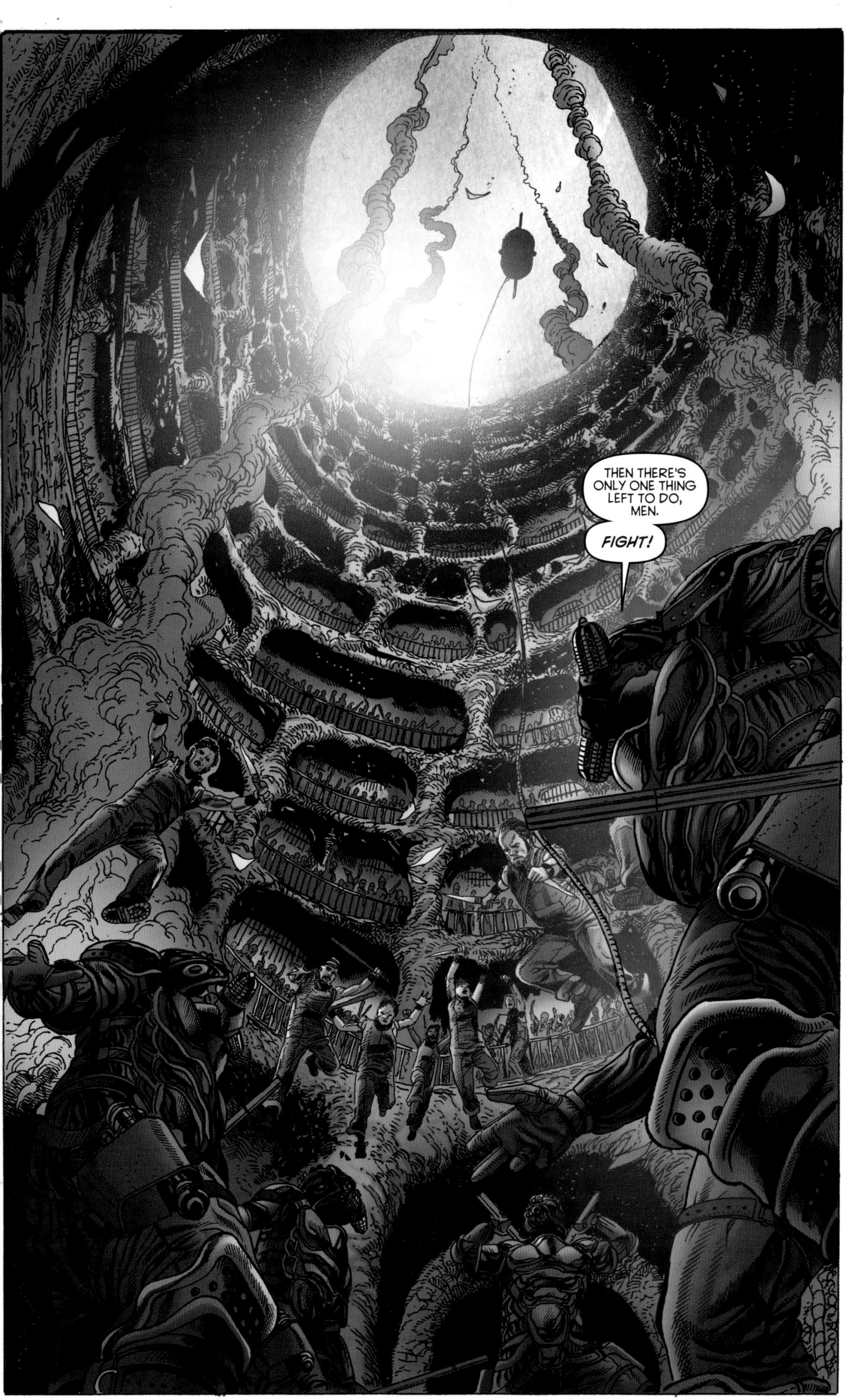
THEN THERE'S ONLY ONE THING LEFT TO DO, MEN.
FIGHT!

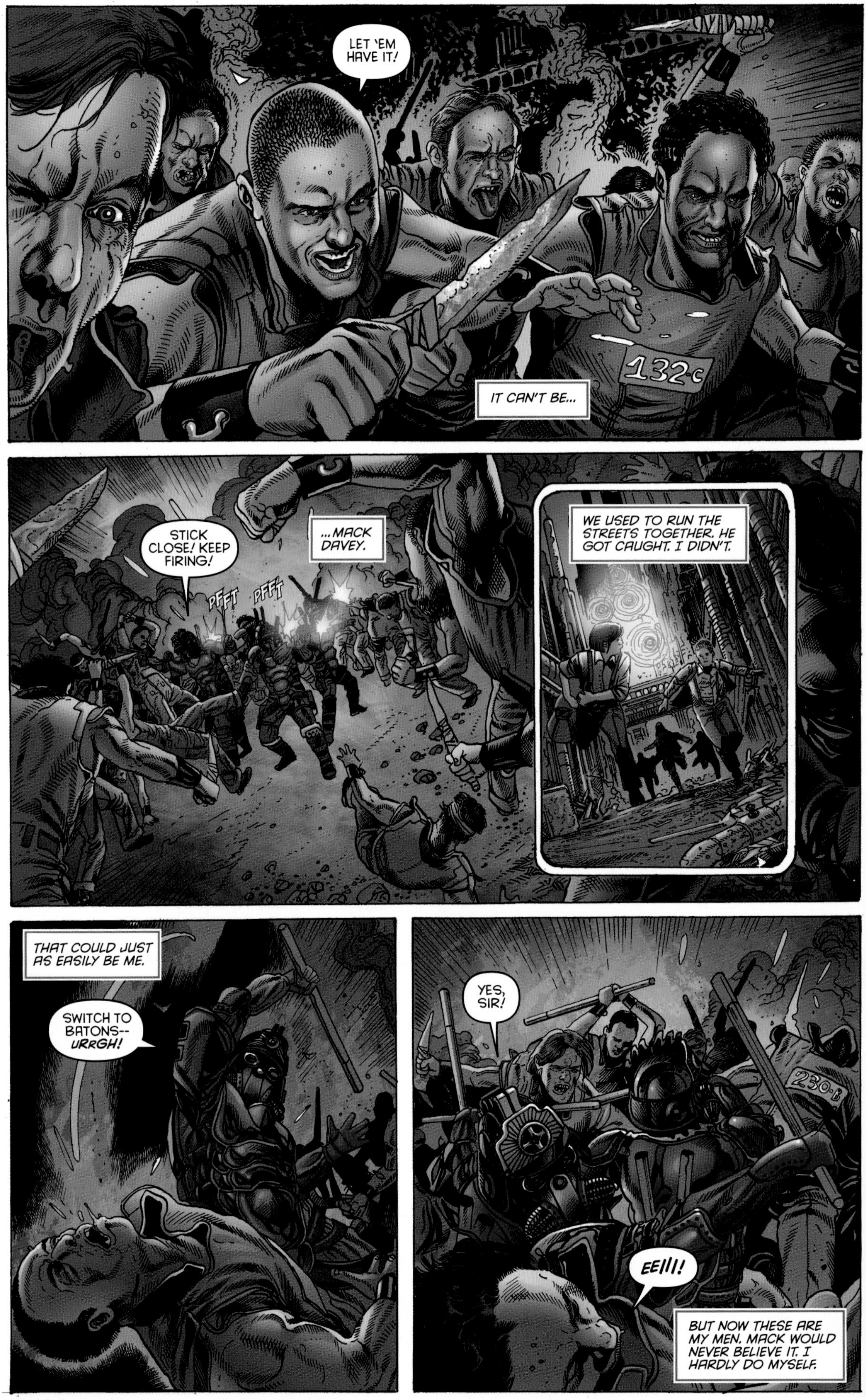
LET 'EM HAVE IT!
IT CAN'T BE...
STICK CLOSE! KEEP FIRING!
PFFT PFFT
...MACK DAVEY.
WE USED TO RUN THE STREETS TOGETHER. HE GOT CAUGHT. I DIDN'T.
THAT COULD JUST AS EASILY BE ME.
SWITCH TO BATONS-- URRGH!
YES, SIR!
132-C
230-B
EEIII!
BUT NOW THESE ARE MY MEN. MACK WOULD NEVER BELIEVE IT. I HARDLY DO MYSELF.

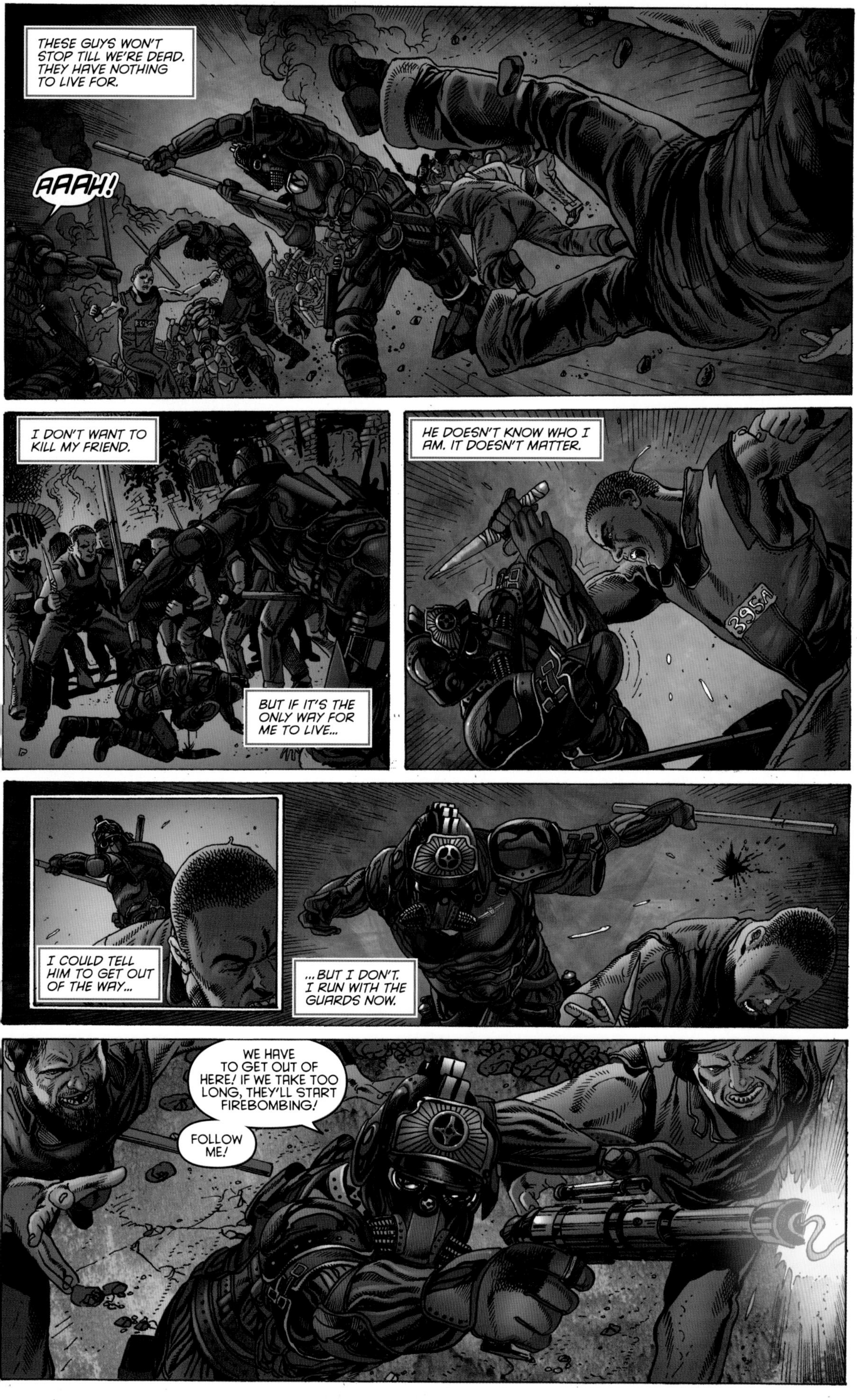
THESE GUYS WON'T STOP TILL WE'RE DEAD. THEY HAVE NOTHING TO LIVE FOR.
AAAH!
I DON'T WANT TO KILL MY FRIEND.
BUT IF IT'S THE ONLY WAY FOR ME TO LIVE...
HE DOESN'T KNOW WHO I AM. IT DOESN'T MATTER.
395A
I COULD TELL HIM TO GET OUT OF THE WAY...
...BUT I DON'T. I RUN WITH THE GUARDS NOW.
WE HAVE TO GET OUT OF HERE! IF WE TAKE TOO LONG, THEY'LL START FIREBOMBING!
FOLLOW ME!

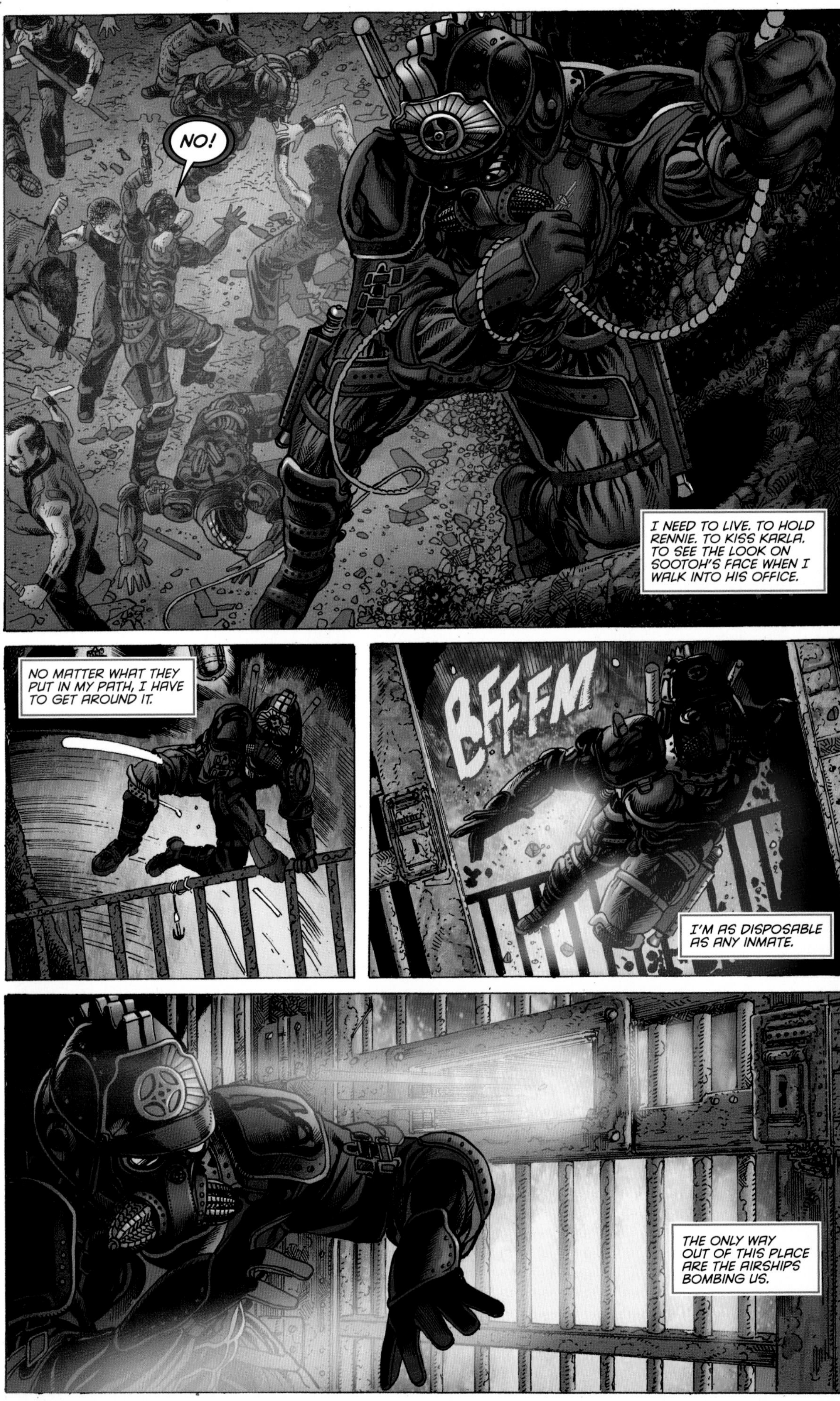
NO!
I NEED TO LIVE. TO HOLD RENNIE. TO KISS KARLA. TO SEE THE LOOK ON SOOTOH'S FACE WHEN I WALK INTO HIS OFFICE.
NO MATTER WHAT THEY PUT IN MY PATH, I HAVE TO GET AROUND IT.
BFFFM
I'M AS DISPOSABLE AS ANY INMATE.
THE ONLY WAY OUT OF THIS PLACE ARE THE AIRSHIPS BOMBING US.

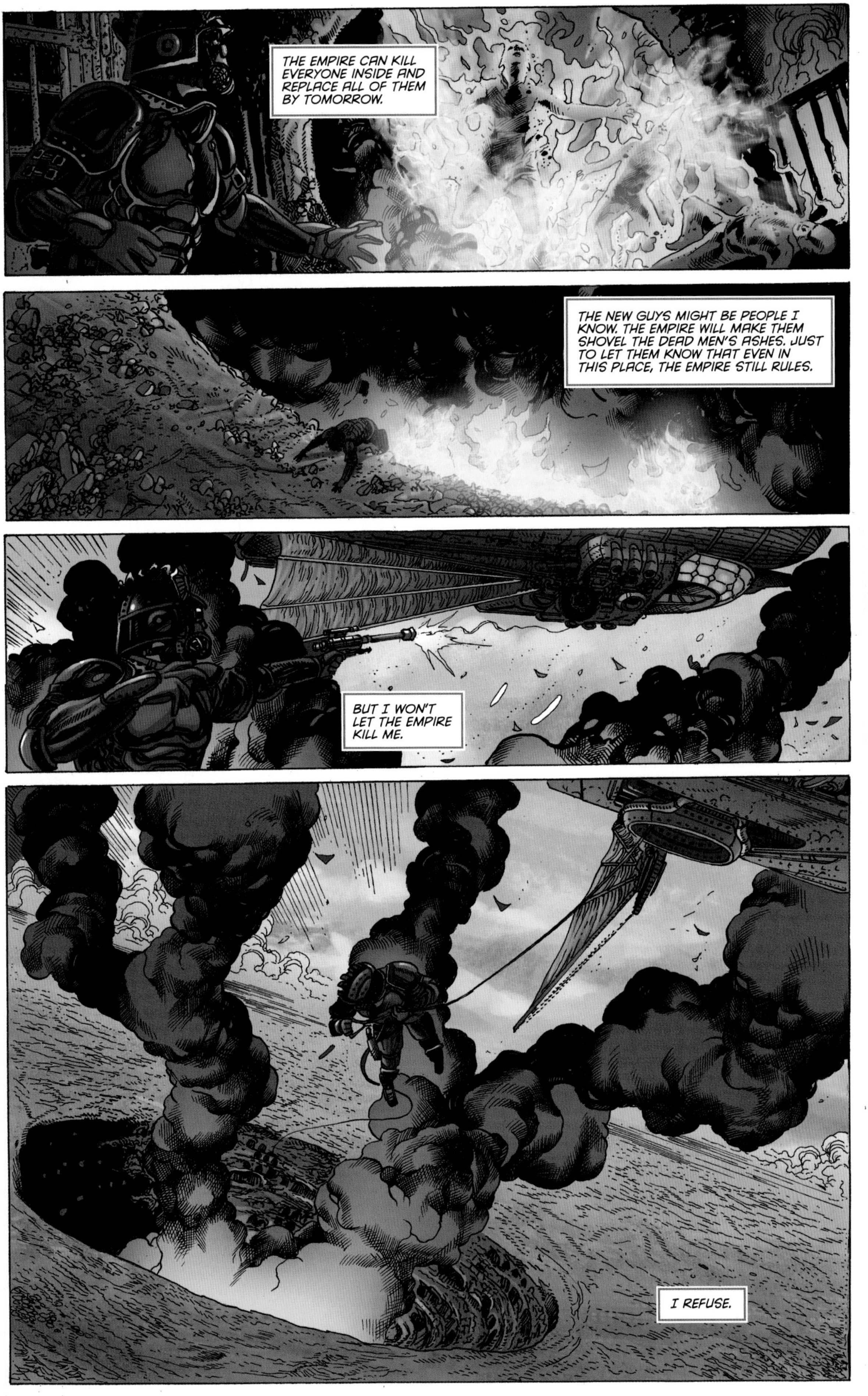
THE EMPIRE CAN KILL EVERYONE INSIDE AND REPLACE ALL OF THEM BY TOMORROW.
THE NEW GUYS MIGHT BE PEOPLE I KNOW. THE EMPIRE WILL MAKE THEM SHOVEL THE DEAD MEN'S ASHES. JUST TO LET THEM KNOW THAT EVEN IN THIS PLACE, THE EMPIRE STILL RULES.
BUT I WON'T LET THE EMPIRE KILL ME.
I REFUSE.

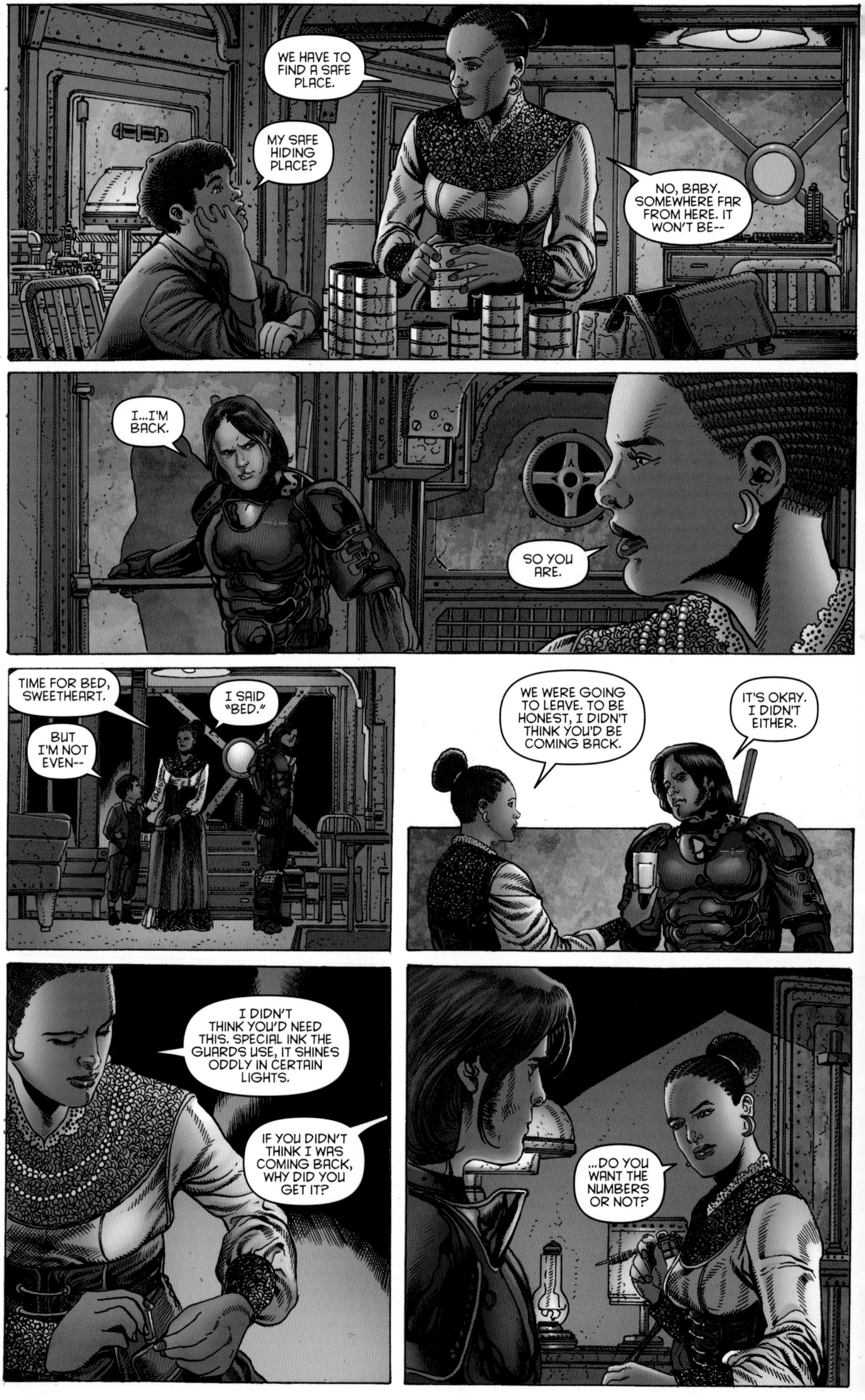
WE HAVE TO FIND A SAFE PLACE.
MY SAFE HIDING PLACE?
NO, BABY. SOMEWHERE FAR FROM HERE. IT WON'T BE--
I...I'M BACK.
SO YOU ARE.
TIME FOR BED, SWEETHEART.
BUT I'M NOT EVEN--
I SAID "BED."
WE WERE GOING TO LEAVE. TO BE HONEST, I DIDN'T THINK YOU'D BE COMING BACK.
IT'S OKAY. I DIDN'T EITHER.
I DIDN'T THINK YOU'D NEED THIS. SPECIAL INK THE GUARDS USE, IT SHINES ODDLY IN CERTAIN LIGHTS.
IF YOU DIDN'T THINK I WAS COMING BACK, WHY DID YOU GET IT?
...DO YOU WANT THE NUMBERS OR NOT?

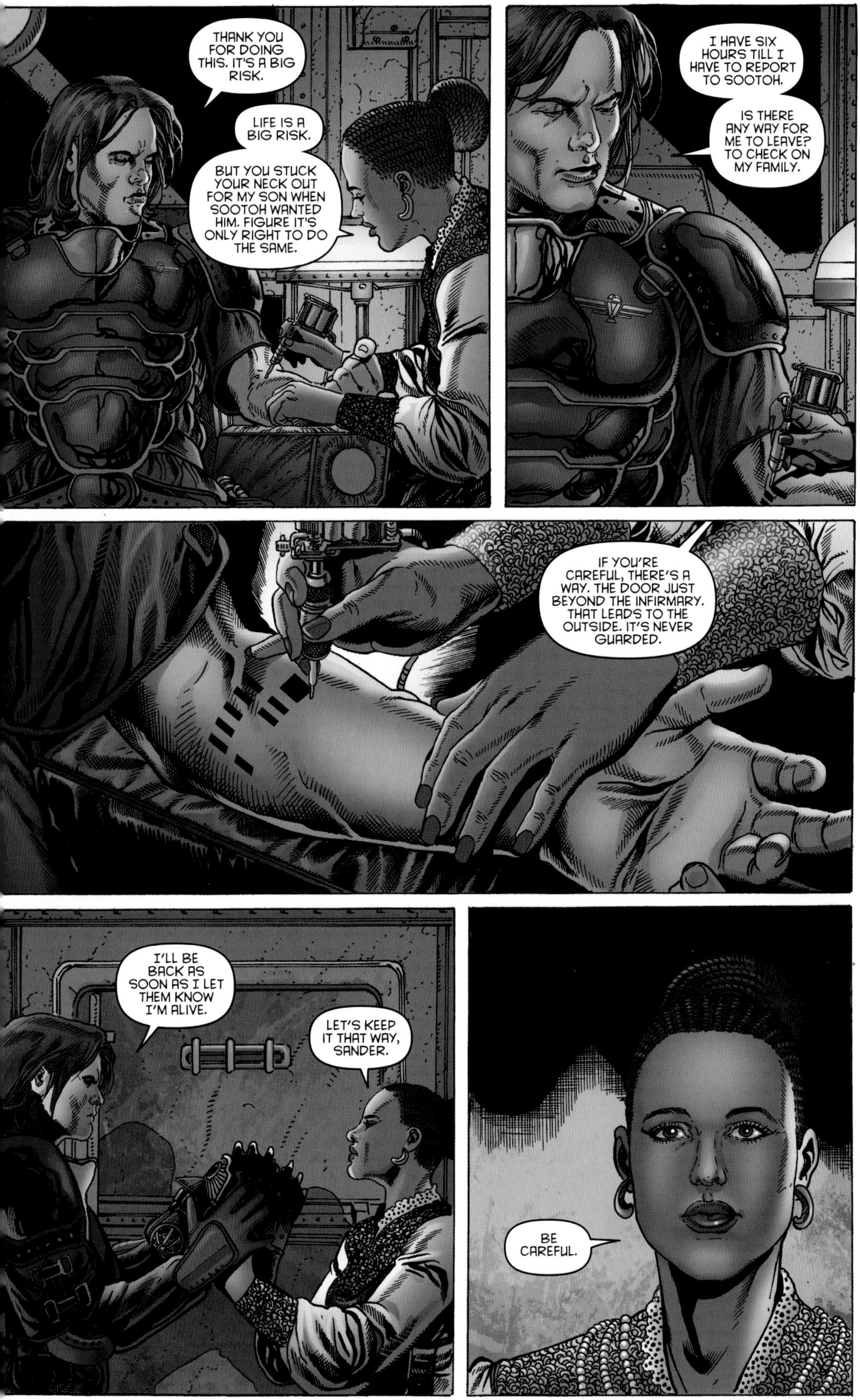
THANK YOU FOR DOING THIS. IT'S A BIG RISK.
LIFE IS A BIG RISK.
BUT YOU STUCK YOUR NECK OUT FOR MY SON WHEN SOOTOH WANTED HIM. FIGURE IT'S ONLY RIGHT TO DO THE SAME.
I HAVE SIX HOURS TILL I HAVE TO REPORT TO SOOTOH.
IS THERE ANY WAY FOR ME TO LEAVE? TO CHECK ON MY FAMILY.
IF YOU'RE CAREFUL, THERE'S A WAY. THE DOOR JUST BEYOND THE INFIRMARY. THAT LEADS TO THE OUTSIDE. IT'S NEVER GUARDED.
I'LL BE BACK AS SOON AS I LET THEM KNOW I'M ALIVE.
LET'S KEEP IT THAT WAY, SANDER.
BE CAREFUL.

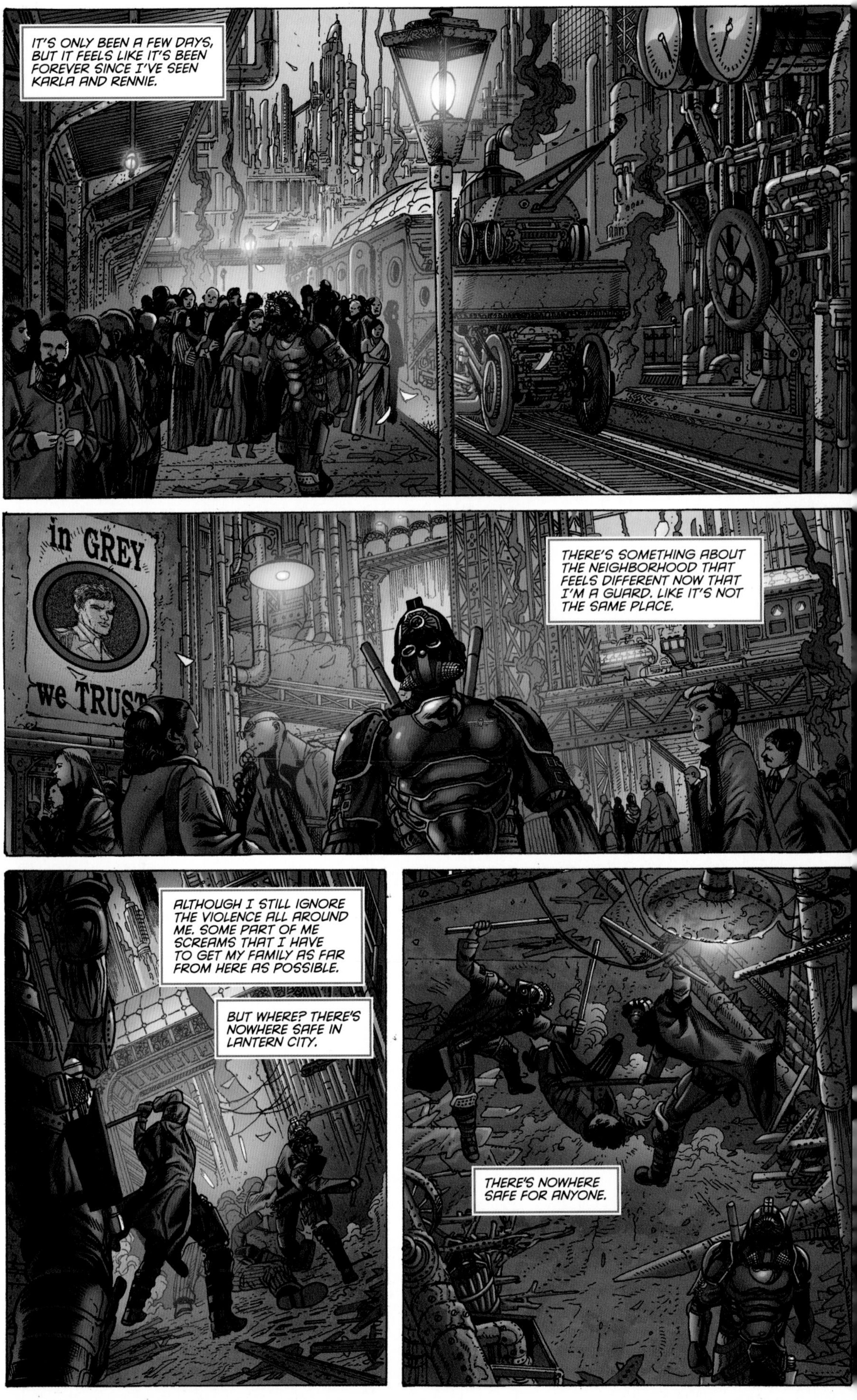
IT'S ONLY BEEN A FEW DAYS, BUT IT FEELS LIKE IT'S BEEN FOREVER SINCE I'VE SEEN KARLA AND RENNIE.
in GREY
we TRUST
THERE'S SOMETHING ABOUT THE NEIGHBORHOOD THAT FEELS DIFFERENT NOW THAT I'M A GUARD. LIKE IT'S NOT THE SAME PLACE.
ALTHOUGH I STILL IGNORE THE VIOLENCE ALL AROUND ME. SOME PART OF ME SCREAMS THAT I HAVE TO GET MY FAMILY AS FAR FROM HERE AS POSSIBLE.
BUT WHERE? THERE'S NOWHERE SAFE IN LANTERN CITY.
THERE'S NOWHERE SAFE FOR ANYONE.

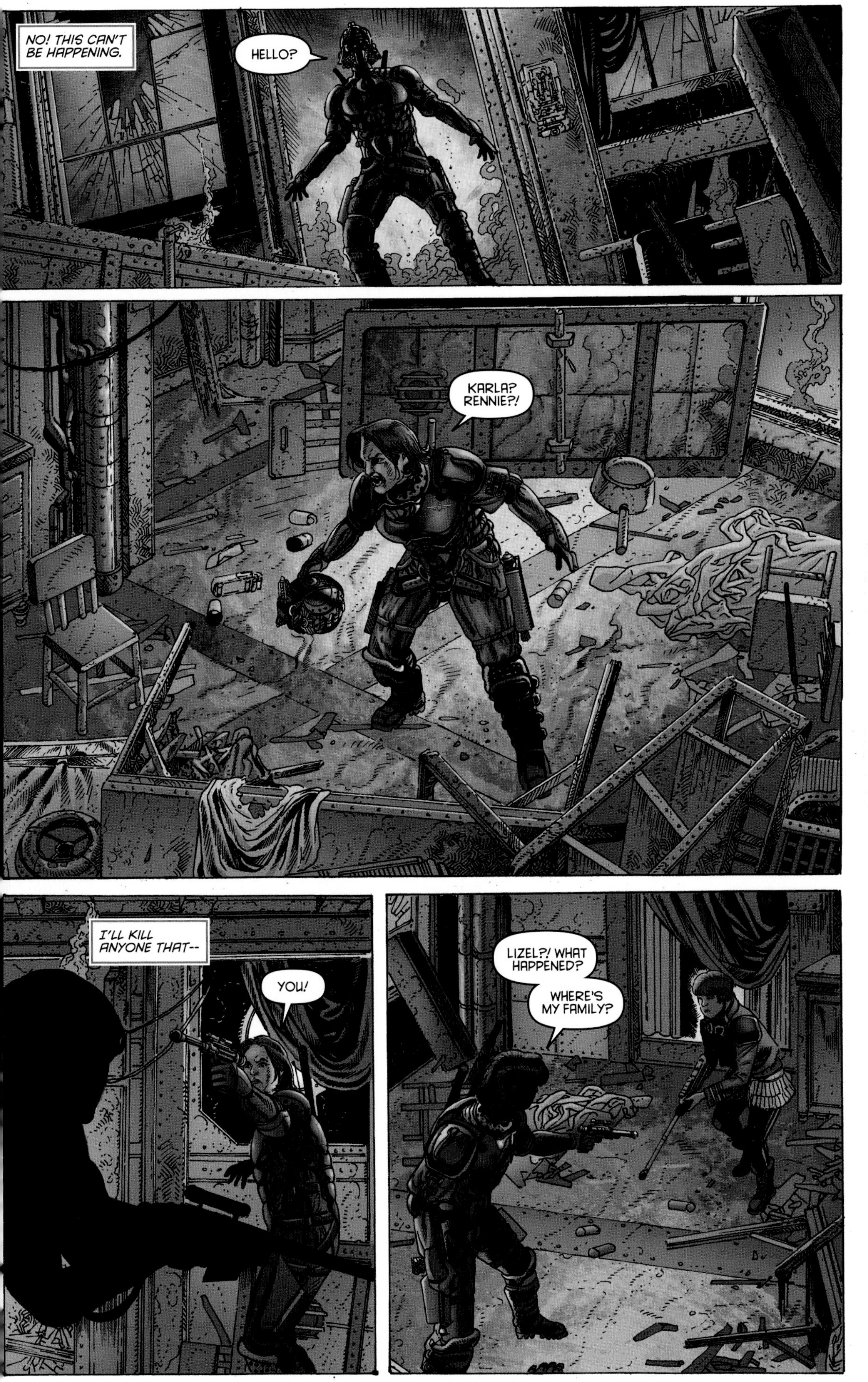
NO! THIS CAN'T BE HAPPENING.
HELLO?
KARLA? RENNIE?!
I'LL KILL ANYONE THAT--
YOU!
LIZEL?! WHAT HAPPENED?
WHERE'S MY FAMILY?

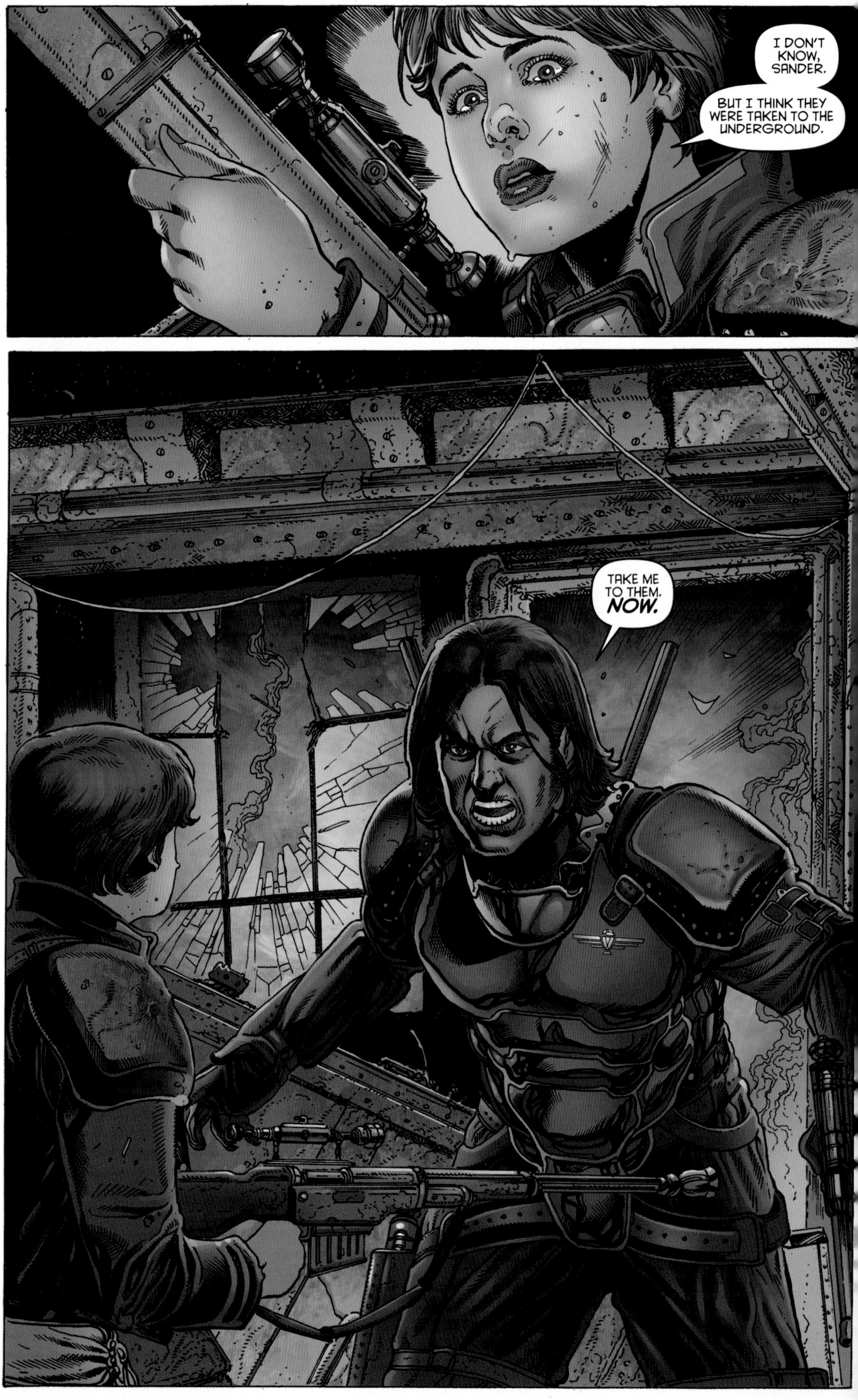
I DON'T KNOW, SANDER.
BUT I THINK THEY WERE TAKEN TO THE UNDERGROUND.
TAKE ME TO THEM. NOW.

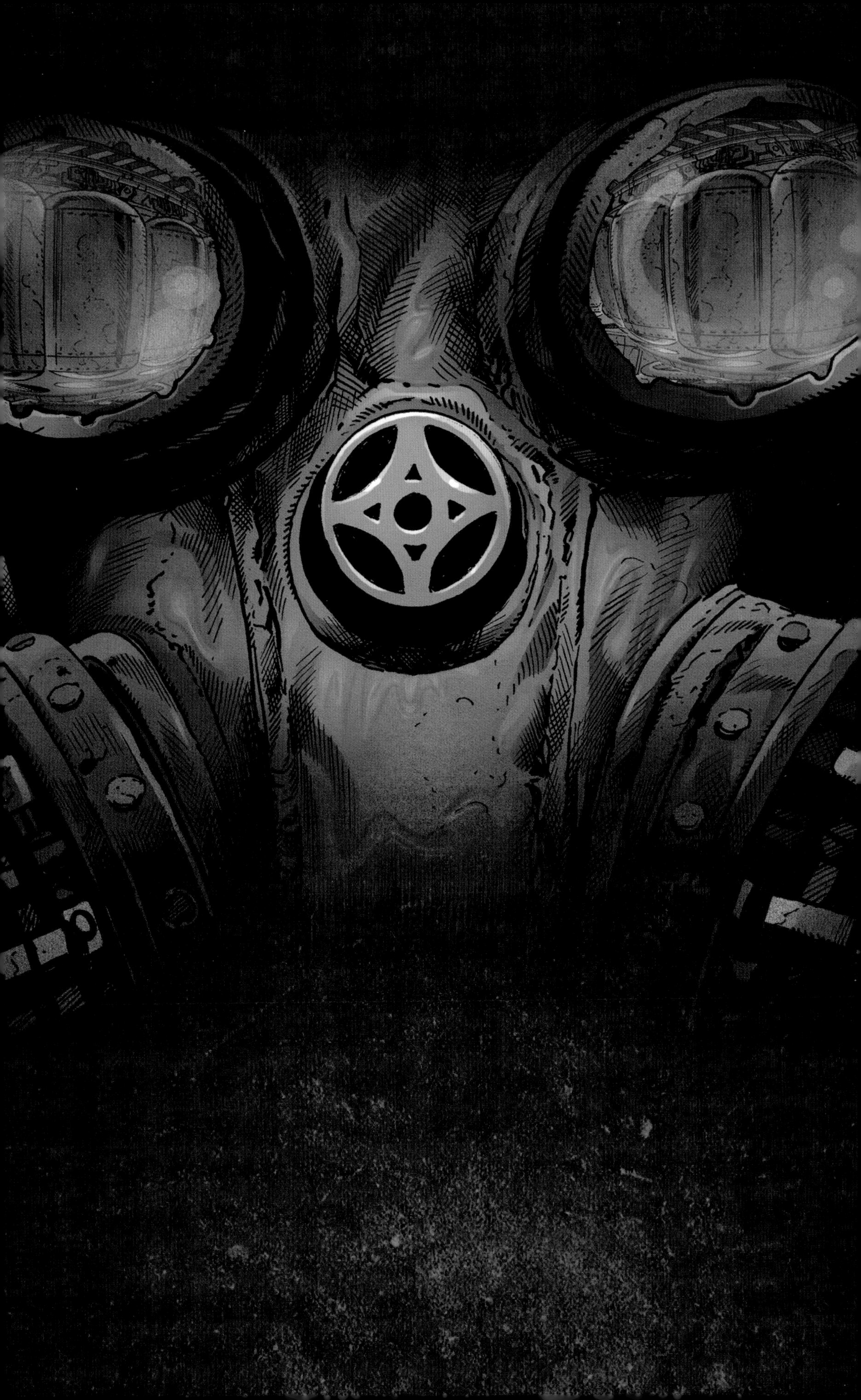

CHAPTER FOUR

THE UNDERGROUND'S A HUGE PLACE. I DON'T KNOW WHERE THEY ARE.

WE'RE RUNNING OUT OF TIME! WHERE DID YOU SEE THEM TAKE THEM?

I--I DON'T KNOW WHAT HAPPENED. IT'S NOT MY JOB TO PROTECT *YOUR* FAMILY!

SO YOU'RE JUST *GUESSING?!*

DAMN IT, LIZEL! THIS IS BOTH YOUR FAULTS, YOU AND KENDAL, AND THAT HICKING GANG OF YOURS!

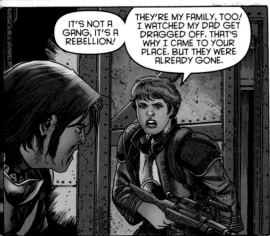

IT'S NOT A GANG, IT'S A REBELLION!

THEY'RE MY FAMILY, TOO! I WATCHED MY DAD GET DRAGGED OFF. THAT'S WHY I CAME TO YOUR PLACE. BUT THEY WERE ALREADY GONE.

LIZEL-- I'M SORRY.

WHAT'S HAPPENING? EVERYONE'S GONE. YOU'RE IN THAT *UNIFORM.*

...TALK TO ME.

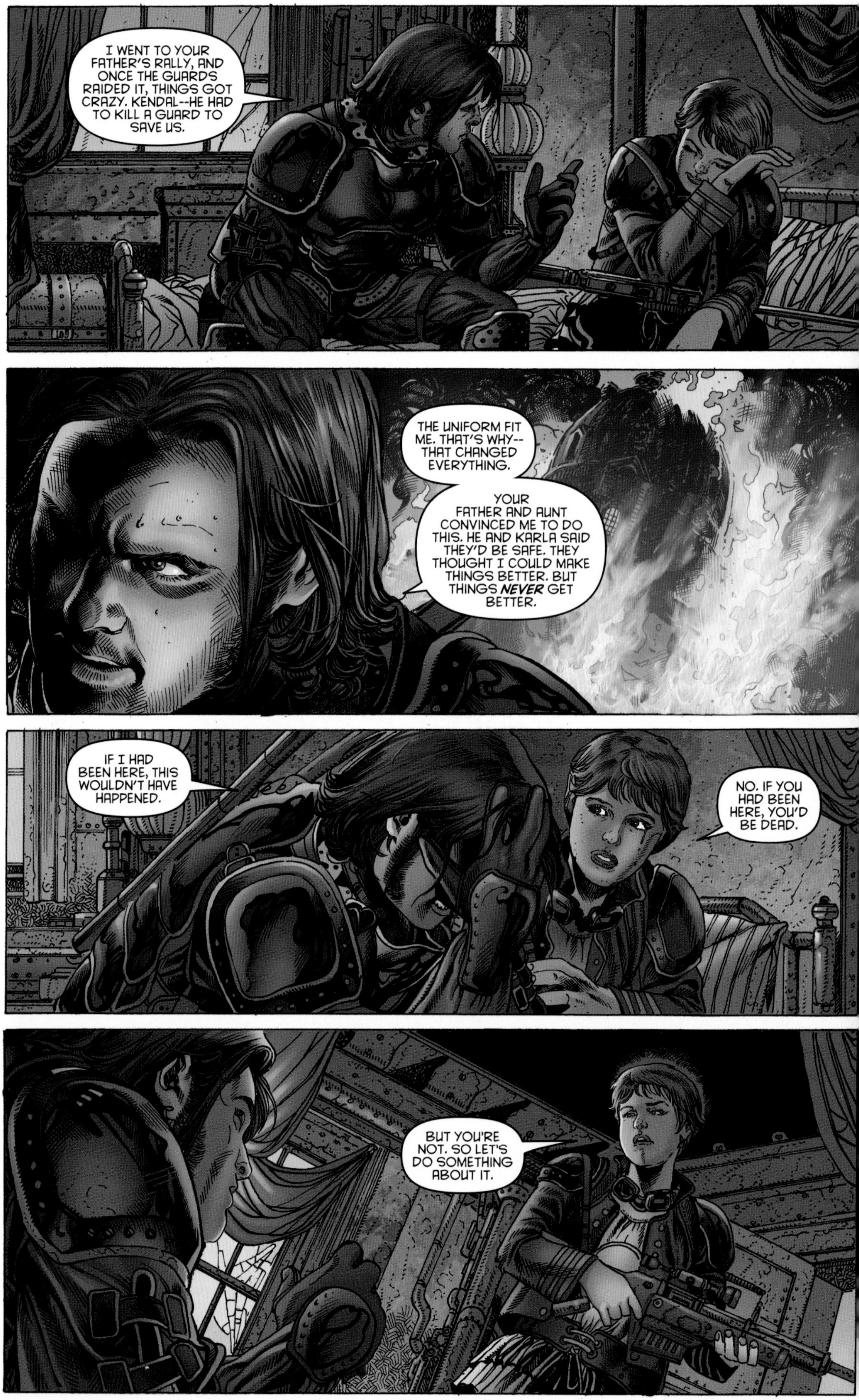
I WENT TO YOUR FATHER'S RALLY, AND ONCE THE GUARDS RAIDED IT, THINGS GOT CRAZY. KENDAL--HE HAD TO KILL A GUARD TO SAVE US.
THE UNIFORM FIT ME. THAT'S WHY-- THAT CHANGED EVERYTHING.
YOUR FATHER AND AUNT CONVINCED ME TO DO THIS. HE AND KARLA SAID THEY'D BE SAFE. THEY THOUGHT I COULD MAKE THINGS BETTER. BUT THINGS *NEVER* GET BETTER.
IF I HAD BEEN HERE, THIS WOULDN'T HAVE HAPPENED.
NO. IF YOU HAD BEEN HERE, YOU'D BE DEAD.
BUT YOU'RE NOT. SO LET'S DO SOMETHING ABOUT IT.

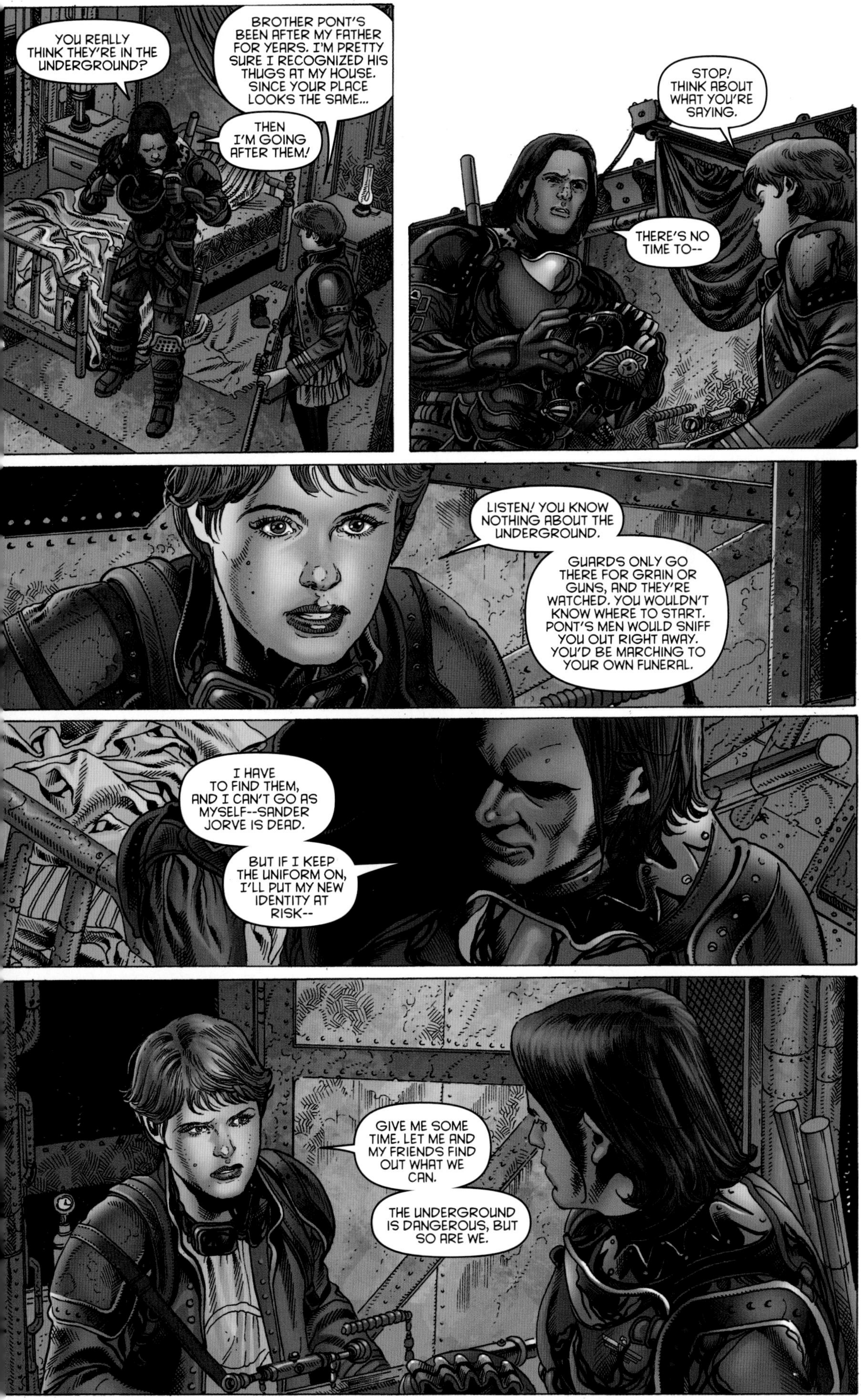
YOU REALLY THINK THEY'RE IN THE UNDERGROUND?
BROTHER PONT'S BEEN AFTER MY FATHER FOR YEARS. I'M PRETTY SURE I RECOGNIZED HIS THUGS AT MY HOUSE. SINCE YOUR PLACE LOOKS THE SAME...
THEN I'M GOING AFTER THEM!
STOP! THINK ABOUT WHAT YOU'RE SAYING.
THERE'S NO TIME TO--
LISTEN! YOU KNOW NOTHING ABOUT THE UNDERGROUND.
GUARDS ONLY GO THERE FOR GRAIN OR GUNS, AND THEY'RE WATCHED. YOU WOULDN'T KNOW WHERE TO START. PONT'S MEN WOULD SNIFF YOU OUT RIGHT AWAY. YOU'D BE MARCHING TO YOUR OWN FUNERAL.
I HAVE TO FIND THEM, AND I CAN'T GO AS MYSELF--SANDER JORVE IS DEAD.
BUT IF I KEEP THE UNIFORM ON, I'LL PUT MY NEW IDENTITY AT RISK--
GIVE ME SOME TIME. LET ME AND MY FRIENDS FIND OUT WHAT WE CAN.
THE UNDERGROUND IS DANGEROUS, BUT SO ARE WE.

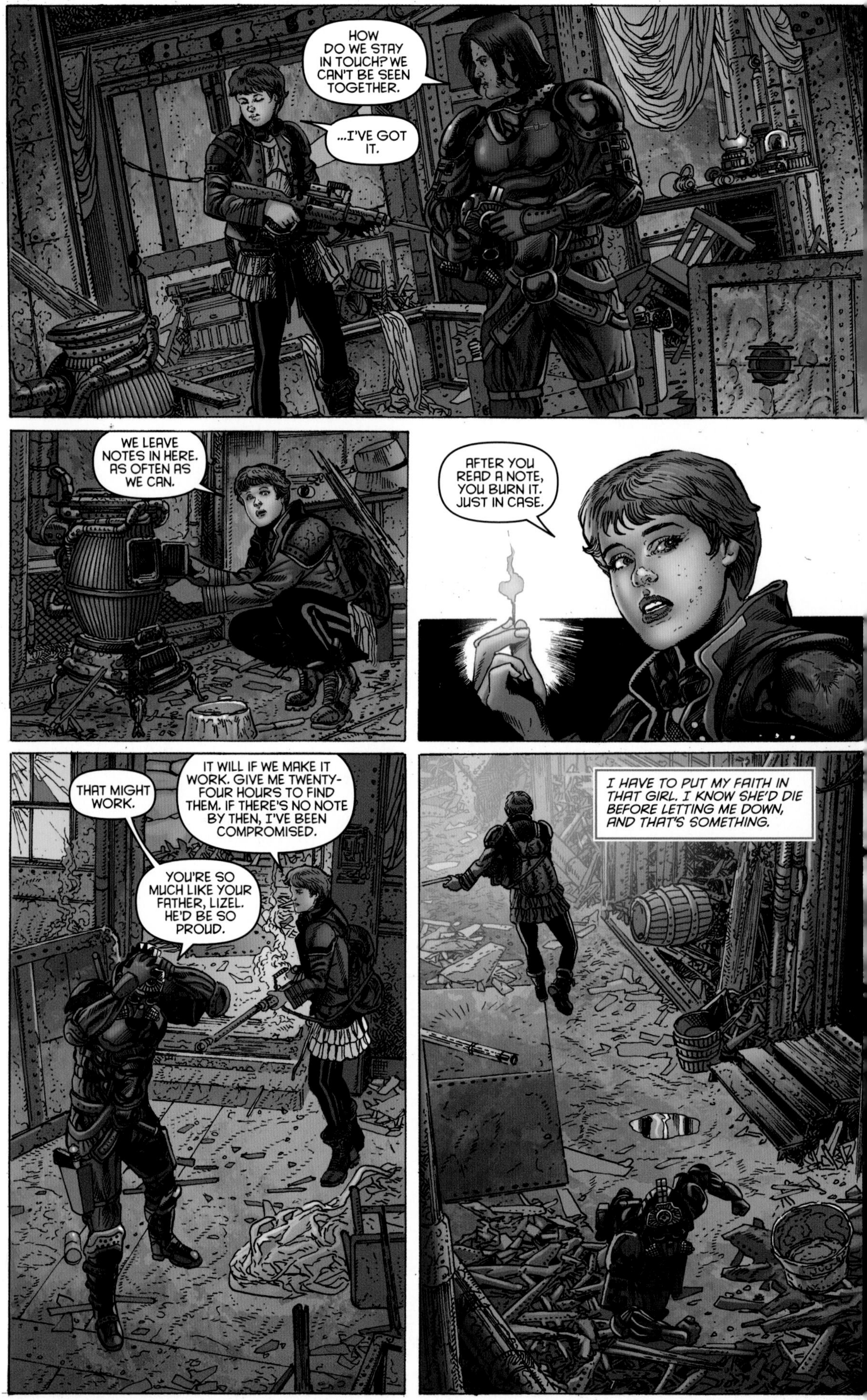
HOW DO WE STAY IN TOUCH? WE CAN'T BE SEEN TOGETHER.
...I'VE GOT IT.
WE LEAVE NOTES IN HERE. AS OFTEN AS WE CAN.
AFTER YOU READ A NOTE, YOU BURN IT. JUST IN CASE.
THAT MIGHT WORK.
IT WILL IF WE MAKE IT WORK. GIVE ME TWENTY-FOUR HOURS TO FIND THEM. IF THERE'S NO NOTE BY THEN, I'VE BEEN COMPROMISED.
YOU'RE SO MUCH LIKE YOUR FATHER, LIZEL. HE'D BE SO PROUD.
I HAVE TO PUT MY FAITH IN THAT GIRL. I KNOW SHE'D DIE BEFORE LETTING ME DOWN, AND THAT'S SOMETHING.

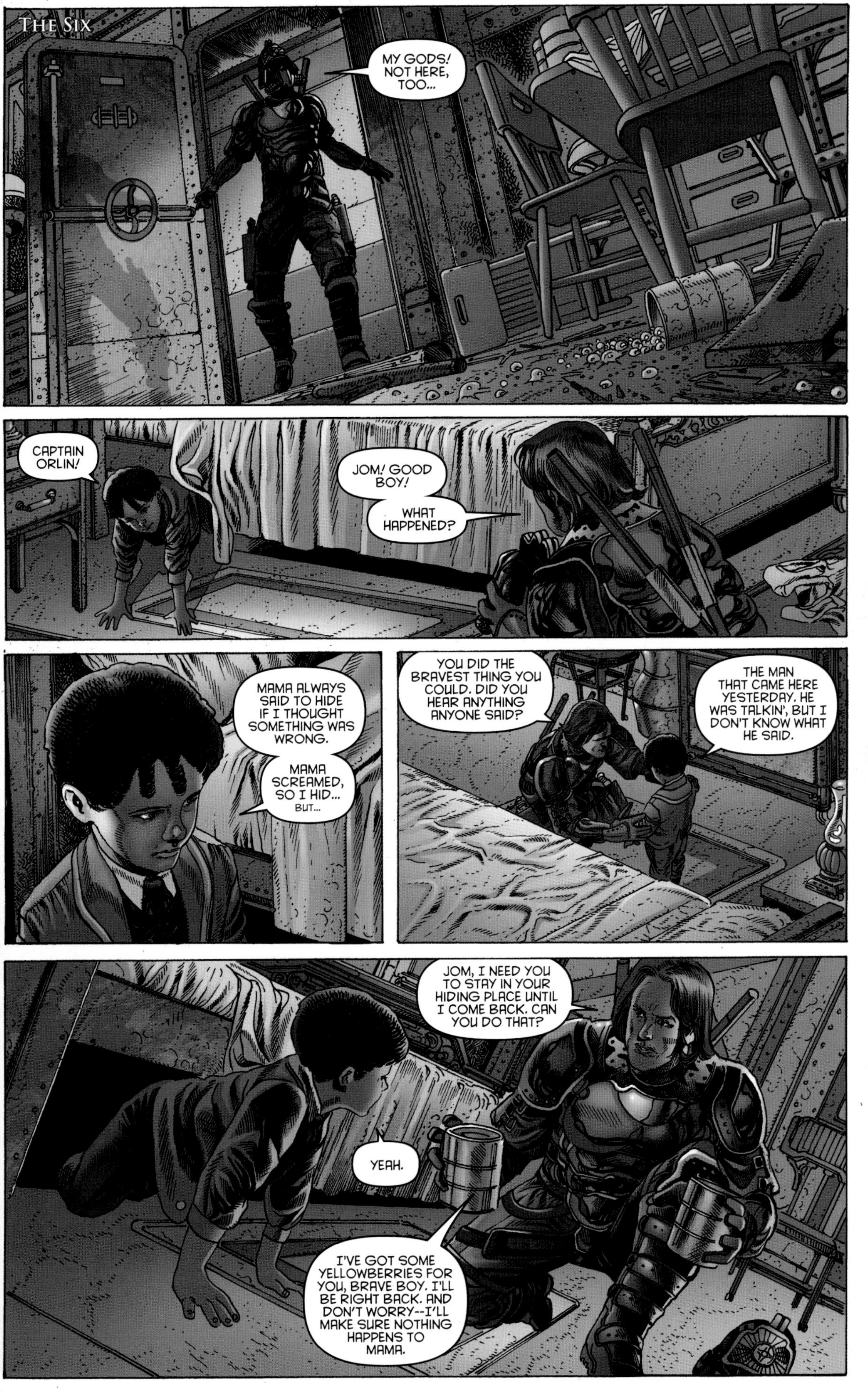
MY GODS! NOT HERE, TOO...
CAPTAIN ORLIN!
JOM! GOOD BOY!
WHAT HAPPENED?
MAMA ALWAYS SAID TO HIDE IF I THOUGHT SOMETHING WAS WRONG.
MAMA SCREAMED, SO I HID... BUT...
YOU DID THE BRAVEST THING YOU COULD. DID YOU HEAR ANYTHING ANYONE SAID?
THE MAN THAT CAME HERE YESTERDAY. HE WAS TALKIN', BUT I DON'T KNOW WHAT HE SAID.
JOM, I NEED YOU TO STAY IN YOUR HIDING PLACE UNTIL I COME BACK. CAN YOU DO THAT?
YEAH.
I'VE GOT SOME YELLOWBERRIES FOR YOU, BRAVE BOY. I'LL BE RIGHT BACK. AND DON'T WORRY--I'LL MAKE SURE NOTHING HAPPENS TO MAMA.

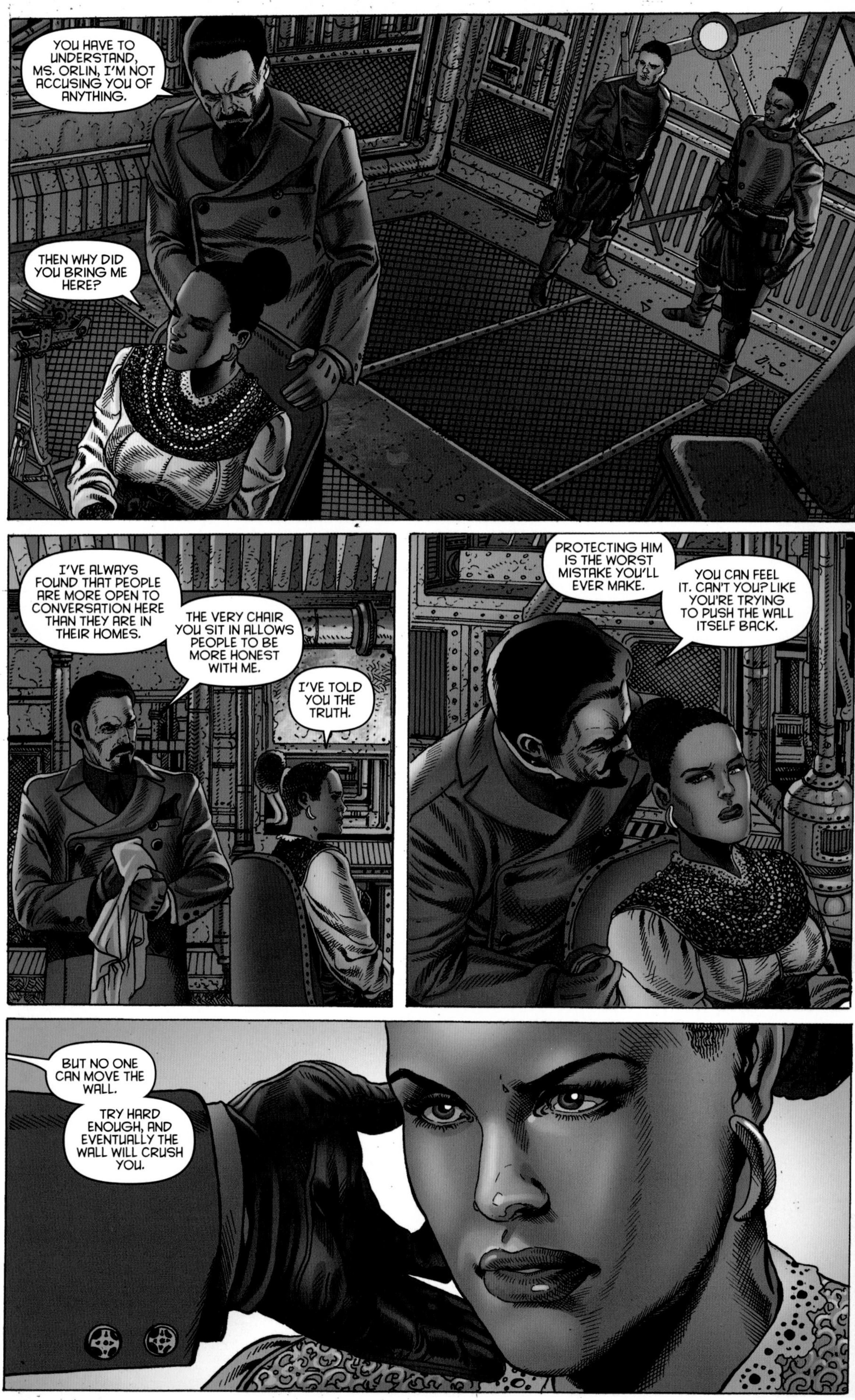
YOU HAVE TO UNDERSTAND, MS. ORLIN, I'M NOT ACCUSING YOU OF ANYTHING.
THEN WHY DID YOU BRING ME HERE?
I'VE ALWAYS FOUND THAT PEOPLE ARE MORE OPEN TO CONVERSATION HERE THAN THEY ARE IN THEIR HOMES.
THE VERY CHAIR YOU SIT IN ALLOWS PEOPLE TO BE MORE HONEST WITH ME.
I'VE TOLD YOU THE TRUTH.
PROTECTING HIM IS THE WORST MISTAKE YOU'LL EVER MAKE.
YOU CAN FEEL IT. CAN'T YOU? LIKE YOU'RE TRYING TO PUSH THE WALL ITSELF BACK.
BUT NO ONE CAN MOVE THE WALL.
TRY HARD ENOUGH, AND EVENTUALLY THE WALL WILL CRUSH YOU.

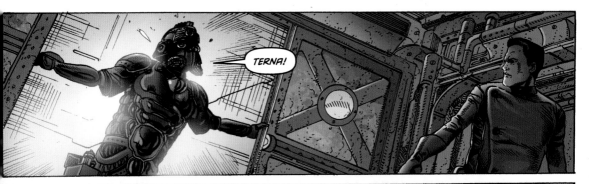

TERNA!

THAT WON'T BE NECESSARY.

WE'VE BEEN WAITING FOR YOU, CAPTAIN ORLIN.

CONGRATULATIONS ON YOUR RETURN FROM THE SPIRAL. THE GUARD MUST BE PROUD OF YOUR SUCCESS.

I HEAR YOU WANT TO SPEAK WITH *ME*, MR. SOOTOH. MY WIFE HAS DUTIES AT HOME.

TOO TRUE. HAVE A SEAT, CAPTAIN.

CA--CAPTAIN. DID...EVERYTHING LOOK OKAY AT HOME?

IT'S ALL RIGHT, TERNA. EVERYTHING IS OKAY.

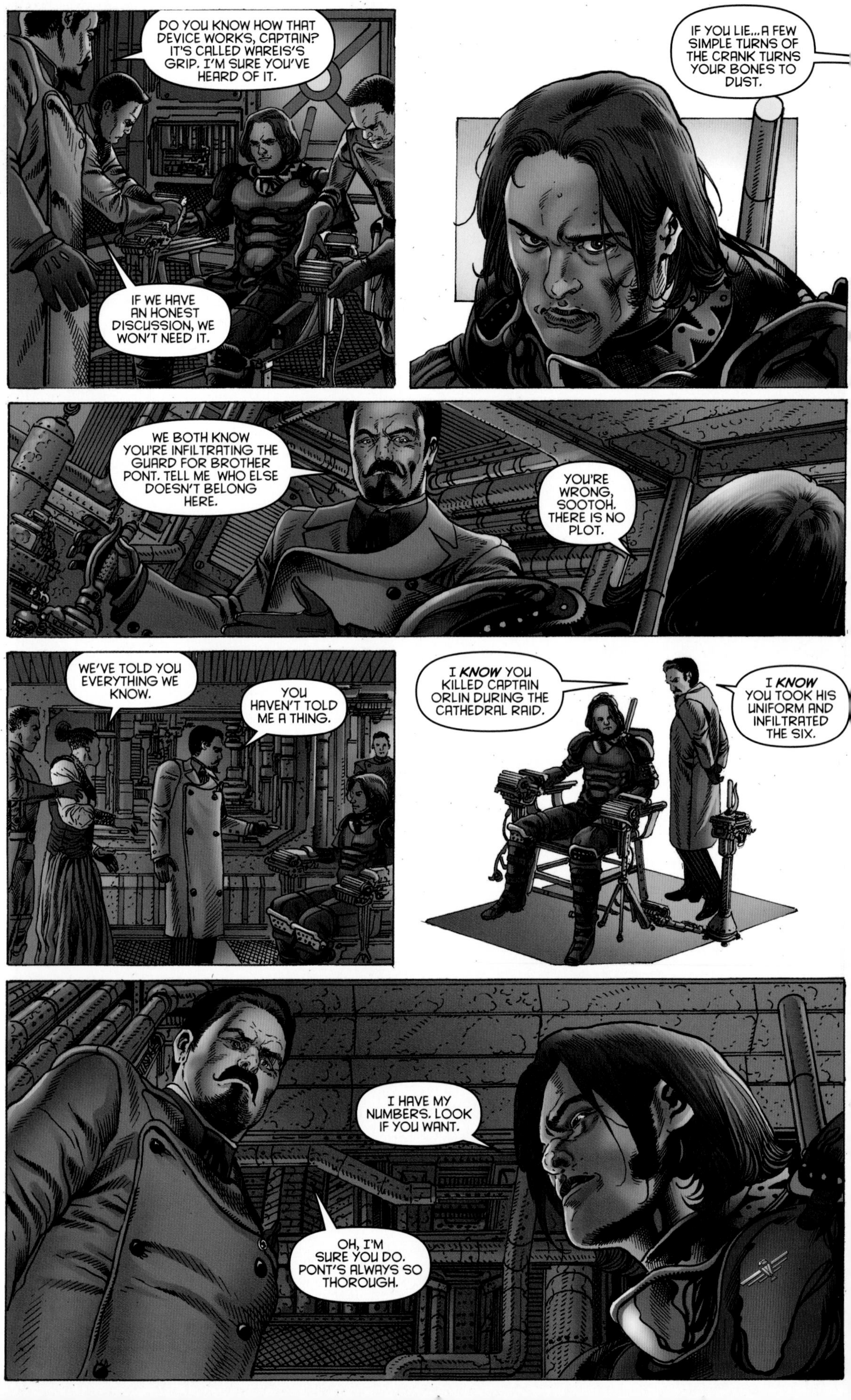
DO YOU KNOW HOW THAT DEVICE WORKS, CAPTAIN? IT'S CALLED WAREIS'S GRIP. I'M SURE YOU'VE HEARD OF IT.
IF WE HAVE AN HONEST DISCUSSION, WE WON'T NEED IT.
IF YOU LIE...A FEW SIMPLE TURNS OF THE CRANK TURNS YOUR BONES TO DUST.
WE BOTH KNOW YOU'RE INFILTRATING THE GUARD FOR BROTHER PONT. TELL ME WHO ELSE DOESN'T BELONG HERE.
YOU'RE WRONG, SOOTOH. THERE IS NO PLOT.
WE'VE TOLD YOU EVERYTHING WE KNOW.
YOU HAVEN'T TOLD ME A THING.
I *KNOW* YOU KILLED CAPTAIN ORLIN DURING THE CATHEDRAL RAID.
I *KNOW* YOU TOOK HIS UNIFORM AND INFILTRATED THE SIX.
I HAVE MY NUMBERS. LOOK IF YOU WANT.
OH, I'M SURE YOU DO. PONT'S ALWAYS SO THOROUGH.

BUT THE LIES STOP HERE. THEY STOP WITH *ME*.

WHAT IS GOING ON HERE?!

GENERAL CANDEN. WE DO NOT HAVE A MEETING SCHED--

DAMN YOUR SCHEDULE!

FIRST YOU SEND A GUARD--MY BEST CAPTAIN--ON A MISSION WITHOUT MY CONSENT!

NOW YOU'RE CLAIMING A CAPTAIN WHO SURVIVED THE *SPIRAL* IS SOME KIND OF THUG FROM THE STREET?! YOUR INVESTIGATION INTO HIM ENDS *NOW*. AM I CLEAR?

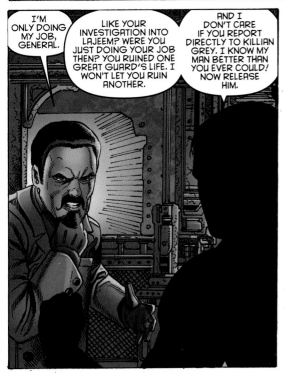

I'M ONLY DOING MY JOB, GENERAL.

LIKE YOUR INVESTIGATION INTO LAJEEM? WERE YOU JUST DOING YOUR JOB THEN? YOU RUINED ONE GREAT GUARD'S LIFE. I WON'T LET YOU RUIN ANOTHER.

AND I DON'T CARE IF YOU REPORT DIRECTLY TO KILLIAN GREY. I KNOW MY MAN BETTER THAN YOU EVER COULD! NOW RELEASE HIM.

CANDEN MAY BE A FOOL, BUT KILLIAN GREY IS NOT. ONE DAY I'LL HAVE ENOUGH EVIDENCE THAT HE'LL EXECUTE YOU FOR TREASON...AND CANDEN FOR INCOMPETENCE.

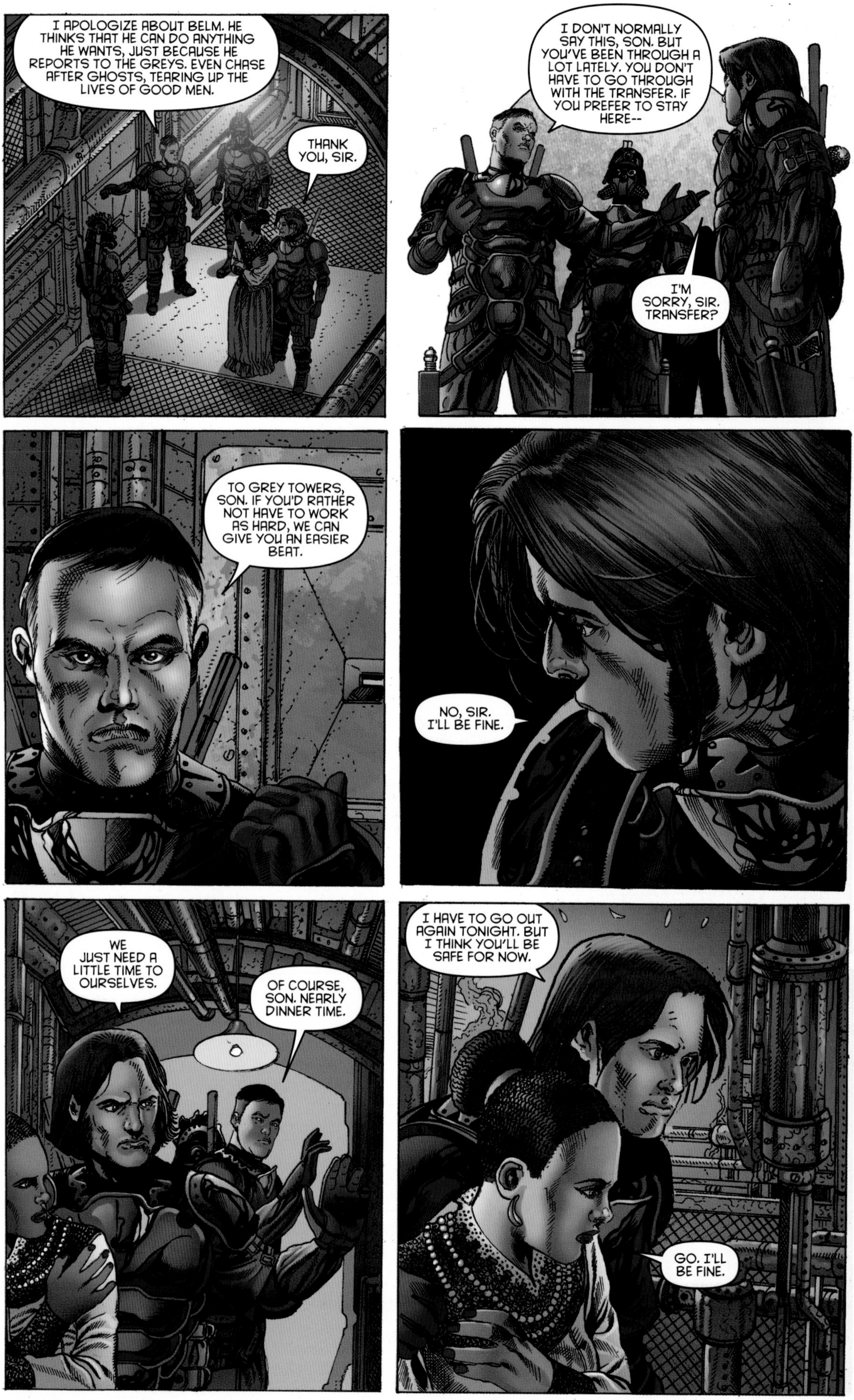
I APOLOGIZE ABOUT BELM. HE THINKS THAT HE CAN DO ANYTHING HE WANTS, JUST BECAUSE HE REPORTS TO THE GREYS. EVEN CHASE AFTER GHOSTS, TEARING UP THE LIVES OF GOOD MEN.
THANK YOU, SIR.
I DON'T NORMALLY SAY THIS, SON. BUT YOU'VE BEEN THROUGH A LOT LATELY. YOU DON'T HAVE TO GO THROUGH WITH THE TRANSFER. IF YOU PREFER TO STAY HERE--
I'M SORRY, SIR. TRANSFER?
TO GREY TOWERS, SON. IF YOU'D RATHER NOT HAVE TO WORK AS HARD, WE CAN GIVE YOU AN EASIER BEAT.
NO, SIR. I'LL BE FINE.
WE JUST NEED A LITTLE TIME TO OURSELVES.
OF COURSE, SON. NEARLY DINNER TIME.
I HAVE TO GO OUT AGAIN TONIGHT. BUT I THINK YOU'LL BE SAFE FOR NOW.
GO. I'LL BE FINE.

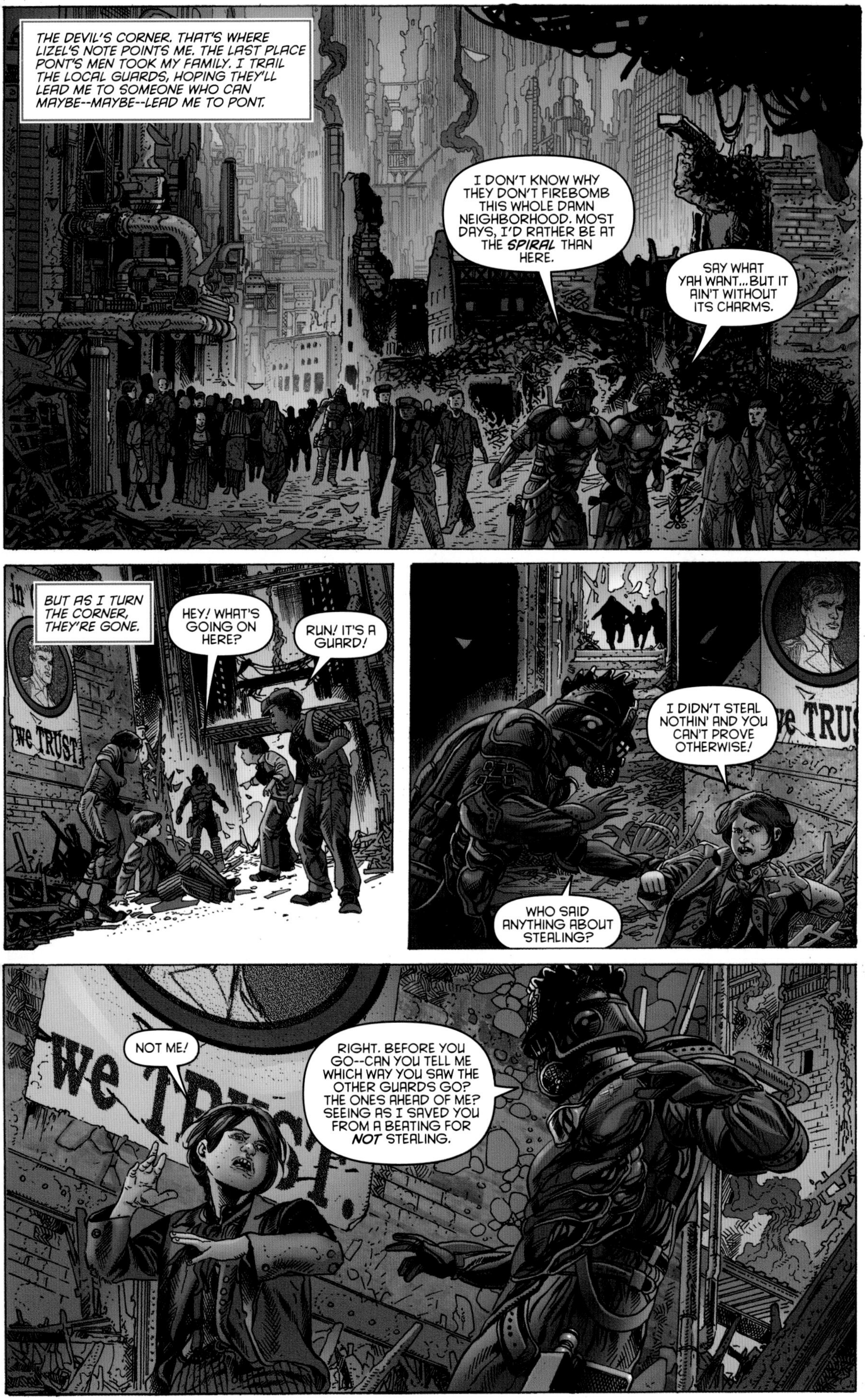
THE DEVIL'S CORNER. THAT'S WHERE LIZEL'S NOTE POINTS ME. THE LAST PLACE PONT'S MEN TOOK MY FAMILY. I TRAIL THE LOCAL GUARDS, HOPING THEY'LL LEAD ME TO SOMEONE WHO CAN MAYBE--MAYBE--LEAD ME TO PONT.
I DON'T KNOW WHY THEY DON'T FIREBOMB THIS WHOLE DAMN NEIGHBORHOOD. MOST DAYS, I'D RATHER BE AT THE SPIRAL THAN HERE.
SAY WHAT YAH WANT...BUT IT AIN'T WITHOUT ITS CHARMS.
BUT AS I TURN THE CORNER, THEY'RE GONE.
HEY! WHAT'S GOING ON HERE?
RUN! IT'S A GUARD!
I DIDN'T STEAL NOTHIN' AND YOU CAN'T PROVE OTHERWISE!
WHO SAID ANYTHING ABOUT STEALING?
NOT ME!
RIGHT. BEFORE YOU GO--CAN YOU TELL ME WHICH WAY YOU SAW THE OTHER GUARDS GO? THE ONES AHEAD OF ME? SEEING AS I SAVED YOU FROM A BEATING FOR NOT STEALING.

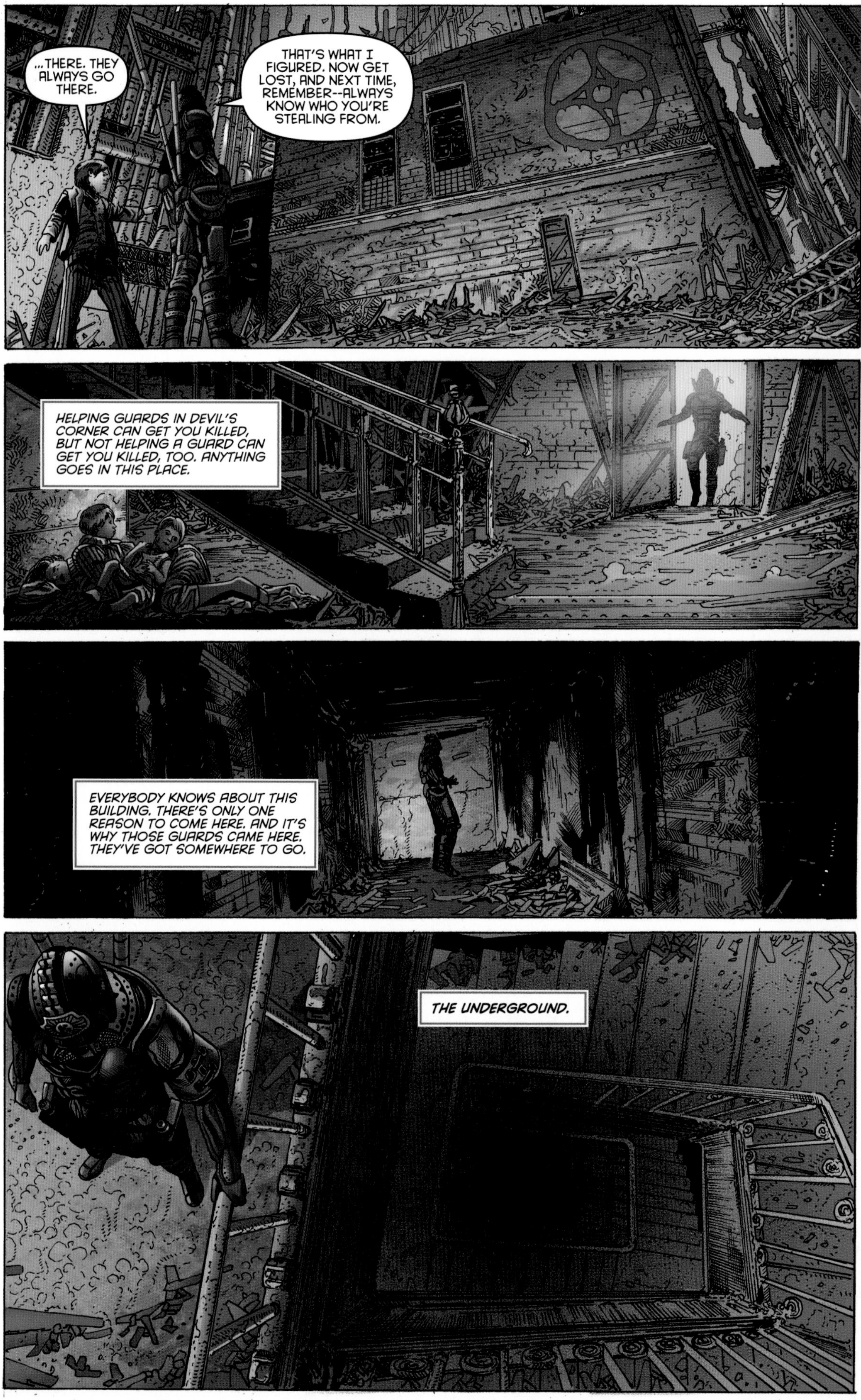
...THERE. THEY ALWAYS GO THERE.
THAT'S WHAT I FIGURED. NOW GET LOST, AND NEXT TIME, REMEMBER--ALWAYS KNOW WHO YOU'RE STEALING FROM.
HELPING GUARDS IN DEVIL'S CORNER CAN GET YOU KILLED, BUT NOT HELPING A GUARD CAN GET YOU KILLED, TOO. ANYTHING GOES IN THIS PLACE.
EVERYBODY KNOWS ABOUT THIS BUILDING. THERE'S ONLY ONE REASON TO COME HERE. AND IT'S WHY THOSE GUARDS CAME HERE. THEY'VE GOT SOMEWHERE TO GO.
THE UNDERGROUND.

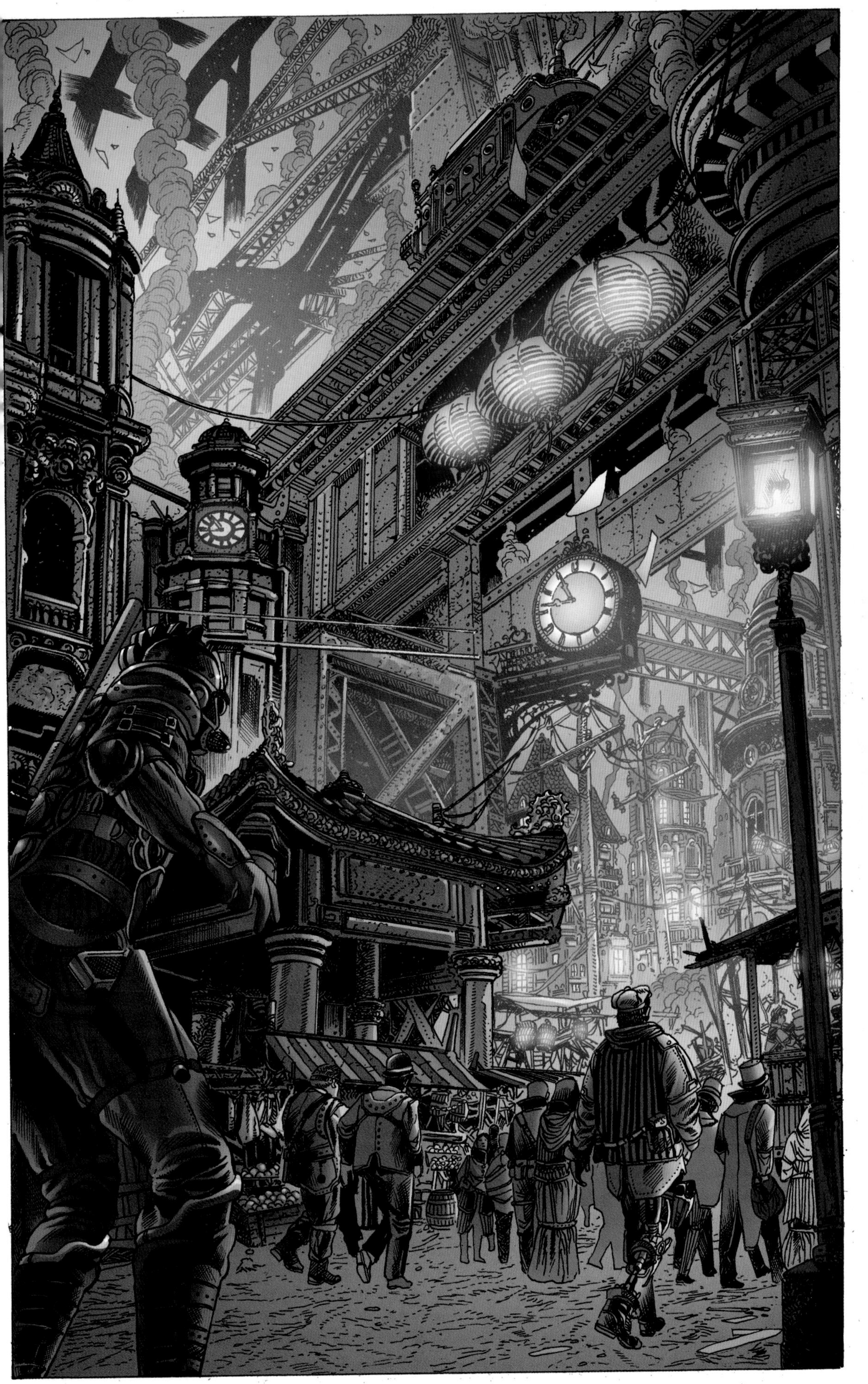

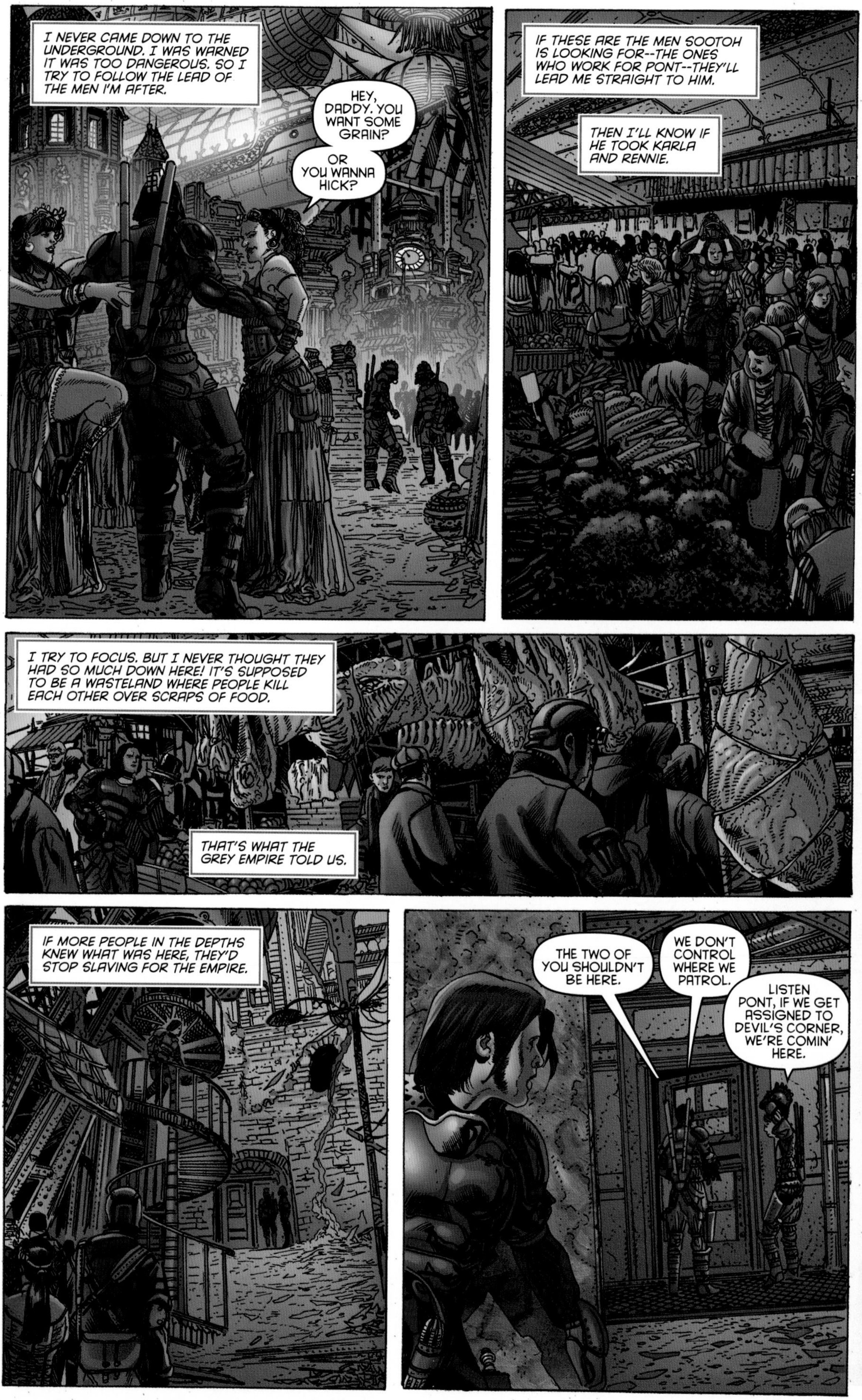
I NEVER CAME DOWN TO THE UNDERGROUND. I WAS WARNED IT WAS TOO DANGEROUS. SO I TRY TO FOLLOW THE LEAD OF THE MEN I'M AFTER.
HEY, DADDY. YOU WANT SOME GRAIN?
OR YOU WANNA HICK?
IF THESE ARE THE MEN SOOTOH IS LOOKING FOR--THE ONES WHO WORK FOR PONT--THEY'LL LEAD ME STRAIGHT TO HIM.
THEN I'LL KNOW IF HE TOOK KARLA AND RENNIE.
I TRY TO FOCUS. BUT I NEVER THOUGHT THEY HAD SO MUCH DOWN HERE! IT'S SUPPOSED TO BE A WASTELAND WHERE PEOPLE KILL EACH OTHER OVER SCRAPS OF FOOD.
THAT'S WHAT THE GREY EMPIRE TOLD US.
IF MORE PEOPLE IN THE DEPTHS KNEW WHAT WAS HERE, THEY'D STOP SLAVING FOR THE EMPIRE.
THE TWO OF YOU SHOULDN'T BE HERE.
WE DON'T CONTROL WHERE WE PATROL.
LISTEN PONT, IF WE GET ASSIGNED TO DEVIL'S CORNER, WE'RE COMIN' HERE.

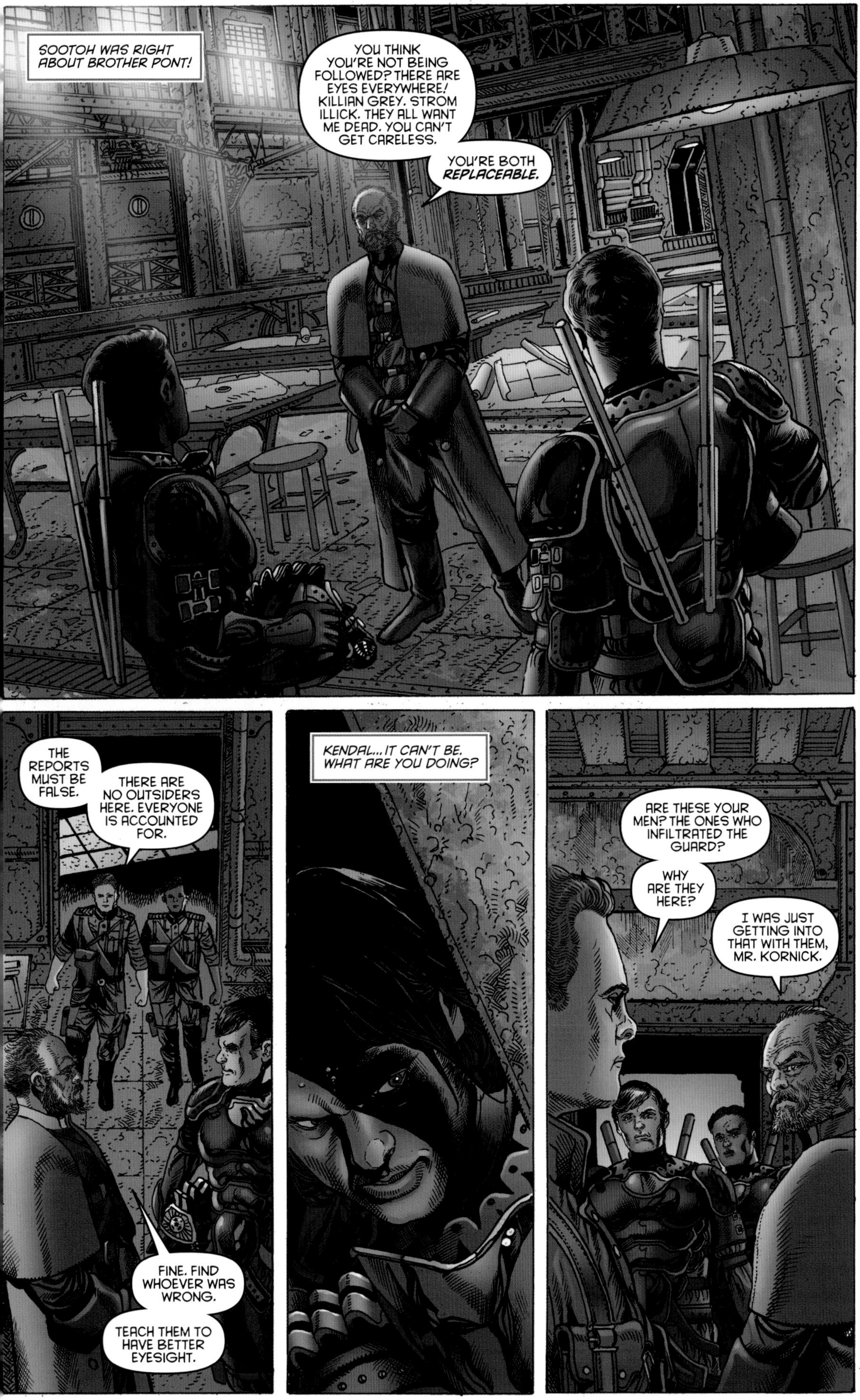
SOOTOH WAS RIGHT ABOUT BROTHER PONT!
YOU THINK YOU'RE NOT BEING FOLLOWED? THERE ARE EYES EVERYWHERE! KILLIAN GREY. STROM ILLICK. THEY ALL WANT ME DEAD. YOU CAN'T GET CARELESS.
YOU'RE BOTH *REPLACEABLE.*
THE REPORTS MUST BE FALSE.
THERE ARE NO OUTSIDERS HERE. EVERYONE IS ACCOUNTED FOR.
FINE. FIND WHOEVER WAS WRONG.
TEACH THEM TO HAVE BETTER EYESIGHT.
KENDAL... IT CAN'T BE. WHAT ARE YOU DOING?
ARE THESE YOUR MEN? THE ONES WHO INFILTRATED THE GUARD?
WHY ARE THEY HERE?
I WAS JUST GETTING INTO THAT WITH THEM, MR. KORNICK.

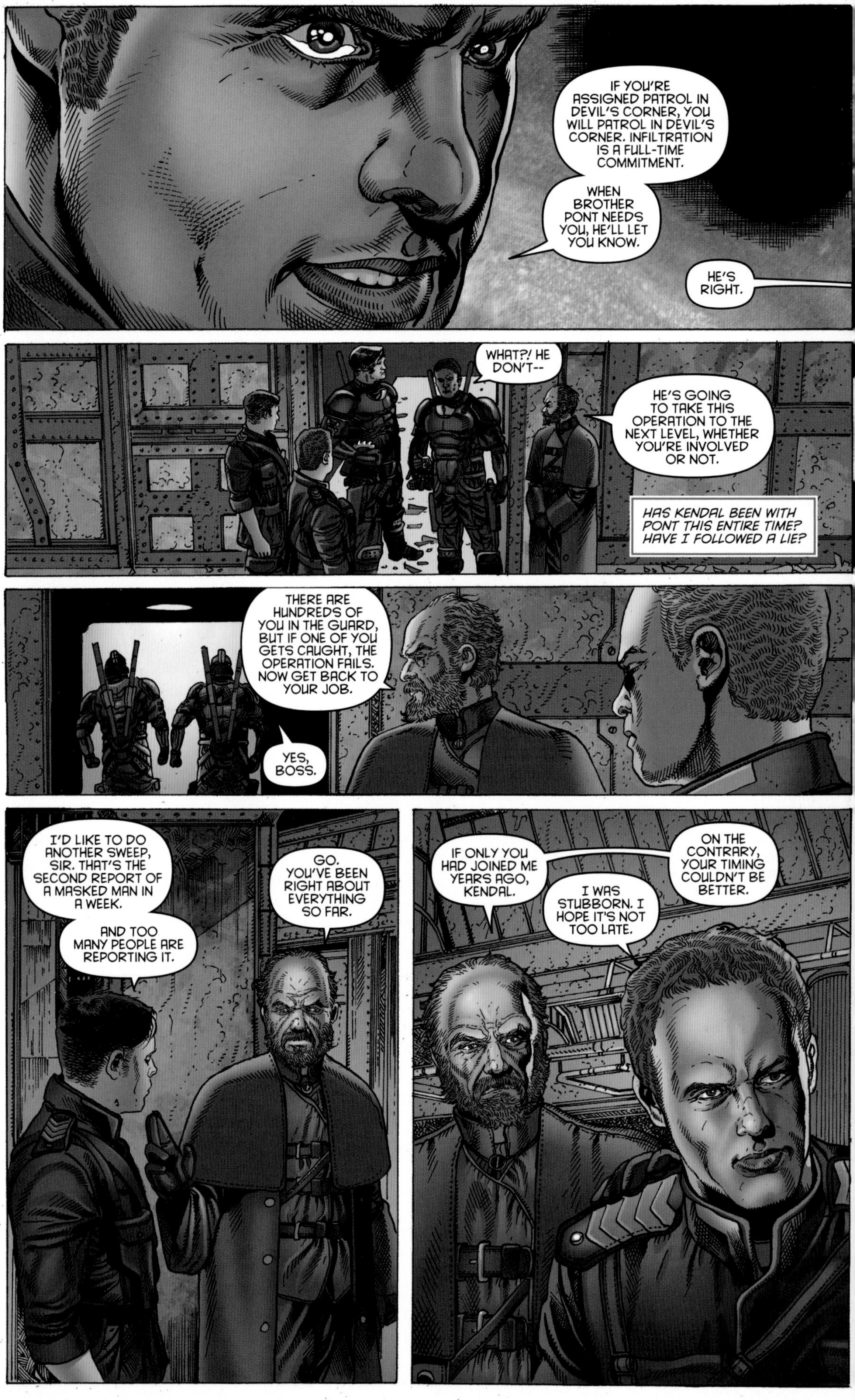
IF YOU'RE ASSIGNED PATROL IN DEVIL'S CORNER, YOU WILL PATROL IN DEVIL'S CORNER. INFILTRATION IS A FULL-TIME COMMITMENT.
WHEN BROTHER PONT NEEDS YOU, HE'LL LET YOU KNOW.
HE'S RIGHT.
WHAT?! HE DON'T--
HE'S GOING TO TAKE THIS OPERATION TO THE NEXT LEVEL, WHETHER YOU'RE INVOLVED OR NOT.
HAS KENDAL BEEN WITH PONT THIS ENTIRE TIME? HAVE I FOLLOWED A LIE?
THERE ARE HUNDREDS OF YOU IN THE GUARD, BUT IF ONE OF YOU GETS CAUGHT, THE OPERATION FAILS. NOW GET BACK TO YOUR JOB.
YES, BOSS.
I'D LIKE TO DO ANOTHER SWEEP, SIR. THAT'S THE SECOND REPORT OF A MASKED MAN IN A WEEK.
AND TOO MANY PEOPLE ARE REPORTING IT.
GO. YOU'VE BEEN RIGHT ABOUT EVERYTHING SO FAR.
IF ONLY YOU HAD JOINED ME YEARS AGO, KENDAL.
I WAS STUBBORN. I HOPE IT'S NOT TOO LATE.
ON THE CONTRARY, YOUR TIMING COULDN'T BE BETTER.

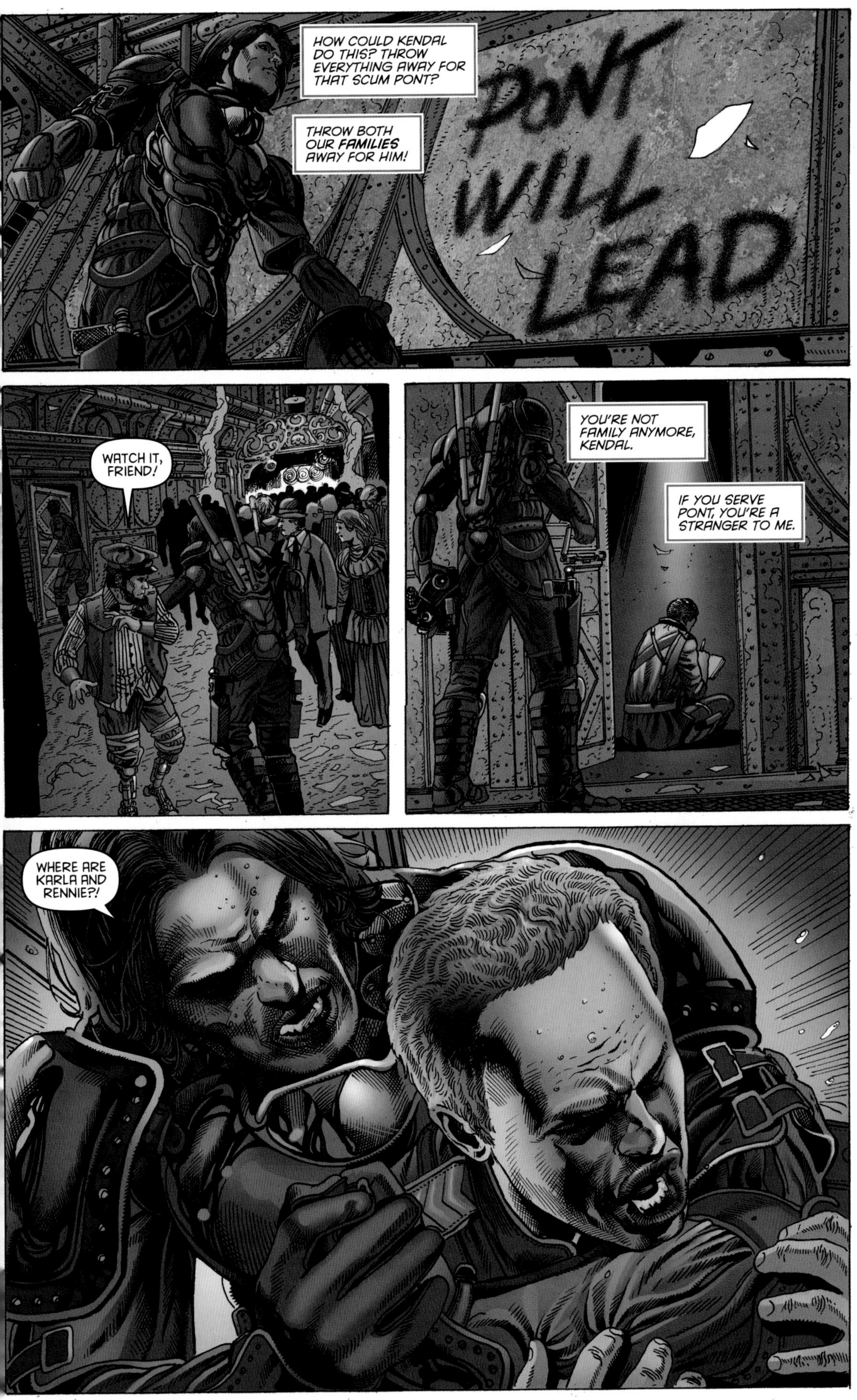
HOW COULD KENDAL DO THIS? THROW EVERYTHING AWAY FOR THAT SCUM PONT?
THROW BOTH OUR FAMILIES AWAY FOR HIM!
PONT WILL LEAD
WATCH IT, FRIEND!
YOU'RE NOT FAMILY ANYMORE, KENDAL.
IF YOU SERVE PONT, YOU'RE A STRANGER TO ME.
WHERE ARE KARLA AND RENNIE?!

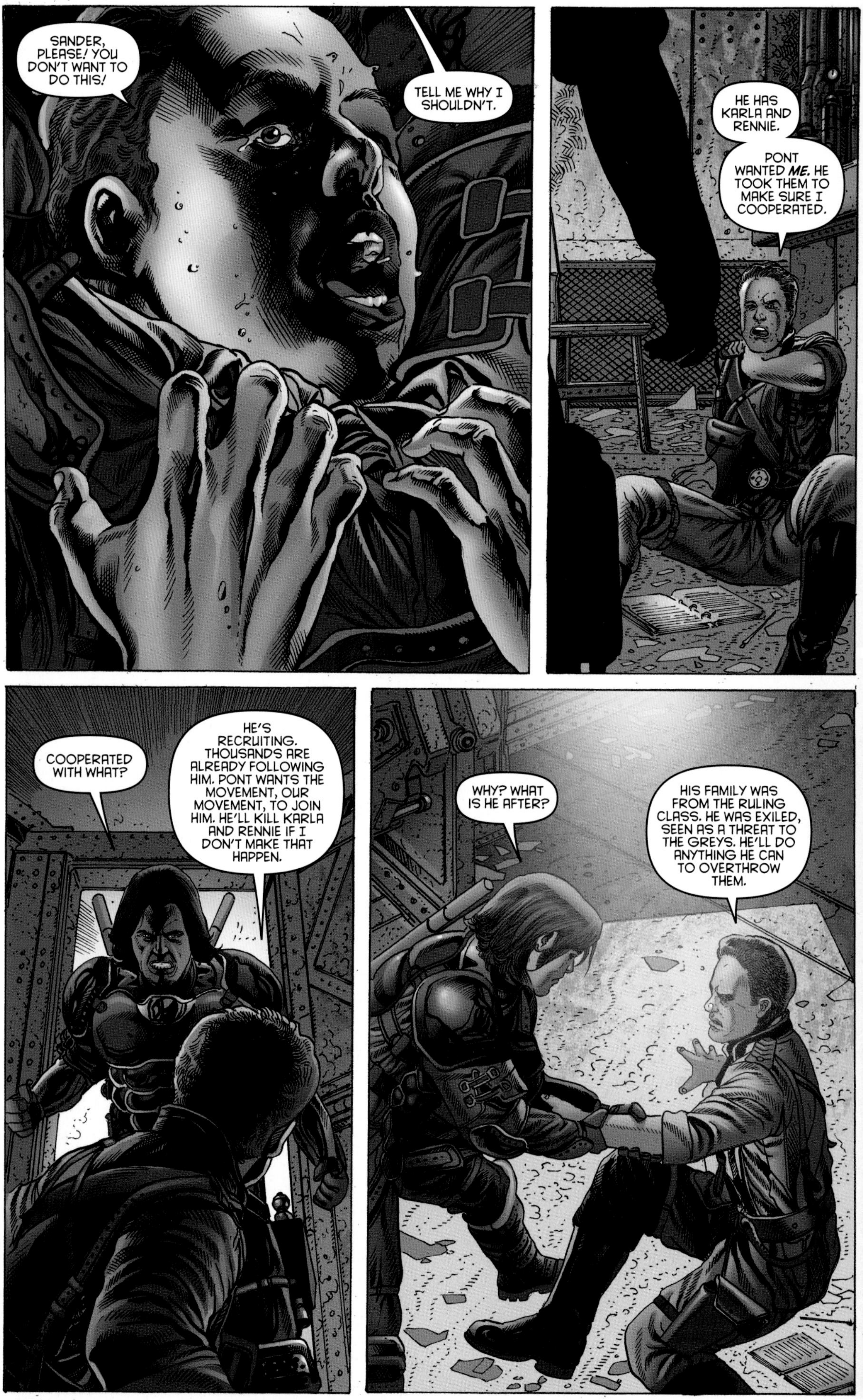
SANDER, PLEASE! YOU DON'T WANT TO DO THIS!
TELL ME WHY I SHOULDN'T.
HE HAS KARLA AND RENNIE.
PONT WANTED ME. HE TOOK THEM TO MAKE SURE I COOPERATED.
COOPERATED WITH WHAT?
HE'S RECRUITING. THOUSANDS ARE ALREADY FOLLOWING HIM. PONT WANTS THE MOVEMENT, OUR MOVEMENT, TO JOIN HIM. HE'LL KILL KARLA AND RENNIE IF I DON'T MAKE THAT HAPPEN.
WHY? WHAT IS HE AFTER?
HIS FAMILY WAS FROM THE RULING CLASS. HE WAS EXILED, SEEN AS A THREAT TO THE GREYS. HE'LL DO ANYTHING HE CAN TO OVERTHROW THEM.

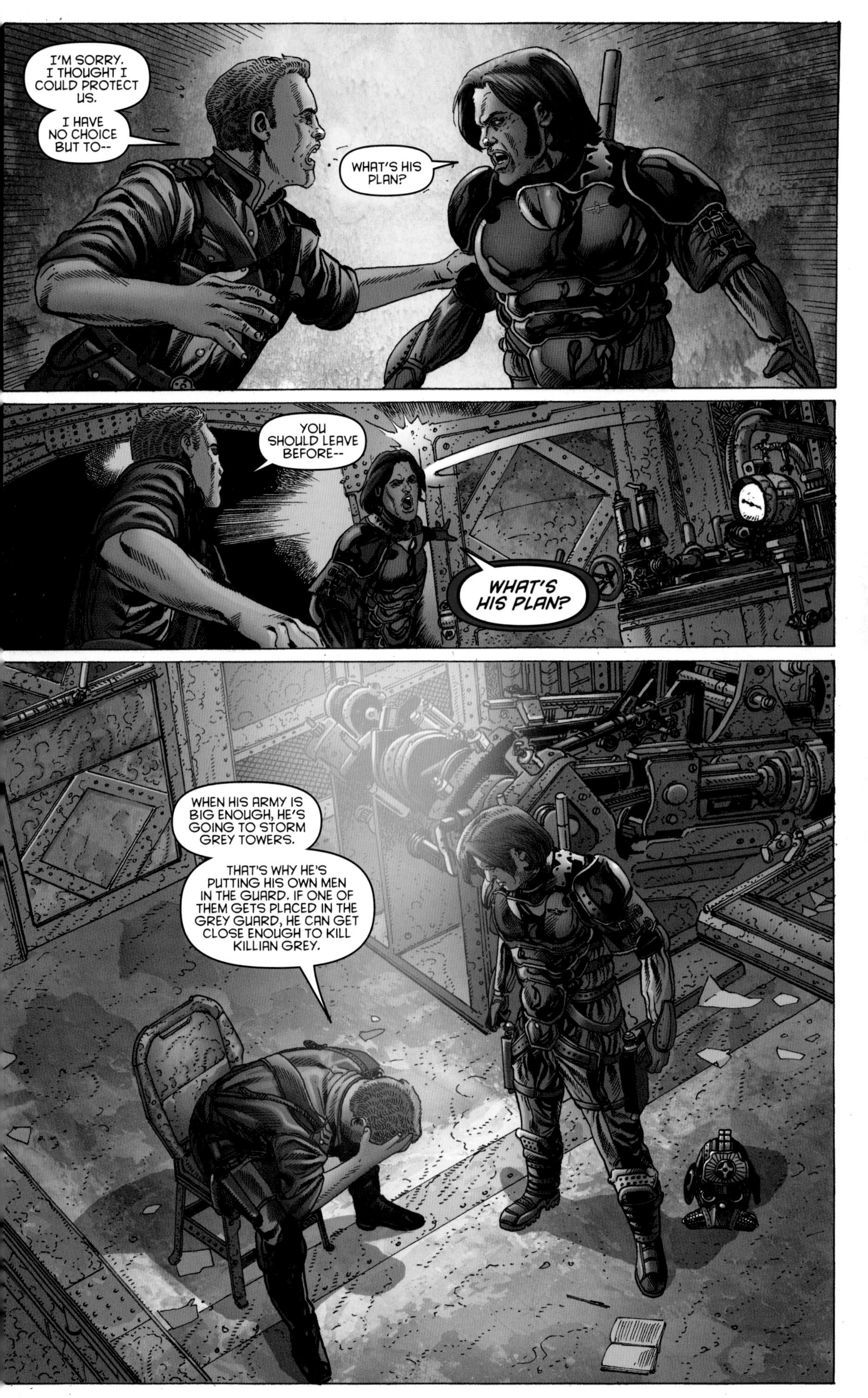
I'M SORRY. I THOUGHT I COULD PROTECT US.
I HAVE NO CHOICE BUT TO--
WHAT'S HIS PLAN?
YOU SHOULD LEAVE BEFORE--
WHAT'S HIS PLAN?
WHEN HIS ARMY IS BIG ENOUGH, HE'S GOING TO STORM GREY TOWERS.
THAT'S WHY HE'S PUTTING HIS OWN MEN IN THE GUARD. IF ONE OF THEM GETS PLACED IN THE GREY GUARD, HE CAN GET CLOSE ENOUGH TO KILL KILLIAN GREY.

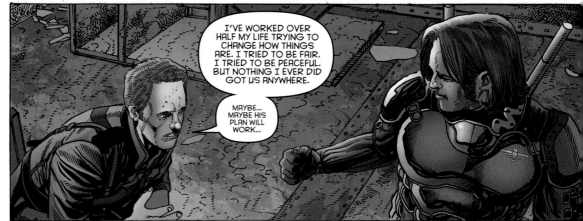

I'VE WORKED OVER HALF MY LIFE TRYING TO CHANGE HOW THINGS ARE. I TRIED TO BE FAIR. I TRIED TO BE PEACEFUL. BUT NOTHING I EVER DID GOT US ANYWHERE.

MAYBE... MAYBE HIS PLAN WILL WORK...

YOU'RE NO BETTER THAN HIM.

PONT KILLS KILLIAN AND MAYBE HE GETS POWER. MAYBE YOU GET POWER, TOO. BUT NOTHING GETS BETTER FOR ANYONE ELSE!

WHERE IS HE KEEPING RENNIE AND KARLA?

I DON'T KNOW. TRULY. BUT YOU SHOULD GET OUT OF HERE. PONT WILL KILL YOU.

SANDER, I'M SO SORRY.

IF ANYTHING HAPPENS TO THEM, I WILL KILL PONT. AND *YOU*.

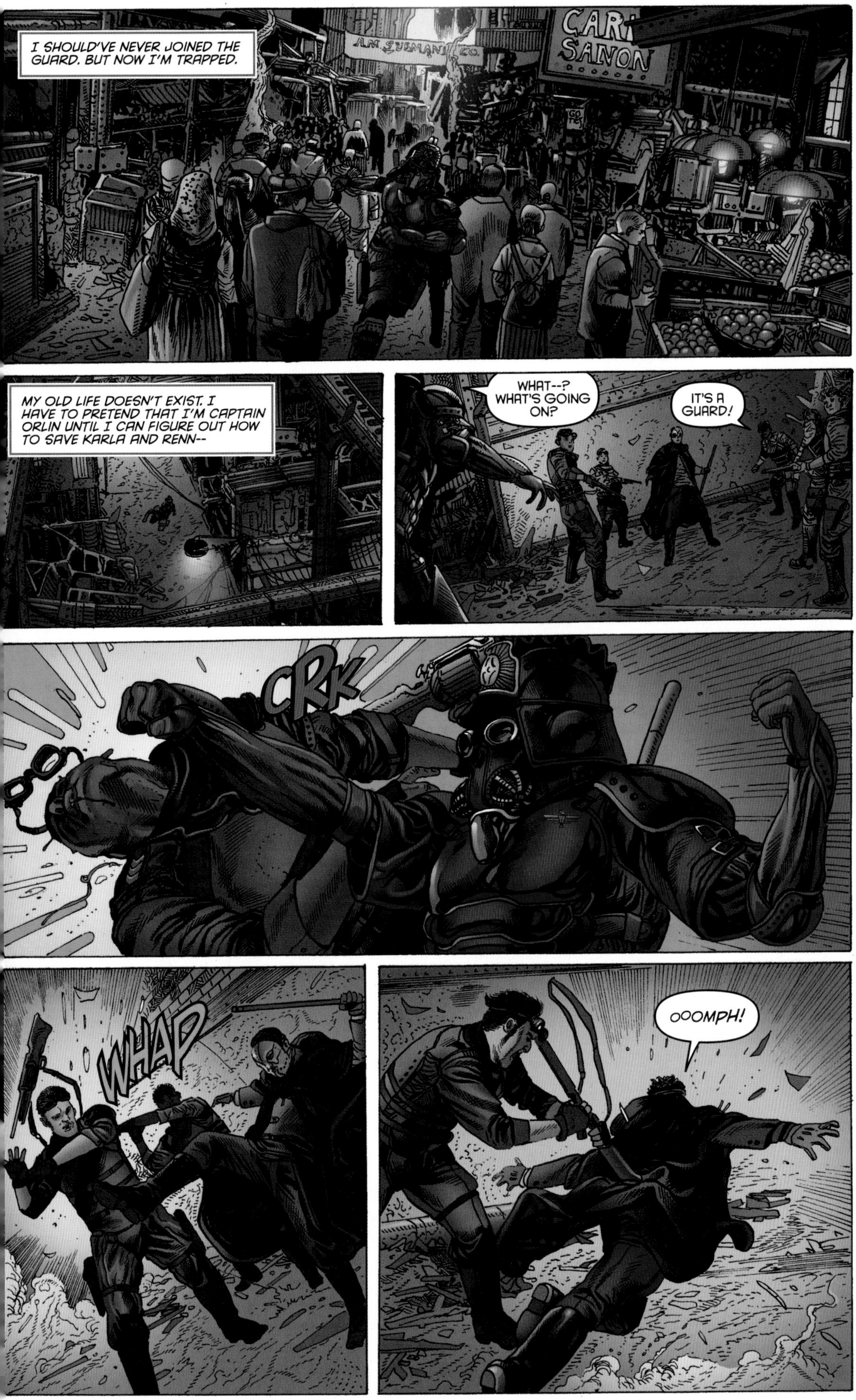
I SHOULD'VE NEVER JOINED THE GUARD. BUT NOW I'M TRAPPED.
A.M. SUSMAN & CO.
SANON
MY OLD LIFE DOESN'T EXIST. I HAVE TO PRETEND THAT I'M CAPTAIN ORLIN UNTIL I CAN FIGURE OUT HOW TO SAVE KARLA AND RENN--
WHAT--? WHAT'S GOING ON?
IT'S A GUARD!
CRK
WHAP
OOOMPH!

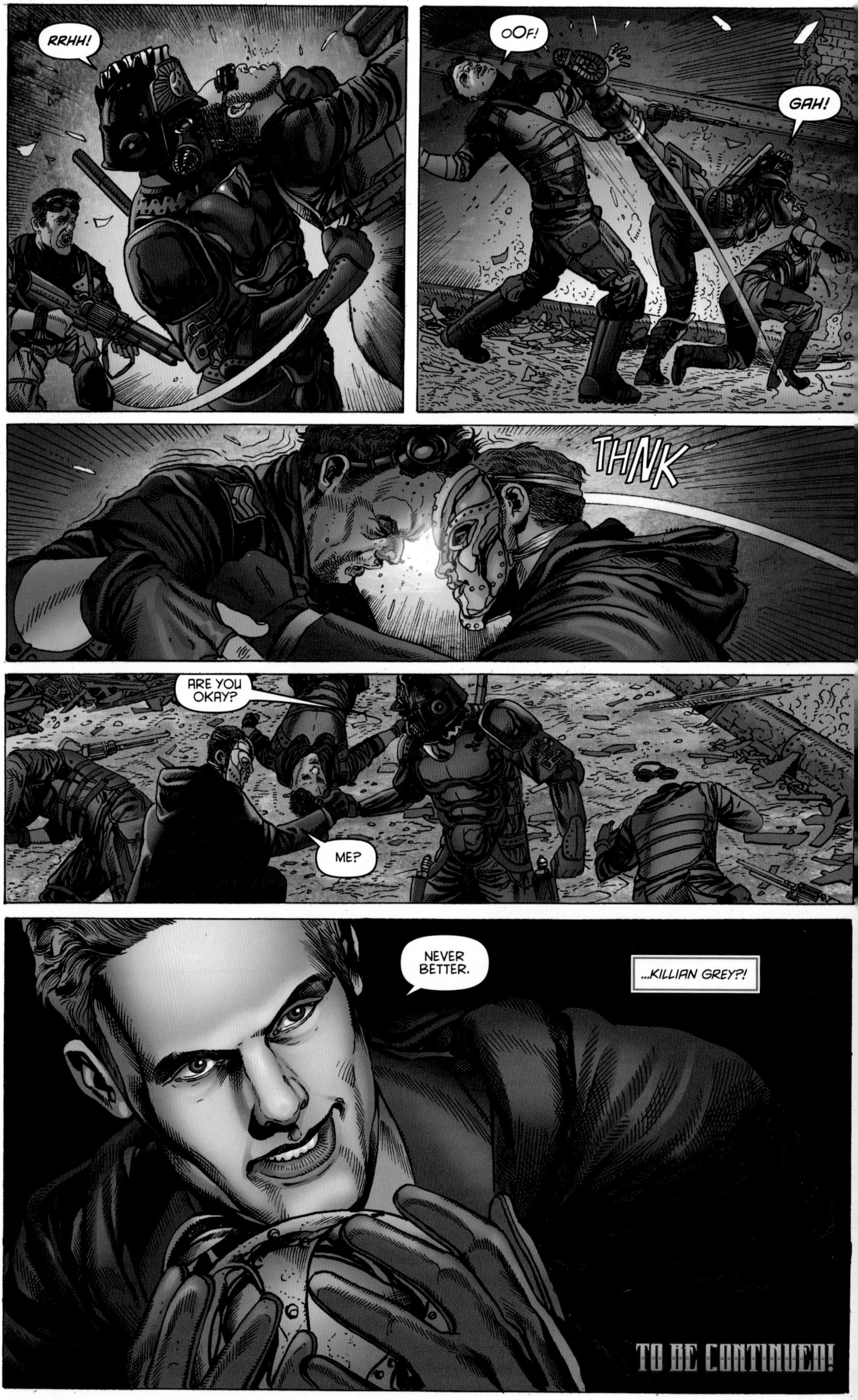
RRHH!
OOF!
GAH!
THNK
ARE YOU OKAY?
ME?
NEVER BETTER.
...KILLIAN GREY?!
TO BE CONTINUED!

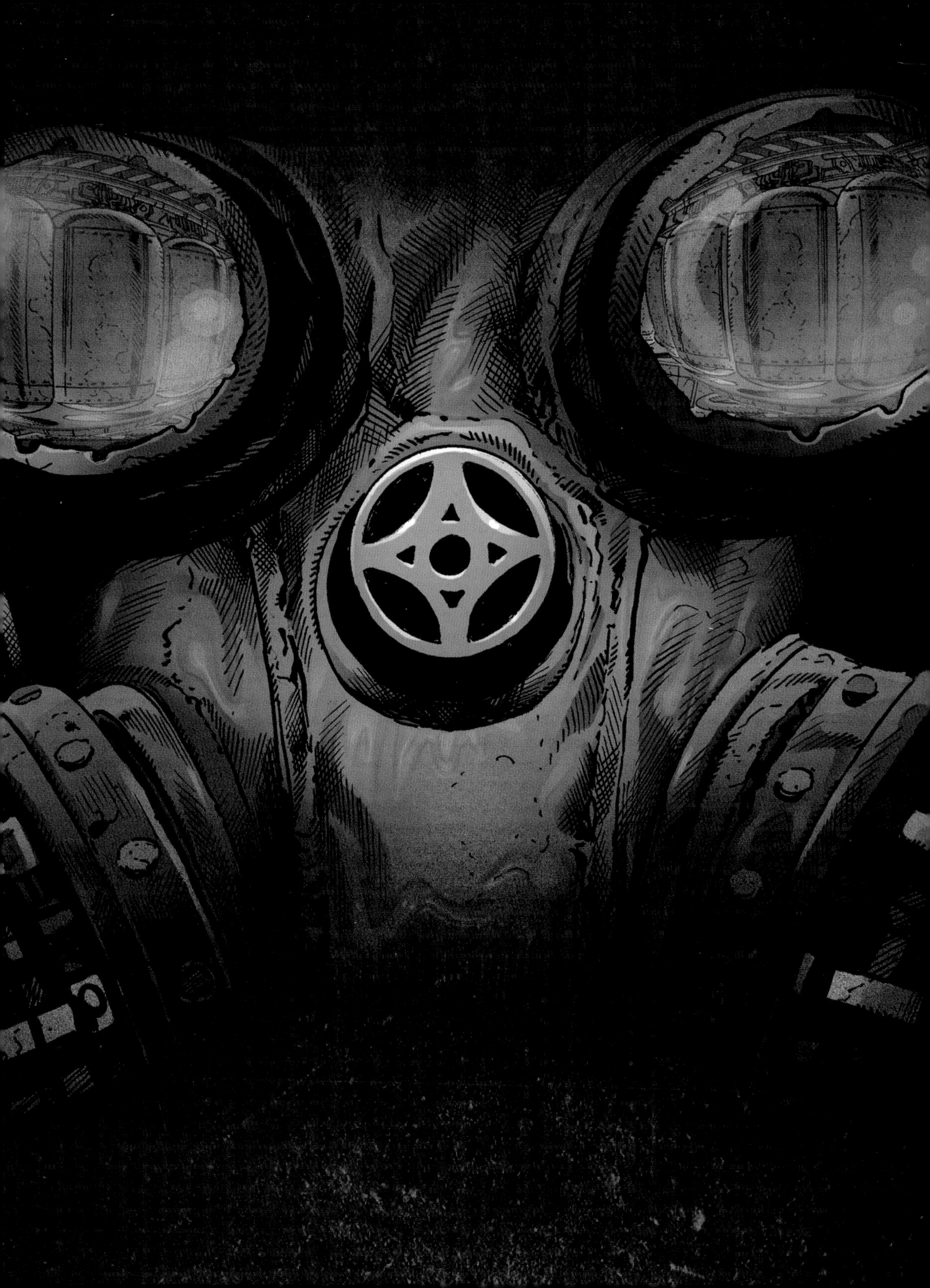

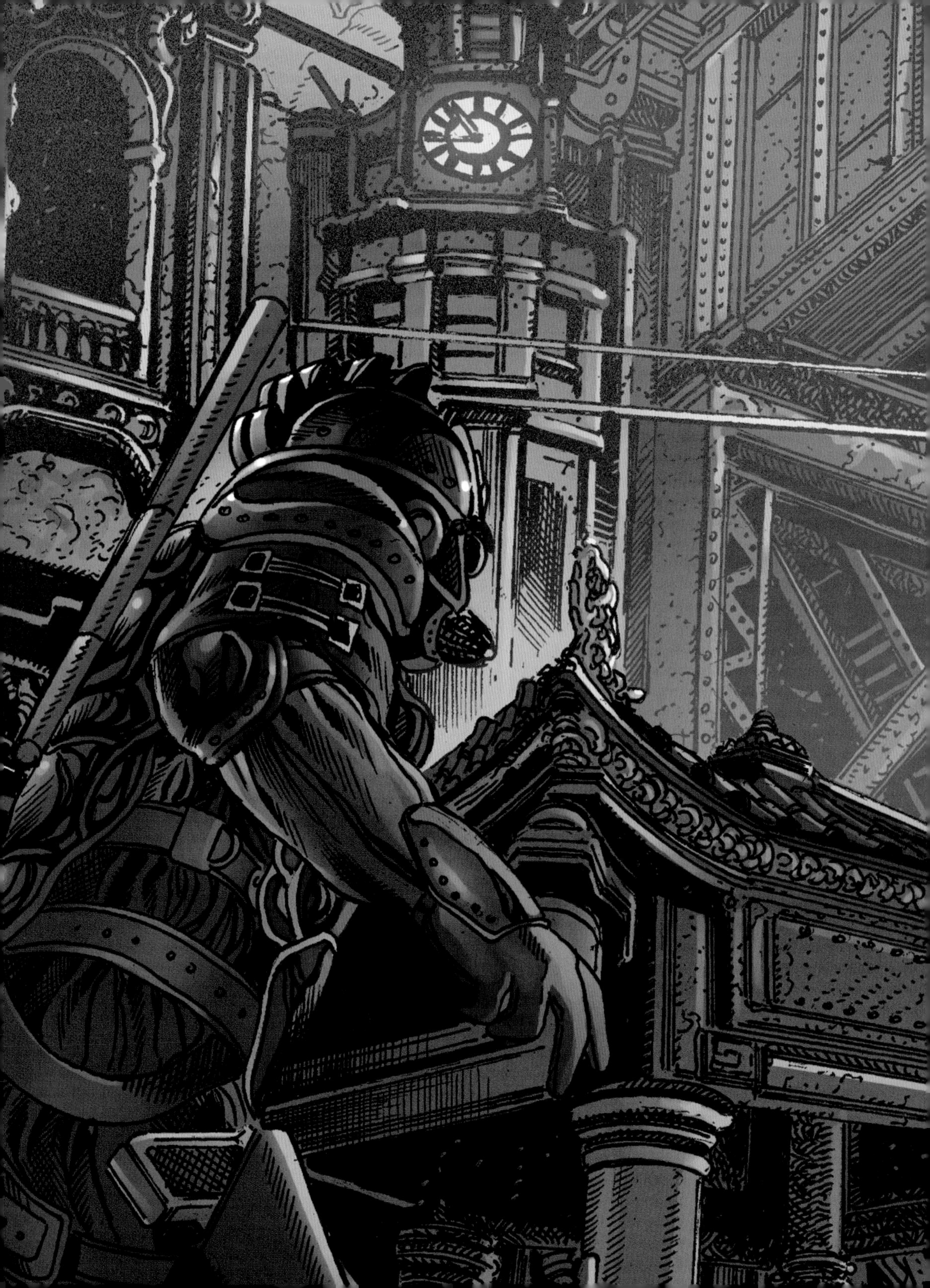

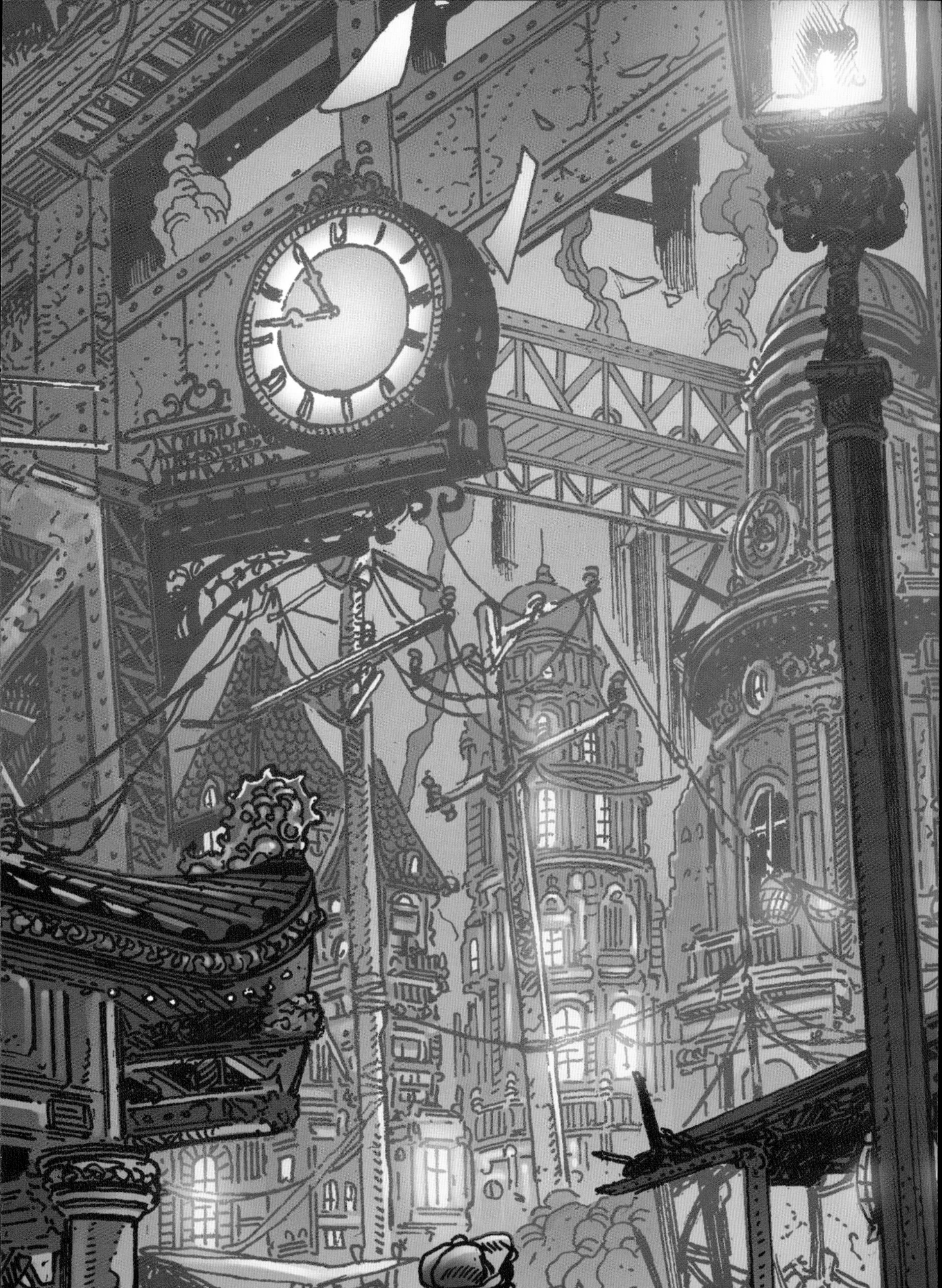

COVER GALLERY

ISSUE ONE COVER BY
BENJAMIN CARRÉ

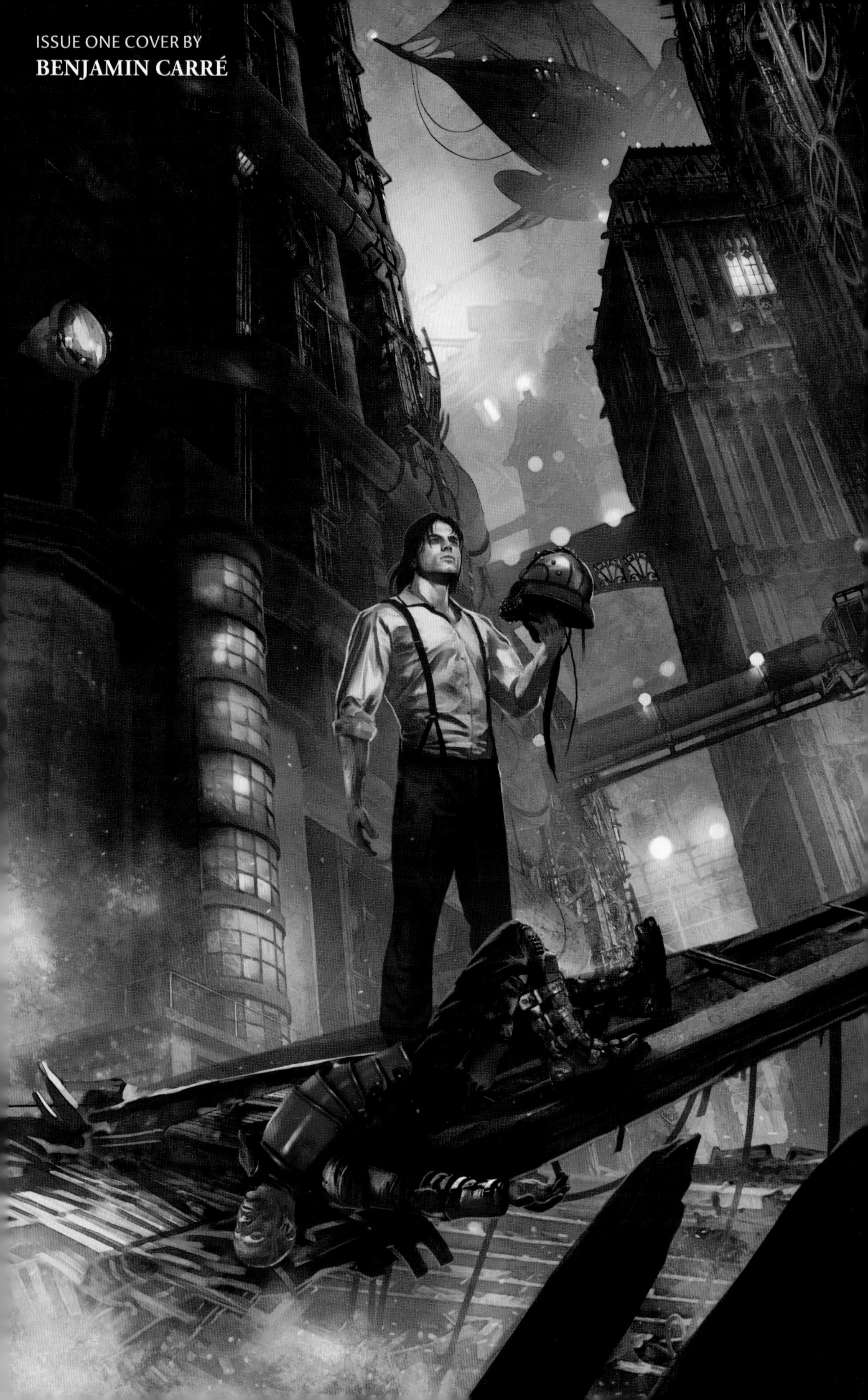

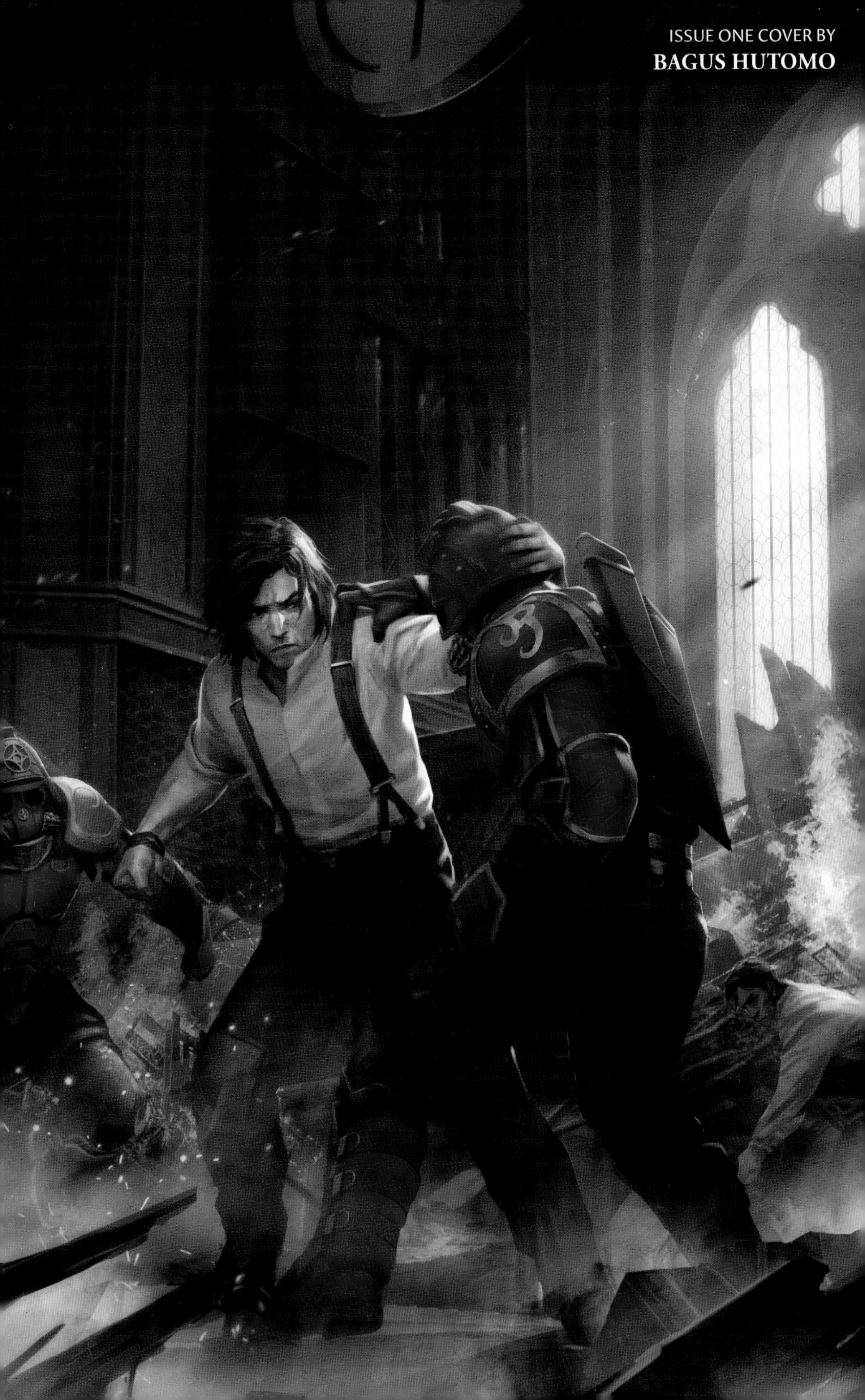

ISSUE ONE COVER BY
BAGUS HUTOMO

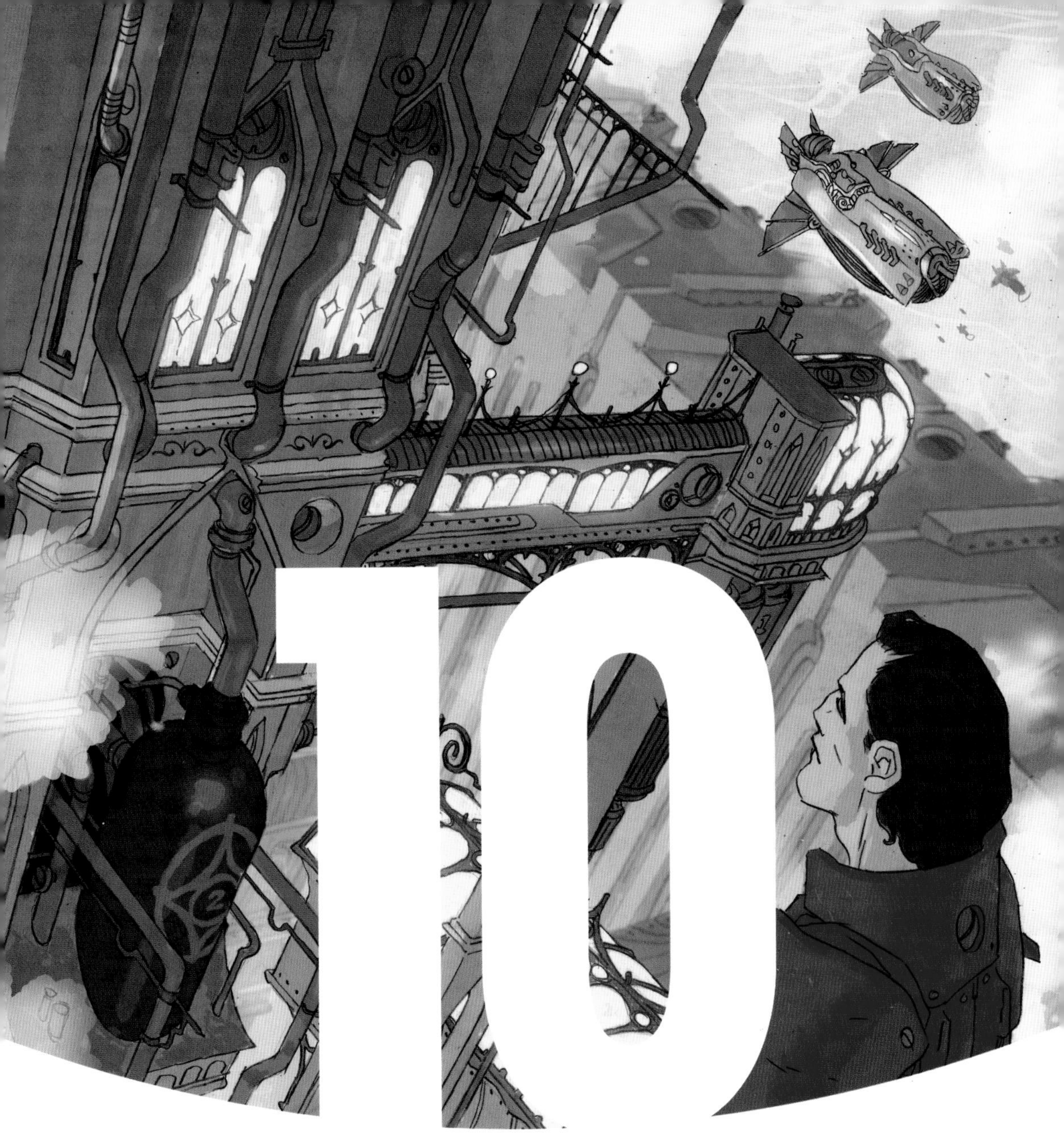

ISSUE ONE BOOM! TEN YEARS VARIANT COVER BY
BEN CALDWELL

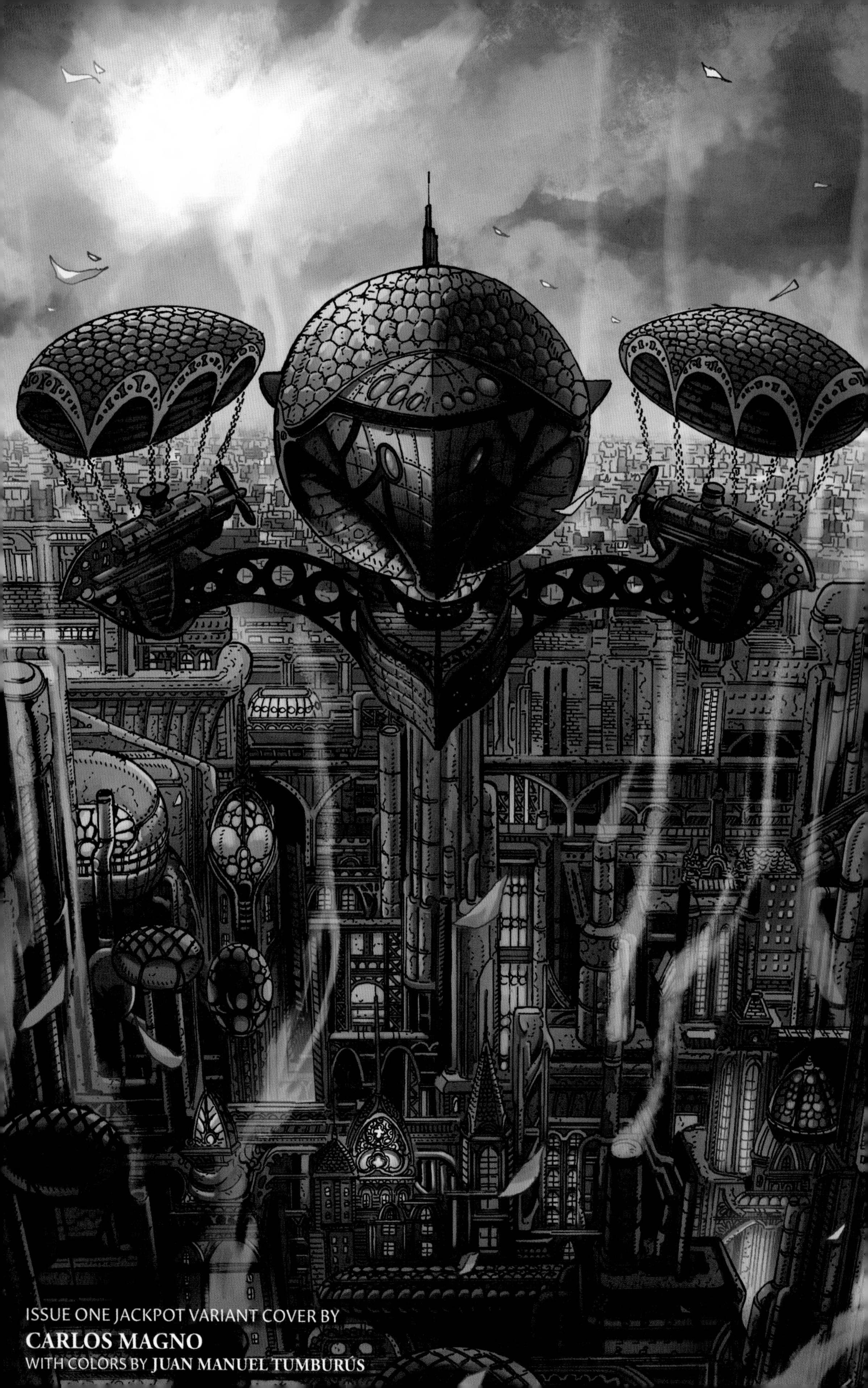

ISSUE ONE JACKPOT VARIANT COVER BY
CARLOS MAGNO
WITH COLORS BY **JUAN MANUEL TUMBURÚS**

ISSUE ONE UNLOCKED RETAILER VARIANT COVER BY
BRETT WELDELE

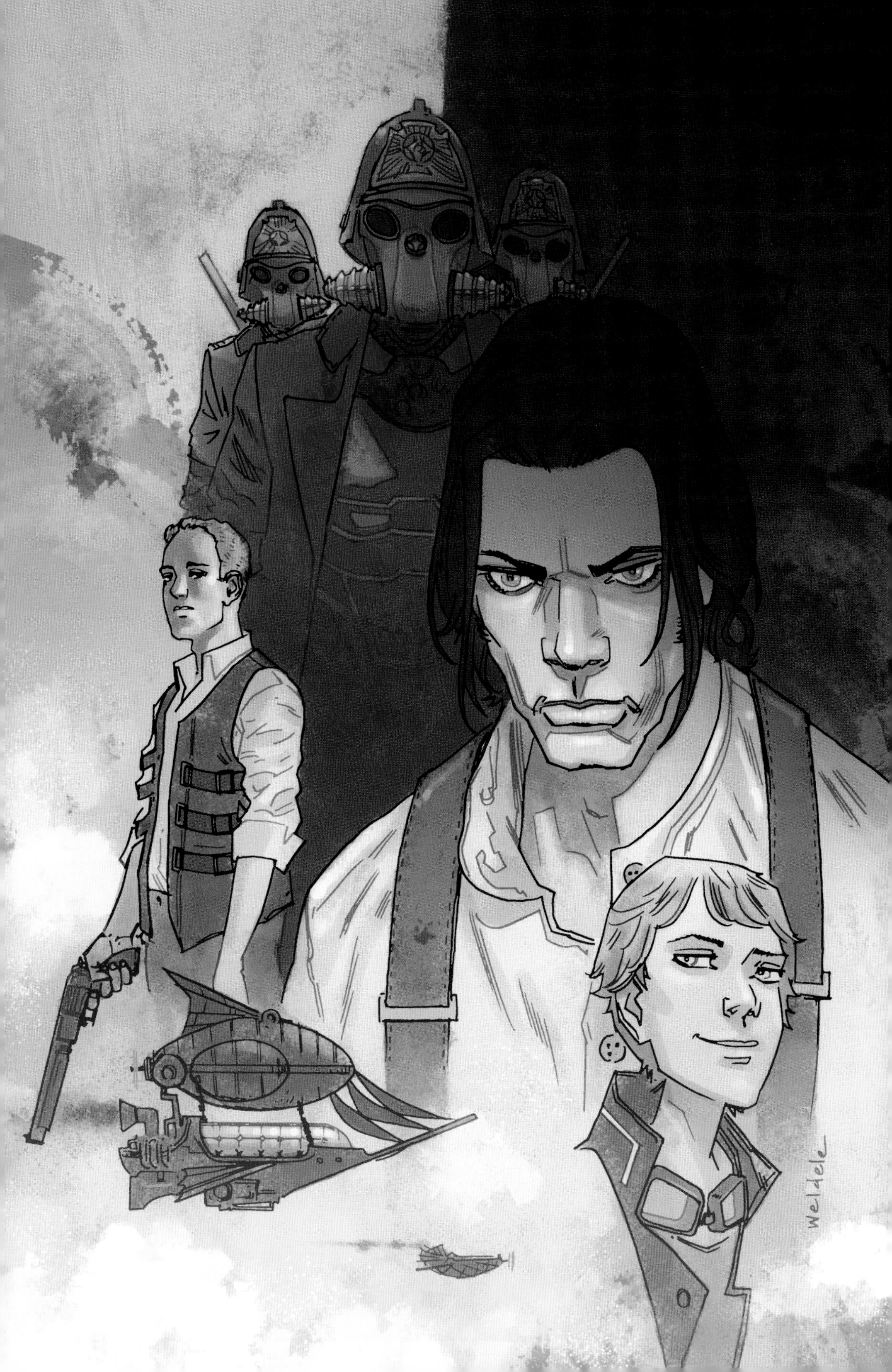
weldele

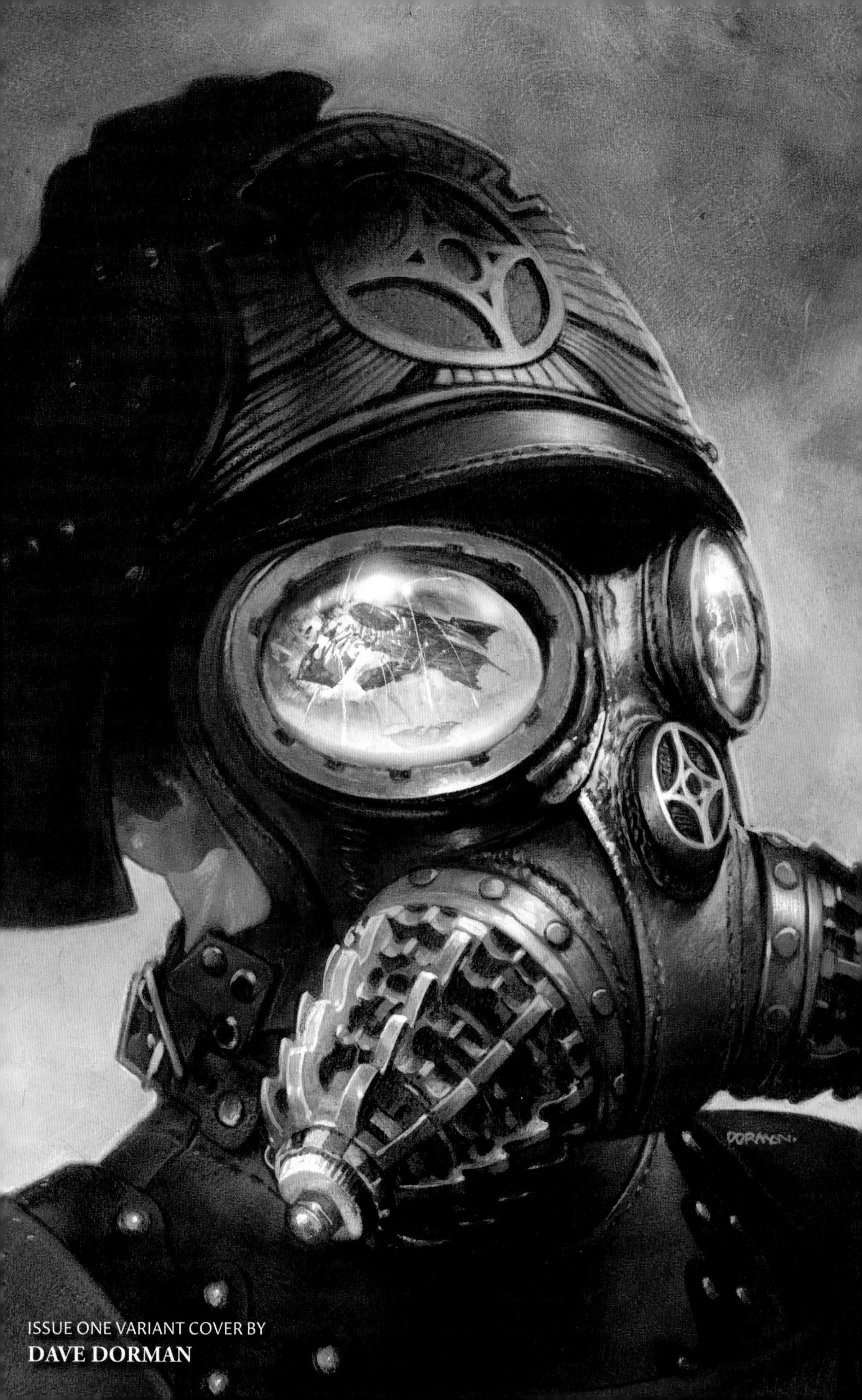
DORMAN.

ISSUE ONE VARIANT COVER BY
DAVE DORMAN

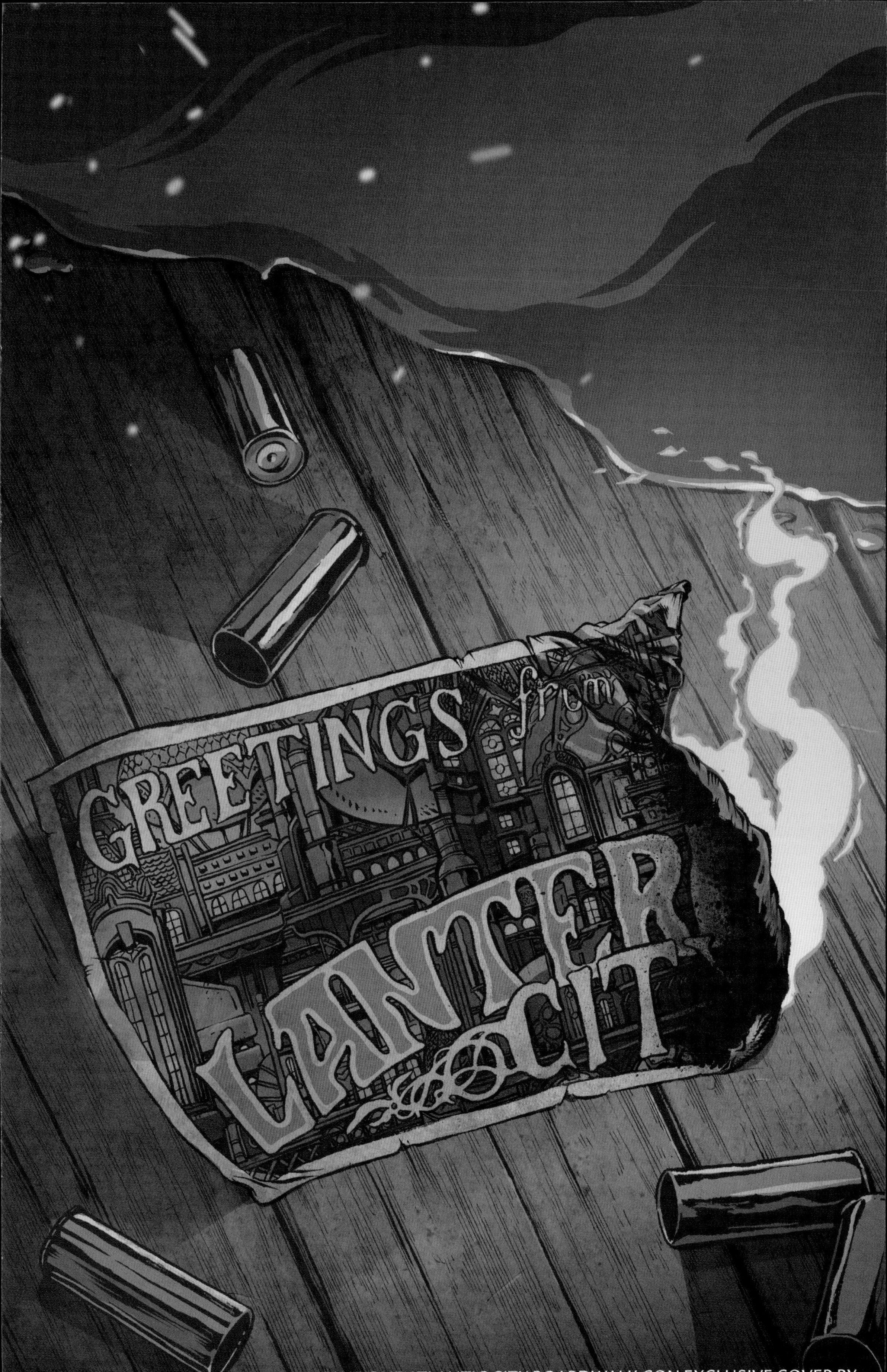
GREETINGS from
LANTER
CIT

ISSUE ONE ATLANTIC CITY BOARDWALK CON EXCLUSIVE COVER BY
CONOR NOLAN

ISSUE TWO COVER BY
BENJAMIN CARRÉ

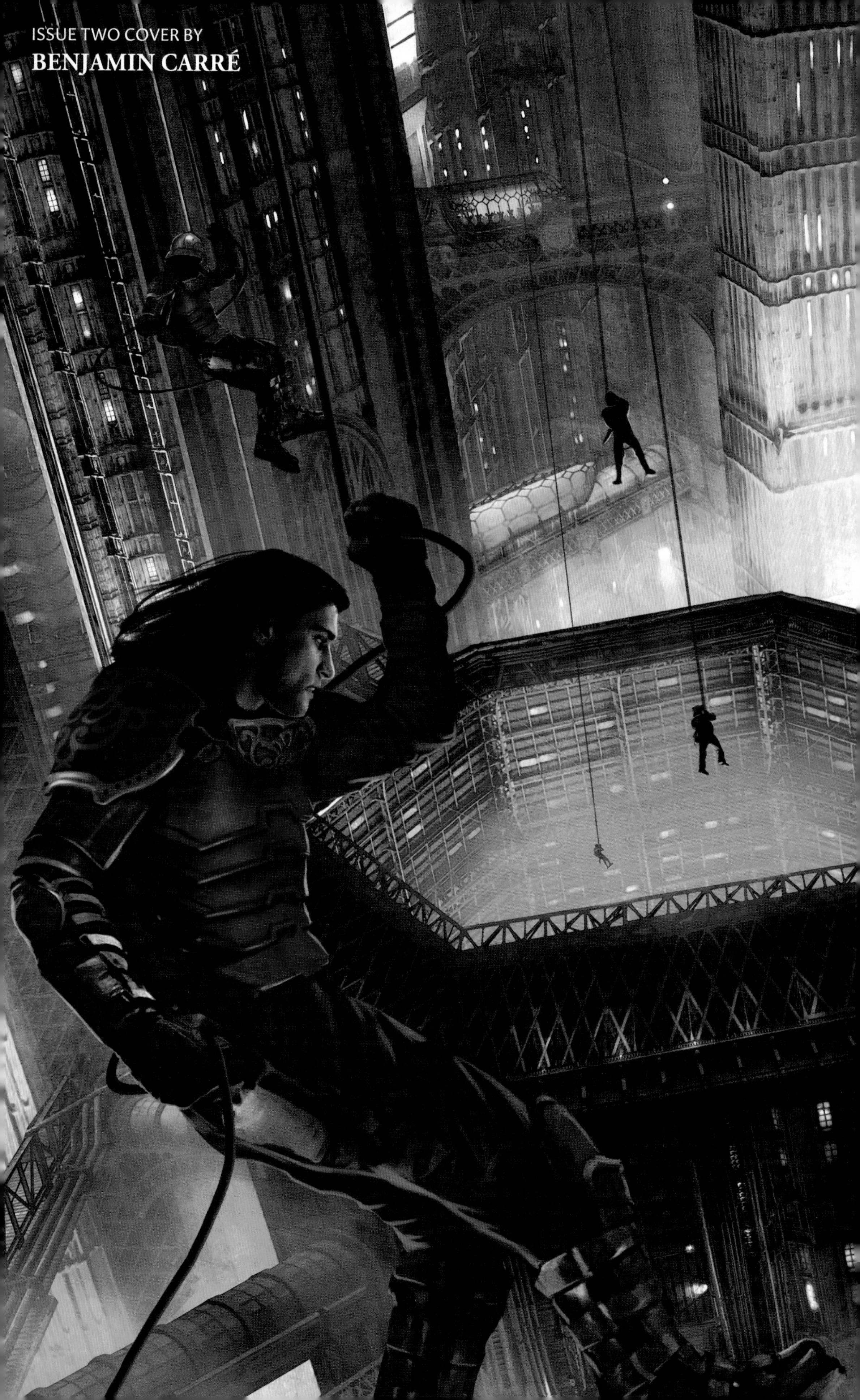

ISSUE TWO SAN DIEGO COMIC-CON EXCLUSIVE COVER BY
JAKE WYATT

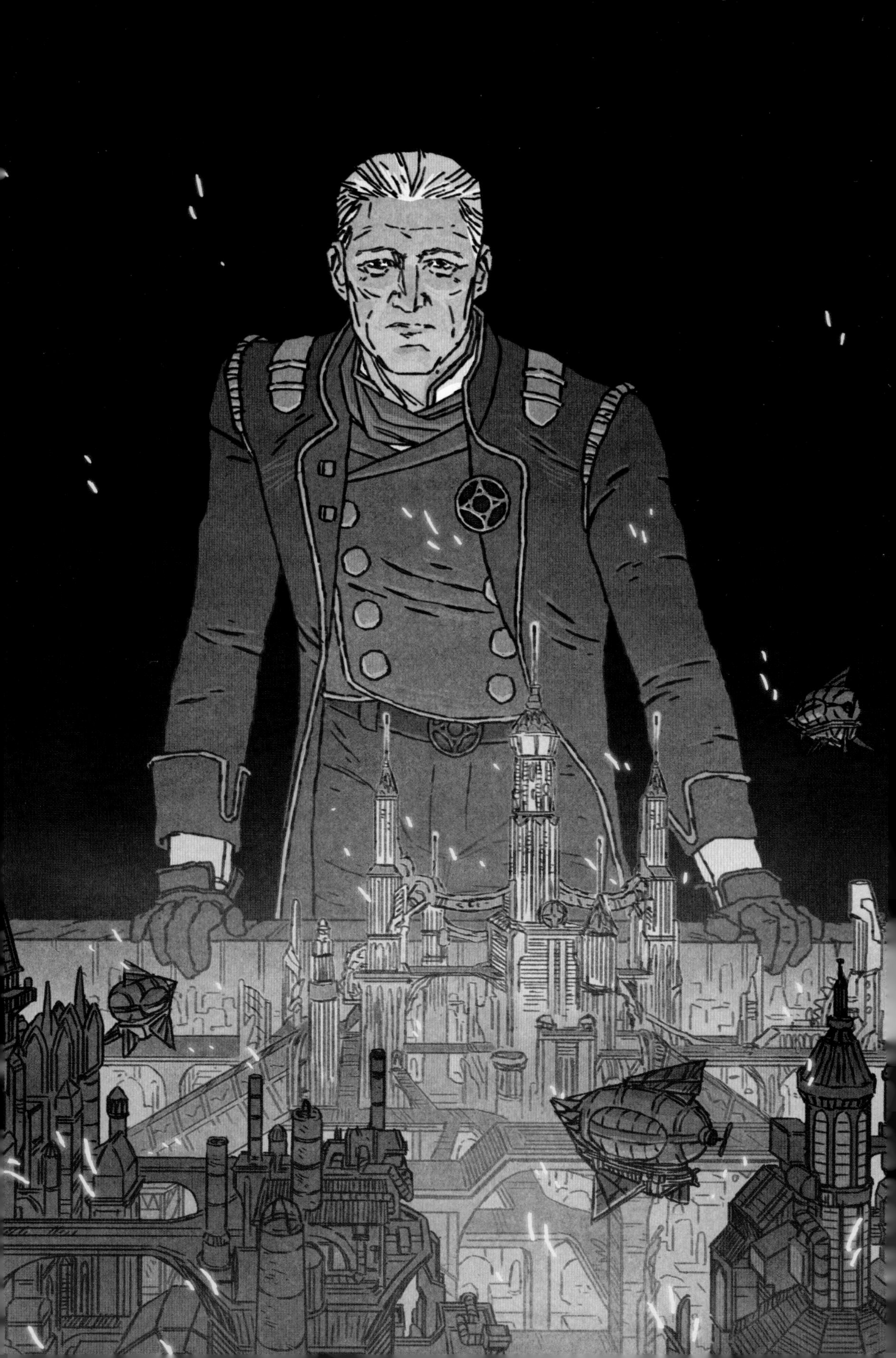

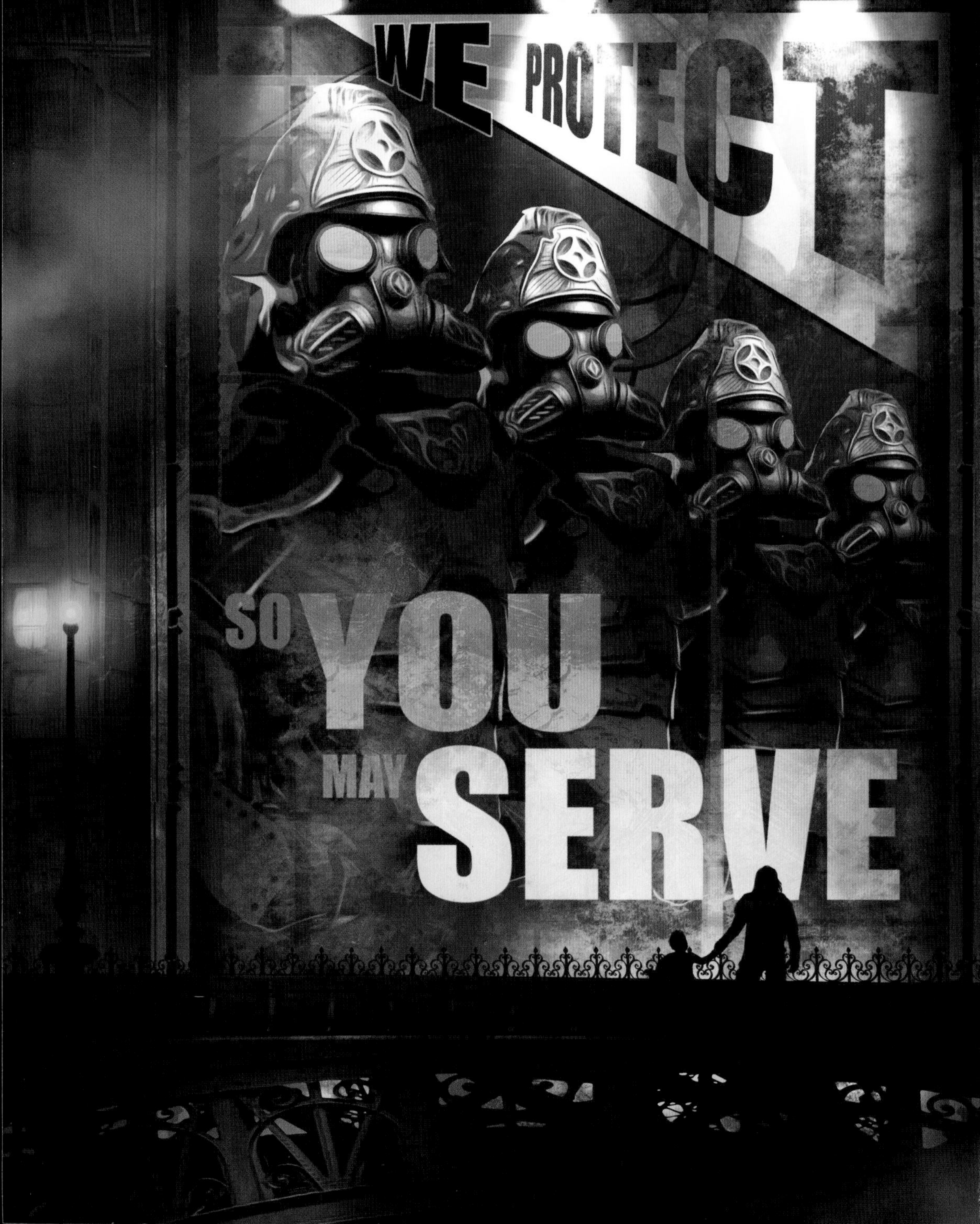
WE PROTECT
SO YOU
MAY SERVE

ISSUE FOUR COVER BY
BENJAMIN CARRÉ

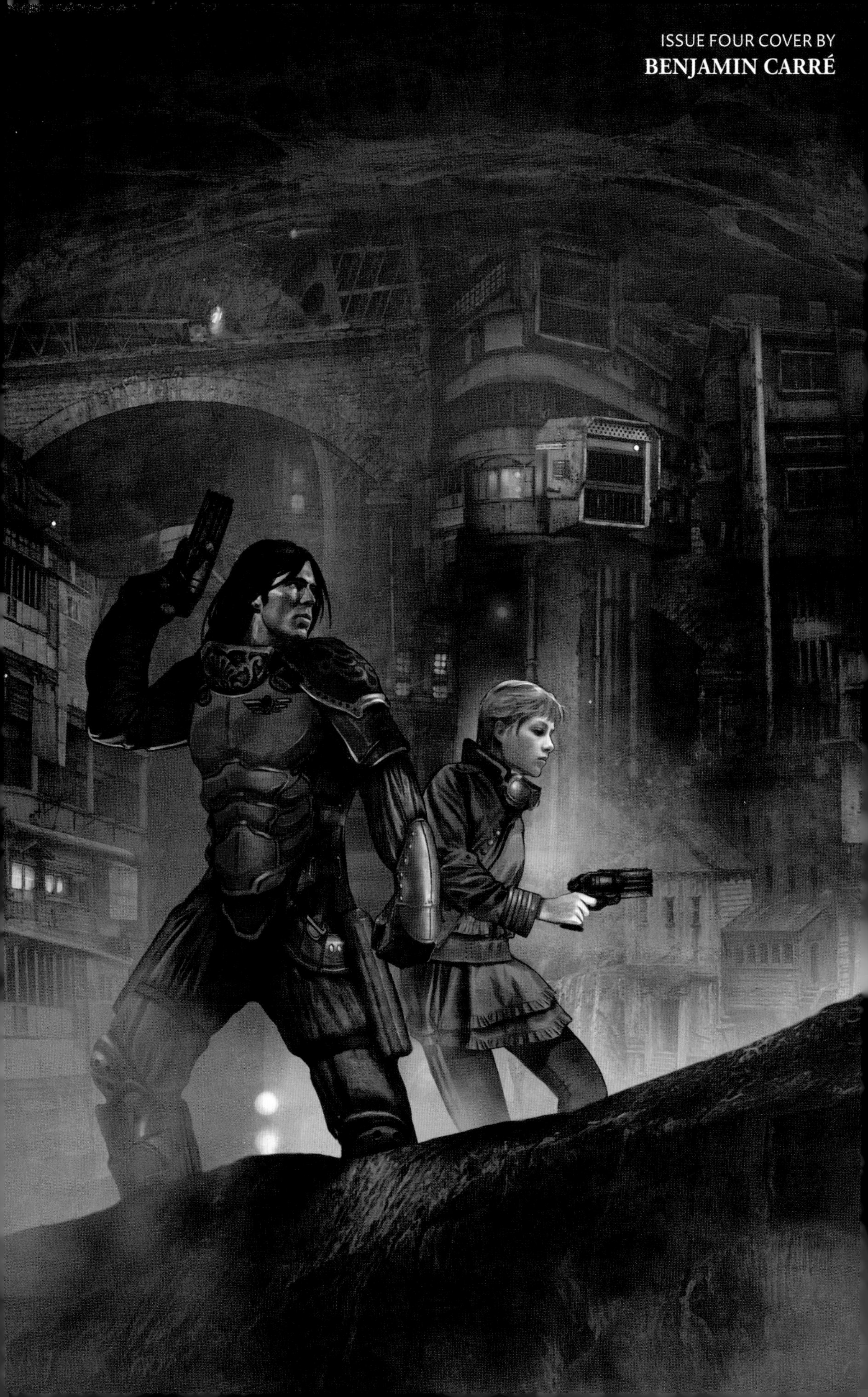

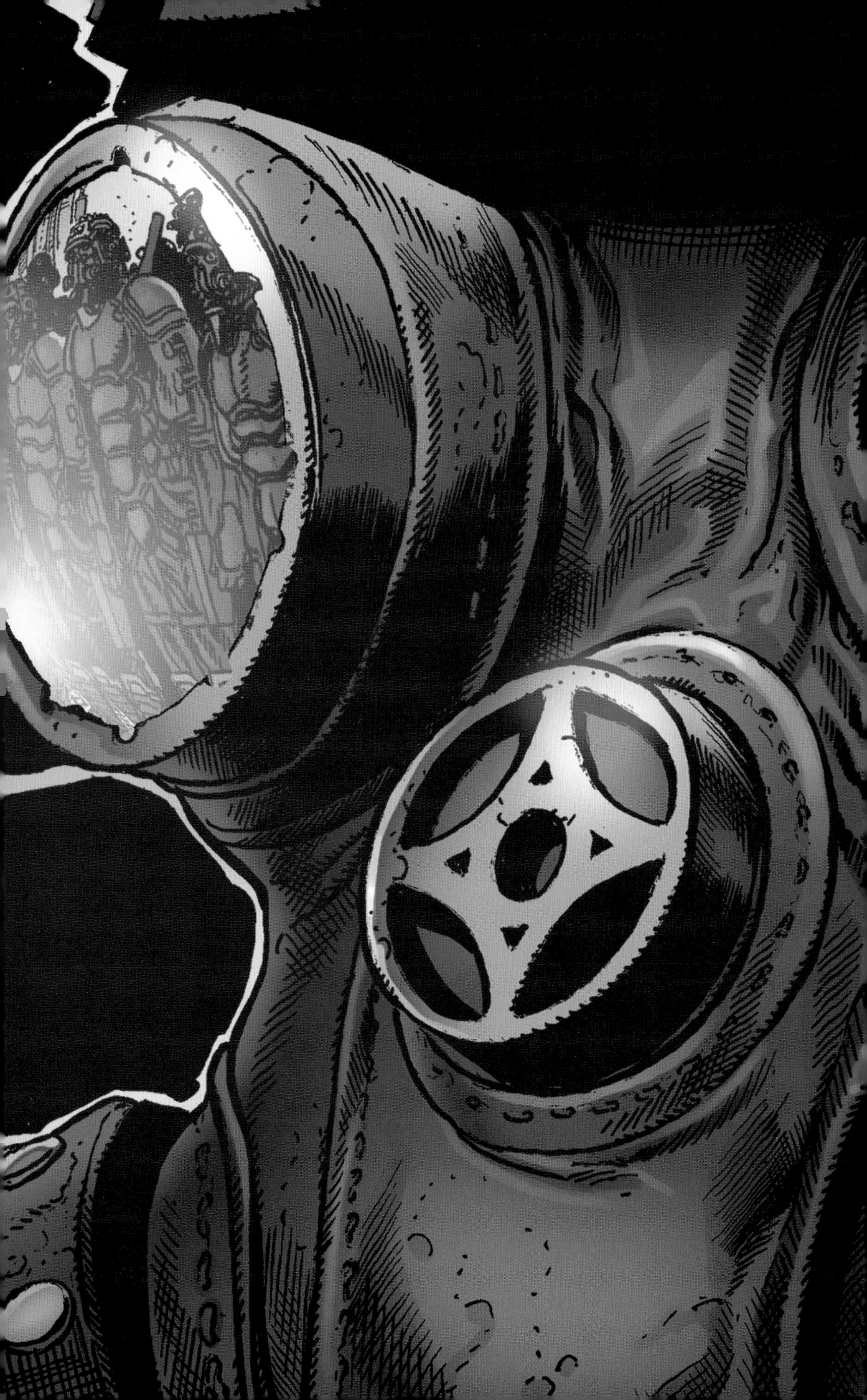

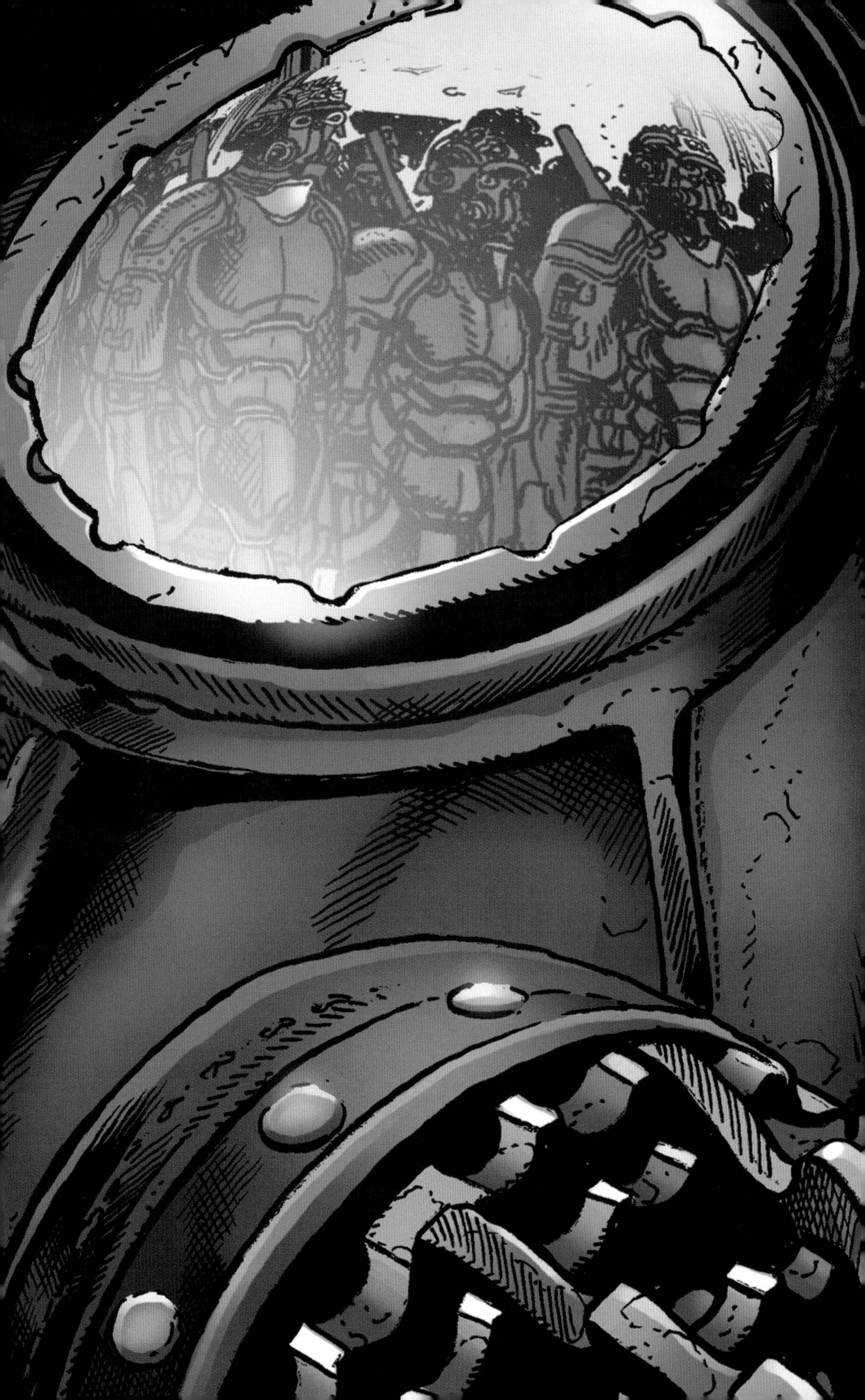

BUILDING LANTERN CITY

Sometimes the really big ideas start off very small. That's how it was with *Lantern City*. One little thought became the cobblestone of a street, which grew into a city of steam and expanded into a universe of characters, classes, and unexpected heroes who rise from the depths.

While it might not be immediately evident from the oppressed workers trudging through dark Neo-Victorian streets, the entire core of *Lantern City* revolves around love. Across all dimensions and in every time that humanity has existed, love has been the single most powerful force that drives who we are and influences our most important decisions.

I was on a cross-country flight from New York to Los Angeles when I wondered how far someone would go to be with the person they love the most. Not just how far they would fly or drive, but would a person be willing to throw away everything they believed in, from religion to science to reality itself, to be with the person they loved for just one more minute. It is this question that informs each and every action of the citizens of Lantern City. There have been many twists and turns since then in the development of the epic of *Lantern City*. One critical stop along the road was meeting Stephen Christy, President of Development at BOOM! Studios at San Diego Comic Con. By July of 2014, Matt, Bruce, and I had been to many conventions, met thousands of fans, and spent countless hours developing the stories and characters you see now. We put our heart and soul into every plot twist and turn. We knew that people out there would respond to the human struggles that took place behind the great wall of Lantern City. We knew that building the world and getting as many eyes on it—and hearts in it—as possible was key to the success of the franchise. That convention was

different from the rest. It planted the seed that became a partnership with BOOM! and Archaia that re-opened our eyes to the power of the comic book page.

Stephen, and soon after, Filip Sablik and Matt Gagnon, believed in the world we had built and were excited and ready to bring our adventure to fans all over the world. In a few short months, we saw the world from our imagination unfold in front of us in amazing detail through Carlos Magno's unforgettable illustrations of Sander, Karla, Kendal, Lizel, and the evils of the Grey Empire and Lantern City Guard. It was all there, the gleaming Grey Towers, the soot-stained factories, the light glinting off the Guards' goggles. Every inch was brought to life by Chris Blythe's explosive coloring, rich with depth and filled with volumetric lantern light. We read Matt Daley's, Mairghread Scott's, and Paul Jenkins's words and followed Sander's heart-wrenching struggle within the text expertly and dramatically laid out by Deron Bennett. This was it, the team that was building the future of a genre. Backed by our phenomenal editors, Rebecca Taylor, Dafna Pleban, and Mary Gumport, we had a team that gave us everything we needed to show everyone the stuff of our dreams.

What I love most about the world of *Lantern City* are the endless possibilities for dynamic stories that we are able to tell. We created a rich history to pull from that started with Isaac Foster Grey's rise to power two hundred years before the events of this book. Every generation of people that followed have their own struggles, triumphs, and love that will stand the test of time.

—**Trevor Crafts**
2015

THE WORKING CLASS AND UNDERGROUND

Members of the working class keep Lantern City running, but their hard work is met with inadequate compensation and oppressive conditions—all in the name of security. A growing number of them are not only dissatisfied with their conditions, but are forming a movement against the Grey Empire for rights that they once had.

Many working class citizens have already divorced from the Grey Empire, living in the vast Underground of Lantern City. While they aren't under the thumb of the Empire, everyday life is very frightening: every meal is a struggle, and violence is an expectation. It is a world where only the fittest survive.

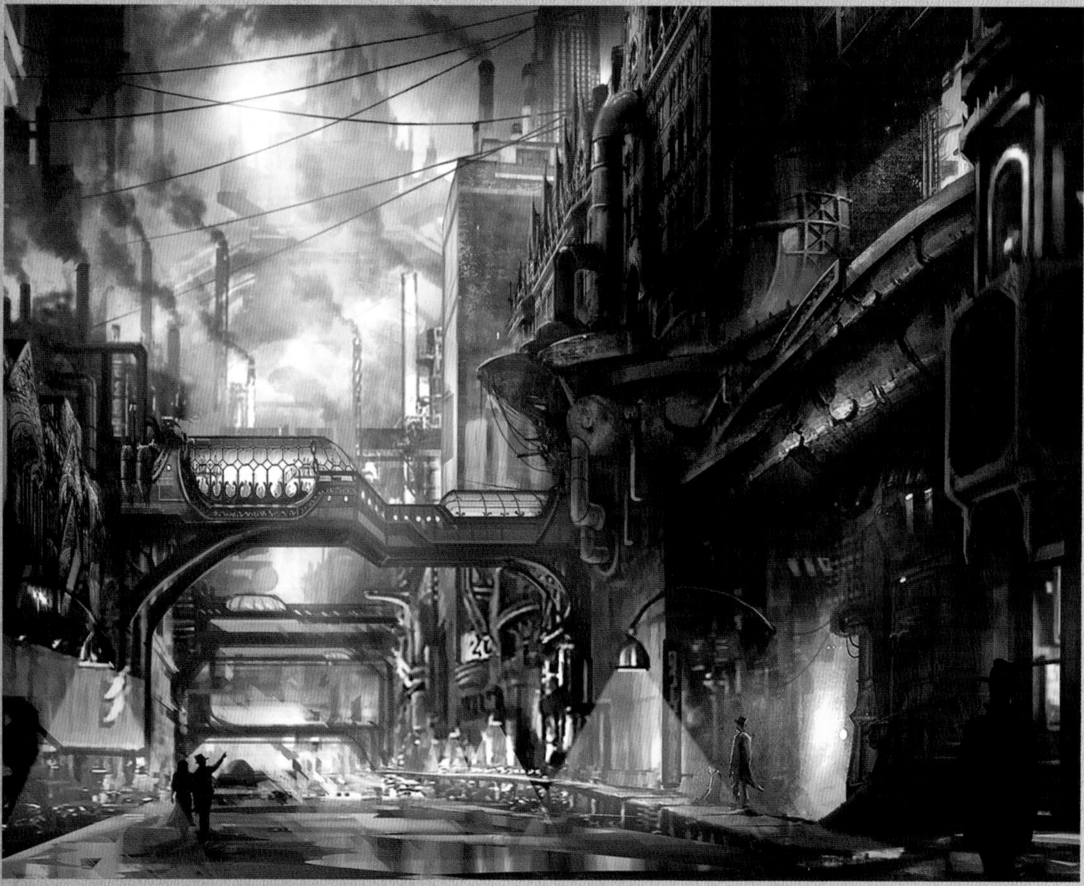

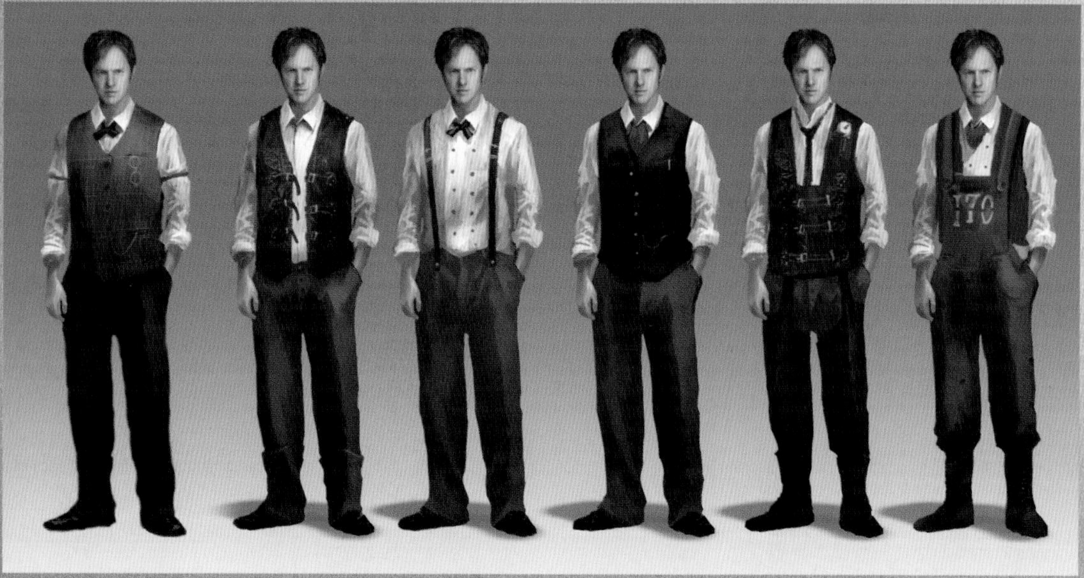
170

THE GREY EMPIRE

Although they are the ruling class of Lantern City, the foundation of their power is beginning to show its cracks. This is a group of people jockeying for power and influence, lying and betraying to gain it, all while trying to maintain the dying belief that the ruling class is keeping the entire city safe.

Killian, the current emperor of Lantern City, has an attitude and style that is starkly different from his father's, creating a great sense of tension and unease within the ruling class. This apparent disregard for tradition has begun to force them to slowly face the inevitable: change is coming. As it unfolds, they scramble for every last morsel of control they have over the city.

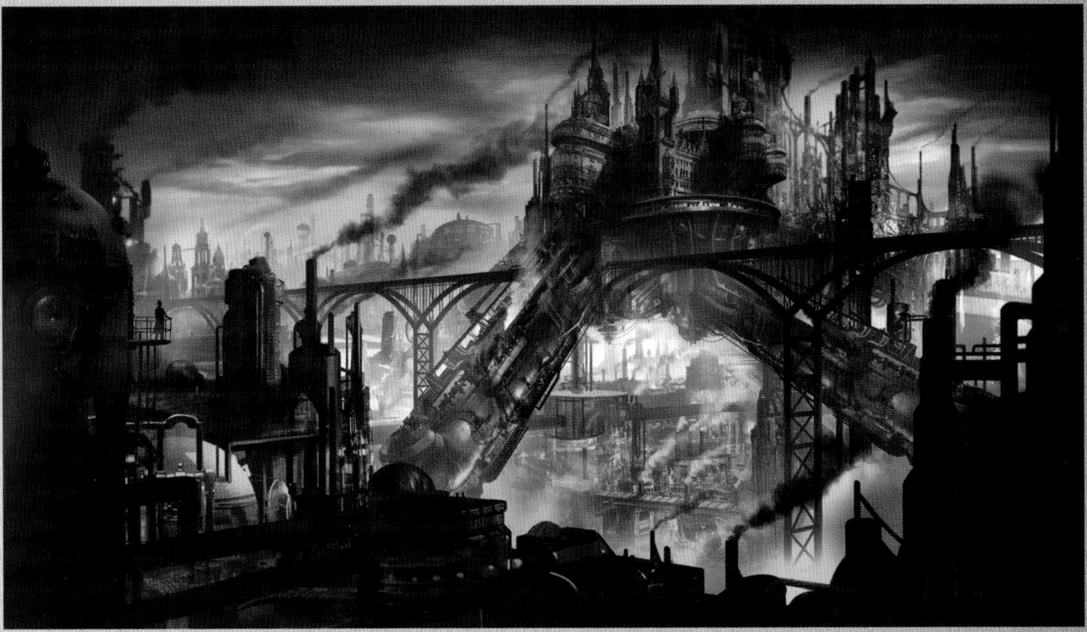

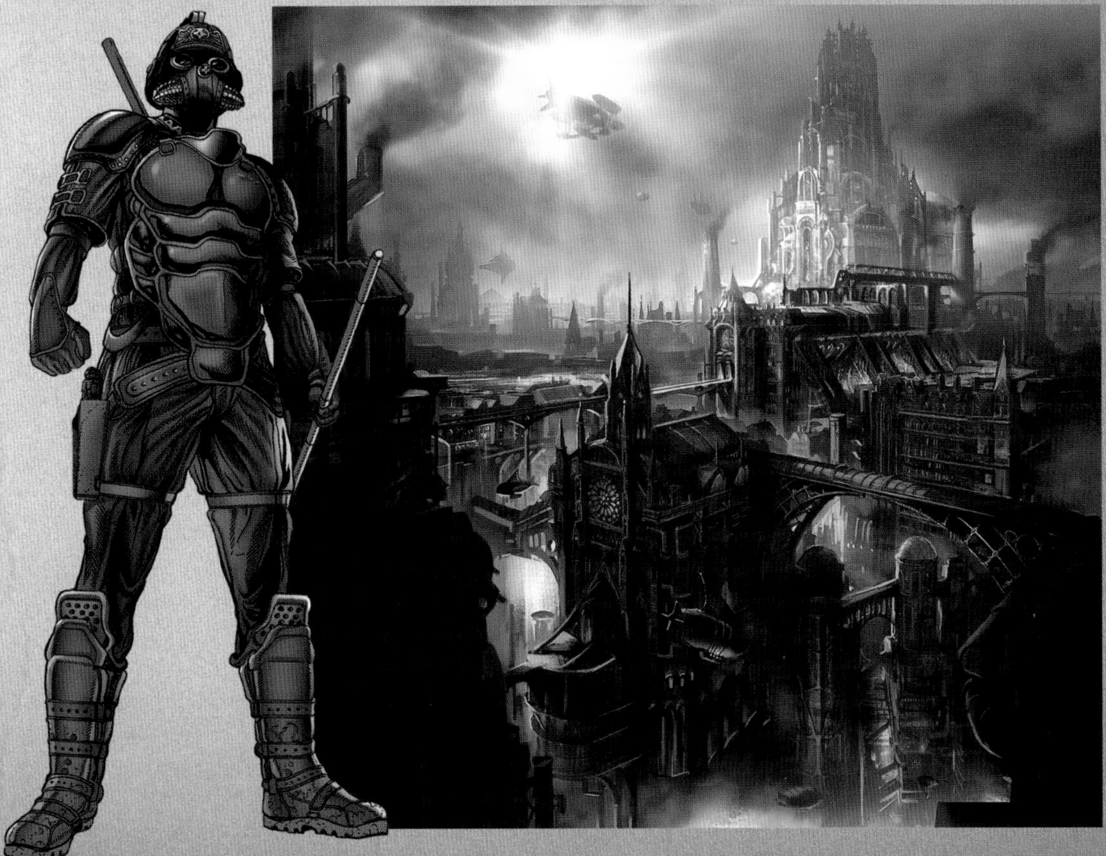

TRANSPORTATION

Lantern City has always been known as a beacon of innovation, where the most talented scientists, architects, inventors, engineers, and intellectuals worked and made great contributions to the urban landscape. This is most obvious in the city's design: how strongly constructed the buildings are, the convenience and security of the elevated ruling class sections, and how close the city is to its agricultural source. One of two great public works projects in the city's recent history, both of which were stalled in their ultimate expansion, the streetcar network was intended to improve transportation around the vast metropolis.

The streetcars, once imagined to crisscross throughout the entire working class sections of Lantern City, only cover a small subsection of the city at present. There is hope that with better representation for the working class, the full streetcar network will finally be realized.

The numerous airships, all owned and operated by the ruling class (many of them by the Grey Empire), fly throughout the skies of Lantern City, representing equally the dynamism and vanity of the city's innovations. The airships, while still widely used, are more status symbols than a necessary mode of transportation. The utility of the airships is never questioned because of their great importance in helping Lantern City survive the Great War.

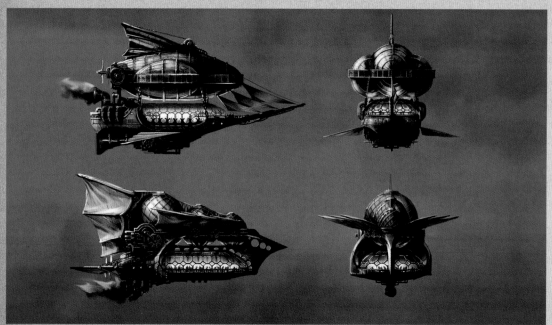

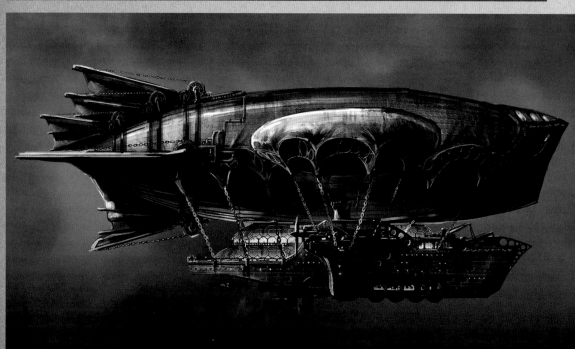

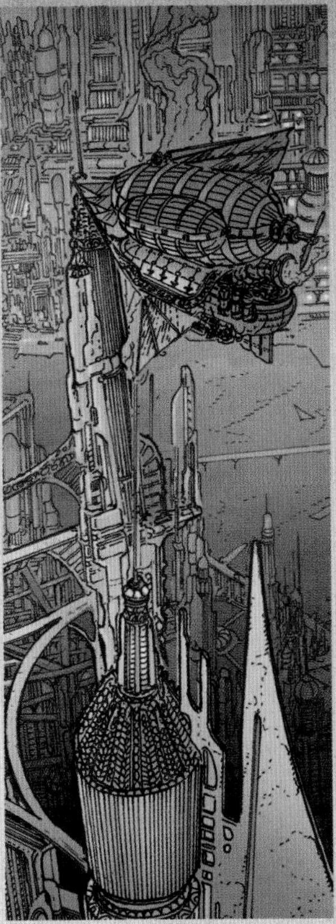

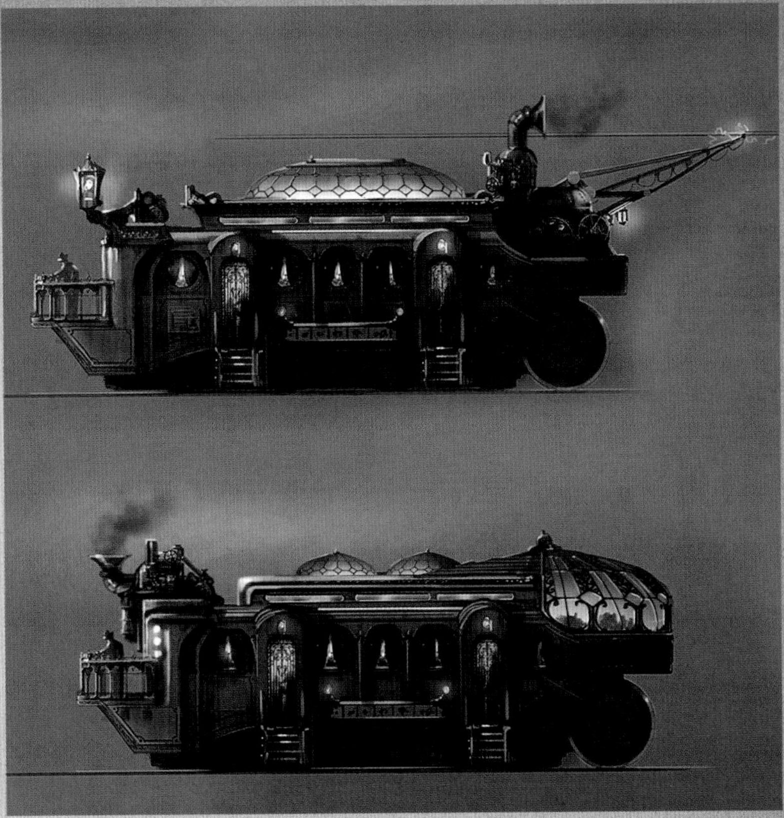

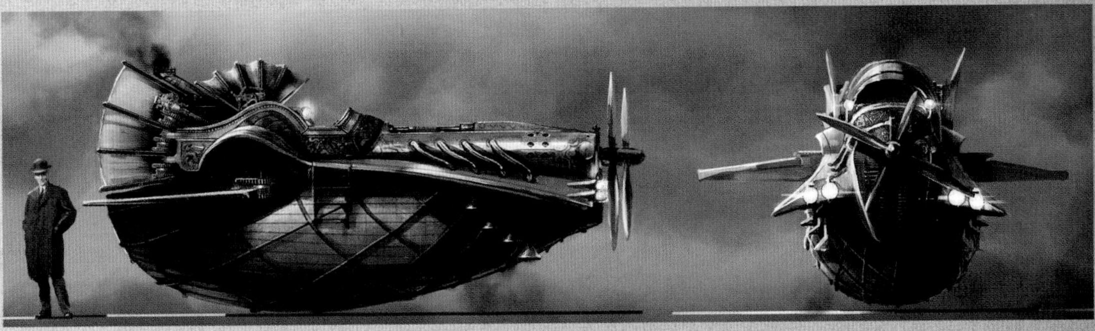

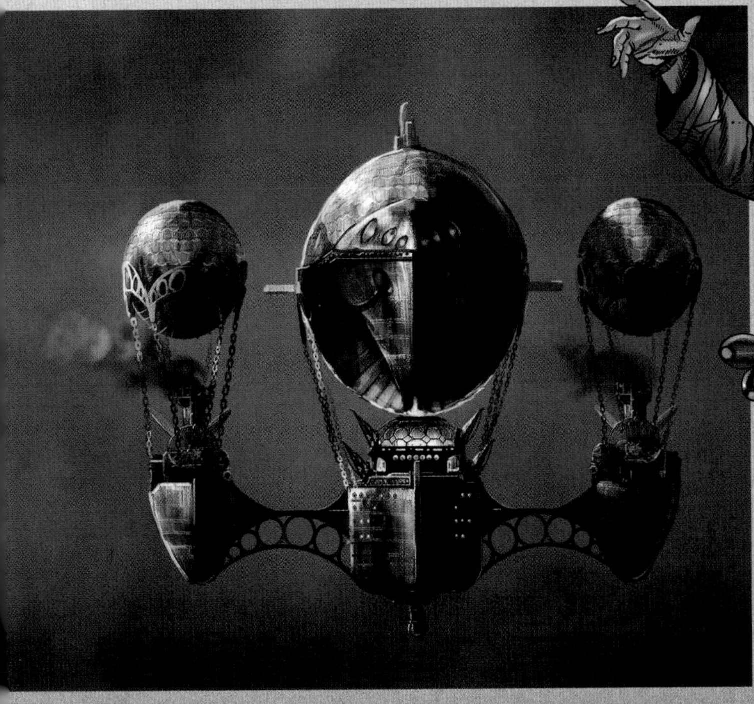

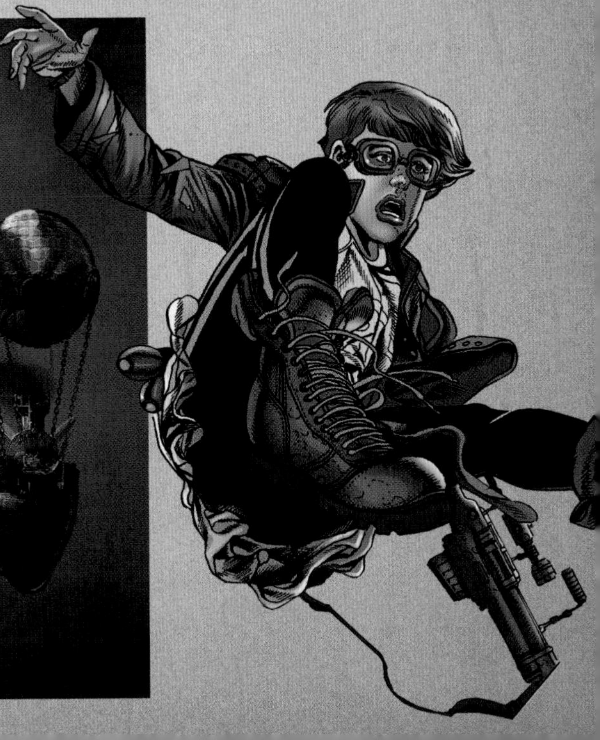

SANDER-CIVILIAN-B

SANDER JORVE

Born into the roughest area of Lantern City (known as "the Devil's Corner"), Sander has fought for survival every day of his life. At the age of six, he lost his father, who became a victim of the Lantern City Guard. Sander and his mother scraped by for nearly a decade, stealing and scrounging for food, moving from place to place. Eventually, Sander was able to escape the Devil's Corner and start life anew. He settled into a grueling working class existence, slaving away in the fields outside the city's walls, finding his only solace in his marriage to his wife, Karla, and his young son, Rennie. Sander is street smart and works on instinct. Both Karla and Sander's brother-in-law, Kendal Kornick, see greatness in him, but finding his own true path and understanding his real potential will be the greatest challenge he will ever face.

KENDALL-B

KENDAL KORNICK

Few working class citizens of Kendal's generation ever have an education, but Kendal was fortunate enough that both of his parents worked directly for the ruling class. They acquired an education for themselves and stole books to teach Kendal. His education helped him to succeed in all of his jobs: first in the fields outside the city, then in the factories, and finally in the primary prison of Lantern City. At night, he started to teach other working class citizens how to read. He also studied the biographies of all the great leaders in Hetra's history.

As conditions worsened gradually for the working class citizens of Lantern City, Kendal emerged as a leader to fight for their rights. He has many qualities that a leader needs: empathy, charisma, and an ability to motivate the masses. He is also a dynamic speaker who attracts great crowds to his speeches. Kendal is confident that the working class citizens can regain the rights they have lost during the reign of the Grey Empire, but he fears the consequences of being the face of the revolution.

LIZEL KORNICK

Though Lizel was born into the working class, her father, Kendal, ensured that she was educated and aware of the world around her. She is smart and a woman of action. Acting before she thinks can land her in troubling situations, but through skill, intelligence, and a little bit of luck, she usually manages to come out on top. She shares Kendal's passion for revolution, though their methods do not always align: Kendal wants a peaceful movement, and Lizel, along with her gang, believes that sometimes violence is the only effective language when the world needs to be turned upside down.

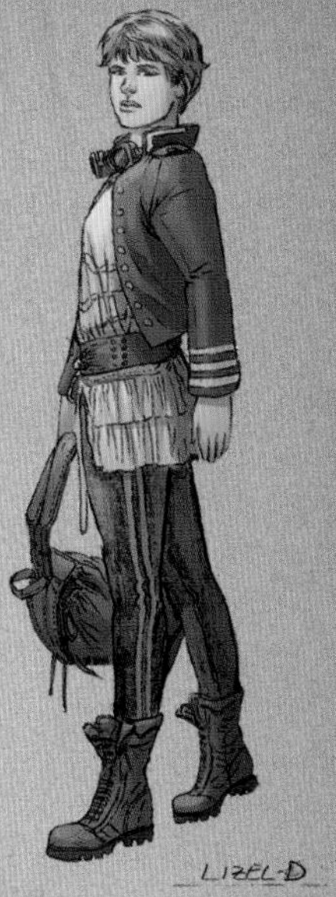
LIZEL-D

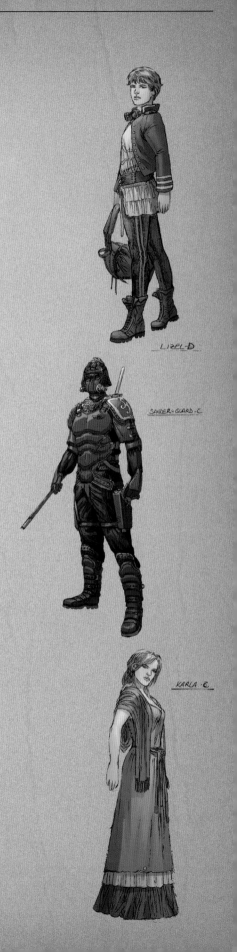

LANTERN CITY GUARD

The Lantern City Guard is the well-trained military branch of the Grey Empire. They ensure that there is order within the city, especially within the working class districts, and they patrol the Wall and the fields outside the city. Becoming a member of the Lantern City Guard is difficult because so many working class men want to join, far more than the Guard needs. It is an esteemed job with many benefits, although it does not place members into a higher social class. There are countless potential dangers to the job, but these risks are worth taking in order for working class men to avoid a job in the dangerous, abusive factories or fields.

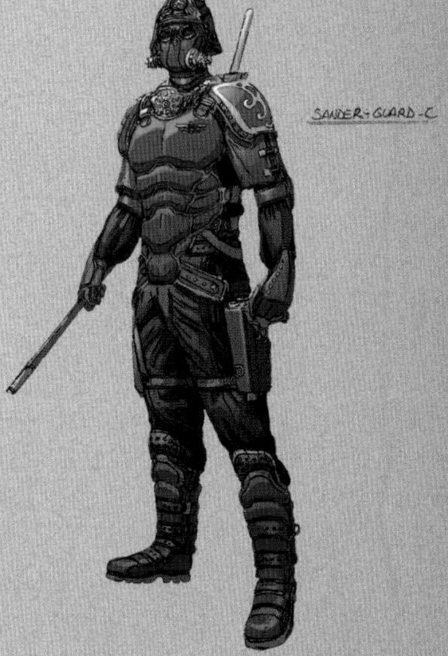
SANDER-GUARD-C

KARLA JORVE

Karla's (and Kendal's) parents ran illegal schools in the Depths for the working class, teaching people of all ages how to read and defying the terrible ramifications they would face if caught by the Lantern City Guard or the Grey Empire. Since this was her idea of normal, Karla always knew what a great sacrifice change—especially revolution—requires. As a wife and mother, she is conflicted, because she finds herself torn between immediate loyalty to her husband Sander and their son and allegiance to her brother Kendal and his revolutionary cause. This conflict pulls her into a dark and twisted world that forces her to become more than she ever imagined.

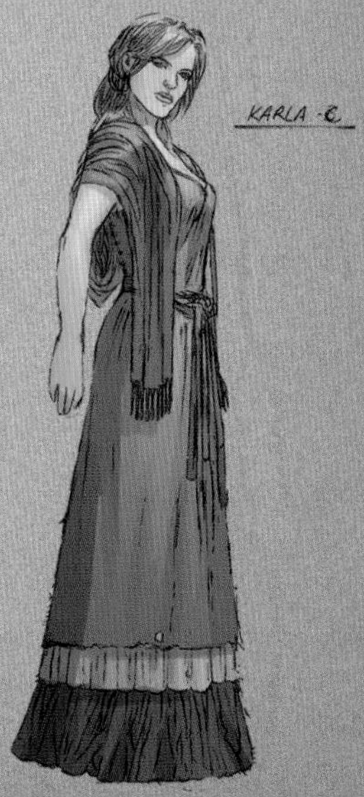
KARLA-C

TREVOR CRAFTS is the creator of *Lantern City*, and is no stranger to building worlds. Winner of the LATV Festival and numerous industry awards, including an Emmy˚, Trevor has spent his career creating dynamic stories with striking visuals featuring strong characters. Now CEO of Macrocosm Entertainment, he has acted as producer, writer, and director for projects *Like Experimenter* (2015), *Manson Family Vacation* (2015), *Enemy of Man* (2015), *Deep in the Heart* (2013), and *Smokewood, Nevada* (2013). You can get updates from Trevor and follow Macrocosm at www.macrocosm.tv and through Twitter @trevorcrafts.

BRUCE BOXLEITNER was cast as the lead role in Disney's cult film *TRON*, which garnered him science fiction fans worldwide. In 1994, Boxleitner joined the cast of the popular TV series *Babylon 5* as John Sheridan. Boxleitner again starred with Jeff Bridges in *TRON: Legacy*, and Boxleitner reprised his role in *TRON: Uprising* on Disney's XD TV network. The veteran actor has appeared in numerous recurring roles on TV series, including *Cedar Cove*, *GCB*, and *Heroes*, and has guest-starred on *NCIS* and *Chuck*. In 1999, Boxleitner authored *Frontier Earth* and in 2001, its sequel *Frontier Earth: Searcher*, published by The Berkley Publishing Group. Follow Bruce on Twitter @boxleitnerbruce.

MATTHEW DALEY is a screenwriter who, when asked by his grandparents at age ten what he wanted to be when he grew up, answered confidently, "a writer, historian, or comedian." He wasn't too far off, finding himself in adulthood writing for film and television (winning an Emmy˚ along the way). He has always been attracted to genres, especially horror and sci-fi, and recently wrote the horror movie *Flay* (2015). He wrote the *Lantern City* prequel novel *Rise* and is currently at work on the *Lantern City* comic book series. Follow Matt on Twitter @matthewjdaley.

MAIRGHREAD SCOTT is a comic book and animation writer. She has written for such books as *Marvel Universe: Guardians of the Galaxy*, *Swords Of Sorrow: Chaos*, *Transformers: Windblade*, and her first original series, *Toil And Trouble*. Her television work includes writing for the Emmy Award-winning *Transformers Prime* as well as *Rescue Bots*, *Ultimate Spider-Man: Web-Warriors*, *Transformers: Robots in Disguise*, and the upcoming *Marvel's Guardians of the Galaxy*. She lives in Los Angeles with her husband and their comic book collection. You can follow her work at www.mscottwriter.com

PAUL JENKINS has been creating, writing and building franchises for over 20 years in the graphic novel, film and video game industries. Over the last two decades Paul has been instrumental in the creation and implementation of literally hundreds of world-renowned, recognizable entertainment icons. With six Platinum selling video games, a Number One MTV Music Video, an Eisner Award, Five Wizard Fan Awards, and multiple Best Selling Graphic Novels, Paul Jenkins has enjoyed recognition on the *New York Times* bestseller list, has been nominated for two BAFTA Awards, and was even the recipient of a government-sponsored Prism Award for his contributions in storytelling and characterization.

CARLOS MAGNO is the oldest son of Zenite and Paulo Sergio, and he has two young sisters, Thaís and Fernanda. He has a degree in Fine Arts from Escola de Música e Belas Artes do Paraná, Brazil. His comic works include *Zombie Tales* (BOOM! Studios), *Captain Universe* (Marvel Comics), *The Phantom* (Moonstone Books), *Countdown*, *Green Lantern Corps*, *Cyborg* (DC Comics), as well as a two-year run on *Transformers* (IDW Publishing). His favorite works include *Planet of the Apes* with Daryl Gregory, *Deathmatch* with Paul Jenkins, *Robocop* with Josh Williamson, and currently, working on *Lantern City*. Carlos lives in Sao Jose dos Pinhais with his wife Ingret and his two children. See more of Carlos's work at his website, http://www.carlos-magno-comics.com/sobre-nos/

CHRIS BLYTHE has been a stalwart presence in the comics scene for nearly twenty years. During that time, he has been a permanent and influential contributor to 2000 AD in the UK, along with working with DC, Marvel, Dark Horse, Nintendo, and Hasbro on hundreds of titles including *Star Wars*, *Aliens*, *Action Man*, *Transformers*, and *Need for Speed*. His critically acclaimed self-published graphic novel, *Angel Fire*, was translated for the mainstream by Casterman and Carlton Books as well as being optioned to become a movie. You can see more of Chris's work by visiting http://ceebee73.deviantart.com/

DERON BENNETT is an Eisner and Harvey Award-nominated letterer, and has been providing lettering services for various comic book companies for over a decade. His body of work includes the critically acclaimed *Jim Henson's Tale of Sand*, *Jim Henson's The Dark Crystal*, *Mr. Murder is Dead*, *The Muppet Show Comic Book*, *Darkwing Duck*, and *Richie Rich*. He has also ventured into writing with his creator-owned book, *Quixote*. You can learn more about Deron by visiting his website www.andworlddesign.com or following @deronbennett on Twitter.